Siege

Edge of Empire: Book One

ALISTAIR TOSH

First published by Sharpe Books in 2022.

To Jenny, for eternal patience and encouragement.
And for all the detours to muddy, remote, historic sites.

CONTENTS

Part 1
Chapters 1 – 24
Part 2
Chapters 25 – 45
Part 3
Chapters 46 – 68
Acknowledgements
Author's Note

PART 1

AD 139 Northern Britannia

1

Lucius Faenius Felix, Trubunus of the First Nervana Germanorum, could not believe that the first man he killed would come from amongst the ranks of his own cohort.

He sat astride his horse, Epona, near the dais, facing into the centre of the parade ground to the west of the fort. The black mare tossed her head and expelled a great snort, seeming to react to his mood. Lucius knew he had been foolish, but there was now nothing to be done other than endure what was to come.

He had been determined to ensure that the preparation of the site for the huge command tent went well. The orders had arrived the day before. The Governor's staff, it seemed, had decided that none of the forts at the western end of the Wall were large enough for the needs of both running a troublesome province and planning for the coming campaign. A temporary headquarters would be built and Lucius was to supply the manpower.

The orders had been specific and detailed. The ground was to be levelled, a well was to be dug and latrine trenches prepared. He had left through the main gates at the start of the morning watch, trotting Epona along the southern road towards the chosen site.

Walking his mount through the growing earthworks, all had seemed to be progressing well. Squads of men had been hard at it with pick and shovel. He'd been unable to locate the Centurion in charge and none of the men had seen him. Feeling his annoyance rise he'd continued his search and had approached a hump of ground behind which the latrines were to be sighted.

He heard a shout followed by voices raised in anger. But it wasn't Latin they spoke, rather the language of the Nervii, the native tongue of most of the cohort's fighting strength.

Cresting the rise he saw two cavalrymen standing in a half dug trench. Both were stripped to the waist, the pair less than an arm's length apart as they quarrelled. Neither was aware of Lucius's appearance, so lost were they in their argument. One of the men stepped out of the trench. Avitius. Lucius recognised him immediately. The trooper had been up in front of Lucius for disciplinary infractions more than once, almost always related to drink. The other he didn't know, but at that moment Lucius thought he heard the name Gavo amongst Avitius's expletives.

Avitius struck first.

A short punch flashed hard into Gavo's stomach. He doubled over with the impact, but quickly recovered.

Gavo leapt at Avitius, who wasn't fast enough to prevent his assailant's arm lock around his neck.

'You men.' Lucius raised his voice. But they didn't hear him. Lucius dismounted and strode towards the pair, crossing the short distance quickly. He grabbed Gavo by the arm. 'Stop this.'

Enraged, Gavo turned unseeing and pushed Lucius, who stumbled backwards. His heel caught on a discarded shovel, accelerating his fall. Both Gavo and Avitius looked on in horror as their Tribunus disappeared into the ditch.

'You men stay where you are!' The shout had come from some distance away but was unmistakable. Adalfus Hesta, the Nervana's First Spear. Lucius pulled himself out of the ditch, his face flushed.

'I'm sorry, sir. I didn't realise—,' Gavo began, now speaking in heavily accented Latin.

'Shut your mouth, trooper.' The shout now so close it made even Lucius jump. The First Spear reached Gavo, vine stick in hand, grabbed a handful of the now terrified man's sweat-soaked hair. 'It's the death penalty now, you fool,' the First Spear said, the words hissed through clenched teeth.

That evening in his office Lucius had the most painful conversation of his young life.

'He assaulted an officer, sir. It's a capital offence, he must die,' the First Spear said, quietly but firmly. Resigned.

'But he didn't realise I was an officer. The look on his face said as much and I surprised him from behind,' Lucius tried to keep the anguish from his voice. He was the senior officer but even so knew the First Spear's word was law in the Nerva. Lucius was in awe of him.

'It doesn't matter whether he meant it or not. He did it. He's a drunk and a layabout. Not to put him to death would have the men thinking they can do what they like.'

'First Spear, we go to war in a matter of weeks. To execute one of the cohort would have a detrimental effect on the men, just when we need them at their best.'

The First Spear prickled. ‘They’ll be at their best, sir, or they’ll have my vine stick up their arse.’

‘The First Spear is right, sir.’ Caius Martis, the Praefectus Ala, spoke for the first time. Both sat on the opposite side of Lucius’s desk; and were so different in appearance, with the exception of their long fair hair typical of the Nervii. The Praefectus, commander of the Nervana’s cavalry, was tall and slimly built, the First Spear shorter by a head but with the neck of a bull. ‘You’re a man of honour, sir. Your desire to spare trooper Gavo’s life does you credit. But you have no choice in this matter.’

‘But surely I could commute the death sentence to field punishment?’ Lucius said, in desperation. ‘It would still send a strong message.’

The First Spear shook his head slowly, saying nothing for a moment, before looking once more at Lucius. ‘No, sir. It must be death. A lesser punishment will not serve and will be seen by the men as a sure sign their new commander is weak.’

Lucius lowered his head. He was beaten. Raising it once more he looked at the two officers. ‘Very well, let it be done,’ he said, cutting the First Spear off with a wave of his hand as the older man opened his mouth to respond. ‘Dismissed.’

The two officers stood and saluted. As he reached the doorway the First Spear turned back.

‘You must learn from this, sir.’ He held his stare for a moment longer before nodding once to Lucius and was gone.

Now as the first of the Sun’s rays broke above the horizon, casting long shadows across the parade ground, Lucius shook himself from the memory and looked at the silent ranks. Every eye seemed to be upon him.

‘Bring out the prisoner!’ The First Spear’s voice boomed from where he and the Praefectus stood side by side on the dais. Four men marched into the square. Three strode alongside one another, two of whom were dressed in full kit, spathas at their hips, helmets and chainmail shining. The third, held between them, was stripped to the waist, wearing only troos and boots, hands tied behind his back. Gavo’s face was white and drawn. To the rear of the three marched a Decurion, the white feathered plume of his cavalry officer's helmet gleamed in the low sunlight.

The small party halted in the centre of the square. The Decurion spoke quietly from behind the three, his words unheard by those watching, but a moment later Gavo lowered himself to his knees, aided by the other two.

'For assault of an officer, trooper Gavo is sentenced to death.' The First Spear's voice thundered once more. There was a collective intake of breath from the assembled ranks, then a hum of conversation.

'Silence in the ranks!' The First Spear's shout cut off all sound. All except the whimper that escaped from Gavo. 'Bring out the execution party.'

Five men stepped forward from the front rank, close to the dais. Chosen from Gavo's own turma, each man selected by the drawing of lots from amongst the troopers of the thirty strong cavalry unit. They wore only tunics. Instead of spathas, each held a heavy wooden practise sword in hand. All marched in single file towards the condemned man. Bringing up the rear of the five was Avitius, face drawn, dark rings circled his eyes, shimmering with unshed tears.

Raising his head Gavo spoke to Avitius, his words unintelligible, but the quaver in his voice carried to Lucius. Avitius nodded, unable to speak as tears finally escaped to run in two rivulets down his lined face.

'Begin,' the First Spear yelled.

Avitius's movement was so fast Lucius almost didn't see it. Stepping forward he hammered his wooden sword onto the top of Gavo's skull. The crack of bone was heard across the square. Avitius followed up with a second blow just above the nape of the stunned prisoner's neck as he fell forward. As Gavo hit the packed earth, Avitius swung twice more in quick succession, striking the side of his exposed head. Lucius recoiled as Gavo's bulging eyes seemed to stare directly at him. Avitius struck a final crunching blow, but by then the trooper's life had already left him.

Avitius stepped back, dropping the wooden sword. His head hung to his chest as his shoulders shook. No other man of the execution party had moved. All stared dumbly at Gavo's body, practise swords hanging limply by their sides.

Lucius swallowed back bile, fighting not to add to the shame he already felt. Even the grizzled First Spear took several moments to come to himself.

'Execution complete. Execution party, remove the prisoner.' Four men moved quickly, lifting the body of Gavo to carry him towards the fort. Avitius had remained still and the Decurion spoke quietly to him. Avitius shook his head.

The Decurion turned to the two escorts who still waited nearby. Both strode to either side of Avitius, held him under the arms and walked the grief-stricken trooper away from the scene.

The First Spear waited until the centre of the square was clear once more. His silent gaze took in the men before him. His unspoken message was clear.

'Cohort!' he bellowed. 'Cohort, dismissed.'

Individual officers shouted orders, preparing to march their units back to the fort. But Lucius neither saw nor heard any of this as he sat frozen on Epona's back. Instead he stared unblinking at the centre of the square, where Avitius's practise sword, smeared with blood and hair, still lay.

2

Two weeks later

Lucius stood at the rear of the Governor's command tent, staring into his wine cup and feeling self-conscious, as he usually did when in the company of so many grizzled veterans. He led his own cohort of a thousand men, but despite the months of winter training he still felt an imposter.

'Tribunus Felix!'

Lucius turned sharply, because the speaker's voice was instantly recognisable as belonging to Marcus Verus, Legatus of the Sixth Vitrix, to which Lucius and his auxiliaries were attached.

'Sir.' Lucius came briskly to attention. The sudden movement sloshing wine from his cup, forcing Verus to step back briskly to avoid his boots receiving a soaking.

'Relax, young Felix. You look like a cat on a hot plate. Are you not enjoying our Governor's fine wine?'

'If I'm completely honest, sir, I haven't touched a drop,' Lucius said. The older man appraised him with what looked like a grimace, but after the months he had been in his company, Lucius now recognised it as a smile.

Verus's voice dropped to a conspiratorial whisper. 'How so? Don't you feel at ease amongst your brother officers?'

'It's not so easy, sir. They're veterans, their positions have been hard won in battle against the Emperor's enemies.'

Verus took a long swallow from his cup, studying his subordinate before only partly suppressing a belch.

'To my mind, Felix, you're not like the young men of title who have come to us on the Cursus Honorum. You have humility, and a willingness to learn. You've shown talent, which is why I gave you the command of a double strength cohort, not because your uncle and I were friends. I've watched you lead your men in training and in the field, I've seen you draw on the experience of your cohort's senior officers, which shows a wisdom beyond your years. You've yet to be tested in battle, that's true, but if you remember what you've learned, take on board some of the advice from that fierce First Spear of yours, you'll be just fine. Now tell me, how are your Germans? Are they ready?'

Lucius twitched a smile. There was no doubt Verus was a hard task master and didn't suffer fools. He had seen more than one of his peers nearly reduced to tears when unfortunate enough to draw Verus's ire. But Lucius had not known him to be vindictive.

'Indeed they are, sir. They're happy to have left the constant drills in the cold and wet of winter behind them, and see some real action at last. We've received the last of the replacement horses too. All sound beasts.' Verus nodded, the smile-grimace creasing his face once more.

'Well, young Felix, I'm glad your men are so keen. I believe our Governor is finally about to announce his first move.'

There was a noticeable rise in the volume of the conversation amongst the gathered officers. Increased activity could be heard deeper within the tent's interior.

'Come to attention for your general, Quintus Lollius Urbicus, Governor of the emperor's province of Britannia.' The voice of an aide boomed around the open space. All conversation ceased. Verus turned to face the dais that had been set up for the occasion.

'We'll speak afterwards, Tribunus. I'm giving you that chance to test yourself.' Hearing the formal tone, Lucius nodded briskly as the Legatus moved through the gathering to stand before the low platform. What did Verus mean? How would he be tested?

An instant later, in strode their commander. Urbicus was, to Lucius's mind, the most striking of men. The Numidian was tall, broad, and lean, with skin darker than any of those present. A thick, well-groomed black beard curled across his chin. Springing swiftly onto the dais, he paced, catlike back and forth, taking in the men around him. He attempted, it appeared to Lucius, to look each of them in the eye. His gaze briefly landed on Lucius, who had to use considerable willpower not to look away. Finally he settled, legs apart, his arms clasped loosely behind his back.

'At ease, gentlemen,' Urbicus's voice, deep and low, carried easily. 'I see from the number of empty jugs that my wine is to your liking?' He flashed a smile. Polite laughter rippled across the room, the tension too great for there to be any real mirth.

'Well, this will be the last for a while.' Urbicus let the thought take hold for a moment. 'Now that we've put down the little insurrection of the Brigantes, we move on to deal with the tribes of Caledonia. Our campaign north will not simply be one of vengeance, dealing a blow to Rome's enemies only to withdraw with nothing to show for it but a few slaves to enrich ourselves. No!' Urbicus snapped. Lucius jumped slightly and he wasn't alone. 'Our emperor has commanded we extend his province of Britannia, and finally bring that troublesome land permanently under his rule.'

There was an outburst of conversation, with looks of surprise exchanged between some.

'Gentlemen.' Urbicus raised his voice only slightly, but all speech stopped instantly. 'We are going to put an end to the depredations of the northern tribes, who've been a continual thorn in Rome's heel. You've drilled your men hard. You are ready.' Urbicus's eyes roved across the gathering once more.

'We'll move swiftly. Grinding our enemies into the dirt of our new province. At dawn tomorrow, we will advance beyond the Wall and the great Sula estuary. Expect action within the first day. The Novantae, I'm told, aren't shy types like the Brigantes.' This time the laughter was full throated, even amongst the veterans.

Urbicus's tone became serious once more. 'This tribe has laid waste to a number of our castrae. One not fifteen miles from where we stand.'

Lucius saw the anger rise on the faces of those around him. But he felt only a chill of fear. Would he get through this without bringing dishonour to his family?

'So,' Urbicus continued. 'We will extract a high price for their impudence.' There was a moment's silence. Some officers leaned forward in anticipation of the Numidian's next words. Lucius smiled despite his own apprehension, seeing Urbicus working his audience like the actors he'd seen at the theatres in Malaca and Acinipo.

'We anticipate that the Novantae will behave as expected and obligingly gather their forces at their hill, which I'm told is a comfortable day's stroll from the Wall.'

The Governor of Britannia let the tension build. When he spoke again there was no mistaking the menace in his voice. 'And let me be clear. We're going to give our emperor a victory to be remembered. One whose glory will be retold across the empire and beyond. Some of you were with me in Judea and know what must be done. We'll hem them in on their dunghill and hold them there as if in a vice. I want none to escape. If there are any left alive when we're finished they'll make a nice first batch for the slave markets.'

'Marcus,' Urbicus snapped. 'Are the Sixth ready to move?'

Verus quickly swallowed the mouthful of wine he had just taken. 'Yes, sir. Tribunus Felix will lead out the ala of the First Nervana before first light. He'll initially scout the way ahead, before splitting his force. Half will move to observe the Novantae's hill, the rest will cross the Anam into Novantae lands, along the river valley, and encourage any stragglers to join their brothers. The Nervana's centuries will follow close behind and secure the river crossings at the Itouna and Isca. Then await the main force.'

Lucius froze, stunned by Verus's words. He was to lead the advance? A knot of fear twisted his stomach. But was it fear of facing the enemy? Or fear of shame and failure?

3

It had been a long day. Now late in the evening, Cai was weary. Cradling his cup at the table, he thought through what he should say.

Cai was an imposing figure, taller than most, but unlike many of the men of the Nervii was slim rather than broad. His long fair hair gave testament to the shared tribal roots of the men he was about to address. Through habit he pulled his hand over his beard. Well, there was no putting it off. He'd keep it simple.

Cai rose and walked to the centre of the officer's mess. Smiling broadly at the gathering, which included the full complement of the cohort's senior men, other than those on duty. Many of the faces looking back at him he had known since the day he joined the Nervana. Even one or two from his own village. He turned on the spot, arms raised, gripping his full wine cup from which two fat drops escaped, tracing lazy, red lines along his forearm.

'Brothers,' Cai said. His voice came as a croak. 'Brothers,' he tried again. The room quietened. 'Raise your cups to young Berengar, first born son of our illustrious First Spear, who came screaming into the world this day. May he have a long life and a strong arm.'

'Long life and a strong arm.' came the merry response, men raising their cups before swiftly downing the contents.

'And may he take his mother's looks.' The room erupted into laughter.

The First Spear slowly rose from a bench, joining his friend in the centre of the room. Other than their long fair hair, the difference between the two men could not have been more marked. Adal was half a head shorter than Cai, with broad shoulders, his chest topped with an ox-like neck partly hidden by a great bush-like beard.

'Thank you, brothers. Your warm congratulations are appreciated.' Adal stared to the back of the mess. 'And yes, Centurion Aelius, he does indeed favour the look of his mother.' Laughter filled the room once more. Adal raised his hand for quiet.

'I'm sorry to dampen the celebratory mood, but the Nervana has been given the honour of being the first to take the fight to the blue-faces.' A full throated roar arose from the assembled officers. This time Adal allowed the noise to die down naturally before continuing. When he did speak, all humour was gone from his voice.

'I want us to show those women in the Sixth what real soldiering looks like.'

'Too fucking right we will, sir.' Aelius again, whose words this time were greeted with the thunder of massed fists on benchtops.

'The Praefectus here,' Adal nodded at Cai. 'Will be taking his lads out before first light, to deal with any of the bastard's who might be keeping a watch on the river fords. The infantry will follow at double pace, to secure and hold each crossing until the pretty boys of the Sixth and Twentieth follow on in their own sweet time. We'll be travelling light, with rations for two days only. Make sure your men have their kit strapped down tight, and keep their mouths shut as we move.' Adal's sharp stare held in the room. All at once he broke into a smile.

'Now, let's have one final drink on me,' Adal held his arms open towards the doorway. A cheer from the gathering rose as mess slaves appeared, moving amongst them with jugs of wine.

Not long after, the assembly began to break up, each officer returning to his unit to make the final preparations. Cai left off talking to one of his men to join Adal, who now sat alone, seemingly deep in thought.

'Well,' Cai said, taking the bench opposite. 'A fortuitous day Adal, to have the blessing of a first-born son on the eve we go to war. If that isn't a sign from the gods I don't know what is, eh?' Cai saw his boyhood friend nod, but continued to stare at his, still full, wine cup. 'What ails you, brother?'

Finally raising his head, Adal looked at Cai, seeming to consider his next words. 'We've been like brothers all of our lives.' Cai made to interject, but Adal stopped him with a wave of his hand. 'I've few memories worth the name that don't include you in them. We've drunk, whored and fought at each other's side since we left our village as lads.'

'What is it, Adal?'

'You must think me a morose bastard,' Adal said, 'especially on the eve before we go into battle once more. It's just that I feel...you know...other than our friendship I've not had anything worth losing. Now I have my boy and a fine woman.' Adal stared into his wine cup once more. 'I don't fear death, you know that. But for the first time I feel my mortality. What would become of them if…' Adal's voice trailed off to a whisper.

Cai smiled. 'Adal I've lost count of the scrapes we've—' Before he could finish Adal reached across the table and gripped Cai's forearm.

'If the worst happens,' Adal said, stared intensely at his friend. 'I ask you to do one last thing for me.' Cai nodded but said nothing. 'I've written a Will and deposited it in the strongroom. I've left all I have to Alyn. If I don't return, will you see it done? And watch over my family when you can?'

'Of course, brother. But there'll be no need. You'll return to them once we've dealt with the blue-faces'. It seemed to Cai that a great weight was lifted from the other's shoulders. But Adal continued to hold firmly onto Cai's arm, staring intently at his friend, until finally he nodded.

'My thanks,' Adal released his grip and picked up his cup. 'It means a lot,' he mumbled.

For a while longer they sat in silence, until Adal stood and retrieved his vine stick, which he'd propped against the bench. 'Well then, Praefectus, shall we visit with our young Tribunus? Let's see if he has any final orders for us.'

Lucius yawned, pushing the note tablet aside. It was late and fatigue competed with both fear and excitement. He would not sleep.

Since handing his letter of introduction to Verus he'd barely had a moment to himself. For the most part he was glad. It prevented his thoughts returning to the terrible events of the previous Autumn. But now in the flickering lamplight of his small office he closed his eyes and let his mind drift back to that time of grief and loss.

They had been hunting, following the tracks along a pine covered mountainside and had seen nothing but ancient ibex droppings all morning. Finally towards noon, thinking about resting for a while, they came upon a small clearing. There at its centre, cropping on the green scrub, was a roebuck. The short branches of its antlers stood proud, the deer's reddish brown hide bright in the late morning sunlight.

Lucius had signalled to Marcus that he should take the shot. The boy, grinning with excitement, had slowly lifted an arrow from his quiver.

Manus shook his head. He untied a small horn from his belt and made a circling motion with his hand. Lucius understood. The roebuck faced away from them, making a killing shot unlikely. Manus raised the horn to his lips. Marcus had pulled back his bowstring all the way to his chin and nodded. Manus blew a short blast, the sound mimicking the bark of a female. The deer lifted its head and looked their way, his interest piqued. Manus blew once more, the deer turned side-on to them, preparing to explore. Marcus loosed. An instant later the deer had dropped, the arrow buried deep behind its shoulder.

'A great shot wouldn't you say, Manus?' Marcus had said repeatedly on their return journey, turning to look at the man behind them, who rode with the small deer tied behind his saddle, its narrow head lolling with each movement.

'Indeed, Dominus. One of the best I've seen.'

'Did you hear that, Lucius? One of the best he's seen and Manus would know, wouldn't he?'

'Yes, little brother,' Lucius said wearily. It had been a hot day and he longed to plunge into the frigidarium of their home's bathhouse. They followed one of the estate's tracks and cresting a rise the valley had come into full view. There in the middle distance was their father's villa, perched on the northernmost hillside, its whitewashed walls gleaming like a beacon guiding them home.

It was another hour before they finally reached the outbuildings that surrounded their home, where they had been met by two slaves who led their horses away.

'I'm off to tell father about my kill,' Marcus had said, as he started pacing towards the villa.

'Oh no, little brother,' Lucius said, grabbing the boy by the shoulder. 'You know father's rules. The one who makes the kill must gut and hang it.'

'But that's slaves' work,' Marcus protested.

'Don't be a brat, do what you're told. You'll have plenty of time to regale father over the evening meal.' For a moment it had looked like Marcus was going to argue the point, but finally with a humph he had stormed off to one of the sheds to retrieve the knives. Lucius had exchanged smiles with Manus, the older man shaking his head in mock disbelief.

Lucius crossed the cobbled yard, heading towards the smaller of the villa's entrances on its western side. Turning the corner of the sprawling building he entered the garden, with its low hedges and the smell from the lavender beds his mother had so loved. He smiled at the memory of her, sitting under the shade of the veranda as she enthusiastically discussed her new plans for it with father.

Entering the arched doorway he had turned into the atrium, the columns of its three sided walkway made of the local white marble, the fourth side open to the vista of the plantation. Lucius strode along the longest side, before, near to its end, turned into a narrower corridor, from which the family's private rooms ran. In its far corner was his father's study.

He gave the heavy wooden door a cursory knock before pushing it open. 'Father I—' Lucius began. The room was empty. The desk was covered with scrolls that rustled gently with the evening breeze from the open window. He turned to leave but stopped, confused by a familiar smell. What was it? Then it came to him: the aroma from that morning's kill. Blood.

Turning back he saw it. Pooled on the plain, tiled floor, emerging from behind his father's solid wooden desk the dark red liquid was just beginning to congeal.

His stomach filled with a feeling of dread. He dashed across the study to the other side of the desk. The sight would be forever burned into his memory.

His father lay on his front, his head to the side. Dark brown eyes open wide, his mouth gaped, frozen in a wail of silent agony. But what had fixed Lucius's horrified gaze was the broad, red patch that had spread across the back of his father's white tunic. The bloody point of his old gladius protruding through it.

'Father. No.' The words burst from deep within his chest. Grief swept over Lucius. He turned his head away, no longer able to look upon the scene. His sight came to rest on a scroll spread out on the desk, its ends held open by two wax tablets. A message had been scrawled, in his father's hand, at the top of what looked like a legal letter.

Forgive me my sons

Lucius's mind raced. His father had laughed with them as they had set off on the day's hunt before first light. He had teased Marcus about not talking too much or he would scare away the game. Lucius could not reconcile that memory with the scene before him. *Why would his father take his own life?* It was true he had been in poor temper in recent months, but over the last few days he appeared to have recovered his normal good humour.

Lucius turned to the open window, his mind numbed, his view of the olive groves blurred as the first tears filled his eyes. He froze. His breath caught at what he saw. On the tiled ledge, below the window's wooden frame, was the print of a hand. A bloody print.

Kneeling once more by his father's body he turned over the right hand, surprised by how warm it still felt. Looking at the palm he saw its familiar callouses, fingertips ink stained from long hours spent in his study. But no trace of blood. Moving quickly, he raised his father's left hand, which had been partly trapped under his hip. That too was clean.

Lucius sat on the tiled floor, resting his back against the plain plastered wall. He stared at the bloody blade, his tears forgotten, as anger began to fill him.

The sound of hobnailed footsteps echoing along the principia's colonnaded walkway snapped Lucius back to the present. The chink of chainmail accompanied each stride. The Nervana's headquarters building bustled with heightened activity ahead of the cohort's departure but even so the sound was unmistakable. The footsteps halted and the heavy wooden door to his office reverberated with a firm double rap.

'Come!' Lucius ordered.

The Praefectus, followed by the First Spear, entered the room, both coming to attention before him, saluting smartly in unison.

'Ah, good evening gentlemen. Pull up a chair, would you.'

The two officers retrieved camp chairs from the corner of the room. Lucius took a wine flask from a small table placed against the wall, filling cups for each of them.

'Before we start, let us honour the birth of the First Spear's new son. What have you named him, First Spear?' Lucius felt the familiar awkwardness in the presence of the two veterans, but since the death of Gavo he had been determined he would never again show weakness.

'Berengar, sir,' the First Spear said.

Lucius raised his cup. 'To Berengar. Health and a long life'.

'Health and a long life,' they echoed in unison, each taking a long swallow.

'My thanks, sir.'

'How is your wife, First Spear? Does she fare well?

Adal beamed at Lucius. 'Yes, sir. She comes from strong Carvetti stock, already up and about when I left.'

Lucius couldn't help but return the smile; the older soldier's joy was infectious. The three exchanged pleasantries for a while longer. He had come to rely on the surefooted guidance of the two men, who were so different from him in many ways. Despite being in their middle years, evidenced by the lines marking their bearded faces, neither showed the first signs of grey. Lucius's darker skin and short wavy brown hair gave away his Hispanic roots. His thin but muscled body spoke not only of these last months of hard training, but also of the years growing up on his father's estate. Before his world had changed.

'Well gentlemen, shall we get to it?' Lucius said. Pulling a map from its leather case, unrolling it on the desk, placing a note tablet at each of its corners. 'We've been over the plan several times now. We know what we must do. But have we missed anything?'

'No, sir,' he said, 'It's pretty clear. We've made regular patrols beyond the Wall. There's been no sign of blue-faces along the old military road, at either of our objectives. The crossings don't appear to be watched. Little more than a few stray cattle have been reported. Until we push further north. Then they appear on their little horses.'

Lucius acknowledged with a brief nod.

'Good. Now as you know, First Spear, once the Sixth have passed over the ford at the Isca here,' Lucius pointed unnecessarily to the place on the map, 'you will follow.'

'Understood, sir,' Adal said. 'We'll make sure none of the

laggards in the Sixth get lost.'

'Once the ala is beyond the sands of the Sula we'll divide the force here.' Again Lucius pointed at the map. Cai and Adal looked, but they knew the plan. 'I'll lead four turmae west, crossing into the Anam Valley. You, Praefectus, will take your force east, scouting the ground near the hill. Your turmae will be clearly visible to the Novantae. But you're not to engage the enemy, if it can be avoided. Is that understood?'

'Yes, sir,' Cai said with a curt nod.

'We want any stragglers along the Anam valley to flee to the safety of their hill,' Lucius continued. 'The Governor's plan is to finish them in one swift action.'

Lucius saw the two friends glance at one another. Adal cleared his throat.

'I take it, sir,' he said, 'we still don't know the strength of the force we're up against?'

'No,' Lucius said with a frown, letting his frustration show for the first time. 'Although it's clear our enemy knows we're coming. How's the mood of the men?'

As was their way, Lucius observed the Praefectus wait for his colleague to respond.

'Spirits are high, sir,' Adal said. The men are glad to finally be getting stuck into the blue-faces. Some of the newer lads are a bit nervous, but the veterans will be a steadying influence on them.'

'My lads are ready,' Cai said. 'We even had time to get most of the replacement horses broken in.'

Lucius looked across his desk at the two veterans.

'Well, I think we're as prepared as we can be,' he said. 'Please do try to grab a little sleep before we move. It's going to be a long day.'

Dismissed, both men stood, saluted smartly and left. Lucius listened to their retreating footsteps.

'Gods, I pray I don't let them down,' he murmured

He moved then to the small shrine set up in an alcove. He lit the oil lamp with a taper. In his right fist, he took hold of two clay statuettes. In his left hand he gently held another of a woman on horseback, slowly rubbing his thumb along the animal's side.

'Divine Epona, mighty and swift. Help me bring honour to my family and my cohort. Father, Mother, watch over your son and I swear that should I survive the trial's ahead, I will restore our family's standing and take vengeance on those who took our lands.'

4

Adela nudged Cai's shoulder. He patted his horse's nose fondly, well used to her behaviour. He had named her after a girl from his village he'd once been sweet on, in part because of the mare's long blonde mane but also her sharp, often unpredictable temper. The memory of the girl made Cai smile. He had not thought of her for some time and did not know why she had come to mind at that moment. By now she would be long married, with a brood of children at her feet.

'Patience now girl,' he said, moving his hand in long strokes down her neck. 'We'll be on our way soon enough'.

Cai heard a crunch of hobnails on the road behind him, breaking his reverie. It was still dark, but he recognised the distinctive outline of his friend.

'Come to wish me a fond farewell, have you, brother?' Cai said.

Adal barked a laugh. 'No. I've come to check you've tied your saddle straps properly. I don't want you falling off pretty Adela here and breaking your neck, or worse, having to walk for a change'

'My thanks for your concern,' Cai said, 'but never fear. The straps are tied tightly as the tongs of your money belt.'

Adal snorted. Cai could just make out his teeth as he grinned in the near darkness. 'For slandering my generosity you can buy the first round in the mess upon our return.'

'And how is that different from usual?' Cai returned

Adal looked up at the star-filled sky. They stood a spear length apart and a few paces from the nearest of Cai's men, but when Adal finally spoke he stepped closer, keeping his voice low. 'Well, brother, it's almost time for us to be on our way. Remember your promise. Watch over my family should I not return.'

'You know I will. But enough of this gloom,' Cai said, embracing his friend. 'I'll see you below the hill at day's end. If, that is, your soap dodgers can get their fat arses up there fast enough.'

Adal laughed once more, before slapping Cai on the arm and walking away. 'See you at the hill,' he said over his shoulder.

Cai listened to Adal's retreating footsteps as they crunched along the roadway. His friend's mood was unsettling. He'd not known him to be like this before an action. But then, he reasoned, Adal had never been a father. Cai was so deep in thought he didn't hear the approach of another set of footsteps.

'Good morning, Praefectus Ala,' Lucius said, his helmet's plume silhouetted against the faint light from the fort.

'Sir.'

'Shall we be on our way?' Lucius said, who was leading Epona, his own black mare.

'Yes, sir,' responded Cai, punching his fist in salute across his chain-mailed chest.

'The First Nervana will prepare to mount.' Cai's voice was loud in the early morning air. He heard the creak of leather as the riders gripped their saddle horns and braced to mount. He waited until each of his Decurion's repeated the order to their own turma.

'Mount!' His shout accompanied an instant later by massed grunts as nearly two hundred and forty men sprung into their saddles. A few of the horses were skittish and it took a short while to get them under control, but even so all men were quickly settled and the eight turmae ready to move.

'The ala is ready, sir,' Cai said. Even after all these years he felt the familiar excitement.

'Thank you, Praefectus. Give the order.'

'The First Nervana will advance at the walk.' Again he waited until the instruction was repeated, even though he knew his voice carried to the rear.

'Advance!'

Kicking Adela into motion he moved alongside the Tribunus, the chinking sounds of tack, chainmail and weaponry loud in the still of the early morning.

By the time they reached their first objective, the Itouna river crossing, the sun had not yet risen, but the light had improved sufficiently for the ala to move at a trot. They quickly splashed past the blackened, wooden stumps in the slow-moving water, all that remained of the bridge. There was no sign of the enemy to slow their progress and less than half an hour later the second objective came into view. Seeing nothing on the far bank, Cai nudged Adela to the water's edge, letting her pick her own way into the dark, languid flow of the Isca.

'It looks like our legionary colleagues are going to get a bit wet on their way through,' Lucius said, in mock solemnity from Cai's side.

Cai beamed, appreciating the humour but also because he could see his young commander developing the auxilia's professional disdain of the citizen soldiers. 'It would seem so, sir. Let's hope the poor darlings don't catch a chill.'

As Lucius reached the river's northern bank two troopers emerged from behind the concealment of a small copse of stunted trees. They were part of a half section of scouts sent ahead of the main body. Lucius brought Epona to a halt, the nearest trooper nudged his mount forward and saluted.

He recognised Avitius. The memory of the execution flashed, unwelcome across his mind. The trooper had avoided the lash, but was still on fatigues. Avitius stared at Lucius, his face outwardly calm, but his hate-filled eyes telling a different story.

'Report, Avitius,' Lucius commanded.

'Sir,' Avitius croaked, spitting to clear his throat. 'Begging your pardon, sir. We advanced at speed as ordered and for a time saw no sign of the enemy. Although it's heavily wooded to the east, mind. We skirted close to the fort but could see no sign of movement within the ruins. It wasn't until we got to around three miles from the main objective, that we were spotted by a band of the hairy...enemy cavalry. Perhaps ten in number. They chased us back down the road, but gave up after a mile or so. I don't think they were seriously trying to catch us, sir, just letting us know they were there. If you know what I mean? I left the other two lads a couple of miles back, out of sight, to keep watch.'

'Very well,' Lucius said. 'What activity could you make out on the hill?'

'Not a lot, sir. There wasn't much light at that point, but we saw a lot of campfires on its top. Must be thousands of the bast—enemy up there, sir. You'll be able to see for yourself in a minute. The road crests a rise a short way further along. It's in sight most of the way from that point.'

Lucius turned Epona to face Cai. 'Right, Praefectus, it seems the enemy is behaving as we hoped. We'll proceed as planned and split the ala here.'

'Yes, sir,' Cai acknowledged the order with a brief salute. 'Good luck.'

More than half of the mounted force had emerged from the river and were formed up along the military road. Lucius returned to its head. Turning Epona to face the column, raising his arm. 'Turmae one to four will advance at the trot!' he yelled.

'Advance!'

Cai watched as the Tribunus turned his mount from the road in the direction of the Sula estuary, whose familiar silver slash could now clearly be seen as the sun broke the eastern horizon. He saw his commander adjust direction again to take the snaking column towards the mouth of the Anam, not yet in sight.

This was the part of the plan Cai still brooded over. He had tried to convince the lad that he should lead the incursion across the Anam. But the young officer wouldn't hear of it. This was to be his first real taste of battle. Cai worried it would be too great a test.

He waited until the last of his own detachment emerged from the Isca. He didn't share the Tribunus's confidence. Experience had taught him that the enemy always had a few surprises of their own.

'Trooper Avitius, a word,' Cai said, his voice low but commanding. He trotted Adela away from the road a short distance, Avitius bringing his own mount alongside.

'Sir?' Avitius said.

'If I see you staring like that at the Tribunus again I'll have the skin off your back,' Cai said, his voice a low growl.

'I don't know what you—'

'Shut your hole, Trooper. I won't save your arse again. Now get back in line.' Avitius saluted, giving Cai a sullen look.

'The men are ready, sir.' Salvinus, his Duplicarius, called from nearby. The double-pay man hawked and spat onto the road's surface.

'Thank you, Salvinus.'

Staring back down the line, Cai saw his men observing him, eyes dark in the depths of their helmets. Steam rose from the wet bellies of their mounts, giving them an otherworldly look.

'Shields!' Cai thundered.

5

Cai halted his force at the crest of a rise. The column would be in full view of the Novantae defenders atop their hill. With the Sula at their backs he had kept the four turmae on the old military way. Not long before they had passed the blackened, skeletal remains of the fort. The two scout lookouts re-joined them there, reporting no further movement. For much of the last hour their objective could be seen on the horizon, drawing ever closer, standing proud and alone. He had heard that its distinctive flat top could be viewed from some points of the Wall. Now he could believe it was so.

Minutes earlier they had watched as a group of horsemen broke from the cover of the forest to the east. The riders had withdrawn quickly towards the hill's summit and Cai had observed how easily the rider's short, sturdy mounts ascended the gently rising slope to what appeared to be the main gateway. For a while he scrutinised activity on the hilltop. The Novantae had made preparations.

At the hill's western extreme a circular palisade had been constructed. The timbers looked stout, perhaps the height of two men. Within he could make out the straw peaks of two large round huts, trails of light smoke snaking lazily upwards through their roofs to merge with the smoky fug which lay across the summit.

The remainder of the defences, however, were less daunting. From the palisaded enclosure, and along the hill's southern face to the far eastern edge, the enemy had erected what looked like a sturdy stockade fence of the type used to corral horses or cattle. Perhaps no more than chest height. Tricky when defended by so many spears, but far from insurmountable to a determined assault.

Unlike the approach to the hill's gateway, the western and eastern slopes were steep, with scarped, rocky sides nearer the summit. It would be impossible for an infantry force to ascend and keep formation. If the Sixth were to take the hill quickly, they would just have to knock on the front door.

Cai shielded his eyes from the brightness of the rising sun on his right shoulder. Although still some distance away he could discern the massed spears of the enemy. Despite his long years of service with the Nervana, facing many of the empire's enemies, he felt a flash of fear.

'Trooper Avitius. Report.' Cai called over his shoulder.

The horseman emerged from the line, halting before Cai, saluting as he did. He had known Avitius since joining his first turma as a young groom. Avitius had taken him under his wing and had taught Cai a great deal. The pair had become firm friends, but rank had now put a distance between them.

'Find the Legatus. The Sixth should be crossing the Isca by now. Inform him Tribunus Felix has reached the Anam with his force and I'm taking mine closer to the hill's base to get a better view of their defences. Any questions?' For a heartbeat the veteran looked like he might protest. Cai knew he hated to miss out on any chance of action.

'No, sir,' Avitius said, with a look of resignation.

Avitius turned his mount and quickly disappeared down the rise. That'll keep the old goat out of trouble, Cai thought. He considered his next move. The Legatus would want to know what lay on the other side of the hill. But that would necessitate taking his force close to the hill's base, passing between it and the brooding, forest's edge. Taking his entire command it would afford greater protection, but they would be less nimble. A smaller force would be at greater risk but could get out of trouble quickly. He made his decision.

'Decurion, Mascellus!'

'Sir.' Mascellus quickly reached his side.

'I want to take a look at the ground to the north of the hill. I'll take my turma to the east and attempt a circuit of its base. You'll lead the rest, advancing as far as that rise to the southwest. I'll re-join you there.' Cai pointed towards a small hill surmounted by a copse of stunted, wind bent trees. It looked like a promising position to keep watch over the Novantae at a safe distance.

'Understood, sir. But shouldn't I join you with my lads? Thirty more troopers would be a help in a tight spot.'

'Thank you, brother, but no. Speed will be our best defence. Now before we move, get the men to break out their rations and take a piss if necessary. I have a feeling this will be our last chance for some time.'

Cai heard the comforting murmur of the familiar conversations between comrades and guffaws of laughter as some wag made a humorous remark at the expense of one of his mates. Removing his helmet and liner he felt the cool morning breeze, smelling its saltiness as it was blown in from the Sula. He pulled his hand through his sweat-matted hair.

His thoughts turned to Adal. He smiled to himself, knowing his friend would not be in the best of humour after wading across two rivers and then waiting around, cold and damp, for the Sixth and Twentieth to arrive in their own sweet time.

Cai was not one to worry much about the gods, who played with men's lives, but he looked around him for some sign all would be well. He marked a flock of gulls winging their way towards the distant estuary. He shook his head at his own vanity, slipping his helmet back on. Why would the gods bother with him?

'Mount up!' He heard the order repeated by the Decurions.

'Ready, Decurion Mascellus?'

'Ready, sir.'

'Well then, let's see what we can see, shall we?' Turning Adela to face his men he hawked and spat to clear his throat.

'First Nervana, we are going to show these sheep-humpers what real warriors look like.' He noticed many of his men, even some of the veterans, sit taller in their saddles.

'Shields and spears at the ready,' he yelled.

Each man settled his shield onto his left arm once more before sliding the long lance from its sheath, leaving the two throwing spears untouched. Reins gripped in the left hand. They were ready.

'The first turma will advance at the trot. Advance!'

Cai nudged his horse into movement, Adela briefly tossed her head in protest, the blonde hair of her mane brushing Cai's face. But she settled quickly. After a short distance, Cai raised his spear point to indicate a change of direction to the right. The column quickly adjusted, the thirty men moving down the gentle rise at a steady pace. As they advanced, the Novantae's hill gradually filled their vision, but he still kept a wary eye on the forest's edge. Its impenetrable depths not much more than a long arrow's flight from their position.

Cai could now better discern the men of the Novantae crowding the hill's ramparts. All appeared to watch the small advancing enemy force. The first jeers carried to them across the still air. Would they attempt to rush his turma from the hilltop? Cai could almost hear Adal's voice. 'Bloody reckless fool.'

As the column reached the edge of the eastern escarpment the ground softened, the horses throwing up great clods of dirt with each stride. Cai judged his men were outside the range of the enemy's hunting bows, but, as the turma progressed, some of the hill's defenders made speculative attempts, arrows falling some distance short. The bowmen soon gave up. Cai could feel the hill's brooding presence almost like a living thing, the steepness of the eastern hillside temporarily hiding the tribesmen above from view. But still the men of the turma could hear the jeers.

Warriors came into view again. Some had climbed over the chest high barrier, taking them close to the steep escarpment's edge. For the first time Cai had a clear sight of his enemy. Most were bare chested, painted with intricate blue patterns. Some wore cloaks of widely differing colours; most carried spears. Some had swords at their hips. But all looked impressive.

One, a mountain of a man, had advanced further than the others. He bellowed a great war cry, throwing his arms wide. Then in a flash of movement he hurled his spear with a mighty grunt towards Cai, whose plumed helmet made him a target, the barbarian thinking to win himself glory. Cai watched, unconcerned, sure the spear would fall well short. But was shocked, an instant later, as the spear pierced the soft ground not five paces from his shield side. Adela whinnied, tossing her head at the sudden slopping sound so close by.

A great cheer arose from above, the big man turning in a circle, arms raised, like a gladiator in the arena, acknowledging his adoring public.

But the turma continued on at a steady pace, gradually adjusting direction as the hill's base curved towards the north facing side. Cai's attention was now so intent on the hillside that he was stunned as he was thrown across Adela's neck. His mount screamed, stumbling, her two front legs sinking alarmingly into bog. He only stayed mounted by grabbing tight to her long mane, but still it took all his strength to stay in the saddle, forced to drop his lance as he did so.

Righting himself, he hauled on Adela's reins. With an effort she pulled her front legs clear of the mud. Cai quickly looked around. All was in disarray. Troopers struggling to control their horses, fighting to free themselves of a sucking quagmire.

Jeers from above assailed them once more. The Novantae could see their hated enemies floundering. A knot of fear gripped Cai's stomach, it was only a matter of time before the enemy seized on this opportunity to rush the chaotic Roman ranks. He frantically searched for a way out of the bog. There, just ahead and no more than a spear's throw away, the terrain began to rise slightly. Would that be firmer ground? Turning back might be a greater risk. Now alive to their enemy's plight, the warriors above were unlikely to let them pass unharmed a second time. There was only one real option.

'Nervana. Onwards.' he yelled.

Cai pointed the way. Retrieving his fallen spear, protruding point first from the mire, he kicked Adela into a squelching, struggling walk, towards the higher ground. The turma followed, all semblance of a column lost. Continually glancing at the hilltop, he slowly made progress. Each laboured step producing sucking sounds as Adela fought her way out of the stinking morass.

Finally, with an exhausting effort, Adela pulled herself onto firmer ground. Turning in the saddle Cai saw his unit strung out behind him. How could he have been so foolish?

As more of his men escaped the bog, Cai moved Adela further up the small slope. For the first time the whole northern edge of the hill came into view. There was a further gateway to the hill, its approach less steep. The ground along the length of the hill's base rose and fell—and was why he had not seen the large war band approaching it from the north. Alerted by their brothers on the hilltop, they now blocked the turma's route of escape.

'Bollocks.' The exclamation came from behind. Cai turned to see an arrow protruding from the shield of a trooper. The Novantae had seen their opportunity.

The same trooper's voice spoke again. 'Shit. We're fucked.'

6

'Shut your mouth, Cordus,' Salvinus snarled.

The last of Cai's men had reached the firmer ground, both horses and riders, breathing heavily from the effort. They needed to rest, but there was no time. They must move now and there was only one choice.

'Form line abreast in rank.' Cai shouted.

The order was repeated by the double-pay men, but after months of continual drill his troopers were already on the move. The formation quickly took shape. More arrows came from above; most overshot.

'Advance at the trot.'

Grasping shields firmly, each man adjusted the grip on his lance, holding it upright. The noise from the ramparts reached a new crescendo at the sight of the Romans now trapped by their brother warriors.

The two lines moved forward in unison, horses and riders still puffing heavily from their efforts in the bog. The line of the war band ahead of them was strung out, but on seeing their enemy's intent, those that had them formed a rough barrier of shields. Most were bare chested, but a handful wore what looked like leather vests.

One stood out from the rest. Even at a distance Cai could see he wore good chainmail, his helmet reflecting silver flashes in the morning sunlight. A great bushy grey beard burst from under his chin strap, coming to rest upon a barrel of a chest. A black mouth gaped as he roared commands, readying his men. Their warchief.

The ground began to level out. Cai raised his spear high, taking a deep breath.

'Charge!'

A responding bellow escaped the throats of his men. Spears came level to the ground and a thunderous sound rose up from the earth, drowning out the noise from the hill.

The waiting enemy grew rapidly in Cai's view. There were gaps along their line, except at its centre on either side of the war leader. His hearth warriors gathering around their chief. These men carried heavyweight spears, and most held small, rectangular shields of wood and animal hides. They would provide little protection. Yet they stood their ground. The bearded war chief, taking in Cai's white crested helmet, fixed him with a stare.

The chieftain cast his spear aside and slid his sword from the scabbard slung across his back, flinging his arms wide. With the sword and shield held aloft he bellowed a great war cry, the sound coming from deep within his wide chest. Even with the thunder of the charge in his ears, Cai heard it.

At the centre of the turma's now ragged lines Cai guided Adela towards the war chief. Now barely a good spear throw apart, their eyes locked. Gripping his lance tightly, steeling himself for the impact, he directed its point towards the mailed chest of his enemy. The grey bearded face contorted in rage and hate. At the last moment the war chief threw his shield aside and made a mighty sword swing, aiming for Adela's legs.

But she was a war horse. All horses baulked at a solid line of spearmen but she cared nothing for a lone swordsman. At the instant of collision Adela took one mighty stride, launching her front hooves at the chest of the war chief.

The impact threw Cai backwards in his saddle. His lance was lost, torn from his grip; by what, he did not know. The sound of shrieking men and horses filled his world. He pulled himself upright using a saddle horn, his right hand was numb. But he was through the enemy line.

His head rang. He swayed, unsteady, and it took considerable effort to rein in Adela. Pain shot agonisingly from his shoulder. He swivelled in his saddle, looking left and right. With relief he saw most of his men had also passed through the enemy's ranks, some fighting to control their mounts; others were even now turning their horses to look back at the chaos. Bringing Adela about, he took in the scene.

Only a handful of warriors now stood at what had been the centre of their line. Screams split the air as bodies of the dead and dying lay in a writhing, bloody tangle. There were casualties too amongst his troopers. Cai couldn't discern which men had fallen but three horses lay on the ground, one thrashing, attempting to rise. The pitiful sounds of the dying animal mingled with those of men.

One horse lay on its side midway between Cai and the Novantae line, a spear protruding from its chest. Its rider had been thrown some distance by its fall and now sat on the soft ground, legs spread wide, staring dumbly ahead as blood ran from below his helmet's rim, streaking his face red.

It was Salvinus. The Duplicarius didn’t move, oblivious to his own peril.

‘Sir, the hill.’ a trooper called from behind him, a note of panic in his voice.

Men from the hilltop streamed through its northern gateway, shrieking and howling as they came, running headlong towards their now disorganised enemy.

‘Prepare to retire,’ Cai bellowed, as he kicked Adela into a gallop towards Salvinus, whose head had flopped onto his shoulder as if dozing. The first of the enemy reached the base of the hill as Cai pulled up next to his Duplicarius.

‘Salvinus, give me your hand.’ Cai leant down, holding out his arm.

‘Wha…’

‘Take my hand man.’ Cai became frantic as warriors raced towards him.

‘Sir?’

‘Duplicarius, take my fucking hand.’

As if waking from a deep slumber Salvinus raised his hand to Cai, who pulled him to his feet.

‘Now get up behind me.’ To his frustration Salvinus stood there, with a confused look, as blood oozed from under his helmet.

‘Sir, I don’t…’ Cai grabbed him by the neck of his chainmail shirt hauling him over Adela’s shoulders. A warrior threw his spear. Cai raised his shield just in time, the point penetrating its rim. Throwing the now cumbersome shield aside, he pulled on Adela’s reins, preparing to break into a gallop. But he stopped, startled by what he saw as his eyes caught movement in the mass of bodies left by the turma’s charge. There, amongst the dead and dying stood the war chief, his helmet lost, blood matting this great beard, staring silently at Cai with hate filled eyes. A severed head held aloft in his left hand, a red smeared sword in the right. One of Cai’s men: he couldn’t tell who.

A groan from Salvinus brought him back to himself. Kicking Adela hard he looped around, heading back towards his men, the

Duplicarious bouncing precariously in front of him.

'Fall back!'

Riding through his disorganised men, Cai had no thought of getting them into any kind of formation. They either followed or they died.

7

Lucius took in the scene before him. After dividing the ala they had reached the Anam by mid-morning at the point it emptied into the Sula. They followed the river's eastern shore as it snaked its way through the wide valley, the water's languid movement like dark honey poured from a jug.

He shifted his gaze from the river back to the small settlement. Four peaked roofs showed above what looked like a well-maintained palisade, but no smoke rose from within. Once again it appeared the locals had abandoned their homes well in advance of their arrival.

Following the now familiar routine he sent a squad of four riders ahead. Just to be sure. He watched as two troopers disappeared through the open settlement's gates. The second pair circled the exterior looking for any sign of the direction they might have gone. It wasn't long before the four riders reappeared. One man broke away from the group. Trooper Betto, Lucius recalled.

'Report, Betto,' Lucius said, following the exchange of salutes. Lucius was continually surprised by the pride that showed in men's expressions when he called them by name. Even amongst some of the veterans. He had come to understand the value of it, working hard to remember individuals.

'Empty, sir. Just like the others, everything of value has been carried away and the hearth fires are cold.'

'Did you see any signs of where they went?'

Betto nodded, still breathing heavily from the quick ride from the settlement. 'Yes, sir. Again there are two trails, one heading west and the other east.'

'Thank you, Betto.'

They're sending their women and children west away from the coming battle, he thought. It was the only answer. Lucius ordered a short rest.

He dismounted and led Epona to the water's edge. The black mare had been given to him by his uncle before he had left for Britannia. His uncle had told him tales of the cold winters he and Verus had experienced as junior officers on this northern edge of the empire. Lucius had fretted that Epona might not endure it. But he need not have worried. She had performed well during the winter training.

Now looking across the wide river valley, he noted the deep greens of the floodplain and the dark of the forest on the hills beyond. He knew some would see this place as beautiful, indeed he recognised that it did have its own brooding beauty, but it did not compare with the magnificence of the lands around his childhood home. The great mountains that surrounded his father's estate, whose olive plantations nestled in their embrace. A home now lost to him and only his uncle's kindness saving Lucius and his brother from destitution.

Lucius shook himself of his melancholy. He adjusted his chainmail that had been rubbing against his neck. 'Decurions on me.' he shouted as he led Epona away from the rivers' edge. Remounting.

'Gentlemen,' he began. 'We'll ford the river here and continue to follow it until the sun reaches its zenith. We'll then turn south east and drive any enemy stragglers towards their hill. Make sure your men remain alert. We must not be drawn into complacency, just because the Novantae appear to have abandoned the land.'

'Decurion Mascellus,' Lucius addressed the most senior and oldest of the three. 'Take two sections and scout ahead of the main column. The land appears more wooded, so don't advance more than a mile ahead of us at any time.'

'Understood, sir,' Mascellus said.

Once across the river the terrain quickly changed. The flat river valley they had passed through for much of the morning began to rise and fall in gentle grassy waves. Small thickets of trees that, at first, had appeared sporadically now came regularly, to the point it was difficult to see clear ground more than a bow shot ahead. Unease began to settle on Lucius and he sensed the same in his men.

Mascellus had been sending back regular reports, but some time had passed since the last and Lucius was becoming concerned. He was considering forming his force into a skirmish line to locate the scouts when he saw a trooper appear out of the trees riding at a gallop. He moved Epona out of line to intercept him. The trooper pulled up hard, his mount's hooves throwing up great clumps of soft earth.

'Trooper Manix, sir. We've come upon a lake not half a mile distant. There's a large settlement with a fortified enclosure on a promontory on its western edge. We've not entered the settlement, sir, but from a distance it looks deserted.'

Lucius nodded his understanding, even though the man's Latin was heavily accented, made worse by his breathlessness from the exertion of a hard ride.

'There's more, sir,' Manix continued. 'To the east and north the land rises above the lake where we observed more huts. They're part hidden by woodland but we could see smoke rising from amongst them.'

Lucius's heart began to race, but from excitement, not fear, he realised with surprise.

'Very well, lead the way, Manix.'

'Just over here, sir.' Manix spoke from his side, leading them through a thicket of silver birch. And there, glimpsed between the trees, was the lake. Lucius took in the sight of it. A feeling this was a sacred place struck him. The lake's surface was like black glass. Dense stands of reeds lined much of its eastern edge. Most of its oval circumference was cradled by gnarled and stunted trees. He saw the enclosed promontory on the western bank Manix had reported. It was a strong defensive position and would cost his detachment dearly to take it. But it too looked to have been abandoned. No smoke rose from its interior. There were further dwellings hugging the northern edge, appearing to sprawl back into the woods beyond.

What struck Lucius most sharply was the silence. There was no sign of life. Even the birds seemed to have abandoned this place, as if by the command of some unseen god.

Manix led them along the lake's eastern shore, coming upon the advanced sections, who had taken up a concealed position. The hill they watched was peppered with the same stunted trees that surrounded the lake. Interspersed among them Lucius could make out the pointed roofs of dwellings. Smoke rose languidly through the thatch. This was the first sign of life they had come across since entering the lands of the Novantae. And of course, it was a trap.

Decurion Mascellus appeared out of the dense brush on foot, squelching over the waterlogged ground. He spoke in a low voice as if he was within the precincts of a temple and Lucius could understand why.

'We've been observing the hill for some time, sir. There's been no movement, nor a sound. But the fires continue to burn.'

Lucius sent a runner to bring his senior officers to him.

'It looks like our enemies have set a trap for us to walk into, sir,' Mascellus said.

'Undoubtedly,' Lucius said, reaching under his helmet's neck guard to scratch an itch that had been bothering him all morning. He stared at the hill, his mind a fog of indecision. His orders were clear: he couldn't leave a potential enemy force at their rear. But he had no idea what was ahead of them. He might be leading his men to their destruction.

He made his decision. 'As hunters what should we do with traps, Decurion Mascellus?'

Mascellus looked at Lucius with a wide wolflike grin. 'Spring them, sir.'

Lucius returned his grin, feeling more confident, before fixing his gaze once more on the hill.

'Right then, this is what we'll do.'

8

Lucius nudged Epona forward. The men of his turma followed. They had spent some time stripping the lake's shoreline of reeds and now every man carried a smouldering firebrand. On his orders troopers called insults to each other and generally made the noise of men who didn't expect trouble.

Entering the settlement they passed empty cattle pens and low storage huts. The smell of dung strong in the air. Finally they reached the first of the round dwellings. In pairs his men dismounted and entered each in turn. All re-emerged shaking their heads, confirming what he had expected. The Novantae's ambush would not come from within the village. The thirty horsemen picked their way between the low buildings, maintaining the pretence, although to Lucius's ear each jovial call was filled with tension.

Now was the time to get the enemy's attention. He tossed his burning brand onto the nearest roof. His men followed his example, moving deeper into the settlement to fire the huts there. The thatch was dry, catching quickly, dark smoke rising in columns as flames spread. The turma continued to search and fire dwellings, knowing by doing so they were cutting off their own route of escape.

'Sir, over here.' The voice came from just ahead.

Lucius spurred Epona towards the shout and found himself in what must be the centre of the village. A large flattened area spread seventy or eighty paces across east to west and twice as wide north to south. At its far end was a wooden platform, which reminded Lucius of the temporary stages set up by travelling performers who had visited his local town. Except for one startling difference. Mounted on a post at each of its corners was a skull, each topped by a cavalry helmet.

From his position he could see the helmets were of an older design and the skulls themselves had yellowed with age.

Lucius walked Epona to the centre of the clearing taking in the rest of the settlement ahead of him: a maze of huts and animal enclosures. He could hear a fast running stream to his left that must run into the lake below. This was the worst ground for cavalry to pick a fight. But the plan was now in motion. There was no going back.

Turning Epona in a slow circle he surveyed the growing destruction. Most of the huts they had passed by were now ablaze. All thirty men had reached the clearing. Looks of trepidation passed between some, heads turning right and left seeking a glimpse of the enemy.

'Where the hell are they?' He was beginning to wonder if the locals had decided against taking on mounted warriors after all. He didn't have to wait long for an answer.

A blast of a horn sounded sharply from above them. Joined instantly by the blare of others. Maniacal warcries of massed tribesmen joined the warhorns.

'Form up.' Lucius screamed. Troopers who had been momentarily frozen by the sound moved into action. The men of his turma quickly assembled into a loose horseshoe formation, with the open end near the now-blazing buildings at their rear. Lucius was at the leading edge of the formation, some ten paces from the macabre platform. His mind filled with the growing cacophony of warcries, mingled with the deep warbling of the warhorns.

'Ready spears.' The turma lowered their long lances as one.

The sound increased in volume and intensity. Fear filled him. There were too many, surely? But the village beyond still hid the enemy's approach. Then all at once they were upon them.

The Novantae burst from between the huts, running headlong towards the waiting troopers. But the narrow spaces between the dwellings and animal enclosures funnelled the mass of warriors. Slowing their momentum and preventing them from assaulting the stationary cavalry as one.

'Remember your training, and remember help is on its way.' Lucius yelled above the clamour. The warriors emerged onto the open area, their faces twisted in hate, spears raised as they ran uncaringly at the small enemy force.

'Now!'

The thirty men kicked their mounts into motion, warcries in the language of the Nervii filled the air. Spears levelled, they surged into the first of the enemy. The impact was instant as lances were thrust into faces and unarmoured bodies. But now, each man of the turma was on his own in a fight for survival.

Many of the blue painted warriors were drawn to Lucius's helmet plume. He was their enemy's war leader. But the crush of men emerging from between the buildings, combined with the press from the Nervana's horses meant that for the time being, Lucius and his men could only be assailed by one or two Novantae at a time.

The first warrior to reach Lucius had disappeared quickly from sight under Epona's hooves. The next assailant was short and wiry with a long pleated, red beard. He ran at Epona, swinging a long, vicious looking sword in a downward arc, aimed at the mare's head. Lucius stabbed his lance point into the Novantae's exposed chest, the warrior's own motion driving it deep, his shriek cut short as he too disappeared from view. Lucius had to yank the spear's shaft hard to free it from the sucking chest wound.

An instant later he raised his shield reflexively, deflecting a spear thrust that slid over its rim and glanced against his helmet. He couldn't bring his lance to bear so did the only thing he could. He rammed his shield downwards, its rim smashing into the warrior's spear, forcing it from his grasp. Lucius kicked Epona hard, driving her chest first at the warrior, who was thrown backwards into the crush of screaming tribesmen. Now Lucius could use his lance, and he stabbed it viciously into the flailing man's throat. Blood sprayed up its shaft, the hands of the dying warrior grasped it in his choking agony. He looked pleadingly up at Lucius, the recently tattooed face not disguising that he was barely out of childhood.

As the man-boy fell, Lucius was forced to release his grip on the spear, its point firmly wedged in the victim's neck sinew. Quickly he drew his spatha, its honed blade glinting in the light of the flames behind him. He had a single objective: to hack at any enemy who came within reach. He mustn't allow himself to be dragged from Epona's back: that would mean his death.

A horse screamed to his right and in a brief glance saw a grey and its rider pulled to the ground, both disappearing into a mass of stabbing spears. Lucius swung and cut his sword left and right, all the while shrieking like a madman.

An agonised bellow escaped his lips as pain shot across his ribs below his raised shield arm. Lucius slashed his sword blindly to his left, splitting the spear's shaft. He followed through by smashing the lower edge of his shield onto the skull of his attacker, who had fallen forward off balance. With a crunch of bone he was gone.

Lucius had never felt such pain. He could only hope his chainmail had taken the worst of the impact.

'Where the hell is Mascellus?' Lucius cursed. He jabbed his sword point at the face of the next warrior. The thrust did not connect but forced him to flinch away. But the crush of his fellow tribesmen pushed him forward once more, giving Lucius a second chance. This time the point sank deep into the Novantae's eye socket. Lucius wrenched the blade hard to extract it. The warrior was already dead as the sword point came free.

But the press of wild eyed, bellowing blue-faces was relentless. His turma's end was certain. For the first time Epona whinnied in fear as she was pushed backwards, her front legs lifted from the ground by the mass of moving bodies.

Fortunately Lucius's men and horses were now so tightly packed the nearest warriors could not bring their weapons to bear.

Nevertheless, multiple hands clawed and grasped at Epona's harness. Panic engulfed him.

His head rang. His sight fogged over in the blinding light of pain. Something had struck hard at the side of his helmet. His strength and consciousness began to rapidly ebb. Confused and disorientated, one single thought filled his mind. Stay in the saddle. Releasing his spatha, he grabbed Epona's mane with his right hand. His shield, still somehow attached to his arm, he used to cover his head. With the last of his strength he held on.

The world around him began to darken. Epona stumbled, her back legs slipping under her. Clinging desperately to her mane, he awaited the death blow.

9

Cai paced amongst the low trees on the hill's summit. The sun was now long past its zenith.

'Where the hell is he?' he muttered, not for the first time. He had barely been able to take his sight from the horizon since his turma had reached the meeting place, rejoining the rest of his force. For some hours they had watched the great plume of smoke rising in the distance, now fading to a dark smudge drifting lazily into the cloudless sky.

The lad had got himself into trouble, but how bad was it? He had considered dispatching a scouting party but knew it would be too great a risk to send a small unit. There was nothing for it but to wait.

All was quiet. His men spoke in low voices, sensing his mood. Even the blue-faces on the hill had grown bored of calling their challenges to the watching cavalry.

'Rider approaching from the south, sir.' The shout came from Salvinus standing at the other side of the thicket. The double-pay man's head was heavily bandaged, but he had finally washed the encrusted blood from his face and other than a thumping headache, seemed to have no serious injuries.

'How's the head Salvinus?' Cai asked, as he crossed to where he stood.

'It feels like I have an unbroken stallion trying to kick its way out of my skull, sir. But my old mam used to tell me I was thick headed. So I'm sure I will be fine come morning.'

Cai smirked. 'Good to know,' he said. 'But have a medicus take a look at it anyway.'

'Will do, sir.'

Looking beyond Salvinus, he watched the approaching rider as he left the military road, swiftly ascending the slope towards their position. Cai recognised him. One of the Legatus's staff officers. The rider must have picked out Cai's crested helm as a moment later he steered his mount towards his position. Pulling up as he reached them, horse and rider breathing heavily.

Cai saluted. 'Good afternoon, sir.

'Good afternoon, Praefectus,' the officer returned, with a slight lisp. 'Marcellus's the name, I must speak to your Tribunus.'

To Cai he looked young, barely out of adolescence. He had grown a wisp of a beard, its fluffy curls failing to hide his spot-covered chin. His armour looked expensive though, no doubt bought by his indulgent father.

'He hasn't returned yet from his foray up the Anam, sir. We've been holding position here but there's been no sight of his force. Although from the smoke on the horizon it looks like he's stirring things up.' Cai flicked his thumb over his shoulder.

The young Tribunus stared blankly at the distant rising smoke. This was not what he had expected and bit his bottom lip, pondering what to do next. It eventually struck him.

'Very well, Praefectus, it will have to be you. The Legatus wants a briefing in person on the lay of the land here. Enemy defences, strength and so on. The Governor has set up a temporary headquarters near the ruined fort. The old man will no doubt want you to brief him too.'

'Very good, sir. Let me give instruction to my second in command,' Cai said.

Shortly afterwards Cai and Marcellus galloped their horses down the military road, hooves clattering over the metalled surface. It was not long therefore, that the ruins of the fort came into view as they crested a final rise.

To the south was a scene Cai had not witnessed for some years. A legion preparing its camp; the Sixth in this case. The quiet pasture they had passed through in the early morning light was now transformed by deep ditches and the movement of thousands of men who swarmed across it like ants.

Marcellus led him to the camp's centre, where a large temporary awning had been set up. Officers moved about a number of tables. In the middle of it all was a man instantly recognisable, his grey beard cut through by a pink scar, easily discernible even at a distance.

Dismounting, both men strode smartly into their commander's presence. They stood at attention, waiting for Verus to finish conversing with a group of staff officers. After a moment he looked up, recognising the Tribunus and indicated for them to come forward with a flick of his hand. Cai took a deep breath and gave his best parade ground salute. The young man next to him opened his mouth to speak but Verus cut across him.

'Where is Tribunus Felix, Marcellus? It was him I wanted to see.' Verus's scar turned a dark shade of red.

'The Tribunus wasn't available, sir. I have brought his Praefectus Ala in his stead.'

'Praefectus Martis reporting, sir,' Cai said. 'The Tribunus has not yet returned from the Anam valley. We had expected him some time since, but it looks like he may have encountered some resistance. We've been observing smoke rising to the north for some time.'

'Very well, Martis, you'll have to do. We are to brief the governor on the lay of the land around our objective. Start by running me through it.'

'Yes, sir.' Cai had thought through what he would say on the ride along the road. He recounted the approach to the hill and what he had seen of the defences.

'What of their numbers?' Verus interjected.

'Difficult to tell, sir. But given I could see heads watching us across the entirety of the ramparts. I would estimate two to three thousand.' Cai coughed to clear his throat.

'A moment, Martis.' Verus poured a cup of wine from a jug set on a small campaign table, before handing it to Cai.

'Thank you, sir.' Cai accepted the cup gratefully, taking a long swallow

'Continue, Praefectus.'

'Sir. The ground at the hill's eastern base is soft and difficult for cavalry to manoeuvre in. We almost came a cropper there. The ground on the northern approach is firm enough, but there's dense forest within an arrow shot of it.'

Verus interrupted again. 'You took a turn around the entire hill?'

'Yes, sir. My turma only though. We had a short engagement with an enemy band. But we finished the patrol without further difficulty.'

Verus gave Cai a long searching look. 'That was well done, Martis.'

'Thank you, sir.'.

'Is that all?' Verus said.

'Just one more point, sir. We observed enemy horsemen

withdrawing to one of the southern entrances to the hill. It's clear the approach is not difficult. If I may venture a view, sir. If we use ballistae to destroy their flimsy palisade, a strong force of cavalry could take the hill in short order.'

Verus frowned and Cai wondered if he had said too much.

'That's my summation, sir,' Cai said, swallowing the last of the wine.

Verus stared in the direction of the Novantae's hill, hidden from view by the rise on which the ruined fort rested, before turning to look at Cai directly.

'Martis, you'll give that same brief to the Governor. Marcellus, fetch my horse.' The young Tribunus ran off to do Verus's bidding, Cai thought the young lad looked relieved to be out of his Legatus's presence.

'He has set up his headquarters with the Twentieth. They're preparing their camp over the ridge there.' He nodded towards where the land rose gently further to the south.

'Praefectus, a word to the wise,' his voice lowered. 'I have known Urbicus for some years. I fought with him in the Judean campaign and have some experience of his preferences when engaging with the enemy. Particularly when assaulting prepared positions.' Verus came to stand next to Cai.

'Confidentially, Martis, our general desires most of all to present our emperor with a great victory. But most importantly, provide a good story that can be retold to the noisome old farts in the senate.' Verus placed his hand on Cai's shoulder.

'So as in Judea, we will assault that pebble of a hill with overwhelming force, using both legions, bringing all of our ballistae, large and small, to bear. The auxilia will also play their part.' The older man gripped Cai's shoulder firmly. 'Therefore, Martis, heed me on this. When you give your summation don't offer your thoughts on how best to take the hill. Even if you and I may agree on its sense. Understood?'

Cai nodded once. 'Understood, sir.'

'Good. Now let's go and see the man himself.'

10

In the dark Lucius's mind was filled with a buzzing, like angry wasps. Blood pulsed in his ears and a dull pain throbbed on the side of his head. Why could he smell smoke?

'Sir,' came a distant voice. Was someone trying to hail him in the night or was he dreaming? 'Sir, are you with us?'

Ah, it was Mascellus. But why was the Decurion in his dream?

His shoulder was being shaken. Who was trying to wake him in the middle of the night? Cold water splashed across his face. He took in a sharp intake of breath at the shock of it, choking as the liquid hit the back of his throat, too dry to swallow. Spluttering and coughing he opened his eyes to the bright light of day. Searing pain filled his head, the noise from the wasps reached a new height. He groaned, the blackness almost taking him once more.

'He's awake,' Mascellus said. 'Help him sit up.'

Hands levered his back and head into a sitting position. Lucius opened his eyes carefully to see Mascellus's concerned face looking back. The Decurion held a canteen to his dry lips.

'Drink, sir.'

Lucius took two swallows and tried to speak. 'What…' He choked. He hawked and spat. 'What happened? Where are we?'

A look of relief appeared on Mascellus's lined face. 'We're still in the Novantae settlement, sir. You took a hell of a blow from a spear shaft. I saw it from across the clearing. Big red headed bastard he was. Look.' Mascellus held up Lucius's helmet. Two of its white feathers were bent, and on its left side was a long dent, that a smith would have to hammer out before he could wear it again.

Lucius tried to stand. Pain shot through his left side.

'You also took a cut to your ribs, sir,' Mascellus said. 'Your chainmail has been ripped through. The wound isn't deep but it'll hurt like Hades to ride for a while.'

'Help me up,' Lucius said, ignoring the dizziness and the pounding in his head. He could not afford to be a casualty.

Men on either side gripped him under his arms. He hissed through clenched teeth as icy pain stabbed at his ribs once more.

Standing unsteadily, with Mascellus's support, he gingerly touched his head. He winced as he felt an egg-shaped lump above his left ear.

'Thank you, Mascellus. I think I can stand on my own now,' Lucius said, more irritably than he intended.

He looked around. They were still in the clearing at the centre of the settlement. Bodies lay everywhere. Mainly the blue painted Novantae, but he also picked out the chainmail of a number of his own men. There were wounded troopers too, being tended to on the far side of the open space.

'Give me your report, Mascellus.'

'Yes, sir.' The Decurion paused briefly to gather his thoughts. 'As planned, sir, when I heard the first sound of the enemy I ordered the men forward. Decurion Stonea did likewise from the eastern flank. However after only a short distance into the advance through the woods we hit dense undergrowth, forcing us to pick our way through. Our lines became ragged. Once we finally closed in on the edge of the village I had to get the men to dress the line so we could hit the enemy hard rather than arrive in ones and twos.' Mascellus's voice became craggy and took a long draft of water from the canteen, handed to him by Lucius, before continuing.

'As we reached the clearing your lads were in deep shit, being pressed on three sides. Only the fires at your back prevented complete encirclement. I ordered the charge and it seems Decurion Stonea simultaneously did likewise from the other side. s

So more by good fortune than judgement that we hit the enemy flanks hard as one. The blue-faces tried to put up a fight but were too tightly pressed. It didn't take long for panic to set in and they made a run for it. We pursued them but the woods prevented us from inflicting major casualties. The bulk were able to swim the Anam. It's too deep here for cavalry.'

'What casualties?'

'Eleven dead, eight from your turma, sir. Fifteen wounded. Thirteen will be able to ride out of here. The others I doubt will see the day out.' Mascellus looked at his feet. 'I'm sorry I couldn't get to you sooner, sir. I…'

'Put it from your mind, brother,' Lucius said, 'I know you'll have driven your men hard to reach us. But sometimes the gods like to laugh at our plans.' A thought came to him.

'Where's my horse?'

'Corralled with some of the others, sir. She's unharmed other than a few nicks here and there. Remarkable given she was in the thick of it.''

Lucius nodded with relief. 'Help me over to her will you, Mascellus? I feel as weak as a newborn calf.' The Decurion gave Lucius his shoulder to grasp.

'We need to get the hell out of here. Make sure the wounded are seen to, and quickly. I don't want to be caught out here when night falls,' Lucius said, as they walked to the corral. Each step a trial. 'We'll return for the dead when we've dealt with the Novantae's hill.'

'What of the two seriously wounded, sir?' Mascellus asked. 'The ride could finish them off.'

'There is nothing for it, Decurion. If they're unable to ride unaided, tie them to their mounts as best you can and trust in the gods.

11

Cai and Verus were escorted through the huge command tent's interior. Clerks and junior officers worked with a purpose at desks and there was a continual buzz of conversation. A guard pulled aside a drape at their approach and they stepped into Britannia's administrative heart.

More campaign tables were scattered around the room. All covered with scrolls and stacks of tablets. All except one. At the rear of the large space was a solid oak desk whose surface was hidden by an unrolled map, its corners held down by a wine jug, an unsheathed pugio and two wine cups. Behind the table stood the man they had come to see. Quintus Lollius Urbicus, Governor of the emperor's province of Britannia. And general of its army.

Cai observed Urbicus from his position behind the row of senior officers. All waited in silence for their commander to speak. In his long service Cai had become accustomed to the melting pot of cultures that was the Roman army, even here at the empire's very edge. But he had never seen anyone like him. This big Numidian stood out in the misty isles of Britannia.

Urbicus looked up from the map. His eyes eventually settled on Verus, who had told Cai to wait where he was until called forward.

'Ah, Marcus, there you are. Do we have a view of what the Novantae have in store for us?'

'Yes indeed, sir. I've received a report from the Praefectus Ala of the First Nervana. He surveyed our objective this morning. I've asked him to brief you directly.' At that Verus turned to Cai, waving him forward.

Cai's legs felt like lead weights. He was about to make his report to the most powerful man in the province. A friend of the emperor. At that moment he would have rather faced a band of screaming Novantae single handed than to be in the presence of this most striking of men. He managed to step forward without stumbling. Now he stood in front of the huge desk no more than a spear's length from Urbicus, who scrutinised him as he made his salute.

'Praefectus Martis, sir.' He remained at attention waiting to be addressed. The Governor continued his scrutiny as if trying to take the measure of a horse he wished to buy. Cai had to work hard not to avert his eyes and maintained his gaze over the shoulder of the Numidian, who despite Cai's own size, stood a hand span taller.

'At ease, Martis. Let's have your report, warts and all. We have an old map here that portends to provide a view of this hill of the Novantae. It would be useful if you could refer to it as you move through. Aeneas here can make notes.' Urbicus indicated an older man, his hair almost white and certainly long past military age. He looked Greek to Cai's eyes.

'Yes, sir.' Cai began, speaking carefully, knowing his Latin was often less than perfect. He repeated what he had told Verus. This time excluding his view on the ease with which the hill could be taken. Urbicus listened intently as Cai spoke, occasionally interjecting with a question or at times asking Cai to indicate where on the map certain points were. When Cai described his turma's actions on the hill's northern side, Urbicus's head snapped up, raising an eyebrow at Verus. The two men silently exchanged nods. Unaware of the scrutiny, Cai concluded his report.

'I've left my lads keeping an eye on the hairy...the Novantae, sir. They were behaving themselves up to that point.'

'Thank you, Martis. That was a great deal more detail than I had hoped for. You are to be commended for your quick thinking. Not to mention bravery.' Urbicus stroked a hand through his lush, black beard. 'One final question. Other than the enemy force you engaged, did you see any sign of others attempting to join their fellows?'

'No, sir, my Tribunus took his turmae up the Anam valley to roust out any stragglers from their hiding places. He hasn't yet returned, but from the smoke we saw rising from the north, he may have engaged a significant band.'

'Very good, thank you, Praefectus.' Urbicus returned his attention to the map. Cai took it as the signal he was dismissed. Coming to attention he saluted and stepped back to allow the senior officers to envelop the table once more. He had been forgotten, so he stood at the rear of the gathering, continuing to observe the Governor. Urbicus still surveyed the map, speaking in quiet tones to his freedman. Finally the big Numidian looked up.

'Well, gentlemen. Thanks to the intelligence provided by Praefectus Martis I'm able to adjust our plan.' Urbicus turned to

Verus. 'Marcus, I want the Sixth to build our main assault defences in front of their southern gateways. I know how much you liked the work in Judea.'

Both men shared a brief smile.

'Yes indeed, sir.'

'I want to put the fear of the gods into these savages,' Urbicus continued, 'so our forward ramparts will be placed aggressively close to the foot of the hill. We'll use slingers from the auxilia units and the Hamian archers to keep the barbarians' heads down whilst we prepare. The Sixth's architectae have built three fine ballistae that I want planted in front of our main defences to sweep the entire front of their ramparts.' There was a rumble of conversation. Looks were exchanged between those gathered.

'Yes, yes, I know it's not normal practise to position catapultae in such potentially vulnerable positions. But we want a more glorious story for our emperor, don't we?'

Verus was first to understand his commander's meaning.

'Of course, sir,' he said. 'And I'll ensure there are units positioned to protect them in any case.'

'Your men will be in range of their slingers and those with hunting bows.' This statement was made in a matter-of-fact way by the officer standing at the other end of the table from Verus. Cai didn't know him, but his dress and demeanour suggested a man of importance.

Short in stature, his dark hair was receding. His broad belly pressed hard against his expensive looking, muscled cuirass.

'You're quite right, Gaius and my men will be ready,' Verus responded, not quite hiding the irritation from his voice.

Urbicus turned his gaze on the fat officer.

'Gaius, the Twentieth will advance to the northern edge of the Novantae's hill and construct a blocking castra. You will prevent any attempt by the enemy to flee and stop reinforcements joining, as the Sixth makes the main assault.'

Even from his position at the rear, Cai noted the Twentieth's legatus did not seem pleased with the role he had been given. A red flush appeared on the rolls of his fat neck. But he nodded in acknowledgment.

'Any final questions?' Urbicus asked.

Verus gave a low cough.

'Sir, the east and west escarpments of the hill are indeed steep, but the Novantae could still use them as a route to escape or potentially to assault our flanks. Should we prepare a circumvallation trench connecting the north and south siege works?'

Urbicus looked sceptically at Verus, raising an eyebrow. He looked down at the map as if pondering the point.

'I want to make the assault at dawn on the day after tomorrow,' he said. 'Preparing a circumvallation ditch will add delay. You're correct however in your assessment, Marcus. But I would think a cohort of auxilia positioned at either end of the hill will suffice. Agreed?'

'Yes, sir,' Verus said, 'the First Nervana and the First Hispania can handle that job.'

Bollocks, Cai thought. As Urbicus signalled the meeting's end. Cai strode from the tent with dread settling in his stomach.

'Fuck.' The word slipped from his lips. He must find the Tribunus and Adal. The Nervana had just been dropped in the shit.

12

Cai walked briskly through the camp. The sight and sounds of its construction barely noticed. His mind in turmoil.

'Is this a cavalry officer of the Imperial Roman army I see before me, marching with his own two feet? Surely such a thing has never been witnessed?'

Cai had been so wrapped up in his own thoughts that, at the camp's partly completed gateway, he had nearly walked into the unmistakable figure of the Nervana's First Spear. Cai beamed in delight at seeing his friend.

'It's good to see you plodders have finally caught up,' Cai said. 'You left all the fighting to the cavalry as usual.'

Adal gave him a wry smile. 'Cheeky bastard,' he said. 'We had to wait hours for those lazy wretches in the Sixth and Twentieth to cross the Isca. They must have enjoyed a nice lie-in this morning. By the time they reached us my lads were freezing their bollocks off. I had to march them up and down the military road to warm them up a bit.'

'Well it's good to see your happy smiling face anyway, First Spear.'

'Likewise, brother.' Both men looked at each other a moment longer.

'So what's the plan, Cai?' Adal said. 'Some snotty staff officer, who looked like he'd just left his mother's tit, told me we'll have to wait for orders. Which means the prick didn't have a clue.'

Cai laughed at the thought of what his friend must have said to that particular young officer.

'It seems the governor is determined to have a nice set-piece tussle with the blue-faces and present our beloved Emperor the glorious first victory he so desires,' Cai said, then relayed the details of the meeting with Urbicus only minutes before.

'So,' Adal said, shaking his head in frustration, 'when the Sixth are kicking their way through the front gate the Nervana are to be alone and exposed, like a virgin's arse on her wedding night.' The shorter man scratched his bearded chin. 'We need to speak to the Tribunus. Where is our young commander?'

'It looks like he's getting his first taste of a real battle,' Cai said.

Adal looked surprised. 'He hasn't returned yet?'

'Not at the point I was summoned before the Legatus,' Cai said, before telling him about the distant smoke they had seen.

'Well, he's a good lad and we've done our best to keep him on the right track. He'll be fine,' Adal's voice betrayed his concern

'He'd better be, brother. I really don't want to have to break in another one.'

'What's that, Praefectus? Have you been missing me?'

Both men turned in surprise at their Tribunus's distinctive voice. Neither could immediately reconcile the sound they had come to know so well in recent months with the sight that stood before them. Only the black horse that Lucius led by its halter confirmed his identity. He was almost unrecognisable. Lucius's head was heavily bandaged, and a trail of dried blood ran in a line from his left ear and down onto his neck. The left side of his face was swollen into a carpet of purple shades.

Both men snapped a salute.

'Fuck me, sir,' Adal said, 'It looks like you've had an argument with the wrong end of a tavern owner's club.'

Lucius laughed, immediately regretting it as pain lanced through his head.

'Not that far from the truth, First Spear,' he said, 'and I have the mother and father of all headaches to go along with it. But the tale will have to wait. I must report to the Legatus. He must be made aware we may have more than the blue-faces on the hill to contend with.'

'There's more you need to know before you see him, sir,' Cai said, and quickly outlined Urbicus's plan. When Cai had finished Lucius was silent. Epona nudged Cai gently in the neck in recognition and he absentmindedly ran his hand down her black nose.

Cai broke the silence first. 'We'll be pretty exposed, sir,' he said, 'all on our own as we wait for thousands of the sheep humpers to spill over their ramparts trying to escape the sword points of the Sixth.'

'Perhaps you could have a word with the Legatus, sir,' Adal said, 'see if he'll beef up our ranks a bit.'

'Very well. I'll report to Verus on the pretext of getting

confirmation of our orders. If I get the opportunity, I'll try to gently make him aware of some of the potential difficulties our Governor may not have considered.'

'You should get a medicus to have a look at your head too, sir,' Adal said, his voice almost fatherly.

'Probably wise, First Spear,' Lucius said, glancing back over his shoulder as he led Epona towards the camp's centre.

The two older men watched him go. Only then did they notice the blood splattered rip in the side of his chainmail.

Cai turned to Adal, smiling grimly. 'He'll do,' he said.

13

A gust of wind on the exposed hilltop licked at Lucius's cloak. The bent and stunted trees on its summit offered scant protection from the elements.

'Right, gentlemen, here we have it,' he said, raising his voice as he addressed the cohort's senior officers. The group had formed a loose half circle around Lucius's campaign table, outside of his tent.

'The Nervana,' he said, 'are ordered into blocking positions below the western escarpment. We will take up formation before first light, the morning after next, ahead of the main assault. 'Our colleagues in the First Hispana will in turn cover the eastern end.' Lucius winced as another jolt of pain stabbed inside his head.

'Make no mistake,' he continued, 'when the Sixth breaks through the enemy's defences, we can expect the Novantae to pour down our side of the hill and hit us hard.' Lucius let that sink in before continuing.

'Are there any questions?' None came. 'Thank you, gentlemen. Prepare your men.' He signalled to Cai and Adal to remain behind.

As he waited for the officers to disperse he turned his gaze to the hill. Smoke from multiple fires drifted above its flat summit and ragged singing drifted over on the early evening breeze.

'Pull up a chair,' Lucius said, indicating the folding campaign chairs to the side of his table.

'How's the head, sir?' Adal asked, once they were seated.

'Pounding,' Lucius said, with a wry smile. 'It feels like this bandage is holding my skull together. I just hope I can get my helmet to fit over this lump above my ear when the time comes.'

'Life's a bitch, sir,' Adal said, with a smirk.

'Yes quite. Your wisdom in these matters is much appreciated, First Spear,' Lucius returned with a grin, which turned into a grimace at another bolt of pain.

Cai and Adal exchanged a look of concern, unnoticed by Lucius as he waited for the pain to pass.

'Well,' Lucius continued, 'our orders are clear. However, I do have a couple of concerns.'

'One being, where in Hades are that band you ran into, sir?' Adal said.

'That's one.' Lucius scratched the day old growth on his chin. 'Mascellus pursued them as far as the Anam. He saw many abandon weapons to make the swim, but that doesn't mean they won't regroup and make a nuisance of themselves.'

Adal hawked and spat. 'The last thing we need,' he said, 'is those sheep-humpers taking *us* up the arse while we're watching the hill.'

Lucius nodded, immediately regretting the movement.

'Organise a patrol of turma strength to sweep to the north whilst we still have a few hours of daylight left. We must locate them.' Lucius stood and arched his back.

'Yes, sir,' Cai said.

'Other than the pummelling the cohort are certain to take, what else is on your mind, sir?' Adal asked.

'It's the top of the escarpment itself,' Lucius said, looking at the hill once more. Both Cai and Adal turned in their chairs. Its steep sides had been the subject of a lengthy discussion already between the two friends.

'Do you see that dark mass on the hill's edge just below the enclosure's palisade?' Lucius said, raising his hand to shade his eyes from the sinking sun's light.

'Your sight is better than mine, sir,' Cai said, 'There's definitely something there, but whether it's a midden heap or something more sinister I can't tell.'

'We must assume the Novantae have a nasty little surprise awaiting us,' Adal said.

'My feeling too, First Spear. Which is why I plan to go and take a look for myself, so we know what we're up against. I'll take two men with me and make the climb during the middle watch. Most of the blue-faces should be unconscious from that swill they drink by then.'

The two friends glanced at one another.

'With respect sir,' Cai said, 'you're in no condition to make the climb. You're still in considerable pain from that bash on the head, not to mention the wound in your side you're trying to hide from us.' Cai gave a lopsided grin. 'I'll go. I know the First Spear will argue that it should be him. But he'd be as quiet as a bull before a sacrifice to the Great Mother.'

Adal harrumphed but said nothing.

Lucius returned his attention to the hill. Deep in thought. Whilst Adal gave Cai a look that would have wilted even the most experienced of veterans. Cai kept his eyes on Lucius, affecting not to notice his friend's glare.

'Very well, Praefectus. Pick your men,' Lucius said, slumping once more into this chair. 'The Sixth,' he said, 'and the Twentieth will continue their preparations long into the night, which should keep the attention of any of their sentries.' Lucius stretched his back to ease the pressure on the wound.

'Let's pray the enemy's sentries are as dozy as we hope, or the Praefectus here might find a Novantae's spear wedged firmly up his arse. No matter how quiet he is,' Adal said, an evil grin spreading across his face.

14

The three men picked their way across the open ground. The knee-high tufted pasture was water-sodden underfoot. It squelched alarmingly to Cai's ears with each step and forced the group to slow their pace. Near his right shoulder was Salvinus, who had recovered from his tumble, and Avitius to his left. The old trooper had been as excited as a lad being invited to his first hunt when Cai told him he was coming on the patrol.

To minimise noise, Cai had told the men to remove their chainmail and helmets, and to wear their pugio as the only weapon. But even with the long dagger strapped to his side, Cai felt naked.

Eventually the ground became firmer as it began to rise. They had reached the base of the western escarpment. The three halted. Cai tried to discern any movement or sound from above. Nothing.

'Let's move,' Cai whispered. 'Stay close.'

Almost immediately the ground rose sharply and it was not long before the group was forced to grip onto clumps of the long grass to aid their progress. Thighs burning, breath ragged, they climbed slowly upwards. Gradually the faint light from campfires, burning within the enclosure, enabled them to see the silhouette of its palisade. They were close.

Cai froze. A low murmur of conversation came from above. The others had heard it too. He listened, heart thumping. It sounded like there were only two men speaking, but with no urgency. Just two sentries passing the time. He hoped.

They waited unmoving. Until gradually the voices faded away. Had they shifted along the palisade? They lay still a while longer. Then tapping each man on the shoulder, Cai crept upwards once more.

A bright light bloomed suddenly into life on the palisade.

'Down,' Cai hissed.

All three disappeared into the long grass.

Risking a glance upwards between the scrub, to his horror he saw a blazing bale of straw being tossed over the ramparts. It hit the steep bank, quickly gaining speed.

Sparks flew, casting the hillside in a flickering orange light. The bale bounced and spun rapidly. It was coming directly towards Cai.

It was almost upon them. Cai shut his eyes tight, pressing harder into the soft hillside as if it might swallow him.

'Divine Fortuna, protect us.' He breathed the prayer into the earth, smelling its dampness.

An instant later he felt the flames' heat against his cheek as the bale hissed over him before it continued its journey towards the hill's base.

Eyes still shut tight, Cai's body tensed in anticipation of the searing pain of a spear-point's impact. He lay unmoving. Moments passed.

The bale had finally come to a rest below. The light it cast diminishing as the flames gradually burned low. Until finally all was black. The urgent voices had become whispers, fading to silence.

Had they moved on?

He would have to risk it.

Salvinus and Avitius lay on either side of Cai, their heads level with his knees. He gripped on the shoulder in turn, indicating he would go on alone. He edged slowly upwards. Sliding through the scrub, the shooshing sound of his passing loud to his ears.

He stopped continually. Listening. Expecting at any time the blazing light of another bale, tossed over the palisade. Surely they could hear him? There would be no hiding next time.

Finally, almost unexpectedly, Cai reached an area of low bushes and what he hoped was the point of the rampart near his objective.

Heart racing, he carefully grasped the nearest bush and began to move it aside. Thorns pricked his palm. To his surprise the dense bush moved easily, as did the one next to it. They didn't grow here. They'd been cut and placed to conceal whatever lay beyond.

Cai stopped dead. Voices came from his left, further along the palisade's walkway. He dared not breathe. The voices moved on once more.

He tried to see what lay beyond the bushes. He could discern a dark mass, but there was no telling what it was. He would have to get closer.

Raising his head, he listened intently. The base of the palisade was now no more than a spear's length away. Turning slowly he glanced up. The top of the wooden barrier was faintly visible. But the feared silhouette of a head looking down at him did not appear.

Exhaling slowly, he pulled himself through the gap in the bushes and slid across the flat ground. Smooth ridges of rock scraped against his knees and elbows. The short distance seemed to take an eternity to cover. But finally he closed on the dark shape.

Slowly, he reached out. His hand touched wrinkled tree bark. Rising now to his knees, Cai felt along the rough edge. Tree trunks. Piled on top of one another. Searching along its base now, it didn't take long to find what he was looking for. A stave. He knew enough.

Flat on his belly once more, he made his way back towards the screen of bushes. A sharp screech, immediately to his left, shattered the silence of the night, accompanied by loud flapping of wings. Raised voices sounded from above. Footsteps thumped along the walkway.

Shit!

Jumping to his feet, Cai leapt over the escarpment's edge, into darkness. For a second he flew through the emptiness of the night. Until he landed hard, the air driven from his lungs. But his momentum was unchecked as he rolled downwards, out of control.

Grabbing onto the long grass he finally came to a halt.

'Run,' Cai gasped into the blackness, towards the place he thought Salvinus and Avitius lay hidden. Two faint shadows detached themselves from the hillside, not needing a second invitation. Shouts of alarm followed them. An instant later their path ahead was lit and Cai saw the silhouetted figures of Avitius and Salvinus to his right. He dared not look back as a great bellow of voices came from above.

A spear struck the ground just ahead of them. Avitius, now alongside Cai, was so intent on avoiding the spears shaft, now protruding from the scrub, lost his footing and tumbled headfirst down the slope, cursing as he went.

The ground became brighter still as a blazing bale somersaulted before them, as if in a race to the bottom of the hill.

'Bollocks!' The cry of pain came from Avitius, who had come to rest amongst long tussocks of brush.

Still trying to fill his own hurt lungs, Cai reached the groaning trooper's side. Looking quickly back up the hill he saw the dark, fleeting shapes of men as they leapt over the palisade.

'Let's go, Avitius,' he said, holding out his hand.

'I can't, I've done my ankle. I can't stand. Leave me.'

'Give me your arm man,' Cai said. He hauled the trooper to his feet. Salvinus appeared out of the darkness and without a word moved to support Avitius on his other side.

A sucking noise came from their left. An arrow had buried itself in the soft ground close by.

Go.' Cai said.

They reached the base of the slope. Cai and Salvinus part dragged, part carried Avitius over the soft, uneven ground. Salvinus's foot squelched into a sodden hollow. He stumbled and fell, taking the other two, cursing, with him.

'Up,' Cai commanded. Taking the opportunity to look back into the darkness. The pursuit was close.

An excited shout came from behind them. The enemy had sighted their prey. Another arrow slopped noisily into the watery ground just ahead, swiftly followed by another.

'Hopeless. Couldn't hit the main gate at two paces,' Avitius said.

But the sounds of the pursuit became louder. They were closing in. They weren't going to make it. Cai pulled up. Drawing his pugio swiftly from its sheath. He turned to face the Novantae.

'Let's make sure we take a few of the bastards with us,' Cai said, his voice grim.

'Aye,' Avitius said, freeing himself from Cai's arm. Both he and Salvinus slid the daggers from their belts.

A shout of triumph came from the chasing warriors, seeing their quarry at bay. They closed in for the kill.

15

The three men stood tensed. Pugios gripped in their hands. Ready for the end.

'Front rank! Prepare to release spears.' The command erupted from the darkness.

There was no mistaking that voice. It took only an instant for Cai to react.

'Get down.' he hissed. The three threw themselves onto the sodden ground. Instinctively Cai drew his knees into his chest.

'Release!'

A whooshing sound filled the air above him, as dozens of spears flew past unseen. An instant later, the night filled with agonised screams.

'Front rank. Prepare to release spears.' Adal's voice filled the darkness once more. 'Release!'

More screams from the unfortunate Novantae. But Cai didn't hear much after that, his head buried so tightly against the soft, wet earth. Cold water filled his ear.

'Are you there, brother?' Adal's shout from the darkness, now full of concern.

Cai raised his head.

'Over here,' Cai shouted.

Barely discernible, the silhouette of a Centurion's fan tailed plume bobbed steadily towards them.

'Nervana! Advance. And watch you don't accidentally kill the fucking Praefectus,' Adal bellowed.

'Let's get out of here,' Cai hissed. The three men slid and crawled their way out of the path of the advancing century.

'Well, well what's this I see?' Adal said, as he reached where they lay. 'Grown men playing in the mud?'

The three men looked at each other from their prone positions. As if some unspoken word had passed between them, they began to giggle. Once they started they couldn't stop. It was as if they had been told the funniest of tavern jokes. Avitius laughed and groaned by turns.

Adal stared down at them with a look of bemusement, slowly

shaking his head.

‘Yes, sir,’ Cai said, ‘as you suspected the Novantae are prepared for any unsuspecting units who try to make an assault on this side of the hill.’ Cai was standing in front of Lucius’s campaign table, pulling on his armour and cloak as he spoke. He was glad to feel its familiar weight.

‘Although,’ Cai continued, ‘given the steepness of the rampart it has a dual purpose.’

‘What other purpose, Praefectus?’ Lucius said, giving Cai a look of puzzlement.

‘I expect,’ Adal said, interjecting, ‘the whoresons will release the tree trunks just before they make a run for it. When the lads from the sixth knock on the door of that enclosure.’

‘You can imagine the mess those great logs could make of our stationary ranks,’ Cai said, before taking a swallow from the cup of spiced wine the Tribunus had pushed across the table to him.

Lucius said nothing for a while, deep in thought. He had been standing outside his tent watching the dark shape of the hill as the night operation got underway. With mounting trepidation he saw the light of the burning bales tossed from the ramparts and heard the distant shouts carry across the open ground. He had been greatly relieved to see Cai’s tall figure walking through the tent lines towards him, his friend at his side.

Cai and Adal stood unspeaking, patiently watching their young commander without concern. They were by now used to his habit of lapsing into silence as he worked through a problem. Cai drained his cup, placing it on the table. He turned to Adal.

‘First Spear. When you march out the cohort in the morning, I suggest you take up a position a good fifty paces from the foot of the hill. That should give you enough time to react if anything comes rolling down the hill at your formation.’

‘Aye, sir. We’ll be ready.’

‘Any word from the Legatus, sir?’ Cai said.

‘Not yet. I’ll try to get to him again tomorrow and brief him on this development. He may feel more inclined to beef up our ranks. Especially if this looks like the main route for an attempted break out.’

‘Not forgetting our patrols haven’t found any sign of that war band you came across, sir,' Adal said.

'Indeed.' Lucius retrieved the jug of spiced wine and refilled their cups, Cai and Adal nodding their gratitude. Lucius stretched in a futile attempt to ease the continual pain of his wound.

'How are the men?' he asked

'Good, all things considered, sir,' Adal said, 'the old hands are just getting on with it and making sure the younger lads don't have too much time to fret. But everyone will be a bit nervous this close to a battle. We've got a solid cohort, sir.'

Cai nodded in silent affirmation.

Lucius had expected nothing else, but it was still comforting to hear it. 'Thank you, gentlemen. It appears we are as ready as we can be for whatever the coming days' throw at the Nervana.'

'Here's to that sir,' Adal said, raising his cup, before downing the remains of his wine in one great gulp.

'Well, it appears my jug of wine has been emptied quite effectively, so I suggest we try to get whatever sleep we can before we move.'

When they were out of sight of their commander's tent, Cai put his hand on Adal's arm to stay him. 'Our Tribunus seems to be handling things quite well, don't you think?'

'Aye, he's doing just fine. That skirmish yesterday sounded like it was fierce, so he's already doing better than some of the useless, young pricks we've come across in our time.'

'Too true,' Cai said.

'Thanks for digging us out of the shit earlier, brother. I thought my end had finally come.'

Adal punched his friend playfully on the shoulder.

'Isn't that what I've been doing since your mam was still wiping the snot from your nose?'

Cai laughed. 'But how did you see me and the lads to know you wouldn't hit us, with the blue-faces so close on our tails?'

'I didn't. I just thought if you were too stupid to hit the deck when I gave the order to release spears, then we probably needed a new Praefectus anyway.'

At that Adal turned on his heels, leaving Cai staring open mouthed at his friend's retreating back.

16

'The Legatus is with the governor, observing the progress of the siege works,' said the adjutant, who sat behind a table just inside the command tent's entrance.

Lucius cursed. He had ridden south to the Sixth's camp and would now have to make his way back.

'Which siege works? North or South?'

'Both, I believe, sir. He left some thirty minutes ago. I'm surprised you didn't pass him on the road.'

Lucius pushed Epona as hard as he dared up the now-congested military road. At times he was forced to cross onto the softer open ground to pass trundling supply wagons. He must get to Verus before he moved on to the northern camp. When he eventually left the road behind to reach the siegeworks, the ground became a quagmire. The formerly green pasture had been churned by thousands of hobnail boots, not to mention the supporting baggage train.

As the hill's base came into view he was slowed further by wide lines of mules hauling felled tree trunks from the nearby forest. Frustrated, he now had no choice but to let Epona carefully pick her way towards the works. The air stank of horse shit and his journey was accompanied by the ever-present buzzing of the flies that feasted upon it.

The camp was still out of sight but he could already hear the now-familiar confusion of sound created by thousands of men at work, accompanied by the bellows of officers, no doubt taking issue with any men who were not putting in the required effort.

He became aware of a different buzzing noise, gradually increasing in volume the closer he got. Initially he put it down to more flying insects, clouds of which appeared out of nowhere.

Reaching the top of a rise he pulled up in surprise at the scene before him. This was no mere marching camp. The works were huge. The square shape of the defences was as expected, but what grabbed his attention most were the fort's northern ramparts, facing out to the hill. They were mostly complete, including a tall wooden palisade. Three broad gateways cut through the wooden barrier.

All were easily wide enough to accommodate a column of legionaries marching ten abreast. To the fore of each gateway and protected by their own deep ditches were huge mounds, the platforms that would support the ballistae. The legion's architecture looked like worker ants from this distance as they laboured to assemble the huge frames of each of the stone throwers. Wisely they had already constructed roofed wooden canopies to shield them from the continual assault of arrows and sling stones from the hill's defenders.

Lucius wondered at the decision to place the platforms in such an exposed position outside of the fort's own defences. Although, Verus had stationed a century to the fore of each platform to discourage the Novantae from any attempt to sally and fire the stone throwers.

Lucius at last identified the source of the continual buzzing sound. It wasn't from any shit-loving flies. Two centuries of slingers, including one from his own cohort, were spread out along the rear of the palisade. The men were loosing lead shot continually at any target they picked out or just to simply ensure the defenders kept their heads down. Each lead ball buzzed as it flew invisibly towards its target. The effect on the defenders must be terrifying, he thought.

The ground inside the fort was like much of the land around the hill. Soft and boggy. Now it resembled a ploughed field. A small stream ran through its centre north to south, giving the camp the appearance of being split into two halves.

Pulling his attention from the activity in the fort, he sought out Verus. He spotted a large formation of red-cloaked cavalry outside the ditch, close to the southern entrance. They could only be the Governor's personal guard. He nudged Epona towards them. As Lucius approached the edge of the formation, a trooper disengaged and rode out to meet him, bringing his mount to a halt before him, saluting smartly.

'Duplicarius Secondus, sir. How may I be of assistance?'

Lucius returned the salute. 'Tribunus Felix of the First Nervana Germanorum. I wish to speak to Legatus Verus. If he can be disturbed?'

'Very good, sir. If you could wait here for a moment, I'll inquire.' At that the double-pay-man turned his horse and rode back the way he had come.

Shortly after Lucius watched as the white plumed helm of the Legatus bobbed around the corner of the cavalry formation. Verus brought his mount to a halt alongside Lucius, who snapped off a salute. Verus returned it, speaking curtly.

'Felix, what brings you here? I need you watching over our western flank. What's so important that you must speak to me right now?'

'I'm sorry to disturb you, sir. This was too important to send a messenger.'

'Very well man. Out with it.'

Lucius relayed the events of that night and what his Praefectus had found on the hill's western ramparts along with his view on what that could well mean for the Nervana. He mentioned, too, his concern at the failure of his patrols to locate the enemy band from the battle by the lake.

'Given the ground and the nearness of the forest, sir, I feel it may be prudent to increase our forces on the western flank of the hill.'

Verus nodded slightly, twisting in his saddle he looked back at the hill. Turning back his face thoughtful.

'From our observations the enemy force on the hill is greater than we first thought. More may have joined during the night from the north before we closed that route off. Your elusive band of warriors are likely to have already reached their brothers.' Verus arched his back and flashed Lucius his grimace-smile.

'My old bones protest at long rides in the saddle these days.' He stared appraisingly at Lucius for a while longer.

'Look, Felix, the Governor wants to hit them hard. You must hold the flank. I will try to get you more if I can. But you must hold.'

'Yes, sir.' Lucius snapped a salute, knowing Verus was dismissing him. 'We will do our duty.'

Verus returned the salute before reining his mount around and heading back towards his commander's side. Lucius watched him go with a growing sense of unease. But he had his orders. The Nervana would hold the flank, even if it meant its destruction.

17

The three ballistae lost their fist-sized stone balls in quick succession. A distinct thunk could be heard as the torsion was released. Lucius tried to follow the flight of the nearest, but it proved impossible. He did, however, see some of the damage it inflicted. As the stone passed through the chest-high wicker palisade it tossed up splinters. The flimsy barrier was gradually being shredded.

At such a short range the stones would continue their journey unimpeded, taking a terrible toll on the bodies of any defenders that stood in their path. The Novantae, who earlier had continued to shout their defiance, now sought whatever cover they could find.

Lucius watched from Epona's back on the rise opposite, a short distance from the Nervana's camp. The black horse tossed her head, discomforted by the unfamiliar sound.

He had been watching the crews for some minutes, mesmerised by their speed of reloading. Each five-man team appeared to compete with the others. No doubt bets had been laid on who would fire most projectiles ahead of the main advance.

His position allowed a view of both the hill's southern face, where the main assault would take place, as well as the ground on its western slope, where his cohort had taken up its positions before first light. As he looked upon their ordered ranks, he replayed in his mind his address to them not long before.

He had fought nausea as he trotted Epona to the fore of the waiting centuries. Turning her to face his men, the plume of his helmet had been blown in the stiffening breeze. Hundreds of pairs of eyes stared back at him. They had been standing at ease, their oval shields resting against hips, spears held loosely in their right hands. At the heart of the second rank, the First Spear, the broad brush of his Centurion's crest standing out for both his men and the enemy alike to see. What must this veteran of many battles think of him? Lucius's throat had become suddenly dry. He swallowed.

He knew he did not have the parade-ground bark of the grizzled veteran officer. But Lucius understood these Nervii were as much warriors as those on the hill above them. They would want to hear from their war leader.

Lucius had looked along the ranks, from left to right, slowly, deliberately, letting them know he spoke to them all. Finally he cleared his throat, taking a deep breath.

'First Nervana!' His voice seemed shrill to his ears. 'The Sixth will soon be on the move and will make short work of the Novantae's defences.' There was a ripple of a cheer at this, and a buzz of whispered discussion broke out.

'Silence in the ranks,' came the booming voice of the First Spear.

Glancing beyond their lines, Lucius saw the clouds moving along the Sula had become darker.

'The enemy will be driven to make their final stand on the ramparts above us.' He let that sink in for a few heartbeats before continuing. 'When the end comes and the pressure is greatest, they will make a run for the forest. You know what must be done. None must escape. They will be met by the points of our spears and the cold steel of our swords. When this battle is done the Nervana will have another honour to add to our standard. Hold your nerve, hold your ground and the honour will be yours.' Without thought, Lucius drew his spatha, raising the long sword into the air. 'Nervana.' He roared. And to his surprise the cohort responded instantaneously, spears thrust into the air.

'Nervana! Nervana! Nervana!' The sound erupted from hundreds of throats, including the First Spear. The veteran acknowledged him with a firm nod and what Lucius thought was a smile. Or was it a grimace?

With a shake of his head at the wonder of it, Lucius's thoughts returned to the present. Turning in his saddle, he focussed his attention on the legion's siege fort. The slingers, detached from his cohort, were back in action. They now moved at a slower but steady pace, picking their targets with the heavier lead shot. They had been joined by two centuries of the First Hamians. The archer's movements were languid and their appearance striking, with conical helmets, plate body armour and loose red troos. They had been letting fly, volley after volley, into the interior of the hill for some time. Stacks of arrows were positioned behind them, close to hand.

To the rear of the auxiliary units and completing the onslaught were dozens of two-man scorpio squads. One of the small bolt-throwing ballistae was provided by each of the legion's centuries, distributed west to east across the fort's length. Lucius had seen experienced crews fire off three or four of the short, iron-tipped bolts every minute. He shook his head, awed by the firepower unleashed against the hill's defenders. How many would live to meet the Sixth when they finally made their assault?

He turned his mind back to his own command. With his slingers occupied in the south he had been able to deploy nine centuries onto the hill's western flank. Seven now formed an unbroken line three ranks deep around the base of the hill, with the remaining two in reserve. He could see the familiar figure of the First Spear as he paced in front of his men. But what he said did not reach Lucius.

Lucius had split the ala to protect the infantry's flanks. The Praefectus led four turmae nearest the forest to the north. His own four to the south. The mounted patrols had once again failed to discover any sign of the tribesmen who had escaped the action by the lake. Perhaps Verus was right and they had already reached the hill. But not for the first time that morning, he looked at the brooding, dark depths of the forest's edge. He pushed away the rising doubt. Would the thin line of the Nervana be enough?

Within the siege fort, the men of the Sixth had formed up into three great columns, each three cohorts strong. Officers strode along the formations. The occasional exasperated shout carried to Lucius. It wouldn't be long now.

The weather had begun to change. The wind had picked up further and he felt the first, light drops of rain. The dark clouds he had watched roll in along the Sula's silver waters covered the battlefield with their gloom, the waters of the estuary now turned grey.

Bringing an unexpected feeling of relief, the trumpeted blasts of the legion's buccina's split the air. The bright, polished and curved brass horns could be seen clearly even on this dull day. One final long blast set the three formations into motion.

The jangle of armour and weapons, combined with the squelch of four thousand pairs of marching feet, created an incongruous sound. The head of the three columns, all ten men wide, quickly reached the open gateways and approached the ballistae platforms immediately to their fore, whose crews continued their unrelenting barrage.

Lucius did not hear the command but each column split. Each side flowed around the huge mounds like the waters of a river breaking on a great rock midstream. The two parts merging once more as they passed the obstacle.

The buccinas' sounded again, three short blasts. The ballistarii and slingers ceased their barrage, although the Hamians continued to direct their barbed arrows into the hills interior.

Lucius's focus was broken by an other-worldly noise from the hill. It was lower pitched than the buccina's, a haunting, echoing sound that carried across the battleground. Instantaneously hundreds of bare chested, blue painted warriors leapt over their small palisade, which now looked severely frayed. Many carried bows or slings and rained projectiles onto the advancing cohorts. Others threw rocks, gathered from the ancient, tumbled stone rampart, now just a low hump to the fore of the palisade.

The enemy barrage was uncoordinated, but it began to take a toll on the advancing troops. One man collapsed, his helmet struck by a sling stone. Another, on the corner of the front rank of the nearest column, fell, an arrow protruding from his foot. The staccato sound of the legionary's shields being struck reminded Lucius of the hard winter rains of home hammering against the tiled roof of his father's villa.

A long double blast came from the buccinas'. In a trice the columns transformed into the testudo, even though the rear-most of each had yet to exit the siege camps gateways. Shields clashed together along their sides and above heads. The force now resembled three monstrous, snake-like creatures. Despite the increasing gradient of the hill and the assault from above, the Sixth kept up a steady pace.

The testudos' neared their objective. Lucius could not clearly see what was happening with the farthest columns but had a good view of the most westerly. The front ranks were now forced to step over the rocky ruined hump of the ancient stone wall, pulled down after some long-forgotten battle. As legionaries took care not to lose their footing, their movements slowed. Inevitably, gaps appeared. More legionaries fell as the Novantae hurled spears, taking advantage of the disorder. But it didn't last long; as the first ranks reached the chest high palisade a vicious stabbing battle began with the warriors on the other side. Resounding war-cries mingled with screams of agony.

Lucius's heart thumped hard against his chest. He gripped his sword pommel, his knuckles whitening. This was the first, perilous point of the battle. If the Sixth broke through, they would quickly sweep the hill's interior. The Novantae knew this and fought with the wildness of desperate men. The incoherent bellows, the clash of shields, the ring of steel on steel resounded across the battlefield. He could only imagine the horror.

But the ballistae crew's had done their work well. Lucius saw the flimsy, shredded palisade finally collapse under the pressure from the testudo. The first ranks stepped through.

The fierce bravery of the Novantae could not be denied as they threw themselves against their hated enemy. But it was already too late. The weight of numbers drove the Romans forward. The columns more distant from Lucius still fought ferociously to break through.

The Sixth would then turn its attention to the enemy's last redoubt. The enclosure. Its wooden palisade of stout timbers perched on the hill's western edge overlooking the Nervana's position at the base of the steep escarpment.

It was time to go. Turning Epona from the scene, Lucius made his way down the slope towards his command. His mount whinnied in fright as two arrows struck the ground immediately in front of them. He had strayed too close to the hill's ramparts and his plume had made him a target. He directed Epona on a wider loop away from the hillside.

Lucius passed his own four turmae, the cavalry standing in three silent ranks. He moved now along the infantry's front to the First Spears position. All men now stood ready, shields and spears held firmly. There was complete silence but he could feel the eyes of his men following him.

'It will be soon, First Spear,' Lucius called, upon halting Epona. 'The Sixth have broken through.'

'Very good, sir,' Adal responded, but said no more.

Lucius looked for the Praefectus and spotted his white plume. Lucius raised his hand, making a fist. Cai acknowledged with the same clenched fist response. All was set.

Then the storm began.

18

Adela's long fair mane hung wet and lank across her neck, mist rising from her flanks. The horse's ears were pricked, sensing the impending action. The din of the battle from the hill's ramparts above had reached a new intensity.

The storm had been blowing for some time now, soaking Cai to his very skin. Gradually the unrelenting downpour had found its way into every gap. Water dripped from his helmet running in rivulets down his face, with a continual drip from the end of his nose.

The already soft ground around the cohort had turned to bog that would cause its own problems when the inevitable attack came. His gaze shifted once again towards the hill's summit, hoping to discern some sign of what was to come. But low cloud continued to obscure its heights and the sound of men's screams, curses and the clash of steel seemed to come from a ghostly battle in the otherworld.

The men's initial high spirits had now been dampened by the constant downpour and he could see that many in the centuries to his right had hunched into themselves in a vain attempt to shelter from the deluge.

But not Adal. Even from his position on the flank, Cai could see his broad plume standing tall. Occasionally it moved to one side or another as he, no doubt, called words of encouragement to those around him.

Cai led the cavalry wing on the cohort's left flank, his force a spear's throw distance behind the rear rank of the nearest century. He wanted that open space in front of him so his men were able to hit the enemy with impact. It was better than standing still waiting to accept an assault by the Novantae. He had noticed with some satisfaction that the Tribunus had mimicked his position.

'He's learning,' Cai thought.

Cai kept a wary eye on the edge of the forest that curved from the left of their position and partly around their rear. He had dispatched a section of his men into the trees at first light to watch and report any sightings. They had not yet returned.

To Cai's frustration Verus had not strengthened their force with any other units. But he had sent a detachment of four scorpios. Their two-man crews were commanded by an Optio, who, at the Tribunus's suggestion, had positioned the bolt throwers behind Cai's formation. This gave Cai a little more comfort. The Optio had the foresight to erect hide coverings to protect the weapons' mechanisms from the rain.

The volume of noise from above rose once again, sounding closer. For the first time, Cai saw wraith-like figures flit through the low cloud on the slope nearest the northern ramparts. He would leave them to the men of the Twentieth. The deep trench of the legion's blocking camp would offer little hope of escape if the Novantae chose that route.

But as if appearing from behind a curtain, ten more tribesmen emerged out of the low cloud. They came tumbling and sliding their way down the hill's steep western slope, seemingly oblivious to the waiting ranks of their enemy. The slick turf made it impossible for the small band to maintain their feet until they finally reached more level ground.

The warriors came to a stop. Raising themselves from the sodden ground. All stared wild-eyed at the silent Roman lines staring back. Their leader wore mail and a helm that reflected a dull silvery light even in the storm. His great red beard, blood-spattered and sodden. Cai immediately recognised the warchief he had faced on that first day. These few men must be the last of his hearth companions. All gripped a sword. None now held a shield, presumably lost or abandoned in the flight from the battle raging above them.

The chief turned to his men and spoke quietly to them. He touched each on the shoulder in turn. Cai thought he saw the warriors stand taller by turn. Finally all moved to face their enemy. Resigned to their fate.

The chief raised his great sword high, bellowing a warcry, echoed an instant later by his men. Then they came. Careering down the lower slope directly towards the position where Adal stood in the second rank Their war cries carried across the battleground.

Cai heard Adal's shouted a command, muffled by the distance. In a quick, long-practised movement the front rank levelled their spears as one. The men in the second rank raised theirs to shoulder height. The Novantae hit the front line and for a short time all was confusion. He saw Adal raise his shield to take a blow and his friend disappeared from view.

'Shit,' Cai hissed. The line around Adal had bowed inwards with the impact. He feared the worst. But to his great relief Adal's helmet plume reappeared out of the disorder. The line was redressed. The ten Novantae were gone from sight. A wounded soldier was helped through the lines to the rear. The rain continued to beat down.

A great cracking and rumbling noise came from the still-obscured hilltop as if the Novantae's gods shouted their anger. Dread filled him. Cai realised what that sound meant. Fortunately so did Adal and his bellow rose above the din.

'The centuries will retire by the count.' Adal's voice clear and unwavering.

'One. Two. Three.'

All three lines of the infantry formation stepped backwards as one body. Mens' faces lifted anxiously towards the cloud-shrouded hill.

'One. Two. Three.'

Out of the mist tumbled the tree trunks. Dozens of them. Some spun end over end coming to an abrupt stop on the hill side. But most continued to pick up momentum as they careered towards the retreating ranks.

'One. Two. Three.' Adal's voice still steady. He could have been standing on the dais of the parade ground.

As the first of the trunks reached the lower slopes a tumultuous sound of massed, shrieking voices flared from the hilltop. Disgorging from the cloud came hundreds of warriors, slipping and sliding their way down the steep embankment.

The motion of the timber began to slow, reaching the point where the bodies of the ten warriors lay, crushing them as they passed. The soft ground, which had been turned into a quagmire by the storm and the churning feet of the Nervana's centuries, slowed the wooden columns further. Finally the leading edge of the avalanche of timber came to a sudden stop a mere twenty paces from the men of the front rank.

'Cohort, halt.'

The three ranks stopped. They were now level with both cavalry wings. A man in the rear rank slipped to his knee on the slick surface. The trunks had created a morass of timber in a rough line to the fore of the Nervana's centre as the horde continued to spill from the hill's summit. Its leading warriors approached the unintended barrier.

'Front rank,' Adal commanded. 'Prepare to loose spears.'

The line of men drew back their right arms, spears in hand, right leg back, left leg planted. The first of the Novantae had reached level ground but were encumbered by the barrier of trees. Some clambered over the obstacle, others tried to go around.

'What are you waiting for?' Cai said under his breath. 'Kill the bastards.' More warriors reached the timber and were forced to slow and pick their way forward behind their comrades. Then Cai understood. Adal was waiting for just this opportunity. The Novantae had advanced into a snare of their own making. Caught like water behind a dam.

'First rank, loose.'

Cai watched transfixed. A solid dark line arched upwards into the air. The passage of time appeared to slow until the spears reached their zenith and plunged towards the milling warriors. With practised efficiency the second and third ranks passed their spears forward to the men in front.

Screams erupted from the stranded tribesmen as the spear points burst into unprotected bodies. Hardly one missed a target as men writhed in agony, making the scatter of logs look like a thrashing, many-limbed beast in its death throes.

'First rank, prepare to loose spears,' Adal boomed once more. 'First rank, loose.'

Cai couldn't tear his sight from the curved trajectory of this second wave of javelins, as they fell like a deadly rain.

'The centuries will advance ten paces by the count. One. Two. Three.' Cai watched as the three lines stepped forward in time to their First Spears unwavering voice. 'Centuries halt. First rank, prepare to loose spears.' There was a pause.

'First rank, loose.' This time the spears were thrown straight and level. The impact was devastating. The barrier and the ground to either side was an image from a nightmare. Dead and dying men lay everywhere. Pitiful moans and calls for help from the mortally wounded filled the air before the auxiliaries.

But the Novantae continued to pour from the hill. Cai was momentarily confused upon seeing a number of warriors, still on the hill's slope, thrown backwards into their oncoming brothers as if by some divine power.

The scorpios. Cai turned in his saddle to see the crews in the process of reloading.

Still the enemy came. But Cai now saw the immense dam created by the trunks and the bodies of the Novantae's dead had presented the Nervana with an unexpected opportunity. It was time for the ala to press the advantage that Adal's swift action had given them. Cai filled his lungs ready to give the order

'Sir. The forest.'

Cai turned at the urgent shout from Salvinus. Stunned at what he saw emerging from the trees. His worst fears were realised. Hundreds of warriors were emerging from the forest, streaming across the open ground. They howled their war cries.

Cai had to react. His formation of one hundred and twenty men was facing the wrong way. Turning Adela, simultaneously pulling his lance from its sheath, he swept it in the direction of the on-rushing enemy.

'The turmae will wheel from the rear.'

His men moved quickly and with practised ease until the three lines of cavalry faced the forest and the oncoming threat. Cai turned to the trooper next to his shield arm.

'Avitius. Find the Tribunus. Tell him we're compelled to abandon the left flank to engage with a large enemy force emerging from the trees. We need the reserve centuries brought into the fight now or the blue-faces escaping from the hill will get around us. Go.'

Avitius set off in a shower of mud.

The foremost warriors had crossed more than half the ground between the forest and their position. More continued to spill from the trees. Cai looked down the line of his men. They were ready. He had time to give only one order. Gripping his shield tighter he stabbed his spear towards the enemy.

'First Nervana! Charge.' A great incoherent howl burst from his men and he kicked Adela into motion.

19

From his position on the right flank, Lucius had watched the events at the centre unfold. His initial shock at seeing the tree trunks careering down from the hill's summit had turned to awe at the First Spear's swift action as he wrought destruction upon the Novantae.

Epona had stamped impatiently in her desire to join the fight. It had taken a good deal of effort to bring her back under control. Even now her ears were pricked and nostrils flared, snorting great frustrated gusts of mist.

The Novantae still streamed from the shrouded summit, in seemingly endless waves, only to be halted by the breakwater of logs. But it would be only a matter of time before the warriors turned to the flanks, and the waiting cavalry, in their frantic bid to escape the wrath of the Sixth Legion.

His head whipped around at the eruption of battlecries coming from the far end of the line. But the incessant heavy rainfall meant he no longer had sight of the distant flank. He needed to know what was happening.

A trooper was emerging from the gloom. Lucius felt sick with dread. This couldn't be good news. The rider's progress was tortuously slow. The ground boggy and slick with mud, the mount struggled through the morass.

Another fierce bellow arose from the left. This sound he recognised. The Praefectus was engaging. The mud-splattered trooper finally reached Lucius. It was Avitius. Why did the Praefectus trust this man so much? The thought passed fleetingly.

Coming to a halt Avitius breathlessly made his report. 'Sir, a large enemy force has emerged from the forest. The Praefectus is meeting them but requests that the reserve be brought into the fight to stop the bastard's getting around our flank.'

'Very well, Avitius,' Lucius said, 'ride to Centurion Crescens. He is to move the full reserve at double pace and reinforce the left flank. When you're done, return to me.'

'But the fight's over there, sir,' Avitius said, not hiding his rancour.

'Just do it, trooper.' Lucius's voice sounded shrill to his own ears. The veteran set off, mumbling under his breath.

Lucius quickly assessed the battlefield. His turmae had not yet been engaged, the Novantae must know their only route of escape was into the woods. He could not take his men across the front of the field to engage the enemy and support the infantry as that route was blocked by the labyrinth created by the tangle of tree trunks. The left flank would be supported by the reserve. He made his decision.

'Decurion Mascellus!'

'Sir.' Mascellus moved his horse out of the front line, halting before Lucius.

'You will hold the right flank with your turma, whilst I take the other three to the centre ground at the rear to act as a mobile reserve.'

Mascellus, rivulets of water dripping from his helmet, looked at Lucius with concern and spoke in a low voice.

'You want me to hold the right flank with only thirty men, sir?'

'Yes, Decurion,' Lucius said, unable to keep the annoyance from his voice. 'The enemy will make a run for the forest beyond the left flank, so with luck you won't be engaged. But we'll just have to risk it. Understood?'

'Yes, sir,' Mascellus said, determination now replacing the concern.

Lucius moved out of the line, turning Epona to face his men. Grim faces stared back at him.

'Turmae two, three and four will follow me at the trot,' Lucius shouted. Troopers turned quickly into line, creating a column three abreast.

'Advance!' In a few short moments, Lucius repositioned his reduced force behind the infantry.

Now Lucius had an uninterrupted view of the battlefield. The two reserve centuries passed their position, double timing across the sodden ground. A murmur of laughter came from the ranks of cavalry as one unfortunate slipped onto his arse in the slick mud, and, red-faced, had to hasten after his mates with an Optio yelling abuse in his ear.

The Praefectus and his men were engaged in fierce fighting and hard pressed as more of the enemy emerged from the forest. But for now they were holding.

Avitius reappeared before him, both he and his horse blowing hard.

'Reporting as ordered, sir.'

'Very good. Stay by my side, trooper. I may have need of you again.'

A ferocious, baying sound drew his attention back to the fore. The Novantae were advancing once more in their desperation to escape, driven on by the crush of those behind. Warriors were forced to pick their way over and through the obstacles but they now did so in huge numbers, coming on like a slow-turning tide. The centuries' supply of spears was exhausted. The fighting in the front rank would now be at close quarters. Blood, shit and death.

More Novantae streamed along the base of the hill towards the west. They had spotted the opportunity to escape through the gap vacated by the Praefectus.

'Move, Crescens,' Lucius said, giving voice to his fear.

'He's going to make it, sir,' said Avitius. Lucius hoped he was right, but had no time to watch, as the Novantae crashed into the shields of the Nervana's centre.

The noise of screams and the resounding clash of metal on metal blocked out all other sound. Shield bosses smashed into blue painted faces; swords, axes and spears crashed onto those same shields. The First Spear's men set about their grisly work, stabbing their swords into the stomachs, legs and throats of their enemy.

Lucius saw the First Spear's helmet move forward. He had stepped into the front rank. The first of the wounded appeared through the rear. Some walked, others crawled as best they could, if their comrades were unable to help them. Reaching Lucius's formation, troopers moved their mounts to allow them through.

'Well done men, get to the rear. Keep going, we'll get help to you as soon as we can.' Lucius's words seemed hollow to his ear.

The two reserve centuries had now engaged with the Novantae. But not before some had slipped through. Lucius counted twenty or more warriors running towards the rear of the Praefectus's force, who fought on, oblivious to this new threat.

'Decurion Capriolus,' Lucius called.

'Sir.'

'Take your turma and support the Praefectus before those blue-faces take them up the arse.'

But, even as Capriolus's force tramped across the field Lucius knew the Novantae would reach Cai's embattled turmae first. The rain had finally abated but the sodden ground made it impossible for cavalry to move at anything above a trot.

'Trooper, Betto. Report,' Lucius had to scream the order over the din of the battle. 'Find the Legatus. Inform him we have been assailed on our left flank by a large force emerging from the forest. I have committed my reserve but we are now hard pressed between two formations. Any support he can give would be appreciated.' Betto gave a grim nod before disappearing towards the assault camp.

The flow of warriors coming from the hill's summit had slowed, but the crush at its base began to tell. In three places the infantry's formation was bowing inwards. There were few points along its length that still had a third rank. The First Spear's helmet plume continued to bob furiously as he fought fiercely in the front rank.

'Turmae will form a single line.' Lucius commanded. He waited as the rear troopers manoeuvred to join the front, armour and tack chinking. In moments one line of sixty horses faced towards the hill. 'Ready javelins.' His men returned their lances to their sheaths, each lifting a shorter throwing spear.

The first gap appeared in the Nervana's line before him. This might be the last throw of the dice.

'Advance.'

20

Adela let out an almost daemonic, whinny. Enraged by a cut from a spear point that had glanced across her chest. She kicked out, crushing the face of her tormentor, who dropped from sight, taking the spear with him. Other warrior's, even in the press, stepped away from this terrifying war horse and its blood and mud splattered rider.

Space suddenly opened up creating just enough room for Cai to swing his spatha. He sliced into the neck of a big man too slow to raise his shield. A splash of his life's blood mingled with the red of his long-braided moustache. Cai pulled his blade from the dying man's neck, accompanied by a sucking noise, before plunging its point into the cheek of another.

Cai raised his shield to deflect a spear blow, kicking out at his assailant, hearing the crunch of bone and yelp of the spearman. A shout of anguish came from his right and he had an instant to see one of his men dragged from his mount, to be swallowed in a mass of stabbing swords and thrusting spears.

His men were being overwhelmed. Their initial charge had driven deep into the enemy's uncoordinated ranks, causing death and destruction. They had advanced to within a spear's throw of the forest's edge but the Novantae's numbers had eventually blunted the attack. Warriors continued to disgorge from its depths. He looked towards the trees. His heart sank. Horsemen had emerged. Perhaps thirty of them.

'They're behind us, sir.' A yell from Salvinus. 'They're escaping the hill.'

Cai did not react. All of his focus was on surviving for a few seconds more. Fighting to stay on Adela's back.

Pain seared hotly through his left knee. His attacker, hidden by Cai's shield. Reflexively he slammed the shield's oval rim downwards. Its edge smashed against a spear shaft. Cai followed through, swinging his spatha across and down to his left. The blade cut deep into the unprotected shoulder of the warrior, who appeared momentarily as a blur of hair and tattoos. But Cai's wild swing had left his right side exposed. A heartbeat later he screamed as pain shot between his ribs, below the armpit.

'Bastards.' Cai heard the shout through his agony. A horse forced its way between Cai and the unseen spearman. It was Salvinus. The Duplicarius swung his sword left and right in a frenzy, kicking out at one warrior who tried to grab his chainmail shirt before slashing his spatha down onto the enemy's exposed skull.

A great crash of noise came from behind them accompanied by a fresh wave of screams. This was the end.

The nearest Novantae to Cai started to back away. Why? He twisted sharply in his saddle, crying out as burning pain lanced through his side. But he had in that instant taken in the scene behind him. Lucius had sent men to support Cai's turmae and they had struck the enemy assailing his rear. But his position was still precarious.

His turmae, what was left of them, were scattered across the field in small groups. All fighting their own battles for survival. But Cai saw he had been gifted an opportunity. In many places the enemy were stepping back. Having been on the verge of victory they had been stunned by the appearance of more of the hated enemy.

'Withdraw, Cai roared, 'withdraw and reform.'

The cry was taken up by Salvinus nearby. Tugging hard on Adela's rein, Cai turned her in the small space that had opened around him. Kicking her hard she leaped forward. The host surrounding Cai's men finally snapped out of their shock at the turn of events.

They pressed in once more. Cai was forced to fend off assailants on all sides, slashing unseeing with his sword, kicking out at the face of a warrior who made a grab for Adela's halter. Arching backwards in the saddle to avoid a spear thrust. Slicing down with his spatha, cutting through the ear of a grey bearded Novantae who screamed, disappearing from view.

Cai fought on without thought, the pain in his side forgotten, blindly driving Adela out of the morass of men. Until, with a shock of surprise, he found himself in open ground once more.

'Withdraw and reform,' he yelled once more, before nudging Adela across the boggy ground.

Cai had an instant to observe the Tribunus with his remaining men in a single line, positioned a short distance behind the infantry.

He was relieved too when he glimpsed the red flash of Adal's helmet plume. His friend was still in the fight. But Cai had no time to linger. Sheathing his sword, he felt along his side with careful fingers, testing the wound. He touched the jagged edges of the damaged links of his chainmail. When he pulled his hand away it dripped with warm blood.

Cai halted Adela, turning the mare to face towards the Novantae once more. Most of the remaining troopers had been able to extricate themselves from the fight and were making for his position. The retreating cavalry were followed by the maniacal battlecries of the enemy close behind.

The horsemen who had emerged from the forest had finally freed themselves from the press by working their way around its western edge. For an instant Cai was confused as three men were thrown backwards from their mounts. A fourth, catapulted over his horse's neck as it collapsed under him.

'The ballistae, sir.' Salvinus was back by his side. Turning to look, Cai hissed through gritted teeth as pain lanced along his ribs. The Optio, commanding, had repositioned his scorpios. The crews were already frantically turning the crank handles, readying to reload. Seconds later a new volley tore into the enemy cavalry. This time the effect was more devastating. Four more horses collapsed as the unseen short bolts buried deep within their chests. Some horsemen behind, moving too fast, were unable to evade the thrashing of the dying mounts and were thrown into the chaos.

The remainder of the terrified horses fought the riders' control, giving the scorpio crews time to unleash more death and mayhem. Only moments after the Novantae horsemen had charged, what was left of them fled the field. Desperate to escape the invisible threat. Shortly they disappeared, swallowed by the sanctuary of the forest.

'Reform the line,' Cai called out, his voice carrying above the din of the battle. There wasn't much time: the Novantae were close. Perhaps sensing victory, or seeing the opportunity to help their brothers escape the hill, they ran headlong towards the disorganised cavalry. War cries filling the air.

Cai's men had formed a ragged line and more were joining. But there was no time to wait. They were exhausted. Some had no shields, others gripped onto ragged remnants. But each trooper held grimly to his spatha. Blood spattered faces giving them an otherworldly look.

Cai slid his sword from its scabbard once more, the congealed gore covering the blade, slowing its removal. His arm ached ferociously as he pointed the spatha towards their enemy, where death awaited them.

'Nervana,' Cai yelled, his voice hoarse.

This time only a ragged cry arose from his remaining men. Some mounts, wild-eyed, pulled at their reins. But as one they moved, kicking up great clods of mud. The gap between the two forces closed quickly. The cavalry punched into the horde of running Novantae with a crunching impact. The first warriors disappeared under thundering hooves. Once more Cai's men drove deep into the horde, bringing death.

But, as before, the inexorable pressure of the enemy's numbers quickly tolled.

Each man fought on for every last, exhausting second of life.

21

The soldier on the First Spear's left fell under a vicious overhead axe swing. The blow to his exposed shoulder, the remnants of his shredded shield unable to deflect it. The veteran Centurion buried his sword into the ribs of the axeman, but Lucius could see there was no one in the second rank to take up the space vacated. The breach would not be closed.

The enemy had seen the opportunity too. Men leapt at the gap in their enemy's line, teeth bared, faces distorted. One slashed his sword at the First Spear who raised his shield just in time, forcing the blow onto his helmet before driving his blade into his assailant's exposed stomach. But he was off balance now. Lucius watched in dismay as another Novantae, following behind, drove his spear point into the First Spear's undefended side, shattering his chainmail. Adal swung his sword in a vain attempt to force the warrior back. But his strength was gone. Finally he collapsed to his knees, head sagging onto his chest. Another warrior swung his spear, its shaft striking the side of Adal's helm. He disappeared from view.

'No!' Avitius cried out, despairingly.

'Prepare!' Lucius bellowed, his voice raw.

Twice his men had galloped to the rear of the Nervana's line, using the force of the arching turn to launch their short throwing spears over the heads of the embattled infantry. The deadly impact had slowed the Novantae and had bought the infantry a fleeting breathing space. But the press of those tribesmen behind had continued, forcing the increasingly desperate warriors relentlessly forward. The cohort's line had continued to thin.

Now Lucius's sixty men were the final meagre formation that stood between the Novantae and escape. Positioned not twenty paces behind the infantry's disintegrating line. Each trooper gripped his long lance and held his shield tightly. The Novantae began to pour through the breach. On seeing the line of horses facing them they tried to run along the narrow channel between the remains of the Nervana's centuries and the two turmae.

'Nervana!' The battlecry burst from deep in Lucius's chest. The responding cry came an instant later from his men. He kicked Epona, driving her at the fleeing enemy. Warriors stared wide-eyed as terror gripped them.

Warriors choked and screamed, impaled on lances and crushed under thrashing hooves. Drawing spathas, when spears were finally lost, Lucius and his men slashed and thrust at exposed flesh, in a frantic last stand. The fight quickly disintegrated into a melee. The remaining men of the Nervana's centuries fought on but now faced enemies front and rear.

The numbers and recklessness of the Novantae was turning this final stage of the battle to escape. Troopers were pulled from their saddles, horses shrieked in fear. Lucius fought on. Stabbing, cutting and thrusting in a frenzy, his arm screaming with the pain of the effort. Nothing could prevent his failure and destruction of the cohort?

A fear-filled shout came from his side. Avitius, shield and sword lost, was being manhandled by two warriors as they tried to drag him from horseback. He held desperately to his mount's long mane, but was hanging precariously over its neck. Lucius kicked Epona hard, driving her through the crush towards the trooper, hacking wildly as he went.

All was lost but perhaps he could save this one man? This man who hated him.

22

Lucius slashed a cut onto the exposed wrist of the nearest warrior who had a firm grip of Avitius's chainmail shirt. His scream was swiftly cut off by Lucius's follow-up stab to his throat. With the pressure eased, Avitius kicked out at the other warrior. Blood spurted across the Novantae's cheek as the trooper's studded boot connected with his nose. The warrior, with both hands covering his damaged face, tripped backwards falling from sight.

Lucius leaned over to help Avitius back into his saddle. The trooper turned, his look of gratitude turning to surprise when he saw who had come to his aid. Finally he nodded his thanks.

Unnoticed at first by Lucius, the rhythm of the battle changed. He heard, without registering, a wave of agonised screams. Not understanding its significance. He continued to fight, wildly cutting his sword, left and right. Twisting in his saddle to avoid a spear thrust, he slashed his spatha at the spearhead, sliding the blade along the shaft and into the warrior's neck. He kicked his boot into the dying man's chest to lever the sword free of the gaping wound.

More screams. This time Lucius glanced up to see warriors falling amongst the mass still to the fore of what was left of the Nervana's infantry. One tribesman stumbled, clutching at the arrow that protruded from his cheek.

Snapping his head to the south Lucius was in time to see a black cloud of arrows in flight. They appeared to hang a moment, before plunging into the defenceless crush of the enemy.

A low rumble like distant thunder came from the south beyond the archers, gradually increasing in volume as if a storm neared. The first of the riders appeared around the curve of the hill's base. More followed. Their ranks were not ordered, the slope and the soft ground preventing it. The Hamian archers ran to get out of their way. An unfamiliar warcry broke the air.

'Hispana!'

The Novantae turned in terror at this new threat. Some looked around in desperation for a route out. Others seeing no way out scrambled up the embankment one more. The Hispana's ala ploughed into the Novantae, tearing deeply into the terrified men.

Most gave up hope and joined their brothers attempting to climb the hill's ramparts. The summit could clearly be seen, the rain clouds now lifted. There stood a tall, dark skinned soldier in shining silver armour looking down upon them. Godlike. On either side of him, along the length of the hill's escarpment, in an unending blood-drenched line, stood the men of the Sixth Legion.

A low moan of despair arose from the hillside. One by one warriors began to throw their weapons to the ground. Some sat heavily on the wet embankment or dropped to their knees in anguish and exhaustion. Death or slavery awaited them.

From his position at the forest's edge, Cai had seen the final events of the battle unfold. Watching as the Novantae on the hill's slope had capitulated. Exhaustion enveloped him and he had slumped across Adela's neck.

The fighting around him had come to an abrupt ending with the intervention of the Hispana. The will to fight, of those surrounding the remains of his force, had dissolved. Cai's men had been in no condition to pursue. Most still sat upon their mounts, eyes staring blankly. Few spoke.

The storm had passed and the sun cast its light and warmth across the battlefield. What had been green pasture in the early morning was now a foul, churned, bog of mud, blood and shit. The stench was unbearable. Bodies of the dead ay strewn across it, friends and enemies alike. Many horses had died too, though a few still lived, whinnying pitiably in their pain. The sound mingled with the pleading calls of wounded men.

As the heat of the early afternoon began to slowly dry out the land, a misty haze arose from the ground. As if the souls of the dead were slowly leaving the shells of their bodies, Cai thought, spirited on their final journey.

Over the next few hours Cai saw to the care of his men and had his own wounds dressed. The sun was dipping rapidly towards the west when he finally led Adela on a slow limping walk across the field to where Lucius oversaw the removal of the infantry's dead. Cai dreaded the answer to the question he must ask.

He hadn't eaten since that morning and was thankful only bile filled his mouth as he passed the heaps of the Nervana's dead. He could not bring himself to search their pale, lifeless faces.

Lucius had his back to Cai and stared up at the hill's summit, appearing not to hear his approach.

'Sir,' Cai said in a low voice, reluctant to disturb the Tribunus from his thoughts nor the dead from their slumber. Lucius slowly turned a haunted look in his young commander's sunken eyes. His face was creased with lines of concern and he seemed older somehow.

Lucius gave a nod and a smile that held genuine warmth.

'I'm glad to see you have survived, brother. But it appears you've not come through unscathed.' He indicated the rent in Cai's chainmail with a nod of his head.

Cai snorted. 'A big bastard pricked me with his spear, and my knee hurts like Hades, but I'll survive. I'm glad you made it through too, sir. It was a close run thing.'

Both men turned to stare at the summit once more, not sure what else there was to be said. But finally Cai looked at Lucius.

'What of the First Spear, sir?'

'He yet lives,' Lucius said, 'he's been taken to the medicus legionis at the direct order of the Governor.' Lucius's voice became gruff. 'His wounds were grievous, brother. You must prepare yourself.'

Cai nodded, unable to speak. His stomach churned. A long silence fell between them, eventually broken by Lucius.

'I've never witnessed such a sight. It was as if Jupiter himself had descended and possessed him. He fought with such ferocity. At times it seemed the First Spear held the line by his own strength of will. It would have broken much sooner if not for him. Urbicus himself observed it from the hilltop.'

Cai gave a slight smile. 'Yes that's Adal. Always in the thick of the fight. Even when we were lads fresh to the cohort, whether it be in battle or in some tavern brawl defending his mates.'

Lucius nodded and tried to speak but the words at first came as a croak forcing him to swallow. 'There are so many dead. I haven't been able to bring myself to start the count.' His shoulders slumped, his head sunk to his chest.

'Not to worry, sir. We'll do it together.'

The sun had set by the time they had the numbers of dead and wounded. He and the Praefectus had walked the battlefield while men had been detailed to cut wood from the forest to build the stacks in preparation for the funeral rites. The night was now lit bright by the flames from the pyres of the dead.

Exhausted, Lucius made his way to make his report. He exchanged salutes with the sentries at the entrance to the Sixth's headquarters tent, making his presence known to one of the clerks. He was led inside and asked to wait at the rear of the tent's large open area whilst Verus finished with the legion's senior officers.

He observed the Legatus deep in conversation with the small group. All were still in their field armour, plumed helmets held under their arms. Initially Lucius tried to listen in to the discussion but his thoughts soon drifted, his eyes heavy, staring blankly into the brazier that burned in the room's centre.

'Ah, Felix.' Verus exclaimed.

Lucius jumped, snapped out of his reverie.

'Thank you, gentlemen, that will be all.'

As they left the officers conversed in low voices. Upon passing Lucius, each in turn greeted him with a grave nod. Lucius found this odd, as most had barely acknowledged his existence on previous occasions. Verus waved him forward. Lucius stepped to the front of the campaign table and saluted.

'I have the count, sir.' Lucius handed over the tablet he had brought with him. The older man stared at it unmoving for a time.

'A real butchers' bill to be sure.' Verus nodded towards the tent entrance. 'They know what you did, Felix.'

'Sir?'

'All of the officers of this Legion and the Twentieth by now know you and your Germans stopped the Novantae's escape. Defending an assault from two directions simultaneously. Remarkable really. Although I'm mightily glad your man found me, and not a moment too soon.'

Lucius nodded but said nothing.

'The Governor knows too. He watched the final moments from the hill's edge. Including the actions of that crazy bastard of a First Spear and your man Martis who held the left flank. How do they fair?'

'The Praefectus was wounded but will recover, sir.' Lucius coughed to clear the lump building in his throat. 'But I fear the

First Spear will not see dawn.'

'That's a damn shame.' Verus fiddled with the tablet, considering his next words. 'Well, the Governor wants to see you in the morning.'

Lucius looked up sharply. He had not expected this. 'Me, sir?' he said, unable to keep the bemusement from his voice.

'Yes you, Tribunus. You're to report to his headquarters at the end of the morning watch. Make sure you've washed that gore from your face and cleaned your kit, eh?'

'Yes, sir,' Lucius said, with growing unease.

'He knows he ballsed up, you know?' Verus said.

'Sir?'

'Urbicus knows he should have reinforced your position before the battle started. But a word to the wise, Felix. If you value your career and perhaps even your life, take that information with you to the grave.' Verus stared at Lucius for a few seconds to ensure his point was made.

'Besides knowing the man as I do,' Verus continued, 'he will feel in your debt. He'll likely want to make amends in some fashion to your advantage.' He closed the tablet, placing it on a pile next to him. 'Now, I know you will want to get back to your men. Good night, Felix.'

'Good night, sir.' Both men exchanged salutes and Lucius strode quickly from the tent, not knowing what to make of his commander's words.

23

Cai walked slowly through the camp, his heart heavy. Of the nearly one thousand men of the cohort that had started the day, barely four hundred had survived the battle. More would die during the coming days. Some forced to end their time with the Nervana prematurely, invalided out.

Entering the largest of the hospital tents he asked an orderly for his whereabouts and was led through a flap into an open area holding numerous cots, all occupied. Mateo was a Greek, like many of his profession, and close friend of the Legatus. He was tall, dark of complexion, with greying hair, just beginning to recede at the temples. The medicus was standing in front of a thick wooden table, stained dark, by what Cai did not want to guess. The table's surface was strewn by all manner of metal devices that, to Cai's eyes, looked like instruments of torture.

Cai cleared his throat and Mateo turned, a look of confusion crossing his face.

'I'm Praefectus Martis of the First Nervana.'

'Ah yes, Martis. He's been asking for you.' His tone was not abrupt but held the kind of professional brusqueness adopted by those so used to dealing with friends and relatives of the sick, injured and dying. 'Come with me, Praefectus.'

The medicus ushered Cai to the entrance of the large tent. At the door flap Mateo turned to Cai, a look of compassion in his eyes.

'I'm sorry, Martis,' he said in a low voice. 'Your friend's time is short. The spearpoint he took in the chest also punctured a lung. He's bleeding internally. I believe it carried damaged links from his armour into the wound. But I've been unable to locate them. I made him as comfortable as I could but he would only take a little juice of the poppy. He insisted he wanted to stay awake to speak with you.'

Desolation chilled Cai as Mateo led him outside and across the way to a small section tent. They stopped outside where the medicus turned to Cai once more.

'I'll leave you here. But take this.' He handed Cai a small, stoppered jar. 'Give him all of it when the pain finally becomes too much to bear.' Cai accepted it, nodding his understanding, not trusting himself to speak.

Cai pulled back the tent flap and entered, letting it fall into place behind him. The interior of the tent was dark, the only dim light coming from a small oil lamp set on a table next to the single cot. He approached its side, pulling up a campaign stool that had been placed at the rear of the tent. He sat for a short while looking at the still figure of this friend. His head was propped up on a folded cloak and Cai could see droplets of sweat glistening on his forehead. Adal's face had taken on a grey pallor and his long fair hair lay lank across his shoulders and onto the blanket that only partly covered the darkly stained bandage wrapped around his chest.

Adal's eyes were closed and Cai thought, with a stab of fear, that he may have already passed, until he noticed the shallow rise and fall of his chest. He gently took hold of his friend's hand and Adals' eyes opened. At first they held a glazed look as they stared at the roof of the tent. But all at once they cleared as he became aware someone was in the tent with him.

'Hello, brother,' Adal said, his voice gravely and barely above a whisper. But his lips twitched in a smile. Cai held Adal's hand tighter and smiled back not yet trusting himself to speak, but knowing he must. Taking a steadying breath, Cai forced a smile into his voice.

'What's this, First Spear? Are we having a nice lie-in today?'

Adal croaked a ghost of a laugh which turned to a wince of pain and Cai noticed the dressing on his chest glistened with fresh blood. But the pain seemed to pass quickly and Adals' face calmed as he looked at Cai once more.

'You won't forget your promise will you, brother?' He gripped Cai's hand tight with a look of anguish. A great lump grew in Cai's throat and at first he could only shake his head, as the words would not come.

'No, my friend,' he said after a while. 'I will watch over them both. I swear it on the spirit of my father.' Adal looked at him for a moment longer, before he relaxed, loosening his grip a little.

'Thank you, Cai.' They were silent then for a while before Adal spoke again, a little strength returning to his voice.

'Tell my boy about me.' Cai nodded, not daring to speak. 'Teach him to hunt. Not the way those rich boys do, but in the ways our fathers showed us, with bow and spear.'

'I will, brother. I swear you will be proud of him,' Cai said. Adal nodded and closed his eyes. The friends stayed that way for some time but did not release each other's hand. Cai thought his friend must have fallen asleep and jumped slightly when Adal spoke again.

'Do you remember when we were boys and our fathers took us together on our first hunt?'

'We couldn't have been more than eight summers,' Cai said. 'I was a snotty nosed skinny runt barely able to draw a bow. I was envious of your strength even then.'

Adal laughed gently at his friend.

'You're still a skinny runt,' his voice rasped, 'but I've done my best with you.' It was Cai's turn to laugh gently.

'Indeed you have, brother.'

'But what I remember most,' Adal continued, 'were the nights the four of us sat around the evenings' fire. Listening wide eyed as our fathers told us tales of the battles the Nervii fought against other tribes and the final great one with Rome.' Cai nodded letting the memory fill him.

'I'll be glad to see them again,' Adal said, 'and sit around the fire sharing stories of the battles we have fought together, you and I.' He paused before continuing; the effort of talking was sapping his strength. 'We three will watch over you my friend and welcome you to the fireside when your time finally comes.' The two friends gripped the other's hand tighter as a fat tear fell unnoticed across Cai's cheek. Adal continued to stare at Cai for a while longer but soon closed his eyes, the last of his strength finally leaving him.

Cai stayed by his friend's side. Time passed unnoticed in the dark tent as he kept this final vigil. Images of their past lives together flitted through his mind. He could not remember a time of any length that they had not been in each other's company. A great chasm began to open inside him.

A low moan broke from between Adal's lips and a look of agony creased his face. Cai saw blood bubbling from between his lips and knew his friend's pain was becoming unbearable. Moving closer to his side he eased his arm under Adal's shoulders, raising him slightly.

'Here my friend,' he whispered gently into his ear. 'I have something to ease the pain.'

Adal's eyelids fluttered open and looked directly into the eyes of his boyhood friend. He nodded almost imperceptibly, acknowledging this last act of love and the gift he was being given. Cai raised him a little further and held the small jug to his friend's lips. Adal slowly swallowed its contents, a little of the white liquid escaping to roll down his chin. Cai lay him gently down once more, using a fingertip to wipe away the stray liquid.

Adal's eyes slowly closed and Cai knew they would not open again. He sat unmoving, watching the rise and fall of his friend's chest, as it slowed imperceptibly moment by moment. Until at last, it was still.

His friend's face looked at peace and Cai watched for a while as if he might suddenly wake. Finally, unbidden, a great sob escaped Cai's chest. He bowed his head as tears fell uncontrollably, some dropping onto Adal's hand, which he still held.

24

Lucius was guided through the camp by the duty Optio. Not something that would normally be necessary, but with the Governor present amongst them, additional precautions were being taken by the Twentieth. When they reached Urbicus's quarters, a great canopied tent at the camp's centre, he was presented to the Centurion of the guard who checked a list of names on his tablet then disappeared inside to report Lucius's arrival.

It was several minutes before he returned

'If you would wait inside for the time being, sir. The Governor's running a bit behind.'

Lucius nodded, stepping under the awning and into the tent's interior, removing his helmet as he went. He was offered a chair by an orderly but declined, feeling too ill at ease to sit. He paced the large administration area as clerks worked at desks set up in neat rows.

Time dragged and Lucius was beginning to regret not taking a piss at the latrine trench before reporting. The flap to the inner rooms rose and fell many times as an endless stream of military men, scribes and slaves passed through. All part of the inner workings of simultaneously running a military campaign and a province.

Eventually, after some minutes had passed, a staff officer poked his head through the flap.

'Tribunus Felix?' said the officer with the face of a youth.

'Here,' Lucius said.

'Could you follow me please.' He held the flap open for Lucius to enter. They walked smartly through another area full of more administration staff and more tables, piled high with wax tablets and scrolls.

'The Governor is in conversation with the Legatus of the Sixth. I'll just remind them you're here.' The staff officer entered yet another flap, which swiftly dropped back into place behind him.

'Tribunus Felix of the First Nervana Germanorum is next, sir,' Cai heard the slightly muffled announcement.

'Send him in.' The unmistakable voice of Urbicus. The flap was raised again.

'In you come, Felix,' said the staff officer, revealing only his head as it poked through the gap.

On entering, Lucius paused to get his bearings. In the dull light, cast by several lamps, he saw the backs of two men hunched over a large, intricately carved table. Both appeared to be looking at a parchment. As neither man looked up Lucius strode over the carpeted floor and made his salute.

'Tribunus Felix, First Nervana Germanorum, reporting, sir.'

Verus turned his head and looked at Lucius with a slight smile. 'A moment please, Felix.'

The two men continued their discussion, Lucius forgotten for the present.

'The castra will have to be expanded significantly, sir,' Verus said, 'and defences enhanced. But there's no shortage of building material in the local area. My lads should be able to complete the work within the month.'

'Good, get started immediately,' Urbicus said. 'I want the Novantae lands under our boot before I advance north along the eastern route.'

'Understood, sir.'

With the conversation concluded, the Governor stood upright, arching his back, stretching his arms wide before finally turning to face Lucius. He stared directly into his eyes and it took a strength of will on Lucius's part not to glance away or show his discomfiture. The Numidian's eyes were extraordinary. So dark they appeared black, and almost feline.. He wore a simple woollen tunic, missing the normal broad stripe for a man of his rank, a thick leather belt around his waist. As if noticing Lucius's discomfort Urbicus broke into a wide, white toothed grin.

'I'm glad to meet the officer who held our western flank. You and those mad Germans of yours.' Heat rose in Lucius's face. 'Your cohort has earned its new battle honour.'

'Thank you, sir,' Lucius said, his voice even, not sure what else to add.

'Your cohort has suffered significant losses, but tell your men each will receive a share of the gratuity from the auction of the Novantae slaves. I've already seen to it. Given the size and general condition of the brutes I expect we will all make a great many denarii.'

'That will indeed be welcomed, sir,' Lucius said, for the want of something else to say.

Urbicus turned, reaching for a cup perched on the edge of his big table, raised it to his mouth and took several gulps, some drips escaping the corner of his mouth. Lucius had expected to see the red of wine but was surprised to see it was only water. He turned back to face Lucius once more, saying nothing for a time, appearing to consider his next words.

'Now to the matter of what next for you and your men. You may have caught the end of the conversation between the Legatus and I?

'Yes, sir. Something about rebuilding a fort.'

'I need the Novantae and their neighbours kept firmly under control as I move northwards to enlarge our Emperor's province. A detachment of the Sixth is to rebuild and enlarge the ruins of the castra that sits to the south of our present position. It will act like the hub of a wheel supporting a number of outlying forts to be constructed along the Anam and to the east and west.' Urbicus indicated to Verus he should continue.

'Being a double strength, mixed cohort,' Verus said, 'the First Nervana would be ideally suited as the new fort's garrison. It will also give you the opportunity to recruit and train replacements.'

Lucius understood what he was being given. He would command not just his cohort but all units involved in the suppression of the Novantae. 'Thank you, sir. I don't know what to say. But I'll do all in my power to prove myself worthy of the honour.' Was this the addressing of the debt that Verus had spoken of?

The Numidian gave a rumble of a cough. 'Now there's one final matter.' In his periphery Lucius noticed Verus staring directly at him, as if conveying the importance of the Governor's next words.

'I didn't have the honour of meeting your father,' he said, 'but I knew of him by reputation. He was a faithful and courageous servant of the empire.' Lucius began to feel uncomfortable, unsure where this most powerful of men was about to lead him. 'The Legatus here tells me he was a good friend of your uncle, your father's brother. They served together in the Ninth, in this very province.'

Lucius was aware of Verus nodding confirmation but didn't take his eyes the Governor. 'He has made me aware of your family's situation and the scurrilous way in which your father's estates were lost.' Urbicus paused once again. 'I cannot promise to restore your family's lands, Felix. But, I do have my own resources to explore further on your behalf. If my agents can uncover sufficient evidence, I will bring it before the Emperor. Once I return to Rome.'

Lost for words, it took some time for Lucius to comprehend the magnitude of what the Governor had said. Finally gathering himself he glanced at Verus, who nodded almost imperceptibly.

'Thank you, sir,' Lucius said. 'You do me and my family a great honour.'

Urbicus flashed his broad white smile. 'I have use for young men of talent, Felix. We'll talk again when I'm done dealing with the Caledonae tribes.'

Lucius walked back through the camp, replaying that most unexpected of conversations in his mind. His life had taken a turn in a direction he could not have hoped for.

PART 2

25

AD 149 Hispania Baetica

Vericundus was filled with apprehension as he trotted his family's old horse along the estate's trackway. During the journey he had repeatedly and almost unconsciously touched his black bull cloak pin at his throat for luck. The route was lit by occasional torches that cast an uncertain illumination for a rider. But from the hillside the lights of the villa shone out, marking his destination.

Upon entering the main gateway he was received by two male slaves, one a boy, who took hold of his mount's bridle. The other was dressed in fine clothes and in his middle years.

'Good evening, sir. The Dominus is awaiting you in his study. Follow me if you would.' Without another word he Turned and walked away. Vericundus followed, the odour from the slave's oiled and perfumed hair catching in his throat. He was still as confused as he had been when the note was handed to him that morning, whilst breaking fast with his father and brother.

Their landowner had not spoken to him in all the years he had spent growing up on his father's farm. He had also been gone nearly ten years from the province, serving with the Eagles. He fingered the black bull cloak pin and once again he found himself frantically thinking through various scenarios, each as unlikely as the next.

Entering the villa through a side door the servant led him along narrow corridors, passing what looked like slave cells or perhaps storerooms. Eventually they reached a solid door that his escort unlocked with a latch lifter, holding the door open for Vericundus to walk through, before closing and locking the door once more.

They were now at one end of a four-sided atrium, a slow trickling fountain at its centre. A walkway, framed by pillars of white marble, allowed access to other doorways along each side. The building was silent, not surprising given the late hour, but it only added to his unease. The slave led him to a door, slightly ajar, on the atrium's far side. He rapped twice on the thick wood.

'Come,' a high pitched, male voice answered. Pushing the door open further, the slave spoke to the still unseen person within.

'The son of the farmer, Dominus.' The slave, with a flick of his chin, indicated Vericundus should enter, a waft from the perfumed beard assaulting his nostrils. Stepping through he got his first sight of the landowner, sitting at a large wooden desk, polished dark with age, that Vericundus suspected was worth more than his father's small two roomed farmhouse. The desk faced a large window, its shutters opened wide to the black of the night and the familiar sound of chirping cicadas. The landowner seemed deep in concentration writing rapidly on a small sheet of papyrus.

'Thank you, Silvanus. That will be all.' Although he spoke without looking up Vericundus noticed how his jowls wobbled and the edges of his mouth were slick with dribble. He wore a white tunic, the fat of his arms pressing hard against the edges of its short sleeves. He continued to write without acknowledging anyone else was in the room with him.

'You wished to speak to me, sir?' said Vericundus.

'Wait.' His manner was brusque.

Finally placing his pen in a small pot of dark ink he looked directly at Vericundus. He was seated but Vericundus could tell he was short, his remaining hair shaved clean from his scalp. He sat back against his tall wooden chair revealing much of his upper body. His tunic struggled to contain the huge girth of his belly, upon which he now rested his pudgy hands. He continued to stare at Vericundus with a look that reminded him of the farm's cat eyeing a mouse in one of the outbuildings.

'How long has it been since your cohort was disbanded, Optio?' His jowls wobbled once more.

'You seem to be very well informed, sir?' Vericundus fought to keep his anger under control. He sensed it would not be wise to lose his temper with this man.

'It's a year, is it not,' the landowner continued, 'since you returned to your father's shit hole of a farm and you've been unable to find a new posting. For who will take a junior officer from a disgraced unit?' Vericundus said nothing, feeling his colour rising as a sickly smile crossed the landowners' wet lips.

'Your family is quite something. Not only is the eldest son disgraced, but the father has a great many debts.' He laughed at the younger man's surprise. 'Oh I see, you didn't know? Oh yes indeed, he owed money to quite a large number of people. But not to worry, as a kind and benevolent landlord I've bought up all of his debts.'

Vericundus's heart sank. 'What do you want?' he said, his voice terse.

'Straight to the point like a real soldier.' The fat man leaned forward, placing his elbows on the dark wood of the desk, steepling his fingers under his chins. 'As it happens, I'm in a position to help both father and son out of their current predicaments.'

'And what dirty work is required in order to be beneficiaries of this largesse?'

'Oh it's quite straightforward really,' the land owner said, ignoring the scornful tone of the man before him. 'I've arranged a Centurion's posting for you in a unit in the north of Britannia. There is a Tribunus there, someone from our own province as it happens, who has become an inconvenience to me. You will find him and slit his throat or end his life in any other way you see fit.'

'Murder?' Vercundus said in disbelief.

'Call it what you like. Do this simple task for me and you have your career back with a nice little promotion thrown in. Furthermore I will write papers cancelling all of your fathers debts.' Bile rose in Vericundus's throat. 'But if you fail me,' the fat man continued, his voice filled with menace, 'or any word of this reaches someone it shouldn't. I will see to the ruin of your family.'

26

AD 149 Northern Britannia

Beren sat waiting at the edge of the wood, idly watching a flight of swallows taking turns to drink from a pool of rainwater in the glade below. The swift little birds darted and circled above, before diving in ones and twos, pulling up at the last instant to glide effortlessly above the waters' surface. Their dark breasts almost touching it, before dipping their heads to take a sip and taking flight once more to rejoin their brothers and sisters.

The boy had been waiting in the same spot for what felt an age, hoping to see his friend return before dark. Cai had left that morning at first light. The sun was now low and slowly dipping towards Criffel's distant summit. The mountain was a constant presence as it stood its lonely watch over the entrance to the Sula.

Beren knew he would catch it from his mam, when he eventually got home. Once again returning late, having not completed his chores. But even with the threat of a hiding hanging over him, he couldn't resist the chance to watch the patrol's return. If he were lucky, Cai would let him ride behind him on the final stretch into the fort. He knew his mother's face always lit up when she saw his friend. For some reason he got away with the worst punishments following even the shortest exchange between the two.

Now ten summers old, he longed for the day he would come of age and could join the Nervana. He would train with the horses and men of the ala, perhaps even serve in Cai's own turma. Beren's father had been the First Spear of the cohort. He often thought about him, though he had no memories, as his father had died only a few days after Beren's birth. But living around the fort he had been befriended by many of his father's men. They had told him tales of his heroics. In his mind's eye, he had come to see him as a giant of a man, taking on almost godlike abilities.

His mother from time to time would say he looked just like him, with his long, fair hair and broad shoulders. Which never failed to make his chest swell with pride, drawing soft laughter from her at the sight of it. But there were times too, when he would catch her watching him, a look of sadness in her eyes.

The boy shook himself from his melancholy and resumed his watch across the pool, from which the swallows had now vanished, to the surfaced road beyond. Wishing his friend to appear from behind the distant rise, where the arrow straight route disappeared from sight.

Beren gave the road one last forlorn look as he turned to follow the deer track that threaded back through the trees. A barely perceived noise stopped him. He turned back to look down the road's length. The scene was unchanged and he thought he must have imagined it. But it came again, a metallic chink, accompanied by the sound of distant laughter. Beren stared, his heart thumping with excitement.

The familiar sound became more pronounced until at last the first of the horses crested the rise. He recognised the lead rider instantly, the white feathered plume of his helmet standing out clearly, even in the late evening gloom.

Setting off at a run, as fast as his legs would carry him, Beren quickly passed the pool of rainwater. Haring down the gentle slope, finally reaching the road's edge, where he stood waiting for his friend to arrive. The boy watched as the turma came into full view. The column was split into two groups, the first leading a line of four hide-covered wagons. Each pulled by oxen, forcing the patrol to move at an ambling pace. Beren hopped impatiently from foot to foot.

At last Cai's horse reached where he waited. His friend looked down at him in mock seriousness. His eyes looked dark in the depths of his helmet. Raising his hand, he bellowed. 'First turma. Halt.' Cai ignored the grumbling of the men behind him.

'Well met young Beren. That's a fine spear you hold'.

'He could do some damage with that, sir.' A murmur of laughter arose from the men nearby.

'You should sign him up, sir. He'd scare great Cocidus himself.' This voice Beren recognised. That old goat Avitius, Cai's standard bearer. It was only then Beren realised he was still holding onto the branch he'd been playing with. Heat rose in his cheeks, but he kept a tight grip of his improvised weapon trying not to let his discomfiture show. Cai smiled down at the boy.

'Well my friend, it's getting late and your mother will be

fretting. You'd better jump up behind me, I'll drop you off as we near the village.' Cai lowered his hand. Beren threw the stick aside, allowing himself to be pulled up to sit behind his friend. Cai raised his arm once more. 'First turma. Advance!' Cai's great, blond-maned horse Adela moved gently into motion. Beren bobbed happily at his friend's chain-mailed back, which was partly obscured by Cai's long fair hair as it protruded from under his helmet.

For a while Beren listened to the back and forth of conversations. The easy, mocking familiarity he had grown to love. Even, as was often the case, when he himself would become the target of their gentle jibes. But as ever, Beren was bursting with curiosity and could hold back no longer.

'What're you escorting, Cai? Is it weapons?' His boyish enthusiasm never failed to draw a chuckle from Cai.

'No my young friend. Our weapons and armour are in good condition. We have all we need for the present.'

'Is it salt then? Or chests of denarii?'.

'I think you have an inflated view of how much a trooper is paid, Beren,' Cai said, 'we'll certainly never be rich men.' The boy tried again, enjoying the game.

'It must be oil or wine for the stores then?' Certain this time he has guessed right.

'You're getting warmer.'

Beren harrumphed in frustration, making Cai chuckle once more.

'Tell me young Beren. What do we call our great castra?'

'The Sack of course.'

'Its full name?'

'The Flour Sack.'

'And what do we need to make flour?'

'Grains. Oh.'

'And there you have it. You already know much of our time is spent patrolling the lands of the Novantae. We keep the peace, we make sure supplies reach the other forts and watchtowers. But often a trooper's days are filled with duller jobs. Such as escorting the monthly grain shipment from the harbour at the Castra of the Exploratores. It's nonetheless just as important as riding the wild hills, making sure the tribes behave themselves.'

'But why don't you get one of your Decurions to do the boring stuff?'

'Because, my eager young warrior, my arse gets splinters from sitting behind that desk of mine, for days on end. Sometimes, I just want to put the saddle on Adela and have a boring day riding in the open air.'

The two friends carried on in this way for a time as the fort came into view in the late evening light. Perched on its high rise, it was wedged comfortably into the point where two fast flowing streams met. Its high turf walls were protected by multiple ditches, making it a formidable obstacle, should the local tribes ever tire of Roman rule. The Sixth Legion, Cai once grudgingly admitted, had built her well.

The Sack's internal buildings were constructed of good local sandstone, making life for its inhabitants a comfortable one, especially in the depths of winter. Since Urbicus had constructed the new wall for his emperor, cutting Caledonia in two, life for the most part had been a quiet one. And Cai was glad of it.

A settlement had grown up around the fort, serving the needs of its garrison. Although he tried not to admit it to himself, Cai had been glad when Alyn had shown up one day, a snotty-nosed, toddling Beren in hand. She had not wanted to return to her father's hearth, but instead, with the funds from Adal's will, had built a small dwelling. Now she took in clothing from the cohort, for washing and repair.

Alyn had greeted Cai with warmth whenever they met, but he had sensed a distance that he initially put down to her grief. Now years later, that distance appeared just as difficult to bridge.

She'd had many admirers of course, but spurned most advances. Being the widow of their much-respected former First Spear, no man dared treat her with anything other than courtesy. The one exception had been Camillus. He was a merchant from the lands of the Cornovii who plied his trade in wine between the two walls, passing through the Sack at regular intervals. He had courted Alyn, bringing gifts for her and Beren and for a time they had lived together in her home. When Cai had one day tried to suggest to her it might not be wise to take up with such a man she had told him it was none of his affair and had taken to avoiding him for a time.

Then one day, not long after, he had seen her striding through the village, hair tied back and chin held high. She did not even try to disguise the fist-sized purple bruise on her cheek. Indeed, it seemed she wanted the people of the village to see it.

Cai couldn't remember a time he'd been so angry. 'Where is he?' he had demanded.

'Camillus, you mean?' she had said. 'Oh, he's gone and I don't think he'll be stopping at the village again.'

'But—' he'd begun. She had simply breezed past him, disappearing along a small pathway between buildings.

'Cai!' The hail had come from the smith who stood outside his forge on the main street. As Cai approached, a broad smile had creased the permanently flushed cheeks of the short, muscled man.

'Why're you so happy?' Cai had said brusquely, still feeling frustrated by Alyn's dismissal.

'I had a knock at my door in the early hours of this morning,' the smith had said. 'Young Camillus had an urgent medical problem he didn't want to take to the Sack's medicus.'

'What kind of problem?'

'Well he was struggling to walk you see,' his smile had widened. 'Mainly because he had an eating knife stuck, handle-deep, into the thigh of his right leg.' The smith had roared with laughter. 'I had to pull it out and he whimpered like a child when I cauterised it with an iron.' It had taken a moment before the smith composed himself. 'That lass knows how to look after herself.'

Cai shook his head at the memory. If he was honest with himself, he had been jealous of the young, good looking, trader and was glad to see the back of him. It was some time before his friendship with Alyn had returned to what it was before. But still that distance persisted.

The turma now neared the fort's porta praetoria. The main gate's stout oak doors stood open at the end of the narrow causeway that crossed its ditches.

'Avitius,' Cai said over his shoulder, 'escort the wagons into the fort. Watch the drivers unload this time. The lazy fuckers made a right mess outside one of the granary doorways last month.'

'Yes, sir.'

Cai turned Adela and rode back down the length of the escort, with the boy bouncing behind. Pulling her to a halt at its rear, he called to his Duplicarius. 'Betto, get the turma settled, will you? Make sure the grooms do their jobs properly tonight. It's been a long day for the horses. I'm going to take this young warrior home.'

'Right you are, sir.'

Both men exchanged salutes and Cai nudged his mount from the military road, heading in the direction of the settlement's western gateway. Beren had become quiet, Cai realised. No doubt wondering what punishment awaited him. Their progress slowed as they approached the entrance. A trader's wagon, pulled by two old mules, lumbered slowly in front of them. But finally they reached the gates in the wooden palisade.

Upon entering the village Cai was hailed by many of its inhabitants, men and women alike, all keen to hear the latest news. In a community this small there were few strangers and he spent some minutes passing the time and imparting the latest gossip from the quayside. The first buildings built in the settlement had been mainly the familiar round houses of the local people. But as the years passed more of the solid wooden rectangular buildings appeared, some with shop fronts. A few had tiled roofs but most were thatched. Alyn's home was one such as this.

And there she stood. Cai's breath caught at the sight of her, framed as she was in the doorway. As he approached he soaked in every detail. She wore a rust-coloured dress, flowing down her body, stopping midway between her calves and ankles. It was cinched at her waist by a simple leather belt, displaying the curve of her hips. But what was most extraordinary was the way her long dark hair lay across her shoulders. Often in one plait, today it was allowed to hang free. Her eyes were a soft grey, like the surface of the Sula on an autumn day. Set below a slim, feminine nose were full red lips the colour of rosehips, which this evening seemed to be at war over whether they should smile in greeting to Cai, or grimace in annoyance at her son's disobedience. The boy's head was tucked against Cai's back, in a vain attempt to go unnoticed.

Alyn stepped away from her doorway, Cai halting Adela an arm's length from her. The horse nuzzled into Alyn's neck in recognition. She gently, almost absent-mindedly patted the horse's nose.

'Good evening, Alyn. Look what I found on my travels today.'

Alyn gave the briefest of smiles to Cai before taking in her errant son.

'Berengar, son of Adalfus, we'll speak of this later. For now you'll go down to the well and before filling the pail with water for the hearth, you'll wash your hands and face. Go now.'

'Yes, Mam.' Beren leaped down from Adela and ran to collect the bucket, not wishing to provoke his mother further. Cai smiled at Beren's retreating back, before turning to Alyn.

'He's more like his father with each passing day.'

'He has his father's stubbornness and nose for trouble, if that's what you mean?' But she returned his smile. There was a moment of silence between them. Cai was about to say he should return to his duties. But she spoke first.

'You looked tired, Caius. Will you join us for the evening meal?' She looked at him with a gentle smile. His stomach filled with a fluttering feeling.

'That's most kind, Alyn. It has indeed been a long day. The taste of your cooking would be a welcome change from the officers' mess.'

'Then please, come inside.' Cai dismounted, leading Adela to the rear of the small building, hobbling her in a patch of scrubland, where she could comfortably graze. Walking back, he noticed Alyn's well-organised garden was full to bursting with broad beans, herbs and all manner of green leaves Cai could not place. He was also surprised to see two small apple trees.

Upon reaching the open doorway he paused, wondering if he should knock. The aroma of the cooking food immediately had him salivating. He hadn't realised quite how hungry he was.

'That smells wonderful, Alyn.' She turned from stirring the pot that hung over the hearth fire. She smiled, a blush of red coming to her cheeks.

'It'll be ready shortly. Come sit yourself by the fire.' She indicated a stool to her right before returning to the pot. Placing the helmet at his feet, he turned to watch her work. He noticed her hips' gentle sway as she stirred the contents and had to force himself not to stare. Instead he surveyed the room's interior. It was a single space, but at one end there was a wattle partition that gave her some privacy, when needed. At the other end was Beren's cot, a mound of clothing on the floor next to it. Washing for the cohort, no doubt.

The walls of the dwelling were lined with shelves, filled with all manner of clay pots. There were two large wooden beams supporting the sloping roof, from which hung drying herbs as well as other domestic objects. A real home, he thought.

Cai often felt tongue tied in her presence. He searched his thoughts for something to break the silence.

'I noticed you have two apple trees in your garden. A rare sight.'

'Yes,' she responded, not looking up. 'I bought them from a trader who passed through on his way to the north. He assured me they'd thrive, even in our unpredictable weather. But we'll see. At least they haven't withered away yet.'

The silence had started to build between them once more and Cai was relieved when Beren burst through the door. He carried the pail in two hands, slopping water with every step. The boy beamed upon seeing his friend. Only partly because he thought he might escape the worst of his mother's ire.

'Place it on the floor, Beren, before you flood the place,' she said.

'Sorry Mam.'

Alyn walked across the room, Cai watching as she moved with light, bare-footed steps. She took the bucket and poured some of the water into a large clay bowl, before placing it on the small table at the room's centre. She laid a cloth alongside it.

She turned to Cai with a smile. 'Please Caius, take the opportunity to wash off the dust of the road.'

'My thanks, Alyn. That would be welcome.' He bent over the bowl and splashed his face. His long, fair hair fell forward, almost obscuring the bowl from view. Looking up at the sound of giggling, he realised the boy was laughing at the noises he had been making. Cupping some of the water in his hand, he flicked it at Beren's face. He hadn't noticed Alyn had come to stand near his side and some of the water also caught her. There was an instant of silence before Beren and Alyn burst into a fit of giggles. Cai, caught up in the joy of it, let out his own deep hearty laugh.

When they settled once more Alyn handed Cai a cup of cool ale. Accepting with gratitude he took several deep swallows, nearly emptying the contents. A warm smile lit Alyn's face as she refilled his cup.

'It seems you were in need of that.'

'I didn't realise how thirsty I was. Even uneventful days on horseback are dusty dry work.'

Beren piped up excitedly. 'When I'm grown, I will join the ala. Will you teach me to ride, Cai?'

'Hush now, Beren. Don't pester Caius with your questions. Let's sit and take our evening meal.' Ladling steaming broth into three bowls, she set them on the table, along with that morning's bread cut into chunks. For a while all three ate in silence. Cai was ravenous, but forced himself not to eat as if he were amongst his men.

'When are you going to take me hunting, Cai? You said you would when I reached ten summers. I'm ten summers now.' The words tumbled out of Beren and Cai laughed.

'I'll take you hunting, my young friend. But it's for your Mam to say when that is, not me.'

Beren immediately turned to his mother with pleading eyes. 'Pleeease Mam.'

Alyn frowned and bit her lower lip.

Gods she's beautiful, he thought. 'I'd keep him close, Alyn. He needs to understand the ways of the forest first, before I let him anywhere near a bow. You know I'll look after the lad.'

'Pleeease Mam.'

Her face softened into a smile. She could not deny him. 'Very well. But you must stay close to Caius at all times. Listen to what he tells you.'

'I will Mam, I promise,' Beren broke in earnestly before his mother could say more.

For a time the boy fired questions at Cai. What game would they be looking for? Where would they hunt? Could they build a campfire? Until finally, his mother put her hand on his arm.

'You're tiring Caius with your questions. He's had a very long day already.'

'The lad does have an inexhaustible curiosity,' Cai said, smiling, 'but you're right, Alyn. It has been a long day. I must settle Adela for the night and make my report to the Tribunus.' Was that disappointment in her eyes? 'My thanks for welcoming me into your home. The meal made a most welcome change.'

'You're always welcome at our hearth, Caius.' The lightest of blushes rose in her cheeks.

Cai returned her smile. ‘Well, young hunter. I’ll call for you before sunrise, on the day after the morrow. Make sure you’re ready.’

‘I will, I promise.’

Alyn walked with Cai to the door. ‘Thank you, Caius. I will fear for him, but I know it’s what his father would have wanted.’ Cai looked into her eyes, his stomach fluttered once again at the nearness of her.

‘He’ll come to no harm,’ Cai said.

Alyn touched his arm. ‘Now, I must get this boy to his bed. But not before I give him yet another talking to about forgetting his chores.’ Cai saw Beren blanch.

‘Good night then, Alyn.’ Cai walked behind her dwelling to unhobble his horse. His heart light, still feeling her touch on his skin. Perhaps that distance between them had just grown shorter?

As he walked Adela through the now-dark streets of the village, reflecting on the night's conversations, smiling to himself. How earnest Beren had been about his age. ‘I’m ten summers now.’ Ten years since his birth. Ten years since the battle at the Novantae’s hill. Ten years since the death of his friend. Some of his light mood began to drift away.

27

Lucius folded the letter from Urbicus he had read over and over that day. Finally locking it away in his personal strong box. Sitting in his office in the principia he stared at the blank wall. At this time of the evening the headquarters building was quiet, with only the duty clerk at his desk. This was his first opportunity to fully reflect on its contents.

Urbicus had been true to his word. Over the years he had apprised Lucius from time to time on the findings of his discreet enquiries. Now at last his agents had perhaps uncovered evidence that there was truth to Lucius's belief that his father had been cheated out of his estates. And murdered.

For the first time in a long while he thought there might be hope. But, as ever with Urbicus, anything to Lucius's benefit came at a price and this time it might prove a high one.

Slouching back into his chair, he let his mind drift to the day his father had died. Returning from a day's hunting with his brother Marcus, he had strode with youthful enthusiasm through their home to find his father and tell him about their success, knowing he loved to hear of it. How innocent he had been then.

The image of the bloody point of the gladius protruding from his father's back jolted Lucius back to the present, as always. But the memory of his father's final written words were forever burned into his mind and often would leap forward like a despised uncle at a family celebration. He still had the parchment, hidden in his strongbox.

I am sorry my sons we are ruined

The words had been scrawled on the legal letter, sent by the advocate of his father's creditors. And then there was the bloody handprint.

With a conscious effort Lucius dismissed the unproductive feelings of hatred for his father's tormentors. Instead he reflected upon his developing relationship with Urbicus. The Numidian's campaign to expand the emperor's province had initially progressed well. The southern tribes, through a combination of bribery and threats, had quickly accepted Rome's peace. However those in the far north had other ideas and after two bloody years of campaigning Urbicus had built his wall between the estuaries of the Bodotri in the east and the Clutha in the west.

Lucius had kept his side of the unwritten bargain too and had ensured the Novantae stayed in their great forest, licking their wounds. Other than regular end of harvest cattle raids, they had largely remained quiet.

With the campaign complete, the Emperor's man returned to Rome, having done his master's bidding. It was not long after, sitting at this very desk in his newly rebuilt fort, Lucius had received his first communication. It had reassured him he would keep his word and had tasked agents in Baetica to investigate the acquisition of the Faenii family lands.

The letter had contained a request of his own, and Lucius knew a request from a man of Uribcus's status could not be turned down. It was innocuous enough. When governor, he had acquired a large tract of land south of Deva and Urbicus asked him to employ a reliable estate manager. It was an onerous task but Lucius treated it as a test, taking to it with his usual thoroughness.

After that the letters continued to come, sometimes two or three a year, varying considerably in nature. Some, Lucius concluded, could only be classed as spying on senior officers and officials. Another tasked him with escorting a heavy chest to a chieftain of the Otadini. Although he didn't attempt to open it, he assumed it was another bribe to hold the tribe's loyalty. Lucius never questioned the instructions, carrying them out to the letter, in the hope Urbicus would continue to keep his own part of their bargain.

The sound of hobnailed footsteps echoing through the empty building broke into Lucius's thoughts and he waited for the arrival of the owner of the familiar stride. Cai's tall frame appeared in the doorway, helmet tucked under his left arm.

'Evening, sir.'

'Good evening, Praefectus. You look like you could do with a drink.'

'Well if you're offering, sir, I'd be happy to help you drain your personal wine store.' Lucius laughed, pouring them each a cup from the jug set aside at the back of the room.

Lucius raised his. 'May we kiss who we please and please who we kiss.' Both men took a long swallow.

'You've outdone yourself again, brother,' Cai said. 'How do you find such decent wine at the arse end of the empire?'

'There are many benefits to the requirement for traders to seek my authority before moving their wares north.' Lucius looked at his friend and decided to have a bit of fun. 'Your escort turma returned some time ago, didn't it? I'd have thought you'd have reported before now?'

'I got delayed with other duties,' Cai said, a slight tinge of red appeared on his cheeks.

Lucius smiled mischievously.

'And how are young Beren and the fair Alyn?'

Cai's face now turned a brighter shade of red. 'Both are well,' he said, not quite able to meet his friend's eyes.

Lucius's laugh was full throated this time. 'I'm happy for you my friend, and it's clear as the light of day she is fond of you too.'

'Do you think so?' Cai asked earnestly. 'I'm never quite sure. At times it is like today, being invited to share the evening meal. But there are other times she seems distant, if you take my meaning.'

'It's obvious to anyone with eyes to see. You should do something about it before your time with the Nervana comes to its ending.'

Cai grimaced but didn't reply. Over the years the two men had developed a close friendship. A bond forged in the heat of the battle below the Novantae's hill and through the long months of the rebuilding of the cohort, alongside their new fort. Lucius had discussed some of the tasks Urbicus had asked him to fulfill and his promise of help in the restoration of his family's lands. He even confided the belief that his father had been murdered. Lucius had come to rely on the older man's sensible counsel.

'Did you know it's been ten years? Almost to the day,' Cai said.

'Ten years?' Lucius was momentarily confused. 'Ah yes, of course. Has it really been that long?' Taking the wine jug once more he refilled their cups.

'To the First Spear,' Lucius said, raising his cup, 'may he be enjoying the hunt wherever he is, and may he not laugh too much as we balls-up all his good work.'

'The First Spear,' Cai responded, smiling at the memory of his old friend.

They talked for a while about old times in the comradeship they had both come to value. Eventually Lucius cleared his throat, sitting up straight in his chair which Cai knew from long experience was the signal that a change to a more serious subject was coming. Cai took the seat at the other side of the long table.

'What's on your mind, brother?' Cai said.

'Am I so easy to read?' Lucius asked. Cai responded with a smile and a shrug. Lucius sat forward once more, placing his elbows on the desk.

'It has been increasingly playing on my mind that things in the lands of the Novantae have become too quiet. There have been no raids, no complaints of stolen cattle and our patrols now report they haven't observed any of their mounted warriors for some time. They've been our ever-present shadows all these years. So why stop now?'

'Sometimes quiet is just quiet,' Cai said, but his instincts told him Lucius's concerns were justified. 'But I do know the lads have been getting a bit comfortable in their nice warm barracks. It's about time we gave them a bit of a kick up the arse, to remind them they are still in the army.'

'Indeed,' Lucius said. 'But there's something I would like to show you that gives my suspicions a greater urgency. A letter from the Numidian.'

'He's written again?' Cai said, intrigued.

'He has, but I must ask for your discretion once again, brother, as it also concerns my family.' Cai nodded at once, understanding what was being asked. Lucius removed the letter from his strong box and handed it to Cai, who carefully unrolled it.

There are two matters of the greatest import that you must act upon with haste.

I have a spy placed in a position of influence amongst the Novantae. He has sent word that this most troublesome tribe plans insurrection. Our emperor's newest lands must not be allowed to fall back into its former state of chaos, for to do so would have consequences beyond the shores of Britannia. You must do all in your power to uncover and disrupt their plans. Do this and you will find imperial favour and sympathy for your own family's cause.

This brings me to the second matter.

My agent in Baetica has uncovered a witness, one who can attest to the unlawful means by which your family lands were attained. You must meet with them in Italica. There they will elaborate on their evidence and what must happen next. They will seek you out upon your arrival. I have included orders allowing you to travel by official means once you have successfully completed your task with the Novantae.

Cai puffed out his cheeks, expelling a long slow breath.

'Slippery, isn't he?' Cai finally said. 'No felicitations, nor signature to identify him, only his seal. A Novantae spy? And, by the gods, Lucius, after ten years of doing his bidding he only asks you to complete the smallest of tasks in order that you finally get close to a resolution. If you don't get yourself killed fulfilling that duty.' Cai shook his head.

'You're right as ever, brother,' Lucius said. 'But it doesn't change the fact we must know what the Novantae are up to.' He took another long swallow from his cup. 'I've been giving it some thought. We could kill two birds with one sling stone. The supply run is due to leave in the coming days, is it not?' Cai nodded in response.

'We can take the ala along the coast road of the Sula,' Lucius continued, 'bringing the grain to the castrae along the river crossings. It might disguise our true intent from any watchful eyes. Although the size of our force cannot easily be hidden.'

'True intent?' Cai said, puzzled.

'Yes, brother. Once we have completed the supply run we'll break northwards, moving at speed, deep into the hills to see what we can see. If we find nothing we'll sweep back eastwards. But if the Novantae are up to no good we might just catch them out. But we must move quickly so word of our presence doesn't fly ahead of us. I estimate we'd have to carry supplies for around five days.'

Cai was silent, reflecting. 'We'd have to carry more weight than you might suppose,' he said. 'We'd need to prepare a camp at the end of each day. Meaning each trooper must carry trench tools and a wooden stake for the ramparts.' A mischievous grin broke across Cai's face. 'My lads wouldn't know a camp ditch from a latrine. I'll ask our Gaulish brother to give them some practise.'

Lucius laughed. 'Our illustrious First Spear will love that, even if the men won't. I can almost hear the griping now. But you're right and it'll do them no harm to gain some new respect for their infantry colleagues.' He drained the last of the wine from his cup. 'We'll leave in five days' time. Let's get them hard at it.'

'Five days?' Cai said. 'Good. That gives me time to keep my promise to the lad.'

'Promise?'

'I said I'd take him hunting.'

28

Beren was awake long before dawn, too excited to sleep. He completed his chores quickly as the first hint of light began to touch the eastern horizon. Stars still glimmered in the clear dark sky, and the early morning air was cool but not cold, bringing the promise of a fine warm day. When he walked back through the entrance of his home, a wooden bowl filled with steaming oats sat on the table awaiting him and beside it his mother had placed a small cloth sack.

'I've wrapped some bread and cheese for you and Caius, along with a few slices of pork.'

'Thanks, Mam.' Beren said, through a mouthful of oats.

Alyn ruffled her son's fair hair. 'There are honey cakes too for the pair of you. Try not to stuff them into your mouth in one go for once.'

'Yes, Mam.'

There was a gentle knock on the door and Beren sprang to his feet.

'Good morning, lad. You're ready to go I see.'

Cai stood framed in the doorway. Dressed for the hunt in troos, wrapped tight at his shins with leather straps. He wore a green tunic with a sturdy belt to which was attached his knife and a full quiver of arrows. In his left hand he carried his unstrung ash bow. The only sign he was not a civilian were his hobnailed boots. Even his long fair hair was held back by a thin strip of calf hide, tied around his forehead.

'I'm ready, Cai,' Beren said, leaping from his stool.

'Just wait, young man,' Alyn said, 'you haven't finished your oats.' Cai could see she hid a smile.

'Sorry, Mam.' Beren ran back to the table and gulped the oats down in great dripping spoonfuls.

'There's plenty, Caius, if you would like to break your fast.'

Cai would have loved nothing better than to sit by the hearth fire with Alyn for a while.

'Thank you, Alyn. I've already eaten, and we have a bit of a walk ahead of us if we want to make the most of the day.' She smiled in acknowledgement, handing the small sack to Cai.

'Here's a little food for you both. I know you won't have packed enough.' Cai took it. Their fingers briefly touched. He was lost for words as he stared into her soft grey eyes. A warm smile crossed her lips. Beren tugged at Cai's arm, breaking the spell.

'Come on, Cai. Let's go?'

'Quite right, lad. We'd better be on our way. My thanks for the food, Alyn.'

'You're welcome, Caius. Try to make sure my son doesn't get into too much trouble. I know it will not be easy.'

'Never fear, he'll be safe with me.' Cai smiled and with his hand on Beren's shoulder the pair left the small dwelling. Alyn watched their retreating backs, her son happily chattering away, until they turned down a side path and out of sight.

They took the military road north for a while, before turning east away from its metalled surface and onto open pasture, as the first of the sun's rays broke above the horizon. Beren chatted all the way, rattling off questions Cai barely had time to answer before he was assailed by another.

Beren was breathless as the pair reached the first of the trees, which were younger and grew densely, making progress slow at first. But soon enough they entered the woodland proper, where the trees were tall and strong.

Now they were in the interior; it no longer appeared so dark, as patches of its floor were dappled with light from the rising sun. Cai loved the hunt, but these days there was always one more thing to do.

'Do you know the names of the trees, Beren?'

'I know the oak.' His voice filled with pride.

'That's a good start, but you must get to know them all, as all have their uses. The legions love the ash as it makes strong spear shafts as well as handles for axes and trenching tools. We use the tough but flexible oak for planks and boards, and the palisade that protects the Sack.' Beren nodded along wide eyed. 'But it's also important for our hunt today.' Cai let his words sink, before continuing.

'This forest is full of all kinds of game, including the big deer. They love to eat the low-hanging stems and bark from different trees, especially the saplings. They leave a great deal of damage behind. It's the signs of this damage we must watch for. Do you understand my young friend?'

'I think so.'

'Good. Now let's have a mouthful of water and we'll get moving. But from now we only speak when necessary and even then, only in whispers.' Cai rubbed the hair on the top of Beren's head. 'And I know that will be hard for you, my young friend.' Laughing, Beren flapped away Cai's arm.

Cai restrung his bow and the pair set off at a slow careful pace, moving deeper into the forest, following trackways whenever possible. At times they passed through thick undergrowth, Cai showed Beren how to move branches noiselessly aside. The friends progressed this way for much of the morning with little sign of any wildlife other than the constant twittering of the birds.

Cai would from time to time name the different trees, and test Beren on them as they progressed. They had decided to stop by a stream to rest and eat some of the food Alyn had prepared when Cai heard a snap. He raised his arm to Beren, who froze, a look of excitement lighting his face.

After a moment Cai moved again, to an area of thick bush to their fore, inspecting some of the branches, waving Beren forward.

'Do you see this?' he whispered. Cai held a thin branch for Beren to examine. 'Do you see how the bark has been shredded?' Beren nodded excitedly. 'This has been done by the antlers of a male red deer as he worked his way in to get at the sweetest leaves.' He pointed to the right of where they stood. 'Do you see those trees there? That is silver birch, a favourite of all deer. Do you notice anything unusual?' Beren stared in concentration, turning to Cai with a broad grin.

'The bark has been stripped,' Beren said.

'You have good eyes my young friend. The damage looks fresh. Let's move quietly and see what we can see, shall we?' Beren nodded vigorously, his mouth clasped tightly shut. It was all Cai could do not to laugh out loud at the sight of it. Taking the bow from across his back he lifted an arrow from his quiver, nestling it against the draw string, holding both bow and its arrow together in his left hand.

They crept through the undergrowth, carefully placing each

step, Cai leading, Beren his shadow. They saw more signs. There's more than one deer, Cai thought. After what felt like an eternity to Beren, Cai stopped, instantly moving into a crouch. Beren doing likewise without thought.

Carefully Cai pulled a thin, heavily leafed branch aside and there before them in a small clearing lit by rays from the early afternoon sun stood a do. No more than a spear's throw away. The whole of its dappled light brown body was exposed, its head turned away from where they crouched, tearing strips of bark from a young birch tree. Pulling the branch back a little further he indicated that Beren should take hold of it.

Taking a slow, deep breath Cai drew the bow back until his right hand was in line with this ear. Sighting on the deer he ignored the ache in his arm and slowly expelled the air from his lungs, preparing to release the arrow. But an instant before he let fly a fawn stepped into view from the other side of the tree its mother was stripping, oblivious to the hunters. Cai eased back on the bowstring. Its mother turned, perhaps hearing Cai's sigh. Sensing danger. Her ears pricked and she took flight, its youngling following. Both quickly swallowed up by the dense undergrowth.

'Why didn't you shoot?' cried Beren in frustration. Cai shook his head, placing the arrow back in the quiver.

'You risk angering Cernunnos by killing a nursing deer.' Beren's face still held a look of exasperation as Cai turned and walked away. 'Come. Let's return to the stream we passed and take our rest. I've been looking forward to your mother's food all morning.'

After a few seconds Beren ran to catch up with Cai, who was striding ahead. The pair walked in silence for a while. 'Who's Cernunnos?' Beren asked.

It had been a long morning and even Beren was feeling weary.

'You've done well on your first hunt lad.' Cai sat on an ivy-covered tree trunk. Beren stood on the stream's bank throwing pebbles into its depths.

'But we didn't kill anything,' Beren turned to Cai with a sullen look, before throwing another rock into the stream with a splash.

'Come sit with me.' Cai patted the trunk. Beren stared at the disappearing ripples in the water a moment longer before doing as his friend asked. As he settled beside him, Cai looked off into the dense trees gathering his thoughts.

'I've not spoken of this before, because I judged you were not yet old enough to hear it.' Beren's attention was pricked. It was unusual for Cai to speak this way to him. 'I know some of the old hands in the cohort have told you many stories over the years about your father. Some may have exaggerated his prowess in battle, but if they did it wasn't by much. He was the best and bravest of us. A warrior and a soldier.' Cai paused to clear his throat before continuing.

'But more than that he was my greatest friend and I his. He would have taken a blade for me and I him. You remind me of him a great deal. Not only because you look so alike but because you share so many of his virtues and one or two of his flaws. Including a certain lack of patience.' Cai was silent for a while and Beren thought he had finished speaking.

'Tell me the tale of my father's last battle.'

'I will, another time.' Cai placed a hand on the boy's shoulder. 'But if you will hear it, I want now to tell you about the last time your father and I talked.' Cai drew his hand through his long fair hair. Beren said nothing. Waiting.

'It was in the evening following the battle for the Novatae's hill. I came to the tent where your father lay grievously wounded. We talked for a while of the old days and our boyhood in the lands of the Nervii.' Cai was lost in his memories for a time. 'Before the end, your father asked that I teach you to hunt in the ways of our homeland and I gave him my word that I would.' Man and boy looked at one another as Cai continued. 'This is your father's last gift to you Beren. The only one he could give.' Grasping the boy's shoulder he spoke on. 'I will gladly fulfil that promise if you'll let me. I'll teach you everything I know. I'll show you what signs to look for when hunting deer and boar. We will practise the best ways to approach prey with both bow and spear and how to use them when the time comes.' Cai released his grip on the boy's shoulder. 'But what you must learn above all, my young hunter, is patience.'

'I will, Cai. I promise,' he said earnestly.

'I know you will.' Cai patted the boy's shoulder. 'Now if you'll excuse me, I'm going to leave a gift for the foxes to find.' Beren laughed as he watched him disappear along the stream's edge and behind a clump of saplings near to the water's edge.

Beren, now deep in thought, absorbed Cai's words. The men of the cohort had told him of his father's last battle but not how he had died, wishing to spare him any pain. But now Cai had talked about his promise. He wouldn't let him down.

A snap of a twig behind him brought him out of his reverie.

'Ow,' he yelled. Something had hit his shoulder. He spun around and was in time to see the flash of a pale face and long red hair as it disappeared behind a tangle of bushes. Beren heard the running footsteps of his assailant. Filled with rage and indignation, he set off in pursuit.

'Beren? What is it?' Cai shouted, concern in his voice. But Beren did not hear as he sprang across the clearing and into the undergrowth. He had lost sight of his attacker, but followed the sound of his passage through the brushwood. The woodland began to open up and he caught glimpses of flying red hair. The adrenalin that had coursed through his body in the early part of the chase slowly dissipated and he began to tire. But determined not to give up he continued the pursuit and gradually began to gain. His quarry glanced over his shoulder. Beren realised he was a boy of around his own age. An instant later he disappeared once more into a broad thicket.

Beren heard a scream that was immediately cut off. Slowing as he approached the tangle of bushes he slowly picked his way through, shaken into caution by the sharp cry. Pulling the last of the low branches aside he stepped into an open area of knee-high ferns growing thickly on the forest floor. He should have been able to see the boy, but there was no sign of him.

Treading carefully, anticipating his attacker might be lying in wait, he looked left and right, searching for any mark of his passing.

'Beren, where are you?' Cai's shout was close behind.

'Over here.'

Relief coursed through Beren. He heard Cai pushing his way through the thicket.

'What's going on? Why did you run off?' Cao said, not a little annoyed.

'Someone threw a rock at me. So I chased after him. I think he's a Novantae. I lost him here. He's disappeared.'

Cai removed the bow from his back and nocked an arrow, drawing the bowstring halfway. Ready.

'Are you sure, Beren? You saw a Novantae warrior?'

'Not a warrior. A boy.'

'Oh.' Cai eased the bowstring. 'He must have outpaced you then.'

'No. He's in here somewhere,' Beren said, affronted by Cai's doubt.

'Very well then. Let's see where he's hidden, shall we?' Both moved carefully through the waste high ferns, Beren a step ahead of Cai.

'Hey!' Beren was surprised as Cai grabbed him by the scruff of his tunic, pulling him backwards. 'What did you do that for?'

'Stand where you are. Don't move.' Cai stepped forward, pulling aside some of the ferns. Cai got onto his knees, crawling to the edge of what he could now see was a narrow, dark crevice. Moving to its edge, he looked down. 'He's down here. But not conscious,' Cai said. 'I'll climb down and take a look. You stay where you are.'

Cai slid over the lip. The crevice was as wide as a single stride, its sides were slick with damp green moss. Gradually he lowered himself until he reached a point where he could comfortably drop.

The space was tight. Cai scraped his side against the rock as he reached the boy. Lifting strands of red hair from the boy's face, he saw he was close to Beren's age. His eyes were closed. Carefully Cai examined the boy, feeling along his neck, chest and arms. There was a lump above the wrist of his left hand.

Then, easing his hand under the boy's head he felt the warm slickness of blood. Sliding his arm beneath the boy's shoulders, Cai gently raised him to a sitting position. Immediately he noticed more blood, pooling on the rock where his head had been.

'Damn,' Cai whispered. Laying him carefully back down, he placed his ear to the boy's mouth. His breathing was low and erratic.

'He's badly hurt,' Cai shouted up to Beren. 'He has blood coming from the back of his head and it looks like he has a broken wrist. There may be other injuries I can't see. We can't move him. The sides are too slick and I fear we would do him more damage in the attempt.' Cai thought through his options.

'Beren, do you think you could find your way out of the forest and back to the Sack?'

'Yes, of course.'

'Good. I know you can do it. Run as fast as you can. Find Lucius or men from my turma. Tell them what has happened. They must bring horses and rope. I'll stay and do what I can. Go now. I fear he won't last.'

Without another word Beren broke into a run. Cai heard the sound of his passing as he pushed his way quickly through the thicket once more.

He turned back to the Novantae boy, wishing he had brought his cloak, but he had not wanted it to encumber him. He noticed a slow drip of water from the side of the crevice. Tearing a strip of cloth from his tunic he soaked it. Carefully lifting the boy's head he began to clean the wound as best he could. He wrapped another strip around the boy's head in the hope of staunching the flow of blood. When he was finished he sat back on his heels to wait, praying Beren would find help quickly.

29

Beren ran. He leapt fallen tree trunks and passed through dense brush, not slowing. His mother would be alarmed at the sight of the marks left on his exposed skin. He stumbled countless times, tripped by some unseen obstacle, but picked himself up and ran on. At one point, momentarily panicked, he became lost. But taking a deep breath he calmed himself and retraced his steps until he found signs of their trail from earlier in the day.

Finally, lungs aching, he burst from the forest's edge and onto open ground. He was able to pick up his pace in the clear meadows but after a short while his earlier efforts began to catch up with him. But knew he must not stop. Cai and the Novantae boy were depending on him. Beren gasped for air as he came to the top of a small rise. Looking at the vista beyond, there in the middle distance was the military road.

His heart leapt. Moving along its surfaced length, heading northwards, Beren saw three troopers, each leading another riderless horse. Taking a deep breath he shouted at the top of his voice, whilst frantically waving his arms to attract the riders attention.

'Help! Help me!'

But the riders did not hear and they were rapidly approaching a dip in the road that would take them from sight. Fearing he would miss his opportunity, Beren set off once more, running as fast as his burning lungs would allow, shouting weakly as he went. The first of the riders entered the dip. Beren screamed out in frustration.

'Nervana!'

The rearmost of the three riders turned sharply. He saw Beren and halted. A wave of relief filled the boy. The rider called to his companions, now out of view. Beren continued to leap and wave his arms frantically as the three riders held what looked to him like a heated discussion.

At last, decision made, the front rider broke away and trotted his dappled horse towards Beren, who was now bent double, swallowing great gulps of air. It did not take the rider long to reach him and was glad to see it was Avitius.

‘What’s this about, boy,’ he asked, ‘shouting and waving like a madman?’ Confusion and not a little annoyance coloured his voice. Beren interrupted him before he could go on.

‘Cai has sent me for help,’ he gasped, ‘a boy has fallen in the forest. We need horses and rope, we must go now. He’s badly hurt.’ The words tumbled out in a muddle.

‘Slow down young warrior. Tell me again what has happened.’ Beren took a calming breath and this time spoke carefully.

‘Well you’re in luck this day. We have an abundance of rope and horses. Jump up behind me and we’ll ride back to the lads there and get what we need.”

Sitting behind Avitius, arms wrapped around the old soldier's waist, he bounced along as he guided the troopers’ back through the forest.

‘T’was lucky you spotted us exercising some of the turma’s replacements,’ Avitius said. “A minute or two later and you’d have missed us.’ Now Beren understood why the troopers wore only their white tunics.

They moved as quickly as the obstacles on the forest floor allowed. At times at a steady trot; at others it became too tricky underfoot to move much faster than a walk.

‘It’s just through those bushes there,’ Beren said. ‘You’ll have to leave the horses here and go on foot. But take care, the crevice is hidden from view.’ Beren slid from Avitius’s mount and pushed through the brush.

Cai heard the approach of the horses, accompanied by Beren’s voice.

‘Down here.’ Cai yelled, ‘but have a care.’

Avitius’s smiling face appeared over the lip of the crevice.

‘Got yourself stuck down a hole did you, sir?’

‘Avitius, thank the gods. Did you bring rope?’

‘Aye, sir. Fortuna is with you today.’

‘Good. The boy here’s unconscious and has a head wound. We’ll need to raise him carefully. Cut some spear-length branches and lash them into a stretcher.’

‘Mudenus, on me.’ Avitius shouted, disappearing from sight. Shortly afterwards, Cai heard rustling and grunting as the troopers hacked away at the undergrowth nearby. It wasn’t long before a stretcher made of sturdy-looking ash branches and Avitius's cloak was ready.

'You'll need to get yourself down here, Avitius, to help me lift the lad.' As if hearing himself being talked about, the boy let out a low moan. Cai looked him over. He still wasn't awake, but it was the first sound the boy had made. He hoped it was a good sign.

When they had strapped the young tribesman to the makeshift stretcher a rope was tied at either end and tethered to a horse's saddlehorn.

'Lead him off slowly, Mudenus,' Cai said, 'and listen out for my shout.' The stretcher jerked.

'Steady, you clumsy bastard,' Avitius bawled. It moved again, this time rising gradually as Cai and Avitius steadied it, doing their best to keep it away from the slick rock face. As it approached the lip Cai saw Beren looking down at the boy, who, not much more than an hour before, he had been chasing. The Novantae's skin was very pale and held a damp sheen. His long red hair lay splayed either side of the stretcher.

The Novantae boy wore checked green troos and deerskin boots with leather strappings around his shins. A deep red tunic with long sleeves covered his torso to his waist. But what was most striking was the thick metal ring that circled his neck. Not a closed ring; the two ends in the shape of wolf's heads didn't quite meet at the boy's nape, the animals snarling at one another.

Cai saw Beren reach down and run his fingers along it.

'That's bronze,' Cai grunted as he pulled himself over the lip. Panting with the effort, he offered his arm to Avitius, hauling him up onto the forest floor. 'I think our young tribesman here is no ordinary boy. To wear a torc like that speaks of status amongst the Novantae.' Still breathing heavily Cai turned to the troopers standing by the horses.

'Cut down two branches about twice as long as the stretcher. We need to make a frame to pull the lad back to the Sack. We can't risk carrying him on horseback.'

'I saw the medicus this morning, sir,' Avitius said. 'He's buggered off for the day to visit a colleague posted with the Exploratores. He said it was to scrounge medical supplies for our resupply patrol. But given how much he likes a wineskin, I think he has more than collecting a few extra bandages in mind.'

Cai looked at Beren. ‘We’ll take him to your mother,’ he said. ‘Given the times I’ve seen you with a bandaged arm or knee, I suspect she may know what’s best for the boy.’

They set off at a walk with the Novantae boy strapped firmly to the frame. Cai led the horse on foot, guiding it carefully through the underbrush.

‘Do you think he’ll be alright?’ Beren asked, after they’d been moving for a while. He had been walking beside the litter.

‘It’s hard to say with head wounds,’ Cai said. ‘The bleeding’s stopped. At least on the outside. I’m concerned he hasn’t opened his eyes yet.’

‘Aye, I’ve seen men recover consciousness after a bang on the head,’ Avitius said from astride his mount, ‘but were drooling simpletons for the rest of their lives. Not just that...’ Cai looked over the neck of the horse giving Avitius a flinty glare. The old trooper clamped his mouth shut.

‘We’ll just have to treat him with care and hope for the best,’ Cai said. He made silent prayers to all the gods he could think of. If they couldn’t save the boy, he might not be the only one to die when the Novantae found out.

30

Lucius was standing on a ridge about a quarter of a mile west of the Sack. It overlooked an area of pasture often flooded in wintertime. But at present it thronged with activity.

'Put your backs into it you idle mongrels,' the First Spear's shout carried across the works. 'My old mother could dig faster.'

One practise camp was close to completion. The single ditch had been dug to a depth that a tall man could not see over its lip. An inner embankment, created from the ditch's spoil, now formed the ramparts. The progress of the second camp nearby was some way behind the first and Lucius heard the continual shouted threats of that team's Decurions', urging them on. It was the second day that Lucius had the men of the ala turn out to practise the construction of an overnight camp. Two days extra duties awaited the losing side. Including its officers.

A deep throated laugh came from the man standing next to Lucius. 'Not quite up to infantry standard, sir,' the First Spear said, 'but I think they're getting the hang of it. We should be able to let them out into the wilds on their own.'

'I think you may be enjoying this a little too much, First Spear.' Lucius returned the good humour.

'Not at all, sir. I just enjoy a professional job well done.' Lucius turned to the Gaul and raised an eyebrow.

'I'm sure,' he said.

Marcus Favonius Facilis had been posted to the Sack not long after the battle for the hill, transferred from the fourth cohort of Gauls. The Centurion's of the Nervana, who had survived, were not of sufficient experience to risk an early promotion and a request to Verus had seen Facilus arrive. He was short and broad, much like his predecessor, but instead of the long fair hair he had adopted the Roman style keeping his dark hair closely cropped, his chin clean shaven.

Over the years Lucius had come to like and respect Facilis, whose energy was prolific. He was a fierce disciplinarian, but not cruel, using humour as much as his vine staff to get a job done. Lucius knew his men loved him.

It had taken some time for Cai to warm to the new First Spear, lost as he was in grief after his friend's death. He had been resentful of Facilis, whether he admitted it to himself or not. Cai had buried himself in the day-to-day running of the ala and building it back to strength. Facilis had sensed this and had wisely kept his distance where possible. But gradually the running of the cohort had forced a working relationship to develop. Now ten years on the three worked well together and if there was not a close bond between the two, there was certainly respect.

'Keep them at it, First Spear,' Lucius said. 'We're going to be on our own out there and they need to know more than one end of a shovel from the other. They must be able to dig out defences quickly, even if not as rapidly as your men would.' He gave his subordinate a sardonic smile.

'Don't you worry, sir. Those shovels will feel like extensions of their arms by the time I've finished with them.'

Lucius strolled back to where he had left Epona tied to a fence post. The horse snorted in greeting at his approach and he patted her black neck. Remounting, he reluctantly made his way back towards the Sack, letting Epona pick her own route across the pasture.

The preparations for the ala's departure were endless. It had been a welcome distraction to spend some of the afternoon away from the principia. A light cooling breeze from the direction of the Sula made the ride a comfortable one and Lucius let his mind drift back to the letter from Urbicus. He wondered, not for the first time that day, what it would be like to return to his homeland after such a long time away and to see his brother once more. Would he finally be able to reclaim his father's estates? His estates.

Lost in thought, it was only when the sound of Epona's hoof fall changed as she joined the paved surface of the military road he became fully aware of his surroundings once more. His attention was caught by a small group of troopers, some walking, moving parallel to the road rather than on the easier paved surface. Something struck him as odd about the party and he nudged Epona to a trot to intercept them.

He recognised the distinctive figure of Cai. But why was he leading a horse on foot? The group halted on hearing the clatter of hooves on the road top. Pulling up before them he received a salute from all four, including, to his amusement, young Beren.

'What's this Praefectus? That's an odd kind of game you've brought back from the hunt.' Lucius became serious upon seeing the look of concern on Cai's face. 'What happened?' Cai gave an abbreviated version of events and where he was taking the boy.

'Do you see this, sir?' Cai lifted the edge of the boy's bronze torc.

Lucius grimaced and rubbed his chin. 'We'd better send a section out to locate his people. I suspect we'll soon be paid a visit anyway. Perhaps best to wait until morning though.'

'Aye you may be right, sir,' Cai said. 'We don't want trouble on our hands just before we go on the resupply run.'

'How's he faring?' Lucius could see the white pallor of the boy's face.

'It's hard to say, the bleeding to his head has stopped but he's barely stirred since we got him out. I worry the fall has cracked his skull but until we can locate the medicus, in whatever inn he has decamped to, we won't know.'

'I'll ride ahead,' Lucius said, 'and send men to find him with orders to drag him back if necessary. I suspect knowing the tastes of our medicus he will be found at some hostellery near the dockside.' Lucius nodded to Cai and turned Epona, kicking her into a gallop.

'Right lads, gently does it,' Cai said, 'we're nearly there.' He turned the litter away from the road and towards the gateway to the village.

Alyn waited anxiously at the entrance to her home. As the small party appeared at the corner of the narrow street that passed her home, she rushed out to meet them. With barely a glance at Cai she went to the side of the still unconscious boy.

'Let's get him inside, quickly,' she said, 'I've prepared Beren's cot and have hot water ready on the hearth.' Alyn put her hand on the boy's forehead feeling the warm clammy moisture that lay on its surface. Her own forehead furrowed with concern.

'He hasn't moved mam,' piped up Beren, 'but he's still breathin.' Alyn looked at her son and tried to give him a reassuring smile.

'We'll do what we can for him, never fear.'

Cai and Avitius carefully lifted the boy from the litter, carrying him through the doorway and lowered him gently onto the cot. The boy let out a low moan as Cai pulled the arm clear that had been supporting his neck.

'That's a good sign,' Alyn spoke quietly. 'His spirit is still with us.'

Cai watched rapt as she moved quickly and efficiently around the cot. He had expected Alyn to change the improvised bandage on the boy's head first, but was surprised to see her take a bone needle from a small basket by the fireside.

'Help me remove his boots,' she said. Once the feet were bare she gently scraped the needle's point across the sole of each foot. She nodded in satisfaction as both twitched in turn.

'Good,' she said, 'at least it seems his back is not broken.' Next, using both hands, she felt along each of his legs, repeating the process with his arms. 'I can only feel the break on the wrist. It can wait until we've looked at his head.' Cai wasn't sure if Alyn spoke to him or whether she was simply speaking her thoughts.

'Caius, can you and Avitius gently raise the boy into a sitting position?'

The two men moved to either side of the cot, carefully sliding their arms under the boy's shoulders.

'Ready?' Cai said. Avitius nodded. They slowly raised the boy up, Alyn supporting his head. Then with deft fingers she quickly removed the dressing.

'Beren, bring me the lamp from the table,' Alyn said. Beren retrieved the already lit oil lamp and held it out to his mother. 'No, I need you to hold it for me.'

Alyn carefully examined the wound for a time. Finally she stared directly at Cai, the first she had looked at him fully since their arrival, her grey eyes shining with the lamp's flickering flame.

'The wound doesn't look too deep,' she said, 'but there's a dark swelling at the base of his skull that worries me. I'll clean it and make a poultice that may help reduce the swelling. But that's all I can do. He is in the hands of the gods now.'

31

By the time Alyn had finished, darkness had fallen and the boy lay unmoving. Avitius had left to settle the horses for the night. Cai fetched Alyn a cup of ale from her store. As he handed the dark clay cup to her she gave him a weary smile of thanks. Beren was sitting at the table, his tongue held tightly between his lips as he scraped the root vegetables for the evening meal.

'You've done a fine job for the boy. You're no stranger to tending to injuries, I think.'

'I was the only daughter of six children. My mother taught me early how to treat cuts, scrapes and broken bones. Thankfully none as serious as this boy of the Novantae.'

'Was it your brothers who taught you how to wield a knife?' He had meant it to be in good humour, but when he saw the flash of irritation in her eyes he realised he had overstepped. 'I'm sorry Alyn, I didn't mean to anger you, I only sought to raise your spirits.'

She looked at him for a moment, her face expressionless until she suddenly relaxed. 'No, it is I who am sorry, it's just that it is hard to be reminded of your own foolishness.' Cai was about to respond, but she spoke again before he could.

'No man will come near me now,' she said. 'They either think I will murder them in their sleep or would feel your wrath if they did more than say good morning. And yet you have not made your own approach.' She fell silent, breathing heavily as if it had taken a great effort to say those words.

Cai was stunned, he flushed red, not sure what to say. 'Alyn I…'

'Who do you think he is?' she said, before he could speak further.

He looked at her, confused, then realised she meant the boy. Cai shrugged. 'I'm not sure,' he said, 'but given the quality of his clothes and that torc,' he indicated the ring now propped against the cot, 'he must be the son of someone important. We're sending men out in the morning to spread the word. I just hope the boy survives. If he dies they may blame us for it.'

Alyn nodded. A long dark strand of hair escaped her braid falling across her cheek. 'When do you leave?'

Cai looked up sharply, but relented, unexpectedly pleased to see the look of concern in her eyes. He raised his voice so Beren could hear from where they sat by the hearth.

'It seems our foray into the lands of the Novantae isn't much of a secret around here.' He turned to Beren. 'I wonder why?' Beren looked back sheepishly, a pink flush rising in his cheeks.

'Don't be angry with him,' Alyn said, with a smile in her voice, 'he lives his life around the fort and your men. There's little he doesn't know of the comings and goings in the cohort.'

'So it would seem,' Cai said, returning the smile, relieved to see her humour return. Each held the other's eyes for a moment longer, before her own rising colour made Alyn look at her hands, resting on her lap.

'We leave at dawn on the day after the morrow,' Cai said, whilst Alyn continued to look down, unthinkingly picking at something on the palm of her hand.

'When will you return?' she asked, her voice low.

'All being well in around ten days.'

'You are expecting trouble?'

Cai wondered how much he should share. Was there any point in causing unnecessary alarm? But he also knew Alyn was no man's fool and would likely see through a pretence. He looked at the Novantae boy to ensure he still slept.

'The Tribunus is concerned, and I'm in agreement, that the Novantae have become a little too quiet of late. It's almost feels like they're willing us into believing they have accepted the empire's peace.'

'Could it not be so?' She looked at him now. Cai saw both hope and concern warring on her face and although he was sorry to be its cause, he also felt a thrill that this beautiful woman would care.

'Caius, I—'

There was a hammering on the door.

'Sir, are you there?' Cai crossed quickly to the door, pulling it open to see Betto's wide frame filling the doorway. Over the shoulder of the Duplicarius he saw movement in the shadows.

'Betto? What's going—'

'We found him, sir,' Betto interrupted, indicating with his thumb. 'He wasn't best pleased when me and the lads dragged him from the tavern we found him in. He was a bit unsteady on his feet but the swift ride up the road has shaken him out of his cups a bit.' As Betto moved aside, the light cast from the doorway revealed the rather dishevelled looking medicus. His hair looked comical, standing up on end in places, no doubt from the ride. Despite Betto's optimism the Greek physician still swayed a little.

'Medicus Castellanos. Thank you for coming, I hope we didn't spoil your evening too much,' Cai said.

The normal dark complexion of the physician held a grey tinge, and to Cai's amusement he pulled his shoulders back and tried his best to look dignified as he marched past Betto.

'S'fine. Show me the patient,' he said.

'The boy lies on the cot.' Cai indicated the pile of furs not far from the hearth.

The medicus carefully crossed the room, stopping once to steady himself on the table, where Beren still sat. He wobbled onto his knees at the side of the Novantae boy, steadied by Alyn with a hand on his arm. He nodded his thanks.

In halting Latin, Alyn explained what she had seen and done to aid the boy. The medicus listened carefully, not speaking but nodding regularly to show he understood.

For a few minutes he moved around the cot checking the boy in similar fashion to Alyn.

'Help me lift the boy,' he said. With Cai and Alyn supporting he unwrapped the bandage. He examined the head wound and bruising at length and made what sounded like approving mmm's at intervals. Finally he stood, a little more steadily this time, and turned to Alyn.

'This is good work. I don't see anything I would have done differently.'

Alyn nodded, and with a look of relief, she smiled at the Greek.

'The main concern,' Castellanos continued, 'is the swelling. The boy's breathing is a little erratic, but not too shallow, which is a good sign. As he sleeps we must hope the swelling reduces. For the time being, once you reapply the compress, keep him comfortable. That's as much as we can do for now. If he regains consciousness, help him to drink some water. I'll return at dawn, but send for me if his condition deteriorates.' With that the medicus walked with exaggerated steps back through the door, passing an amused Betto.

'See him back to his quarters will you, Betto?'

'Will do, sir'. The Duplicarious disappeared into the night running after the rapidly retreating back of the physician.

'I'd better turn in myself. There's much to do before we leave.' He ruffled Beren's hair. 'An exciting day's hunting, I think you will agree lad? Even if the game we caught has only two legs.'

Beren giggled. 'When can we go again, Cai?' he asked, eagerly.

'Soon,' he said. 'After I return. You have my promise.' Alyn was standing quietly by the hearth watching him. 'Thank you for all you have done for the boy. I think it may have saved him.'

'Time will tell.' She paused for an instant, unsure. 'Will we see you before you leave?'

'I hope so, though it may be late on the morrow.'

'We would welcome that.' A shy smile touching her face.

'Good night, Alyn.'

'Good night, Caius.'

With that he turned, quietly closing the door behind him. He made his way slowly back towards his quarters with an unfamiliar lightness.

32

Beren woke again before dawn. He wanted to complete his chores before he broke his fast. He hoped his mam would allow him to spend the day with the men of the cohort, watching them as they made their final preparations. Dressing quickly, he glanced at the indistinct bundle of the Novantae boy. He still lay in his cot, unmoving.

The first light of day silhouetted the low eastern hills as he finished his work and returned home, with a pail full of water from the well for his mam's wash and the pot. He placed the water by the hearth and stoked the cooling embers, placing a fresh log at its heart. Casting a look over at the cot, his breath caught. The light of the oil lamp reflected from the open eyes of the Novantae, who stared back at him.

'Mam! 'He's awake.' Beren shouted. The boy continued to stare at Beren unmoving.

In moments Alyn was at the side of the cot, the boy's eyes moving to her, his face relaxing a little at the sight. He tried to raise his head but moaned, closing his eyes once more.

'Lie still.' Alyn gently placed her hand on his shoulder. 'Fetch a cup of water and then you can help me lift him into a sitting position.' Beren quickly returned, handing her the cup. The boy squeezed his eyes tight shut as they raised him carefully to a near upright position. His face flushed red with the effort and pain, but he did not cry out. Alyn held the cup to his dry, cracked lips and he took a tentative sip. As if realising for the first time how thirsty he was he took two more mouthfuls, some of the water sloshing down his chin. The exertion was too much. His head slumped backwards and Alyn and Beren gently laid him down once more.

Alyn placed her palm softly on his forehead and was relieved to feel that the fever heat of yesterday had gone. She moved a stray lock of red hair from his face and he opened his eyes once more at her touch.

'You are safe here,' she said, her voice gentle. The boy nodded almost imperceptibly. 'My name is Alyn and this is my son Beren. What is your name?' Looking from Alyn to Beren, at first it seemed he wasn't going to respond.

'Herne.' The word came as a croak and he swallowed. 'My name is Herne.'

'Well, Herne, you are welcome in our home.'

There was a gentle rap at the door. Herne turned towards it with a look of fear.

Alyn gently touched his shoulder once more as Beren crossed to answer. Castellanos stood in the doorway, his tall frame silhouetted by the light of the rising sun. His eyes looked bleary, but he was clean shaven and wearing a fresh tunic. His dark hair, now hanging in ringlets, was kept under control by a leather strap. The Greek walked past Beren without acknowledging his presence.

'Are you faring better this morning, medicus?' Alyn spoke in Latin, knowing Castellanos had little of the local language. Her words were heavily accented but still failed to hide her annoyance at his abrupt entrance into her home.

'Well enough,' he said. 'Even though we are in the back of beyond, we thankfully have a small but adequate bath house. How is the patient this morning?'

'He woke only moments since and has taken a little water. His fever has broken and has told us his name is Herne.'

The medicus made a grumbling noise at the back of his throat, possibly an acknowledgement. 'Could you tell him I would like to examine his injuries?'

'I understand your tongue, Roman.' All three turned to look at the boy in surprise. For the first time, Castellanos smiled.

'Very well then young man. I'm going to do a bit of poking and prodding, it may be a little uncomfortable but I intend you no harm. Do you understand?' Herne nodded.

Without being asked Alyn moved to the side of the cot to help raise the boy, the Greek nodding his thanks. He unwrapped the bandage and spent some time gently feeling around the base of Herne's skull, murmuring to himself after each prod. Herne winced at times but otherwise kept silent. Castellanos then raised a small oil lamp close to Herne's face and looked into his eyes, gazing into each, continuing his low noises of satisfaction. Finally he nodded, making the grumbling sound once more.

'I think this young man has had a very lucky escape. He has some bruising on his neck which will hurt and be stiff for some time, but nothing appears broken. His eyes are clear which hopefully means there is no internal bleeding, but only time will tell for sure.'

Turning now to Herne, he smiled once more. 'Well, lad, you'll be fine, I think. But you must rest to be sure you recover quickly. It will be painful, but you should sit up and take some food.'

'Thank you, Roman.' A serious look crossed the boy's face.

The medicus laughed gently. 'I'm no Roman young man. I am Greek from the great city of Athens.' He turned and walked towards the door, speaking over his shoulder. 'I'll return this evening to check on him, good morning to you.' And with that he opened the door and was gone.

Alyn stared after him, finally shaking her head in puzzlement.

'Are you boys ready to eat?' Without waiting for a response she turned to the hearth.

Beren sat at the small table, looking at Herne, who stared back.

'How is it that you speak the Latin?' Beren asked.

Pride showed on the Novantae's face who, with some, effort raised himself onto his elbow.

'My uncle had me taught. He says we should understand the language of our enemy.' He fixed Beren with a glare. 'Do you think us stupid, Roman?' Putting emphasis on the final word before dropping back onto the cot, the effort tiring him.

Beren flushed with annoyance, but seeing the look his mother gave him he held back the words that first came to his mind.

'My mam is Carvetti and my father was of the Nervii people,' he said, his chest swelling. 'And why is it that your uncle has you learn the Latin and not your father?' Herne bared his teeth, but Alyn interrupted his response.

'Beren, Herne is a guest in our home and you will speak to him respectfully and I expect the same in return from a guest, Herne.'

'Sorry Mam.'

'Sorry,' Herne said, looking shamefaced, lying back and turning his gaze to the thatch of the roof.

There was silence for a while, the only sounds coming from Alyn as she prepared the oats and warmed yesterday's bannocks. Not taking his eyes from the roof, Herne spoke quietly.

'My father died at the battle of our sacred hill. I never knew him.' Beren could feel his mother's look, but did not want to acknowledge the sadness he would see there if he turned to her.

The silence between the three stretched for a while longer, before Beren responded.

'My father too died at the hill.' Herne turned in the cot to look at Beren and saw the truth of it. The Novantae boy nodded almost imperceptibly.

'Beren, help me raise Herne.' Her voice was hoarse. Alyn fussed around the cot making sure Herne was comfortable, before handing him the now warm bread with honey spread across its crown. Herne made short work of it.

'I think you needed that.' A gentle smile crossing her lips. 'Men from the fort have been sent to find your family and let them know you are well.'

Herne looked at her, his response so low she almost didn't hear.

'My uncle will already know where I am.'

33

Cai stood on the bottom lip of the gyrus fence, observing some of the cohort's horses being put through their paces. Adela was tied next to him and he absentmindedly stroked her neck. A few paces away, Betto straddled the gate to the training ground in order to get a better vantage.

The riders from Cai's own turma were drilling some of the newer mounts. They moved in two loops of four horses each and were continually switching loops at a midpoint. A difficult manoeuvre at the best of times.

'They're shaping up nicely, sir,' Betto said.

'Good enough to take with us do you think?'

'One or two might still be a bit green, but with an experienced hand they'll do just fine.'

Cai nodded. 'Carry on for another hour and then give the men the remainder of the day to clean and repair their kit. I want the ala turned out for inspection at the start of the night watch. Anyone with rusty mail or a blunt blade will have more than my boot up their arse.'

'I'll see to it, sir.'

Cai continued to watch the horses a while longer, enjoying being away from the grind of the seemingly endless preparations. His attention was drawn to the far side of the gyrus. Three grooms were shovelling horse manure into a great pile to be stored and used to feed the barren fields come autumn. One of the boys threw a clump of the dung at his mate, the soft ball striking him on the cheek. An instant later the three, thinking they were unobserved, began a game of chase around the pile in gales of laughter as clumps of brown flew back and forth.

'The little shits,' Betto said, in exasperation 'wait till I get my hands on them.'

Leave them be,' Cai said. 'Let them have their fun while they can.'

'But, sir I...what's going on over there I wonder?' Betto indicated with a jerk of his head to Cai's left.

A small group of villagers were outside the settlement's main gateway beyond the double ditch, waving wildly. Cai cast around, looking for the cause of their excitement. No more than two stadia to the north were three horsemen. Even at that distance he could tell by their bearing they were warriors. The middle of the three handed what looked like a sword to one of his companions before nudging his mount into a trot towards the village. When he was a stone's throw from the villagers, the warrior halted.

'It looks like the brave citizens are making a hasty retreat.' Cai watched, amused, as the villagers walked briskly back across the causeway, disappearing behind the safety of the palisade. The horseman was untying what initially looked like a spear, but as he raised it Cai understood. It was a leafed branch, oak most likely.

'Well what do you know, sir. He wants to talk.'

Cai leaped onto Adela's back. 'Keep the men at it, Betto. I'm going to see what our friend here wants. Although I suspect it might have something to do with the Novantae lad.'

Nudging his mount into a trot he rode towards the horseman, realising as he did so the only weapon he had was the pugio fixed to his belt. He wore no helmet or chainmail. As Cai crossed the open ground it soon became obvious this was no ordinary warrior.

He pulled Adela up a few strides short. Cai raised his sword hand in greeting and to show he came unarmed. The warrior observed him, stony-faced, still holding the branch. He also wore no helmet, his long red hair tied back and braided with a leather strap. His thick moustache drooped below his clean-shaven chin. He wore bronze scale armour. Roman armour. His muscled arms were bare and covered in blue tattoos that curled snake-like from his fingertips to disappear under the armour.

If there was any doubt as to his standing amongst his people, it was dispelled by the torc made of entwined strands of gold encircling the warrior's neck. His white horse was not like the smaller sturdy mounts he was used to seeing amongst the tribes. This was tall and muscular, like those ridden by his own men.

'Welcome. I am Martis, Praefectus Ala of the First Nervana.' Cai spoke in the tongue of the Carvetii, which he knew was close enough to that of the Novantae.

The Novantae gave a fleeting smile, 'I know who you are, Roman.' He tossed the branch aside. 'I watched you at close quarters, ten summers ago at the battle on our sacred hill.

Unfortunately the press of bodies prevented me from reaching you that day. I am Barra, a chieftain amongst my people.'

Cai returned the smile but decided to ignore the barb. 'You've come for the boy?'

'My nephew. You are holding him.' It was not a question.

'He's being cared for in the village by the mother of the boy who found him. He has been treated well, but he's hurt. His head took a forceful blow from a fall. He lay unmoving during the night but woke this morning. He may not be able to travel.'

'I'll judge that, Roman. Take me to him.'

It was Cai's turn to twitch a smile at the other's brusqueness, but he bowed his head in mock acquiescence.

'Follow me then.'

Turning Adela, Cai nudged her towards the village, with the truculent chieftain following behind. Trotting along the causeway and through the solid gates, he led the warrior through a now-deserted main street, turning into the narrow roadway that led to Alyn's home.

She was standing in the open doorway and raised her hand in greeting. Alyn stepped from her home's threshold as the riders approached, looking first at Cai and then at the warrior, addressing the latter directly.

'Welcome to my home,' she said, giving a slight bow of the head acknowledging his rank. 'Please come inside and take your ease.'

For the first time the warrior lost his brusqueness and produced a smile of genuine warmth.

'I thank you for your kindness. But I've come to reclaim my nephew only, and must be on my way.'

Alyn's forehead creased in concern.

'I worry he may not yet be ready to endure the roughness of a journey on horseback. Couldn't he stay for a day or two longer? He's most welcome in my home.' Barra looked at her unspeaking for a while.

'May I enter your home and speak with Herne myself?'

'Of course.' Alyn bowed her head once more, stepping back from the doorway in invitation.

The Novantae dismounted, quickly followed by Cai, both leaving their horses untethered. Ducking his head as he entered, the warchief blinked as his eyes adjusted to the gloom after the brightness of the day. But soon he could make out Herne sitting up in the cot near the hearth.

'So, nephew, it seems you've been up to no good once again.' Although not said cruelly his disappointment in the boy was clear. Herne hung his head, unable to look at the tall warrior.

'I'm sorry uncle, I—'

'We'll speak of this later. Can you stand?'

The boy's face took on a determined look. 'I...I think so.' Herne rolled from the cot onto the packed earthen floor. Alyn rushed to his side to assist him. 'No. I can do it myself,' he said firmly. Gingerly he raised himself from his knees, holding his broken wrist to his chest. Slowly Herne stood, his body curved inward. A gasp of pain escaped his lips as he attempted to straighten.

His uncle watched Herne's faltering movements and moved to his nephew's side. Placing his forefinger under the boy's chin he gently raised Herne's head. Man and boy looked directly into one another's eyes. Beads of sweat stood out on Herne's forehead. He was in considerable pain, but would not acknowledge it.

'Do you think you can ride?'

Alyn opened her mouth to object but upon seeing the almost imperceptible shake of Cai's head, she kept her silence.

'Yes, uncle.'

The chieftain nodded once with satisfaction. And not a little pride, it seemed to Alyn.

'Very well, let us leave.'

Alyn stepped forward and held out a small stoppered flask.

'I've prepared this tonic, it will help with the pain. Let him drink it as he needs on the journey,' she said.

'You have my thanks for the kindness you've shown to my nephew. I'll not forget. Perhaps one day I will have the opportunity to repay it?'

Barra turned to Cai. 'Some of my people watched you carrying Herne with care to your fort. From the look of him, he may have died without your help. He owes you his life and I am in your debt.' The chieftain did not look pleased as he said it.

'I'm sure you'd have done the same for young Beren here. You owe me nothing,' Cai said. Beren had watched silently from his place at the table during the entire exchange.

'No, Roman,' Barra said, his voice firm, 'I owe you a debt. Come, Herne.' Not waiting for a reply he nodded once more to Alyn and strode through the doorway, Herne shuffling in his wake. As he reached the door the Novantae boy turned and looked from Alyn to Beren.

'My thanks,' his voice was quiet and still full of pain. Wincing once more with the effort, he followed his uncle. Mounting in a single leap the warrior held out his hand to Herne, lifting him with surprising gentleness to sit in front of him.

'Remember the tonic,' Alyn said from her doorway. 'Have Herne drink it when the pain becomes too much.' Her look became stern. 'And it will become too much quite quickly.' She also held out a cloak. 'Wrap him in this to keep him comfortable, return it when you can.'

Accepting the cloak, Barra smiled warmly once more, before clicking his tongue and turning his mount. Watching the warrior as he slowly moved down the narrow street, Cai could clearly make out the brand of a charging boar on the rump of the Novantae's white horse.

34

Lucius sighed. It felt like he had been locked into the four walls of his office for days. Pushing the chair from his desk, he retrieved the jug of wine from its usual spot. He was surprised at its lightness. He was drinking too much, he thought, but refilled his cup anyway.

'Good evening, sir.'

Lucius jumped. He hadn't heard Cai's approach through the principia

'Jupiter, brother,' he said, 'why are you sneaking around at this late hour?'

Cai barked a laugh. 'My apologies, have I caught you doing something our glorious emperor wouldn't approve of?'

'Only drinking more than I should, it seems.' Lucius raised the jug as if displaying the evidence. 'Will you join me?'

'I thought you'd never ask.'

Lucius handed a filled cup to Cai. 'To success.'

'To flushing out the sheep-humpers.' Cai took a long swallow.

'Sit, brother,' Lucius said.

Cai took the chair opposite, stretching out his legs, relaxing in the warming glow of his friend's wine. 'I had a bit of a run in with one of those aforenamed sheep-humpers earlier today.'

'So I heard. What did you make of him?'

Cai scratched his chin. He would have to put the knife to his beard before they left.

'Impressive. One of their warchiefs'. Intelligent and an experienced fighter by the looks of him. He wore good plate armour. Roman armour. His horse had the brand of the Twentieth Vitrix and wanted me to know it,' Cai raised the cup to his lips, lowering it once more without drinking. 'He was at the battle for the hill and said he'd seen me there.' Cai raised the cup once more, this time taking several long swallows. 'Lucius, I think your instincts and Urbicus's intelligence are close to the mark. For him to be swathed in Roman war gear he must've been fighting beyond the new wall. Now he has returned. It seems the Novantae may be spoiling for a fight.'

Lucius nodded, 'Send two sections of horse to forewarn the outliers and watchtowers along the military road. They must be alerted and be ready.'

'Well, the ala is ready,' Cai said. 'I carried out a final inspection this evening, we're in good shape. The men are hurting in places they didn't know they could hurt from all the spade work. But they'll be glad of it when the time comes.'

'Indeed,' Lucius said, with a smile, 'Facilis even went as far to say your men's trenching skills were now adequate. Which is high praise from him.'

'The men know we're preparing for something out of the ordinary. We'll have to tell them at some point.'

'Agreed, but let's do it once we've left the Sack behind. The blue-faces no doubt have ears around the fort.'

'Aye, the warchief, Barra made it clear we had been seen returning to the fort with the boy. I would be surprised if the Novantae didn't have eyes within the village.' Cai swallowed down the dregs in his wine cup. 'Talking of which, I promised I'd say goodbye to young Beren before I left.'

'Ah yes. And Alyn too?' Lucius said, delighted to see his friend flush, the redness framed by his long fair hair. Cai was speechless, which made Lucius laugh all the more. 'Go, brother. I won't detain you any longer.'

Cai gathered himself, returning his friend's mirth, raising his now empty cup in a mock salute. 'I'll see you in the morning.'

Lucius listened to the sound of Cai's hobnailed steps as they echoed along the columned walkway until they faded away. He was left alone once more with his thoughts, in the now silent building.

Cai decided to take the longer route via the porta decumana in order to gather his thoughts. Striding through the fort's rear gate, acknowledging the salute of the sentries, he continued over the causeway that crossed the six ditches, just as a returning patrol approached. Men of his own turma.

'Avitius. All quiet I take it?' he said, seeing the standard bearer.

'Nothin' much to report, sir. We crossed the Anam and headed west along the coast. We saw the usual miserable fishing hovels and their sullen occupants but bugger all else. Gods, even their women are pig ugly.'

'I can't see any woman being too ugly for you, Vexillarius,' Cai said.

'Nor their pigs, sir.' The comment from the rear of the column raised laughter from the other troopers.

'Piss-taking bastards,' Avitius said, but his smirk belied his words.

'Well, you lot get yourselves sorted as quick as you can,' Cai said. 'We're leaving at first light.'

'Where're we off to, sir?'

'You'll find out tomorrow, Avitius.' Cai walked on. The men's morale is good, he mused. But it'll be tested in the coming days.

Deep in thought, he was surprised to see he had already reached the gyrus. The sun had set, its fading light making a purple silhouette of the distant, ever present mountain of Criffel. As he approached the settlement's gateway Cai felt the now familiar flurry in his stomach. He had promised the boy he would say farewell before the ala left, but needed little excuse, he realised, to seek Alyn's company.

He had long had feelings for her, and if he acknowledged it, probably since the moment she had appeared that day at the Sack's fledgling settlement. Now, after their conversation of the day before, he began to believe his feelings might be returned.

Passing through the village's main street he exchanged shouted greetings with some of the store owners, those who had not yet closed their shutters for the day. The butcher's shop was already shuttered, he noticed. 'The fat, lazy bastard's no doubt already propping up the bar of the tavern,' Cai grumbled to himself as he turned from the surfaced street and onto the narrower lane leading to Alyn's home.

As her small dwelling came into view the flutter in his stomach increased. Reaching her door he paused to straighten his tunic. Fuck me, it's easier going into battle, he thought.

But before he could knock the door was flung open by an excited Beren.

'You came,' he yelled, surprising Cai by flinging his arms around his waist.

'I promised I would, didn't I?' he said, ruffling the boy's hair.

'Yes, but mam said you might be too busy, what with you leaving on the morrow.'

'Berengar, where are your manners? Let Caius cross the threshold at least.' But Alyn could not hide the mirth from her voice at her son's joy of seeing his friend. 'Please come in, Caius.'

His tall frame forced him to duck under the doorway, with the boy close on his heels. She stood by the hearth, her long dark hair for once not tied back in its usual braid. Instead it lay loosely across her shoulders, the glow from the hearth's fire making it shine. She looked at him directly, with a warm, welcoming smile. By the gods, she's beautiful.

'We've had our evening meal, but there's some broth left in the pot if you're hungry?' she said as Cai took in the sight of her for a moment longer.

'That's kind, Alyn,' he said, 'but I've eaten already.'

'Cai, will you tell us about the patrol?' Beren asked. 'It's more than taking grain to the forts' isn't it? You're going looking for the Novantae, aren't you?'

'Well, my young friend, you still have an ear for the gossip within the Sack. You wouldn't have been talking to that old goat Avitius again, would you?'

'Don't bother Caius with your questions, Berengar, you know he can't say.' Alyn fidgeted with the belt at her waist. 'It's such a lovely evening, shall we take a walk by the stream? If you have time, that is?'

'There's nothing to do that can't wait,' Cai said. 'I would like that very much.'

The three walked slowly back through the settlement, turning at its gate towards the stream running along the south side of the fort and village. They talked of ordinary things for a time as Beren ran ahead. After a while Cai and Alyn stopped under a small coppice of beech saplings at the water's edge. They had been talking almost without pause, but now stood together in silence, watching Beren throwing pebbles at a stick that floated mid stream. Tension built between them as the seconds passed.

Her hand touched his arm. The thrill of it ran through his body. He turned to face her and looked deeply into Alyn's soft grey eyes.

'Oh Cai,' she whispered, 'you will take care, won't you?' And without giving him a chance to respond she suddenly flung her arms around his neck and drew him into a kiss. He wrapped his arms around her waist, pulling her closer still. Hidden within the trees, their lips touched lightly at first, but soon with the force of their desire. As suddenly as it started it came to an end as Alyn broke from his arms, her face flushed.

Cai looked at her in confusion, and she smiled.

'I don't want Beren to see us like this. At least not yet.' With that she turned and walked towards her son, who was still absorbed in his game. She turned back and looked at him with a challenge in her eyes. 'Aren't you coming?'

Cai, still overwhelmed by what had just passed between them, moved towards her. She laughed softly at his bewildered look and waited for him to catch up. For a while the three of them talked and laughed as the evening light gradually faded. For the first time in an age, Cai did not think about the cohort or the Novantae, but simply immersed himself in the joy of being with this woman.

Lucius walked Epona out of the Sack, leaving through the porta praetoria, telling the Optio of the gate's guard section he would be back before dark.

He didn't have a destination in mind, only sought to be free of his duties for an hour. As he crossed the stream in front of the fort, he smiled at seeing Cai and Alyn in the distance, lost in conversation, walking side by side along the bank of the slow-moving water.

Epona snorted. 'I'm sorry girl, am I a little slow for your liking this evening? Let's have some fun then, shall we?' He kicked his mount into a trot and headed in the direction of the Sula. As he ascended the first rise the estuary came into view, its waters silver in the late evening.

He was unencumbered by helm or armour and wore only his leather vest and cloak, his spatha strapped to his side. When he had ridden for around half an hour he found himself close to the estuary's edge. He knew its hidden quicksands and marshes could be treacherous so halted on a spur of dry land to take in the view in the last of the light. The spur protruded some way into the rippling waters, both sides framed by thick stands of reeds.

'It isn't Baetica, is it girl? But it does have a beauty all its own.'

With a start, Lucius turned sharply in his saddle at the muffled sound of hoofbeats. There at the open end of the spur was a rider mounted on a dark brown horse, a patch of white on its broad chest. But what alarmed Lucius was the rider himself. He was cloaked, his eyes hidden within the dark depths of its hood, the lower part of his face covered by a neck scarf.

'What do you want?' Lucius shouted, not quite hiding the fear in his voice.

The rider responded by kicking his mount into motion, simultaneously loosing the javelin he held. The spear flashed towards Lucius's chest. He arched his body instinctively. The shaft glanced against his leather vest to splash into the water beyond. But the rider did not stop. He had drawn his sword and Lucius just had time to free his spatha from its scabbard to parry the downward slice aimed at his head.

Lucius kicked Epona. He needed to get off the narrow spur of land. The speed of the unknown rider's wild charge had taken him past Lucius, giving him an instant to put some distance between them. But his attacker turned quickly to pursue.

As Lucius reached the small rise at the spur's end, he hauled on the reins and spun Epona to face his assailant. Again he was forced to parry a vicious slice, ducking under a backward cut as the rider passed once more. But Lucius had steadied himself. He turned Epona and kicked her directly at the other horse, its rider now frantically fighting to control his mount.

Lucius thrust his spatha the attackers chest. His assailant leaned back and parried. The ring of steel on steel reverberated loudly in the still evening air. But the rider was now off balance. A reverse cut from Lucius forced his attacker to arch back again. This time Lucius felt his blade connect with the rider's throat but saw no blood. Instead his assailant's hooded cloak fell from his shoulders, revealing dark, short cropped hair. Fear-filled eyes stared back at Lucius from above the scarf.

Lucius knew he had to press his advantage whilst he still had one. He kicked Epona hard thrusting his sword instantaneously at his enemy's face. The man attempted a desperate parry, but the move had been a feint. Lucius turned it into a cut, slicing downwards into the masked rider's unprotected upper arm. As the blade cut through muscle, the man shrieked.

Epona's momentum took her past the now-wounded assailant, giving him a blink of time to react. He did what Lucius had not expected: he kicked his dark brown mare and made a run for it. The horse had taken a number of strides before Lucius drove Epona into pursuit.

The light was fading rapidly and his attacker was a dark silhouette as he pounded through the undergrowth of long grass dotted with stunted trees. The rider crashed recklessly on, driven by his need to escape. Soon there was more than a spear's throw distance between the two horses.

Lucius didn't want to risk Epona in the last of the light. Reluctantly he hauled on her reins and she slowed to a halt, snorting her frustration. Lucius listened to the fading thunder of the other horse, as the rider was swallowed by the darkness

His mind raced. Who would attack him here and why? This was no ordinary bandit, nor was it a lone Novantae on the lookout for an easy target. He had fought with a spatha. Lucius retraced his steps towards the spur of land where the attack had begun. Dismounting, he felt carefully along the soft ground in the darkness. Eventually, near the water's edge, he found what he was searching for. The rider's cloak. There was nothing remarkable about it; many of the local people and soldiers alike wore them this far north.

His hand brushed against something cool and metallic embedded in the fabric. The cloak's pin. It hung from a piece of torn material, where his swords point had made contact. Lucius stared at it in the near darkness and finally was able to discern its shape. It was a bull. A black bull.

35

Perhaps Cai was right? His attacker may have been a deserter on the lookout for easy pickings who, seeing Lucius leave the fort, thought he would try his luck. But he couldn't shake the feeling this was something more sinister. The unknown rider had seemed too well fed and armed to be a lawless man on the run.

The rhythm of Epona's swaying movement again lulled Lucius's mind, returning his thoughts to the tense conversation with Cai upon his return to the Sack.

'I'll order a section to hunt him down,' Cai had said. 'We can't have outlaws thinking they can get away with this.'

Lucius had taken a long swallow from his wine cup. His hand had still been trembling as he'd lowered it once more. 'There's no point, he'll be long gone by now.'

'No we can't—' Cai had begun.

Lucius had raised his hand, cutting Cai off. He had looked at his friend for a long moment, considering his next words. On his journey back to the fort his mind had raced. Who would dare attack a Roman officer, let alone the Tribunus of the local castra?

'I can't escape the feeling this was personal,' he had said, before returning his gaze to his wine cup. 'This was no desperate man and look.' Lucius had taken the cloak pin from the pouch at his belt and handed it to Cai, who had stared at it, with a puzzled expression.

'A follower of Mithras perhaps?' Cai had ventured.

'I don't think so, I have seen this bull many times in my homeland. See how black it is and its horns stand proud? It's the symbol of Baetica.'

Cai had shaken his head, incredulous. 'Come Lucius, are you really suggesting someone has travelled across half of the empire just to kill you? The simplest answer is usually the right one. A deserter who thought he had easy pickings and received more than he bargained for.'

A trooper close behind him laughed coarsely, shaking Lucius back to the present. He grimaced at his own conceit. Why would anyone want him dead? But he still couldn't throw off the sense of foreboding.

He took a deep breath of the salty air that drifted on the gentle breeze from the Sula pushing the thoughts aside. It had been a long day in the saddle, riding Epona at the head of the ala. His back ached fiercely. But he was glad to have left his desk behind. He loved nothing more than being on horseback, leading his men.

It was a fine day, and still warm despite the sun being long past its zenith. Lucius was glad of the cooling breeze. This was the third day of the supply run and so far had been uneventful. The ala had spent each of the previous two nights camped outside one of the castrae that ran west along the coast. All were positioned to manage movement through important valleys or at the fords of significant rivers whose waters spilled into the Sula estuary.

Each evening their arrival had been greeted by looks of surprise by the men manning the fort walls. What was so important about these supplies that it required the full strength of the Sack's ala? Lucius had not sent riders ahead for fear of capture, so the commanders' reacted with astonishment as Lucius explained their objective.

'But we've seen almost nothing of the blue faces for weeks, sir,' one had said.

'And that's the point,' he returned. 'What the hell are they up to?'

As the cavalry crested a gentle rise in the road, an inlet came into view, its mouth wide but quickly narrowing to meet the river that emptied into it. Upon reaching the river's edge the road turned northwards to follow its course. The turrets of the final fort were sighted not long after that.

It was the smallest and most isolated of the three castrae to be resupplied, meant to house a force of four turmae, but Lucius knew from the regular reports it was badly understrength. As they came into view of its gates, he saw that the duty section had already turned out on its causeway and from the helmet plume he could make out, the fort's commander waited on horseback to meet them. It was gratifying to see this officer at least was alert to his duties.

A short distance from the fort Lucius gave the order to halt, but nudging Epona forward at a walk. The fort's senior officer met him midway along the causeway that crossed its two deep defensive ditches. Lucius observed they were filled with cut blackberry bushes; their entwined thorny branches would snare any enemy who wanted to take a closer look at the fort at night.

'Welcome sir, it's good to see you. If a little unexpected,' the officer said as they exchanged salutes.

'And you, Nepos.' Lucius knew Nepos, a highly experienced senior Decurion. He was a Tungrian and even after more than two decades with the eagles his accented Latin was harsh on the ears.

Nepo's face showed the signs of long years in the service of the emperor. Long grey hair fanned out from under his shining bronze helmet, whose broad cheek guards only partly hid the left eye. It stared, milky white and unseeing, back at Lucius, the result of a sword slash that had left a livid scar which split his eyebrow and left a hard, red blob under the dead eye. This permanent, bloody teardrop had earned him a nickname no one dared to repeat in his hearing: Crybaby. A spear thrust to the throat in a later battle had not only left him with a puncture scar, but a harsh, gravelly voice to accompany it.

'That's quite an escort for a supply run, sir. Are you by any chance expecting trouble? Or about to cause some for the Novantae?'

'A bit of both. But we can discuss it once I get the men settled. We'll be making camp under hostile territory conditions. Where's the best position to locate it?'

Nepos's good eye widened briefly, but quickly nodded his understanding.

'There's a level area just to the north of the fort, sir. You can use the river to guard the camp's western flank and it's within hailing distance of our ramparts.'

'My thanks, Nepos, I'll visit you this evening.'

'Very good, sir. I still have a supply of some not too disgusting wine.'

Lucius and Cai walked briskly towards the fort's open gate, returning the salute of the sentries. Once inside both officers removed their helmets, carrying them under their arm to indicate no further salutes were required. Cai looked around at the familiar scene. Men sat on the verandas of the barrack blocks repairing their horses' tack, cleaning chainmail or sharpening spathas.

'Nepos runs his command well,' Cai said in approval.

The barrack blocks were similar to those at the Sack, the long buildings split into ten sections, each combining three-man rooms to the rear with the stabling for their horses at the front. All mounts had been well groomed and settled for the night. Cai could barely remember a time where he had not drifted to sleep to the sound of the gentle snort of horses and the smell of straw and dung.

Upon entering the principia the small headquarters building was a hive of activity. The fort's commanding officer sat behind a makeshift timber desk with a sleeping cot directly behind. A plate of bread and cheese had been placed at the table's side.

'My apologies for disturbing your evening meal, Nepos. Please carry on eating as we talk.'

'My thanks, sir. It's been a long day and my stomach thinks my throat's been cut.'

'You wouldn't want that to happen again, brother,' Cai said in mock seriousness, causing Nepos to choke on the piece of bread he had just started to chew. His face turned a bright puce colour but Cai could see it was mirth that choked him rather than annoyance.

Nepos poured himself a cup of wine and swallowed it in great gulps. When he finally had his cough under control he turned back to Cai, giving him a lopsided smile. This, in combination with the milky eye, gave him the look of a wolf ready to pounce on its prey. He poured two more cups, handing them to Lucius and Cai, refilling his own.

'Your good health,' Nepos said, through another mouthful of cheese.

'Not bad at all, brother,' Cai said in surprise.

'I didn't know the Nervii could appreciate half decent wine, I thought you preferred that evil tasting swill you call ale?' Not waiting for Cai's response, the Tungrian retrieved a pair of folded campaign chairs stuffed into the small space between the wall and his cot.

'Now sir,' Nepos said once they were all seated, 'perhaps you could enlighten me on why you've arrived with the Sack's entire ala for a simple resupply run?'

'From the activity in your principia, Nepos,' Lucius said, 'I think you may have guessed at least part of it.'

Lucius and Cai spent the next few minutes summarising their suspicions about the Novantae, omitting the intelligence received from Urbicus. Cai went on to describe the incident with the warchief, Barra. Lucius then outlined his plan. Nepos waited for Lucius to finish, only nodding to show his understanding at important points.

'Your misgivings seem justified, sir,' he said. 'Things had been more quiet than usual, just as you have observed. We stopped seeing signs of their horsemen whenever we struck inland or to the west. But in the last week that all changed. The shadowing of our patrols started once again, but this time in larger groups. I knew those bastard's were up to some mischief, and I was certain it couldn't be good news for us here, stuck out at the end of the line as we are. So before first light this morning I sent out foot patrols to see if the blue-faces are watching the fort.' Nepos drained his cup.

'My lads hunt these hills for the game pot and know them like they know their own horse's rumps. It didn't take them long to find their lairs. There are two groups of five or six warriors each. The nearest are observing our movements here the other watches the road to the east. You can be sure they know of your arrival, sir.'

Cai placed his wine cup on the desk. 'Well, whatever they're up to they may plan to strike here first.'

'There's one more thing, sir. My men observed from a distance, but one of the lads who I trust was sure not all of them were Novantae.'

'How could he tell?'

'He said a pair of them had their skulls shaved and were covered in dark tattoos. The Novantae are too vain to shave their long locks.'

'This might be worse than we imagined.' Lucius looked from Cai to Nepos. 'If our enemies are massing to strike at us, where are they most likely to gather?'

Nepos peered into his cup, his milky eye unmoving. The other roved as if by its own accord.

'Their capital,' Nepos said, 'if that's what you call that dung heap, sits on a peninsula at the far western reaches of the Sula. From there you can see the dark coast of Hibernia, or so a trierarchus told me a while back when a storm forced him to shelter his ship in our bay.' He bit off another great lump of cheese.

'My guess,' he said, spitting crumbs onto the surface of his desk, 'is it'd be impractical to launch an attack from there. The distances are too great.'

'Could they come by sea?' Cai asked.

'I doubt they've the number of boats needed to move enough men. It'd be high risk too; the Sula can kick up a fair storm, with little warning. But they could try to outflank us with a smaller force.'

Lucius pressed. 'We need to narrow our search area. Nepos, you know this land better than any of us.'

'There's one place I've seen,' Nepos said.' If I was trying to hide and feed a large force, that would be the spot I'd pick. There's a large settlement about a day and half's difficult riding from here. Perhaps two with a force of your size, sir. It lies against the western side of a long, narrow lake surrounded by steep sided hills thick with pine forest. It's also close enough to quickly reach our outposts.'

'The question is how do we get the ala there without being discovered?' Cai was thinking out loud, but Lucius responded.

'We'd need to start by dealing with our watchers. 'What's the latest strength report for your unit Nepos?'

'I have ninety-three men, sir. Eighty-five of whom are fit for duty.'

Lucius nodded, his decision made. 'Very well Nepos. It's clear your position here is too exposed. You'll attach two turmae to my own force. Their knowledge of the ground will be invaluable.' Cai could see the grizzled veteran was taken aback, but managed to hold his peace. 'The remainder of your men will escort the supply wagons back to the Sack, taking anything that could be useful to the enemy with them.'

'So we are to abandon the fort, sir?' Nepos could not hide his incredulity this time.

'Yes, Decurion, you must. I would normally order its firing. But that may alert the Novantae to our plans. The smoke would be seen from a long way off.'

'Very good, sir.' The Tungrian understood further discussion on the matter was at an end. 'In that case, let me tell you how I think we should deal with our watchers.'

36

Cai leant against the parapet by the main gate, overlooking the twin ditches. Their shadowed depths were now just emerging in the gloom of the faint predawn light.

'Here they come, sir.' The sharp eyed sentry pointed to his left.

'Coming in!' Came a shout.

'Open the gate,' Cai called down to the men at the base of the steps.

'It looks like they've got wounded, sir,' said the sentry.

As the section crossed the causeway Cai could see a man being carried between two of his comrades. Another, who looked like the silhouette of a bear, carried the limp body of one of his mates over his shoulder.

Lucius had ordered the two sections into the forest, some hours before first light. Each was to make their way to one of the locations of the Novantae watchers and deal with them. They carried spears and swords only, no shields. Chainmail had been allowed but had to be worn under the leather tunic to minimise any noise. The first section had returned half an hour since, almost unscathed, reporting their success.

Cai made his way down from the ramparts, reaching the gate as the section stumbled through, most collapsing in a heap on the ground, taking in great gulps of air, unable to speak.

'Section leader, report,' Cai commanded.

'Here, sir.' It was the big man he'd seen crossing the causeway. He was still standing erect with his comrade over his shoulder.

'You're the section leader?'

'No sir, he is or rather was.' He indicated the body that he lowered gently, taking care not to let the head bump on the ground. 'I'm sorry, my friend.' Cai heard the big man say in a whisper. 'But we'll meet again.'

'A close friend?' Cai asked.

The big man nodded. 'Aye sir, we're from the same village, joined up together a few years back.'

'Both Tungrians?'

'Aye.'

'What's your name trooper?' It took a time for the big man to realise he had been spoken to, but Cai waited, seeing his pain. Finally he looked up.

'Hrindenus, sir.'

'Make your report, Hrindenus.'

'Sir!' The trooper stood erect. 'We dealt with the watchers. There were five of them. We approached from the west making our way through the slopes of the wood. After a while we could smell wood smoke, the fools had lit a fire. We couldn't see it, but the smell drew us directly to them. We killed their sentry quickly enough, he was asleep against the trunk of a tree snoring, would you believe?' The big man shook his head, bemused

'We crept closer and spotted three of them asleep around their fire. But another of them must have gone for a piss. He spotted us and shouted an alarm to his mates. He had sliced his sword through Hediste's neck before we knew it. I skewered the bastard.' Hrindenus nodded at the spear laid next to the body of his friend, a dark stain covering its point. 'The others put up a fierce fight but we were able to deal with them quickly enough. We picked up one more walking wounded.' Hrindenus turned to look at the man that Cai had seen being carried through the gates. He was now sitting having his leg attended to. 'Well, almost walking.'

Cai nodded. 'Well done, Hrindenus. Now see to the care of your friend, and get something to eat. We're leaving shortly after sunrise.'

Cai walked back through the fort in search of Nepos and Lucius. As he passed the barracks, men milled around outside, using the early morning light to adjust their armour and kit in readiness for the day's ride ahead. The horses, still in their stalls, were saddled. Most munched on the grain bags fitted over their noses; some of their riders spoke in low gentle tones to them. Perhaps saying a quiet prayer to the cavalryman's adopted goddess Epona, to keep them both safe this day.

Approaching Nepos's office through the wooden walkway of the principia, Cai heard the conversation before he reached its open door.

'As the eagle flies it's only a matter of ten miles or thereabouts. But the difficult ground on both sides of the river means it'll be a long day of hard riding.'

'Understood, Nepos,' Lucius said, 'but we must reach the river's source by nightfall and make camp at the most defensible spot we can find. We'll then be close enough to reach the lake valley before nightfall the next day. That way we minimise the chances of being discovered.' Lucius looked up as he saw Cai enter.

'What news?'

'The second section's returned, sir. They've reported the road watchers have been dealt with too. Two casualties, one dead, one walking wounded.'

'Who's dead?' Nepos's good eye fixed Cai with a sharp stare. His teardrop scar turned a darker shade of red.

'Hediste was the name I was given. Section leader I believe.'

'Shit. Hediste was a good man. I was going to raise him to Duplicarius.' The Tungrian grimaced.

'That big lad Hrindenus seems like a good man?'

'A bit too fond of a drink and a bar room brawl is our Hrindenus. Not that he's had much opportunity of late.'

'Well, gentlemen, shall we get back to the matter at hand?' Lucius broke in. 'Let's run through the plan one more time. The Praefectus will lead his force across the river ford here and follow its course on the far bank. I'll take my lot on this side, with you, Nepos, acting as my second. Your men know this ground so will act as the lead turmae in both forces.'

Nepos made the now familiar low rumbling sound, a signal he was about to speak.

'As far as is possible,' he said, 'we should keep to the cover of the forest and if not possible at least stay below the skyline.

'The riverbanks are rocky and steep-sided in many places so if one of our forces gets into trouble…' Nepos shrugged.

'Yes, they may be on their own,' Lucius said.

37

Adela tossed her head, impatient to get the day underway. Bending forward in his saddle Cai patted her neck. 'I know, I know, I want to get going too. Just a little longer, my beautiful girl.'

The last of his men were preparing their mounts, checking saddle straps and making sure their lance and two throwing spears were secured in their sheath.

Cai turned upon hearing the familiar creak of the wagons as they left the fort. The first two still held their cargo of grain, the remainder a motley mix of sick and wounded men and those that carried the equipment the Tungrians did not want to leave behind for the enemy.

Once across the ditches the convoy turned onto the road to begin the return journey to the Sack, escorted by the last of the garrison. For a moment Cai longed to join them, remembering that all too brief embrace with Alyn, the touch of her warm, soft lips. He shook the memory away.

'Jupiter, best and greatest, may I do honour to the cohort and my tribe. Divine Epona, watch over Adela, keep her safe from harm.' Cai whispered his prayer into the morning air.

His thoughts were interrupted by the rumbling sound of hooves. Lucius pulled his tall, black mount to a halt beside Adela.

They briskly exchanged salutes. 'Are we ready?' Lucius asked, his eyes were shadowed in the recesses of his helmet.

'Yes, sir. The advanced sections left a short while ago.'

'Good, let's get the lads moving. I'll see you at the end of the day, brother.' Lucius nudged Epona towards his men, who were mounted, waiting in column, two abreast.

A memory came to Cai of the awkward, quiet youth who had appeared all those years ago to command the Nervana. He and Adal had despaired. 'We taught him well, didn't we, my friend?' he murmured.

As the sun's rays broke above the eastern hills, Cai and his force of five turmae forded the river, turning northwards to follow its course.

The advanced sections, drawn from amongst the Tungrians,

ranged ahead, reporting back at regular intervals. After less than an hour Cai spotted a trooper returning down the trail towards him, carefully picking his way along the side of the river, whose rushing, white waters crashed against its steep banks. Hrindenus, he realised.

He really is a bear of a man, Cai thought. With legs dangling low beyond his mount's belly, his fair hair hung loose under his helmet. His beard failed to hide his youth, perhaps no more than twenty-two summers, though he must have been an experienced trooper.

Giving the signal to halt, Cai trotted Adela up the hill to meet the Tungrian.

'Report,' Cai said, as he pulled Alela to a halt.

'Sir. No sign of the enemy so far. The path ahead gets more difficult for a while but evens out after about a quarter of a mile. The route is forced away from the river's edge and into the forest. But it doesn't depart so far that you can't hear its waters.'

'Understood, I'll pass the word down the line,' Cai said. He was concerned the column would become too stretched. But there was nothing for it, he would have to rely on his Decurions to drive stragglers along. 'Any sign of the Tribunus's force?'

'We could hear them for a while, sir. But nothing for some time.'

Cai nodded, lowering his voice. 'Were you able to see to your friend, Hrindenus?' A fleeting look of surprise crossed the big man's face.

'Aye, sir. Me and the lads buried him down by the river's edge below the fort. When we return we'll see to him properly. But I don't think he'll mind where we've left him. He was fond of a spot of fishing.'

The column carried on in the same way for much of the morning. The sky had clouded over and Cai could no longer see the sun's course, but he estimated it was close to the day's midpoint.

'Sir, up ahead.' Avitius saw the scout first. It was Hrindenus once again, but this time he was making haste, even though the ground remained difficult.

'Sir, we've spotted a group of the enemy ahead of us,' Hrindenus said through heavy breaths. 'They're resting in a sheltered spot. It's difficult to make out exact numbers, but I think there are no more than ten of them.'

'Did they see you?'

'No sir. About a half mile up the trail from here the forest begins to thin. We heard someone laugh, some way off, through the trees. A couple of us crawled forward to take a look. After a short distance the forest ends near the summit of the hill we're now climbing. And there they sat out in the open, taking their ease in the shade of a small thicket of trees.'

'Avitius, pass the word down the line that the turmae are to halt here. I'm going ahead to take a look for myself.'

'Aye, sir.'

'Lead the way, Hrindenus,' Cai said.

The trail climbed steeply. After a short while tangles of roots from the thickly growing pine trees crossed the pathway, forcing them to dismount and lead their horses on foot. But it wasn't long before they reached the patrol. Four troopers stood by the mounts, hidden deeper within the trees. The river below was out of sight, but the sound of it was loud in their ears as it crashed across treacherous rocks on its journey to the Sula.

'We'll leave the horses here. I suggest you remove your helmet, sir. You wouldn't want that white plume of yours to give the game away, would you?'

'No trooper, I wouldn't'. Cai cocked an eyebrow and gave the big man a lopsided grin. Removing his helmet and liner, he drew his fingers through the damp and matted hair, relieved to be rid of it even for a few minutes. Leaving everything behind other than his sword, he followed Hrindenus. Almost immediately the trees began to thin, long wheat-like grass filling the ground between. By hand signal Hrindenus indicated they should crouch and move carefully. After only a few steps the big man got onto his knees before crawling through some dense, barbed undergrowth that snagged in their chainmail and scratched at their arms.

'Who goes there?' came a hushed voice in heavily accented Latin.

'It's me, shit-for-brains, and the Praefectus.' Both men emerged into a small open area within and three prone troopers stared back at them.

'Well done, lads,' Cai whispered. 'Where're the blue-faces?'

'If you slide in next to me you, sir, you'll get a better view,' said the middle trooper of the three. 'They haven't budged since Herc went back to find you.'

'Herc?'

'Hercules, sir. That's what we call the big brute. I can't imagine why.'

Cai crawled in between two of the watchers. Carefully moving a thorny branch aside he got his first view of the Novantae. An open area of grassland perhaps three spear throws wide was crowned by a small copse of wind bent pine on its brow. The Novantae's horses had been hobbled and were grazing in the open. They were smaller than those of the Nervana, mainly of a dark brown colour with white patches, but well kept. Cai could hear a low murmur of voices and occasional laughter.

'No sentries?'

'No, sir. We're as sure as we can be there are ten of them. If it's a patrol they're not expecting any trouble.'

'Maybe not a patrol. They could be the reliefs for the watchers outside the fort,' Hrindenus said from behind.

Cai nodded. 'Possibly. Do any of you men know what's on the other side of those trees?'

'We've all been this way a few times, sir,' said the Tungrian on his left shoulder, his voice low. 'To the right the ground drops steeply to the river. On the other side of the copse the forest begins again after a short distance.'

Cai continued to observe the ground before him. 'Could mounted men get around and behind them, by following the river's edge, without being seen?' He looked back at the big Tungrian.

Hrindenus scratched his chin in thought, but eventually shook his head.

'It's too treacherous for horses, sir. But men on foot, moving with care, might be able to make it.'

'Right then,' Cai said, 'you men stay here and keep watch. At the first sign they're going to come this way, get your arses back down the trail as quick as you can.' Then sliding backwards on his belly Cai tapped the big man. 'Herc, you're with me.'

38

The fast-flowing water crashed over the rocks that stood in its path. The noise drowned out most sound from above and Cai hoped it worked both ways as they edged their way along the river's steep bank. He looked back at the men following him. Hrindenus was almost at his shoulder, the big man's presence an unexpected comfort. He was followed closely by Avitius. The wiry old warrior's face was alight with the anticipation of the coming fight. The other eight men moved in single file, stepping carefully.

Lucius had ordered them to carry both their shield and a single spear in their right hands, leaving their left free to grab the long grass and exposed rock of the riverbank. All spathas had been strapped across their backs for ease of movement. The river coursed through a narrow gap at this point, perhaps no more than twenty good strides across. But it flowed fast and deep. Anyone who fell into its depths was unlikely to resurface.

A shout came from above, followed by a coarse laugh. Cai froze. He held his hand up, halting those behind. The shout came again, this time closer. Cai pressed himself into the rocky bank, the smell of damp moss strong as his cheek grazed the slick grey stone. He hoped those behind were following his example. Cai didn't dare look up, praying the steepness of the bank would them.

Someone above hawked and spat. There was a gentle splosh sound as the glutinous blob of phlegm struck the water near Cai's foot. Silence again.

A sound of grunting came next, accompanied by an unintelligible curse. The grunting and cursing went on for an age. Finally a stench floated down to them. For a while, Cai heard nothing but the crashing waters. Then the sound of laughter came once again. The warrior had returned to the others.

Cai risked a glance.

'Dirty bastard,' Avitius said, in a hissed whisper.

Cai signalled to move. It couldn't be much more than half an hour since he had returned to the column and outlined his plan. None of the enemy must be allowed to escape. If they did, the ala's advance into the Novantae lands would quickly become a fight for their lives, through forest their enemy knew well.

To his relief, they reached the point of the river's course where it flowed from the forest's depths once more. They were now on the far side of the open pasture. Cai led the men upwards, carefully negotiating the riverbank's steep sides, into the gloom of the densely packed trees. The way was difficult, progress slowed by thick, barbed and tangled undergrowth.

Finally they came to the point that Cai estimated would be directly behind the warriors. He crept forward until he neared the forest's edge. Lying on his stomach, concealed by the undergrowth, he was able to get a good sight of the Novantae.

They were on the move. Two already straddled their mounts. Cai ran back to his men, uncaring of discovery.

'They're moving out. We need to get their attention. Out into the open. Now,' he ordered.

Without awaiting a response, Cai ran back to the forest's edge, his men hard on his heels. They emerged from the trees and into the long grass, with the sun directly above them, its light reflecting from their helmets.

They formed a wall of shields with Cai at its centre, Avitius on his left and Hrindenus on his right, oval shields touching. The tribesmen had been so preoccupied with the loading of their mounts they had not yet noticed the auxiliaries. Not until, that is, Cai began striking the boss of his shield with his lance stock, quickly taken up by his men.

The Novantae didn't move, stunned by the sudden appearance of Cai's small band.

'Roma! Roma!' Cai shouted the chant, making sure there was no doubt in the warrior's minds that this was their hated enemy before them. For a moment the tribesmen stared in consternation at one another, a number looking left and right as if expecting more men to appear from the forest's depths.

A shout of command came from within the band. A warrior Cai had not noticed previously appeared from within their midst. His head was shaven, with skin darkened by the strange tattoos that covered his body from head to foot. He was smaller than the rest but paced with lithe movements. Cai could see the tight knots of hard muscle on his chest and arms. He was unlike any Novantae Cai had seen before. The warrior ran for his horse, alongside another with a similarly-shaven head, the dark warrior barked an order again, instantly galvanising the others.

As Cai had hoped, the enemy formed a rough line, ready to rush his small force. All had the familiar square shields made of interwoven strips of tree bark; most held swords. The dark warrior had mounted and moved along the rear of the Novantae, peering over at the Roman line. His high-pitched scream rent the air.

'Sounds like baldy's giving birth.' Avitius's words raised nervous laughter from the waiting auxiliaries.

'Spears out.' Cai ordered, his voice steady.

All lowered their lance points and unconsciously shifted closer to one another, their shoulders almost touching.

'Remember lads, we only need to hold them for a short while. But none of these sheep-humpers are getting away. Understood?'

'Sir!' came the shouted response.

The enemy horsemen kicked their mounts into a canter, but to Cai's mind none appeared keen to drive into their wall of shields. The ground rumbled, the horses picking up speed as they quickly closed the space between.

'Prepare!'

The thin line of eleven men raised their spears to chest height, leading with their left legs and bracing with their right. As Cai had expected, more than one of the warriors had been drawn to his helmet's white plume. The horses were almost upon them, but at the last instant the animals balked, swinging away from the viciously sharp spearpoints, leaving the charge in chaos.

'Now!'

All eleven troopers stepped forward, thrusting at any exposed flesh of man or horse. The mount of the first to reach Cai had yanked to its left, exposing the rider's unprotected side. Cai stabbed upwards into his ribcage as the warrior, who, thrown off balance, had attempted to slash down with his sword. The horseman fell from sight, screaming.

An instant later the contorted face of another appeared before him. This one seemed ancient, his mouth gaping, lips flapping against toothless gums. In his battle fury the old warrior made the same mistake as his tribesman, slashing his sword from horseback with the intent of cutting Cai's spear shaft. Stabbing upwards, Cai's lance point punctured the old warrior's windpipe, his horse's motion driving the point up into the skull.

Already dead, the body spasmed as blood ran glutinously down his leather vest and along the spear. As he fell, the shaft, now slick, slipped from Cai's grasp.

To Cai's dismay, the next assailant was upon him before he could draw his spatha. But this one had dismounted. A beast of a man, with long, wild dark hair and a bush of a beard. Instinctively Cai raised his shield as the big warrior's sword crashed into its metal rim. The force driving Cai onto his knees. Agonising pain ran up his arm and shoulder. The only option left to him was to duck further into the shelter of his shield, anticipating the next blow would leave him on his arse and at the Novantae's mercy.

He heard a grunt. The blow against his shield did not come. Cai risked a glance over the rim, in time to see Hrindenus almost casually pull his spear point from the warrior's chest. The Novantae fell to his knees, head slumping forward as if in prayer to his gods.

'Have you finished with your rest, sir?' Hrindenus said as he hauled Cai up by the neck of his mail shirt.

Glancing along both ends of the line, he saw it still held firm. Most of the Novantae had been unhorsed and lay dead or dying at the feet of his men. Riderless horses ran in all directions.

A deep rumbling vibrated through his feet. Cai looked up to see his turma, led by Betto, charging across the brow of the hill. The dark warrior and his companion turned at the sound. Kicking his mount hard he darted forward, making for the forest's edge. The other was too slow. Spooked by the unexpected sound, his horse bucked, throwing him. He landed on his chest in the long grass and was dispatched moments later by Betto's lance point.

'Hrindenus.' Cai shouted, pointing at the fleeing warrior, who was only a few short strides from disappearing amongst the trees. The Tungrian understood. Stepping out of line, he drew back his arm, planted his feet and threw. A grunt of expelled air escaped the big man's lungs as the lance was released.

Cai watched the spear's flight as it flashed across the space between them and the fleeing rider. It moved in a swift, low arc, slamming into the horse's shoulder. The animal made a tortured sound, its front legs buckling under it before rolling onto its side, away from the spear point. The warrior howled as he fell, entangled with his mount. The animal thrashed as it attempted to shake off its agony.

Its cries mingled with the shrill scream of the rider crushed beneath his flailing mount.

'Hrindenus, with me.' Both men ran towards the dying horse. Staying well clear of its legs, Cai circled the animal, spatha in hand. The warrior's eyes were closed. Whether dead or passed out, Cai couldn't tell, but his legs and hips were trapped.

The horse continued to thrash, Cai turned to see Hrindenus, his bloody spear shaft in hand. The Tungrian moved swiftly to the horse's head and with a single movement drove the spear through the base of its neck above the chest and into its heart, mercifully bringing its agony to an end.

Sheathing his sword, Cai went onto one knee by the head of the warrior, placing his hand on the dark tattooed chest. He still lived. Dark bruising bloomed across his stomach. Cai had seen this before, a sure sign the body bled within. The warrior's eyes sprang open.

'Shit.' Cai pulled back in fright. The dark warrior's eyes stared, unfocussed at the sky. In an instant they cleared, like mist evaporating before the heat of the morning sun. Becoming aware of Cai's presence, his head moved almost imperceptibly, his bloodshot orbs locking onto Cai's.

'Roman slave.' The words hissed from between lips pulled tight across black and crooked teeth. 'Taking crumbs from your master's hearth stone.'

'I am of the Nervii and I am no man's slave.' Cai spat the words

The dark warrior wheezed a laugh.

'You fight the eagle's wars. Your tribe has abandoned its pride for a few bags of Roman salt.'

Cai understood the words, but they were in a dialect strange to him.

'What tribe are you? You're no Novantae,' Cai said, losing his patience.

The wheeze-laugh came once more. 'Rome has moved its eye from these lands, and now its people will make it pay for its negligence.'

'Why do you tell me this? Now we are forewarned.'

Again the hiss. 'Because you won't return to your walls of

stone,' his words now a mere whisper. 'Tomorrow you and your horse slaves will be dead and the People will carry your heads before them, as we take back our lands.'

Cai had been forced to put his ear close to the dark man's mouth, as the words grew fainter. Raising his head once more he saw the warrior's eyes stared blankly up at him.

39

Lucius stood on top of the spoil of the south-facing rampart. The construction of the camp was progressing quickly. The defences nearing completion. The site had been well chosen by Nepos, partly concealed in a wide cleft between two low hills.

Further protection was provided on two sides by marshland, the source of the river whose course they had followed since early morning. The men had laboured swiftly, knowing the importance of completing the work before dark.

His force had arrived at the agreed meeting place two hours since. The sun was now low in the western sky, but there was still no sign of Cai. Growing concerned, Lucius had dispatched a section to scouts along the most likely route, but they had yet to return.

'Where are you, brother?'

There wasn't much more than two or three stadia of open ground to the forest. His attention was drawn to a pair of red kites flying gracefully above the trees in languid circles. Even from this distance he could discern their fanlike tales and the rust colour of their plumage.

A puff of black shapes emerged from the treetops, rising towards the two larger birds. At first he thought idly that it was just a family of crows intent on chasing off a threat. But then more black shapes arose, this time closer to the forest's edge. Something disturbed them into flight.

Two troopers stood watch near the forest's edge. Both appeared agitated. One rode forward, disappearing amongst the trees. Soon after he reappeared and looked directly at Lucius, whose white plume would have been clear to see even from that distance. The trooper raised his lance, holding it horizontally. A friendly force approached.

Seconds later, to his relief, Adela's distinctive tan coat and blonde mane emerged. The mare tossed her head, glad to be in open ground once more. Cai nudged his horse towards Lucius, he could see dark stains on his friend's chainmail. Lucius leapt onto Epona's back and rode from the camp.

Both men smiled broadly as they drew up alongside one another.

'You're late, brother. Did you stop for a leisurely repast by the riverside?' Cai laughed wearily.

'No, sir. But we came across a party of Novantae who were doing just that.'

'I presume that isn't your blood,' Lucius said, nodding at Cai's armour.

Cai removed his helmet and liner, feeling the relief of the cool evening air on his sweat-dampened hair.

'I think we may have a bigger problem with the blue-faces than we feared,' Cai said and relayed the events of the day.

'Well, brother,' Lucius said, once Cai had finished, 'these shaven warriors don't appear to belong to any of the tribes south of the Emperor's new wall. Certainly none I've come across. They sound like those who were amongst the watchers we dealt with this morning.

'This changes things, Lucius.' Urbicus's intelligence had been only partly right.

'Damn it. I fear rather than flushing out the schemes of the Novantae, I have just walked the ala into a nest of hornets.'

'Well, night is nearly upon us,' Cai said. 'We can't move again until first light.'

'Agreed. Let's appraise Nepos. But we need a new plan.'

The faint orange glow on the western horizon threw the faces of the three men into deep shadow as they stood close together by the horse lines. Lucius had ordered a cold camp. All men were to rest in their armour, keeping weapons close at hand. Two turmae were on watch at all times.

'The land from here to the lake is similar to what we came through today,' Nepos said, his rasping voice kept low. 'Although there are stretches of dense pine that'll force us to walk the horses at times, slowing our advance.' Even in near darkness, the Tungrian's white orb stood out and Lucius resisted the urge to shiver.

'Given what we now suspect,' Lucius said, 'if there are more than the Novantae gathering against us, we could be risking entrapment and the destruction of the ala.'

'Our outlying castrae must be forewarned too,' Cai said.

'Which we can't do if we're dead,' Nepos grumbled.

'We need to know what the tribes are up to,' Cai said. 'But you're right, sir, the risk is too great. The enemy knows the ground much better than we do.' Cai nodded at the Tungrian. 'Even with our brother here to guide us.' Lucius and Nepos stared at Cai, waiting for him to continue. 'A small force would have a better chance of keeping itself concealed, using the cover of the forest. The rest of the ala should withdraw.'

Lucius nodded. 'But a small force would be at terrible risk. A grim death would await those men if captured. If we do this all must be volunteers.' Lucius spoke as if to himself. 'Very well, this does feel like our best option. I'll take the section—'

'No, sir,' Cai interrupted. 'You must get the ala the hell out of here. Our outlying units have to be warned and if we're correct, we must prepare to block the enemy's advance beyond the Jula. The Novantae will know that the wall of Hadrianus is no longer garrisoned. Just two cohorts of auxilia stand between them and the Britgantes. Only you have the authority to gather what forces we have, sir.'

'But—'

'He's got the right of it, sir,' Nepos said. 'Riders should be dispatched to the boys of the Sixth and Twentieth. But Eboracum and Deva are days away so we can't rely on the legions reaching Novantae lands in time to stop them and whatever allies they've gathered.'

Lucius looked at the near-black outlines of the two men. The irritation at being interrupted ebbed away, to be replaced by a sense of foreboding.

Lucius looked up to the sky as if contemplating the myriad of stars held in its dark blanket. 'Well, it seems I'm outnumbered.' He turned to Cai. 'Very well, brother, find your volunteers, then get some rest. You'll need to leave before first light.'

'Take Hrindenus,' Nepos said, 'he knows these parts as well as any and he's good in a scrap.'

'Thank you, brother. He's already proven his worth today. He's not bad for a Tungrian.'

'Ha!' Nepos let out a great gust of air and thumped Cai on the shoulder. 'Good night Nervian. I'll go and make sure our sentries have their wits about them.' Turning on his heels the grizzled old warrior stalked away, leaving the two friends alone.

Lucius and Cai stood in companionable silence for a while, listening to the sounds of the camp as it settled down for the night.

'I'm sorry it has to be you, Cai.'

'I know, brother.'

'Just don't go and get yourself killed. I don't want to be the one who tells Alyn.'

Cai laughed. 'No Lucius, I'll try to spare you that.'

40

‘All due respect, sir. There’s no way you’re going without me.’

‘I’ve got all the men I need, Avitius,’ Cai said. ‘You’ve done more than enough for the cohort. There’s no need for you to be taking such a risk now.’

‘You think I’ll be a liability, do you? I’ve pulled your arse out of the fire more times than I can count on both hands. I might be overdue for my diploma, but you’re not so far off yourself, sir.’ The face of the old standard bearer was flushed red. ‘You’ll *not* dishonour me in this way.’

Cai held up the palms of his hands in surrender. ‘Alright, alright. Avitius. You can join the other lads waiting at the entrance to the camp.’

‘Too fucking right I can, sir.’ With that Avitius walked casually towards the camp's entrance leading his already saddled mount behind him. Cai watched him go, bemused.

‘There’s life in the old dog yet it would seem.’ Cai spun on his heels. He hadn't heard Lucius approach.

‘You heard, did you, sir?’ Cai could not keep the amusement from his voice. ‘And he’s right. The old goat’s saved my arse more times than I care to remember.’

‘A good man to have with you then.’

Both men stood watching Avitius’s retreating back in the predawn gloom.

Lucius turned to Cai and held out his hand. ‘May Fortuna be with you, brother.’ Both men clasped arms.

‘I’ll see you back at the Sack,’ Cai said. ‘Try not to start without me.’

‘I’ll do my best not to fuck things up while you’re gone.’

‘That’s the spirit, sir.’ With a smile and a nod in farewell Cai went to join his waiting men.

As he approached, Avitius was talking in low tones to Hrindenus. The big man gave a great belly-laugh. Assuming he was the butt of the joke, Cai decided to ignore it.

‘Mount up,’ he commanded, taking Adela’s reins from the trooper who had been holding her, quickly swinging onto her back.

He turned her to face the nine troopers, who looked back from under their helmets, eyes invisible in the half light.

'Remember what I told you last night. We must move like we are stalking prey. Use hand signals only, unless it can't be avoided. If we're discovered, we'll split into pairs and make our way independently to the Sack. Understood?'

'Sir,' came the muted response.

'Good. Move out.'

Cai led them through the camp's entrance, followed closely by Avitius and Hrindenus. As they progressed along the edge of the ditch he looked into the camp's interior. Most of the ala were now mounted, lined up by Turma, ready for the order to leave. Just as he was about to turn back he saw Nepos raise his arm in farewell, the white of his blind eye clearly visible in the gloom. Cai returned it before directing Adela towards the forest's edge.

Above the crunch of the horse's footfall on the thickly covered floor the early morning cacophony of birdsong was in full flow. He let Adela find a path through the undergrowth that headed more or less in a northerly route. If Nepos were correct, it would be late morning before they reached the valley of the lake. He only hoped they had guessed right and their enemy was there.

Cai waved Hrindenus forward. The big man nudged his mount alongside Adela. Cai felt momentarily sorry for the beast, given the weight it was being asked to carry.

'You've been to this valley before?'

'Yes, sir. Last summer, Crybaby — Decurion Nepos sent section-strength patrols a bit deeper than usual into the Novantae lands. I think more to stop the lads getting idle than from any particular suspicions. We were told to keep our distance but observe settlements and report back on any unusual activity. There was nothing much to report.'

'Tell me what you remember about it.'

Hrindenus tried to reach under his helmet to scratch at the side of his head, but eventually gave up.

'Well we didn't go all the way into the valley, sir. It didn't seem wise at the time, but we followed its eastern edge, staying within the tree line. As I recall the lake is wedged between steep sided hills west and east. Both hillsides are covered in dense forest, although there are breaks, so we got a pretty good look at the valley floor.'

The Tungrian was quiet, gathering his thoughts.

'Much of the length of the valley is taken up by the lake, which is about a mile long and narrows to a bottleneck at either end. On the eastern shore there's some farmland wedged between the lake and the forest. But on the western side the forest comes right up to the lake's edge. Though even from our distant position we could make out a number of huts interspersed within the trees.'

'What of the main settlement?'

'That's about halfway along the lake's eastern shore, just north of the farmland. At the time we counted thirty or so round houses built on higher ground and surrounded by a ditch and palisade. There's a small island, perhaps fifty paces distant from the village. It had a large solidary roundhouse also surrounded by a palisade. The island can only be reached by a narrow footbridge.' Hrindenus, failing to reach the itch once again, removed his helmet and scratched the spot vigorously.

'It sounds like it could be the hall of one of their chieftains. What about warriors? What numbers did you see?'

'We estimated there were perhaps three hundred inhabitants, sir. Mainly women, children and the old. But not much in the way of fighting men. As far as we could see there weren't many horses either. It could be they were out hunting, or more likely up to no good. There was no warband to speak of.'

Cai stared at the path ahead, thinking through what Hrindenus had told him.

'We must get close enough to view their numbers,' he said. 'Even better if we can get our hands on one of their men and ask him nicely about their plans.'

The big man gave Cai a look that said and how the hell are we going to do that? But Cai decided to keep his own counsel for a while longer.

'Take point, Hrindenus. We'll follow the route your patrol took last summer.'

As the morning progressed, sunlight broke through to fill the forest with bright rays, giving it an otherworldly feel. Cai's mind drifted to his day hunting in the woods with Beren. He was a fine lad. *A son to be proud of my friend, he thought.* He had been thinking more of Adal recently, and if he was honest with himself he knew why. Alyn.

His attention was snapped back to the present by a sudden movement ahead of him. Hrindenus, now some way to the fore, had halted, arm raised. Cai repeated the silent command, alerting those behind. The Tungrian dismounted, signalling he was going forward on foot. Crouching low, he was quickly swallowed by the dense undergrowth.

After no more than a minute the big frame of Hrindenus reappeared and waved Cai forward.

'What is it?' Cai whispered.

'There's a carcass of a deer hanging from a branch just ahead. There are signs of a hunting party.

'Do you think they've already seen us?' Cai crouched beside him, trying to look into the forest's depths.

'I doubt it, sir. The forest floor ahead thins out to give a view of the way ahead for some distance. There's no sight or sound of movement.

'How far are we from the valley?'

'We should reach its southern end in two or three hours.'

Cai thought for a moment. If the hunting party had left the kill here to collect when they had finished the hunt, then they were most likely west or east of their current position not directly ahead. He reasoned they wouldn't move in a direction that meant they had to double back before returning to the settlement. But what if they weren't from the settlement?

'We'll have to chance it,' Cai said.

He signalled to Avitius, taking a javelin from its sheath on his right side and looking meaningfully at the old standard bearer, who nodded his understanding. The ten men advanced once more, heads continually turning left and right searching for any sign of movement. Every snap of a twig under a horse's hoof or sudden flight of a bird from the undergrowth brought spears up instinctively.

Cai's heart thumped under his chainmail shirt. He forced himself to take slow, deep, calming breaths. Turning in the saddle to check the section was tight, he was greeted by the toothy grin of Avitius. The old bastard loves this, he thought. And he couldn't help but grin back.

After an hour Cai judged the risk of being discovered by the hunting party had passed. He had become aware of the sound of a stream to their right. Upon reaching an area of dense underbrush that provided cover, he ordered the group to leave the trail and water the horses. He positioned sentries to watch the route ahead and behind. That done, he went to find Hrindenus.

The trooper sat with his back against the trunk of a large oak, whose thick branches overhung the stream. His horse was hobbled nearby grazing on a patch of rushes.

He began to rise but Cai signalled him to stay, easing himself down beside the big Tungrian. He groaned with the ache from days in the saddle. He it more often these days.

'This land isn't so bad is it, sir? At least during the summer months. Almost like home.'

'I can barely remember my boyhood home,' Cai said. 'I joined the cohort twenty-five years since. Some of my life's blood has been soaked into this land, which I reckon gives me the right to call it home.'

'Taking one of their women as your wife helps with that too, I'm told,' Hrindenus replied, with a smirk.

Cai laughed. 'Aye.' He removed his helmet, filling it with water from the stream. He drank a few mouthfuls, tipping the remainder over his already sweat-dampened hair.' 'How much farther?'

'Another hour if we continue as we are,' Hrindenus said. 'But it might be a safer bet to leave the path. The forest will be more difficult to pass through and it will lengthen our journey, but less risky I think.'

'A sound thought,' he said. 'We still have hours of daylight left to reach the valley and find somewhere to conceal ourselves before nightfall.'

They remounted shortly afterwards leaving the track behind. The ground they passed through made for tough going, but Hrindenus had been right. It would be very bad luck indeed if their presence was discovered here, Cai thought.

After a while the ground rose sharply, slowing the section's progress further. At one point, around an hour after leaving the stream, they reached a steep slope where great tree roots protruded from its embankment. The men had to spend time coaxing the horses up and over the obstacle.

One horse shrieked its fear. Cai worried the din would alert the

Novatae to their presence. For a while the group waited in an anxious silence, listening for signs of pursuit. The only sounds to be heard were the hiss of the wind as it ruffled the leaves for the trees around them and the ever-present birdsong.

As he was about to give the order to move on, Cai spun around at the noise of rustling behind him. Only to see Avitius relieving himself. The sound of the heavy flow of piss hitting the forest floor mingled with the standard bearer's long sigh of relief. When Avitius noticed the scowl on his commander's face, he offered a guilty smile and a shrug.

The ground continued to rise steadily, the horses snorting great gusts of air with the effort, until finally it levelled out once more. The way ahead was still obscured by the tangled undergrowth, but Cai sensed they had reached the peak of the hill they had been ascending.

They entered a dense area of pine, the forest floor strewn with a carpet of needles, muffling the sound of their passing. The lowest branches were barely above head height, forcing them to dismount.

The thick green foliage prevented much of the sun's light reaching the forest floor, giving a twilight feel to their surroundings. So it came as a surprise when the trees ended abruptly, becoming a low thicket. Cai signalled his men to wait.

Stepping carefully through the brush, thorns pricked scratched his exposed arms. Emerging onto open ground he had the first sight of their objective.

Directly ahead of him was a wide ridge, which they must have been following for some time, but had been hidden by the heavy woodland. To the east were more rolling hills continuing to the horizon. To the west and down a steep slope was a long narrow lake, reflecting silver in the afternoon sun. The far bank was forested, as Hrindenus had described. On the eastern side he could see crop fields. The settlement, however, was still out of sight. Even so, a fug of grey smoke drifted lazily across the lake, which could only be the result of many hearth fires. They must get closer.

Cai returned through the undergrowth. As he appeared out of the bushes his men looked at him expectantly.

'Where's Hrindenus?' he asked

'I sent him back down the trail a bit to make sure we're not being followed,' Avitius said.

'Good thinking.'

The old standard bearer shrugged at Cai, as if it was the obvious thing to do.

'Gather in.' The eight men bunched in around Cai, allowing him to speak in a lower tone. 'The Novantae settlement is close. Perhaps no more than a mile to the north and west. Immediately ahead of us the ground opens up into a wide bare ridge. The forest starts again, perhaps a stadia further along. Before leaving the cover of the trees we'll drop down below the ridge on its eastern side. That will keep us out of sight.'

'But won't we risk being seen by any of the blue-faces watching the hill from the east, sir?' Avitius said.

'We'll just have to pray we don't, won't we, Vexillarius?' Cai gave Avitius a pointed look, receiving a grin in return.

'Yes, sir.'

'I want to find a position that lets us overlook the settlement. We'll use the last of the day's light to see if we can spot what the Novantae are up to.'

A rustling arose behind them. Hands went to sword hilts. Hrindenus appeared pushing his way through the thicket.

'I couldn't see any sign we're being followed, sir.'

'What would a Tungrian know about tracking?' Avitius said. 'Especially a lumbering ox like you.' The big man laughed, cuffing Avitius on the back of the head, almost knocking him onto his knees.

'A lot more than the Nervii, grandfather.'

'Right lads, enough of the levity. You've got time to take a piss and have a swig from your canteens, then we go.'

'Hrindenus, do you know of a location close enough to observe the settlement, without being seen?'

'I think so, sir. If I can retrace the route. We'll have to leave the horses some way back out of sight. There's a place we can conceal them until we're ready.'

'Very well, lead the way. Avitius, you can be the backmarker. Let's put those legendary skills of yours to the test. We don't want any blue-faces taking us up the rear, do we?' Without waiting for a response, Cai turned and followed Hrindenus, smiling as he heard the old veteran's grumbling.

They made quick progress, reaching the trees at the other side of the ridge without incident. The woodland changed once again. Now mainly a mixture of oak and tall red pine, the widely spaced trees let in more light to the forest floor, revealing a covering of lush green ferns that brushed the underbellies of the horses.

Hrindenus pulled up just ahead. Cai raised his arm to halt the rest of the men.

'What is it?' Cai said. The big man pointed through a gap in the trees.

'I think that's it over there, sir. The place where we can hide the horses.'

Cai stared for a long while, but saw only the carpet of ferns. He shook his head.

'It's a cleft in the ground,' Hrindenus said, his voice low. 'Do you see those thin saplings? They mark its edge.'

Hrindenus dismounted, Cai signalling all should follow his lead.

Moments later a great crack in the forest floor revealed itself as if conjured by some old magic. Its floor was flat and wide enough to accommodate their mounts comfortably. About a spear throw in length, there were also two ways in and out, one at either end. They couldn't easily be trapped. The saplings on the lip of the hiding place would provide cover for sentries to keep watch.

'Good work, Hrindenus,' Cai said, 'Let's get down there.'

Once hidden inside the depression, the horses were given their fodder bags and sentries placed. Cai gathered his men around him.

'I'll take three men forward on foot. The rest will remain here, under the command of Avitius.'

'But—'

Cai cut across Avitius. 'I know you want to come, Vexillarius, but I need you to cover our backs. We may need to get the fuck out of here in a hurry.' The old cavalryman still looked like he would object, but finally nodded.

'We'll observe the settlement and if possible take a closer look when night falls. All being well, back here before sun up. It'll be dark when we return, so the watch word will be 'Hairy', and the response 'Arse'. Understood? Any questions? Good. Now get what rest you can, but stay in armour and keep the horses saddled.'

Hrindenus led the way. When Cai looked back shortly after leaving, the hiding place had vanished. I just hope we can find our way back, he thought. The forest darkened as they progressed. But even in the fading light, the Tungrian guided them with confidence.

Eventually the four came to a tall stand of red pine, whose base was obscured by a tangle of blackberry bushes. Beyond this thorny barrier the fading, orange glow in the western horizon silhouetted the dark hills to the west.

'Through here,' Hrindenus said, and without waiting got onto his belly, hauling himself under the thick brush. Cai followed, struggling with the entwined branches.

'Jupiter's balls,' Cai exclaimed.

'Aye, that's some sight,' Hrindenus said.

Despite the failing light, the settlement stood out clearly. But what had really taken Cai aback was what he saw outside of the palisaded defences. On both sides of the lake were many campfires, stretching uninterrupted into the north.

'There must be thousands of them,' Hrindenus spoke quietly.

'Many thousands,' Cai said. It was an astounding sight. 'How could such a force have gathered under our noses?'

'Sir, look at the island.' Cai turned his attention to the enclosure a short distance from the shoreline. There was the solitary roundhouse, Hrindenus had described, and the narrow raised walkway connecting it to the mainland. A tall palisade encircled the island's perimeter, close to the water's edge.

'What do you see?' Cai asked.

'Next to the walkway. Horses,' Hrindenus said. Cai strained to make out what the younger man had seen, his eyesight not what it once was. Then he saw them. Perhaps thirty mounts, all saddled.

'I see them. So?'

'If they were just Novantae horses,' Hrindenus continued, 'wouldn't they be corralled in some way? They must belong to visiting warriors. War leaders of the other tribes perhaps?'

'You could be right.' Cai was silent for a time, before turning to the big man, with a wide grin. 'Can you swim, trooper?'

'Oh bollocks,' Hrindenus said. 'Me and my big mouth.'

A rumble of thunder sounded from the west.

41

The rain fell heavily, its sound drowned out their own footsteps as they crunched on the undergrowth. At least it should disguise our approach, Cai thought.

'With respect, sir,' Hrindenus said, his voice taking on a morose tone. 'Any chance of filling me in on how we're supposed to get through that lot, without being caught and roasted on a spit? Even if we do somehow get by them, there's no cover near the shoreline.' A flash of sheet lightning lit the ground around them, and for an instant Cai could clearly see the Tungrian as they crouched together. His long fair hair lay lank against his face as rainwater dripped continuously from the end of his long nose.

'Everyone shelters from a storm, Hrindenus. Except those that are up to no good, like us.'

The dark clouds had rolled in whilst Cai and the others had waited for darkness. Once he was sure the storm would last, he held back for a while longer, hoping this would give the people of the settlement time to find shelter around their hearths and any sentries would be taking cover too.

He had decided to take only the big man. Hrindenus could easily boost Cai over the palisade. Not to mention having him around would come in handy, if they were discovered. The other two troopers he had ordered to make their way back to Avitius and the others.

Cai and Hrindenus were now concealed at the forest's edge, a short way south of the settlement. There were no watch fires. Another flash lit the ground, followed swiftly by a great crash of thunder.

'There.' Hrindenus touched Cai's shoulder. 'That's why there are no fires here.'

The instant of light had flooded the ground before them revealing a large stock enclosure and the dark outlines of horned cattle.

'We can use the longhorns as cover,' Cai said.

'I don't fancy getting pricked by one of those. They look lethal.'

'Don't worry trooper. They'll probably take you for one of their own. Let's go.'

Hrindenus saw a flash of Cai's wide grin, before he disappeared. The Tungrian followed, crouching low. Reaching the corral quickly, both slipped between its spars. The great beasts sensed the new arrivals, the nearest making snorting noises, but didn't seem alarmed at the presence of the men.

The pair made their way through the longhorns, which in places were standing in tight groups. Pushing and shoving, at times they were forced to use their shoulders to carefully move the cattle out of the way as water dripped from their long hides. But what surprised Cai was the heat coming. Each flash of lightning revealed clouds of steam rising from their broad backs.

Eventually they reached the other side of the enclosure. Cai crouched low against a wooden post, Hrindenus on his shoulder. Another flash that briefly revealed the lake's edge. It was close.

On the island a torch fixed to the palisade faintly lit its western point, still alight despite the downpour. The swim from here was further than he had thought but it was too great a risk to move further along the shore.

'We'll have to leave our chainmail and spathas here,' Cai said, 'hidden amongst the cattle.

'I'm loving this plan of yours, sir.'

The continual downpour had made their chainmail cling to their leather jerkins. Each had to help the other remove the heavy armour.

Cai looked along the shoreline towards the settlement. A dog barked from within the palisade, followed by another in response. The way seemed clear. As he stepped through the wooden spars of the enclosure, lightning flashed once more. Are the gods toying with us? he thought. But in that instant, he had seen the dark outlines of the horses still watched by cloaked figures near to the narrow walkway. He stepped back.

'There are still sentries by the walkway,' Cai whispered. 'But there's nothing for it now. Go.'

Cai dashed for the shoreline, the Tungrian close behind. Reaching the lake's edge they carefully waded into the black water, hoping the storm should mask the sound. When the water reached his waist, Cai pushed off, swimming on his left side in order to watch the shore.

After only a short while, the burden of his leather jerkin and his now waterlogged troos started to weigh heavily and he began to tire. Glancing towards the island Cai saw he had covered only half of the distance. Panic rose. He had underestimated the distance.

Despite the risk of being seen from the shore with each lightning flash, he decided to chance treading water to gather his strength for the final stretch. An instant later he suppressed a laugh as his right foot touched bottom.

Standing slowly, the black water reached no further than the ties for his troos. Looking around he was able to make out the dark shape of Hrindenus, as he too laboured upright, pushing through the lake's surface.

Progress was slower than swimming, but finally they reached the island, pulling themselves onto a narrow line of shingle.

From their observations on the hilltop, there was a low but steep bank, about the height of a man, encircling the island. There was perhaps a spear's length of level ground before the base of the palisade. The plan was for Hrindenus to boost Cai onto the top of the wooden wall and then drop down into the interior. This was madness, he thought. The blue-faces will have you impaled come morning.

Cai tapped the Tungrian on the shoulder. It was time to move. The steep sides of the bank were slick from the continual rainfall. Twice he lost his grip, slipping back to the shingle. But on the third attempt he was able to slither onto the level ground. Both men lay side by side gasping.

Cai forced himself to his feet. Exhausted. His leather jerkin, soaked from its immersion, weighed heavily on his shoulders.

'Let's get it done,' he whispered. The big man moved to lean against the palisade, cupping his hands. Without further thought Cai launched himself into the handhold, gripping the big man's thick neck to pull himself up. He had intended to step onto his shoulder but with a strength that took Cai by surprise he was propelled up onto the palisade in one movement, straddling it, ducking his upper body to avoid any silhouette against the weak light.

He peered along its walkway, it was in almost total darkness, only the guttering flame of the still burning torch on the western end gave a hint of light. The palisade, it seemed, was unguarded.

Sliding silently onto its walkway, crouching low, he listened for movement once more, this time from the island's interior. Looking down into the heart of the complex, all was in near darkness. A soft glow of light came from the far side, outlining the roof of the large roundhouse.

No sound came from outside, but there was no doubting that there were many occupants inside the building. Cai heard the muffled sounds of laughter and drunken singing. A large gathering of now very drunk men. He would have to get closer if he was to hear anything of value.

He stepped carefully along the walkway. The wood crumbled underfoot. Rotten! Cai got onto his hands and knees to distribute his weight. The wooden planking began to creak alarmingly. He froze, expecting to hear voices raised in alarm. But the raucous noise from within the roundhouse continued undisturbed. He pressed on and was relieved when his hand brushed against the spar of a ladder.

Standing, he gingerly set his foot on the first rung. It felt solid. Deciding to risk it he began descending quickly. But the wood was slick from the continuous rain and when only halfway his boot slipped. Cai crashed to the ground, landing on his back, the wind driven from his lungs.

Trying not to moan out loud, he rolled onto his side, panting heavily, a piercing bolt of pain shooting across his back. The ground his head rested upon had been churned by many feet. He spat foul mud from his mouth, smelling shit, trying not to think about whether it was animal or human.

Forcing himself onto his knees, he moved into a crouch and stumbled to the side of the roundhouse. Leaning against its rough, wattled side, he tried to catch his breath. The low overhanging roof at least gave him respite from the rain.

Resting his ear against the wall, the sounds of revelry were louder, but still muffled. He must risk getting nearer to the entrance. Stooping low, remaining within the dark of the overhanging thatch, Cai edged around the building. The footing under the roof's protection was firm and dry.

As he progressed, the dull light he had seen from the walkway gradually brightened and he could discern the ground outside of the overhang. Soon Cai realised he could comprehend a word or two from within. The rain had stopped. The cover of its constant pattering was gone.

His heart raced. He inched further around the wall, guided by its curve. A broad, dark shape came into view, blocking further progress. Cai reached out and felt smooth, bulging wood. A water butt?

Hunched down, hidden in the deep darkness of its shadow, Cai listened for movement. The revelry from within continued, accompanied by the unceasing drip of the roof's runoff into the barrel. He prepared to move into the light.

Someone coughed. Cai froze. A man's cough, from the other side of the butt. His heart thumped hard against his chest, its rhythm pumping loud in his ears. Surely this unseen Novantae would hear it. Cai reached for his pugio, slowly sliding it from its scabbard.

The man hawked and spat. An instant later the sound of laughter grew sharply, before it was cut off once more.

'There you are Barra,' Cai knew that name 'Why do you seek your own company? You should be inside celebrating with the rest of our friends.'

'I needed air.'

The reply was spoken quietly but Cai recognised its owner.

'I know you better than that, my friend. What ails you?'

There was a pause and the sound of swallowing. One of them drank from their cup.

'Why are we still here, Cynbel?' Barra said. 'Why are we not now taking back our lands?'

'Have patience, cousin. We'll be ready soon enough.'

'The Damnonii and the Selvogae are happy to sit on their arses, until they've emptied our food stores and drank us dry of our ale. They'll stay here until all is spent and their welcome passed.'

'Where's this coming from? You fought with the Damnonii after their lands were torn in two by that cursed wall. They, perhaps more than our people, have reason to hate Rome. That daemon Urbicus treated them badly. He took many of their women and children to feed their slave markets. It is why so many from beyond the wall have answered the Novantae's call.'

Barra spat again, but did not respond.

'You lead my people in our eastern reaches. I know you chafe to avenge your brother and for what the Romans did at our sacred hill.

As do I.' The sound of more swallowing. 'In two days, all of the tribes will make the sacrifices and on the following day we move. You've seen how complacent they've become. We'll burn their fortresses on the Sula, then join with our Brigantes brothers.'

'You put too much faith in the Brigantes, Cynbel,' Barra said, 'I don't trust them. Their leaders have become soft under Roman rule.'

'Don't be concerned about their appetite for killing Romans. Once they see the Novantae and our allies have crossed the wall of stone, they'll join us enthusiastically enough. Now come inside, Barra. We don't want to insult our guests.'

'As you wish,' Barra said, with a sigh. A moment later there was a burst of sound, before being cut off once more.

Cai waited until he was sure both Novantae had gone. He peered over the barrel. The dully lit space beyond was empty. He let go of the breath he'd been holding. Shit. Three tribes? He edged backwards, slowly at first, then darted into the darkness, long strides squelching over the muddy ground to the ladder.

'Fuck me, sir,' Hrindenus whispered as Cai landed with a thump beside him. 'You made enough noise back there to awaken the dead from their long sleep.'

'Well it's lucky I didn't send you then, isn't it? You big ox.'

Hrindenus snorted a laugh. 'Did you discover anything of use?'

'Yes. But there's no time now. Let's move.'

They slid into the cold water of the lake, wading with careful steps. Cai kept a wary eye on the shore, but though the rain had stopped there was no sign of movement, only the occasional snort from a horse, near the walkway's end.

Upon reaching the lake's edge, they quickly crossed the open ground to the corral. They felt along the wooden spars, seeking their chainmail and weapons.

'Who's there?'

A voice called from the darkness. Not shouted, but commanding nonetheless. Cai turned sharply to see a faint silhouette framed against the dull light from the settlement. Cai heard the slightest of movement, followed by a grunt. The silhouette dropped from view. Hrindenus moved quickly and quietly to the side of the now twitching body. He drove his thrown pugio in further, ripping through his victim's heart. As Cai joined him the body became still.

The Tungrian had to lever hard to retrieve the dagger. It came free after a final wrench.

'Let's hide him amongst the cattle,' Cai said, 'with luck he won't be found until first light. They might even suspect one of their own'

With an effort, they dragged the body into the centre of the enclosure, the longhorns unconcerned at this new disturbance.

'Get your kit on.' Both pulled on their heavy chainmail shirts, slinging the straps of their spathas across their shoulders.

'What did you hear, sir.' Hrindenus said, when they had returned to the forest's edge.

'I'll tell you as we move. Let's go.' Through broken breaths, Cai relayed the conversation between the two Novantae warleaders.

'Balls,' Hrindenus said, when Cai had finished.

'My thoughts exactly, trooper. We need to get back to the Sack. The Tribunus must know.'

The hillside became steep. Both men doubled over with the effort of the climb, their clothes sodden and chainmail weighing heavily. They stumbled through the blackness, at times forced to feel their way forward between the trees and undergrowth.

'Damn it,' Hrindenus said in a hiss.

'What?'

'I've dropped my pugio. If the blue-faces find it they'll know who killed their man.'

The pair had finally reached the summit.

'There's nothing to be done,' Cai said. 'We won't find it now.'

Cai turned to look at the scene below. There was no movement he could discern in the settlement or the island. Campfires still burned on the far side of the lake, though how they kept them lit after the storm he did not know.

'Like a slumbering beast,' Cai said.

And then the beast awoke. A scream. A woman's scream, came from below, quickly answered by shouts nearer the settlement.

'Bollocks,' Hrindenus said, 'they've found the body.'

'No shit. Run!'

The sounds from the settlement were lost as they moved deeper into the forest. They ran as best they could in the deep darkness. Unseen branches whipped and scratched at their faces. But onwards they lurched, as the tall black shapes of the trees closed in around them.

'Where the fuck are we?' Cai swung around trying to pick out any landmark within the dark. It was impossible.

'We're close, I think.' Hrindenus gave a sharp whistle through his teeth.

'Hairy,' came a hissed call from the darkness.

'Arse.'

'Over here, Tungrian,' Avitius called, emerging from the invisible lip of the hiding place.

Cai moved over to the old standard bearer.

'I've never been so glad to hear your voice, brother,' Cai said.

'The other two lads got back a while ago, sir, so we've been listening out for you.'

'Well we've just kicked the hornets' nest. We're going to have to ride for our lives.'

'Oh goody,' Avitius said, 'I knew I shouldn't have let you go alone with this big lump.'

Cai descended into the cleft calling his men to him. He quickly relayed what he'd heard on the island.

'To give ourselves the best chance of getting a message through to the Tribunus we'll split into pairs. Each to make their way independently to the Sack. And yes, Vexillarius you're with me.' Avitius closed his mouth against the response he was about to make. 'The darkness should buy us some time, they won't be able to track us until first light.' Cai looked at each man in turn, a grin on his face.

'When we meet up at the Sack,' he said, 'the first round will be on me.' Low laughter came from the nine men. 'Now go, and may Fortuna be with you.'

Cai stood silently in the dark, watching the four pairs of riders pull their mounts out of the hiding place and quickly disappear into the night.

'Right then, brother. It's our turn.'

'Right you are, sir. We head east?'

'Not yet. We'll head south for a while. Make the blue faces think we're headed for the Tungrian's fort. We'll cut back east after a couple of hours of hard riding. We might even give them the slip.'

'And my old Ma's a virgin princess, sir. You're going to try and buy the others more time, aren't you?'

Cai's wolflike grin could be seen by Avitius even in the dark.

The Vexillarius grinned back.

'Well, fuck it then,' Avitius said. 'Let's show those Novantae sheep-humpers what the Nervii are about.'

42

There was still no sound of pursuit. For the first hour Cai and Avitius led their mounts on foot through the now sodden undergrowth of tall ferns.

As the faintest of grey light began to emerge from the east, they mounted up.

The forest had changed from tall pine to broad oak and thin silver birch, the ferns gone too, allowing them to press on with less risk to the horses.

They reached a shallow stream, no more than a spear's length wide, but its waters flowed clear from the recent rainfall.

'Let's stop and let the horses drink,' Cai said.

'Aye. I need to take a piss anyway.' Avitius dismounted and Cai heard the sigh of relief and splash of liquid into the stream.

'What the fuck was tha…bollocks.' Avitius cursed as the piss splashed onto his troos.

'Quiet!' Cai hissed

Both men held their breaths. The sound came again. A shout, still far off.

'It looks like they've found our trail. Time to go eh, sir?' The old standard bearer leaped up onto his horse. Cai listened for a while longer but no further sound came.

'It's time to be Nervii, brother.' Cai said, Avitius responded with a leer.

They crossed the stream, riding towards an area of dense bushes a stone's throw away. Entering its tangled depths, they pushed through and out of the other side, before immediately doubling back, reentering the stream. This time however, Cai guided Adela along the channel, against the water's flow, Avitius close behind.

Cai watched the bank closely until he found what he was looking for.

'Here,' Cai said.

Both men nudged their mounts out of the water and across the slab of rock on the stream's edge. Once out Cai kicked Adela into a trot, heading deeper into the forest.

Twice more over the next hour they switched back on their trail.

At one point, the pair dismounted to walk the horses up a dry, boulder strewn streambed.

'That'll fool the bastards,' Avitius had said.

The land began to rise, gently but continually. The trees thinned, allowing them to push the horses harder for a while. They emerged into a clearing. At its far end, Cai saw a tall rise, covered in dark green bracken.

'Let's see what we can see, shall we,' Cai said.

He dismounted at its base and clambered up the slope. Reaching the crest, he took in the view before him, looking back along the route they had taken. Cai could see a considerable distance despite the forest. The cloud cover was broking up, and the morning sun shone through the distant treetops, a thin mist rising eerily from their depths.

There was no sign nor sound of pursuit. Avitius came to stand beside Cai and the pair continued to watch. As the minutes passed Cai's confidence began to grow.

'It looks like we may have lost them, brother,' Cai said. 'So much for—'

'Shit,' Avitius said.

Cai looked at the standard bearer, his eyes fixed on something in the middle distance.

'What have you seen?'

'A couple of flashes in that direction.' Avitius pointed. 'Perhaps two miles back.'

Cai stared intently but saw nothing. Then the flashes came once more.

'It looks like our little tricks have only delayed them,' Cai said. 'What do you think? About an hour behind us?'

'Less,' Avitius said.

Cai pulled his fingers through sweat-dampened hair. His helm still hung from the saddle horn.

'Well, brother,' he said, 'it's time to roll the dice. Let's turn east.'

'I can hear water below us,' Avitius said, 'we can use it to disguise our change of direction.'

Descending the rise they quickly found the stream. It flowed slowly but its water was dark and deep.

'Let's lead the horses, we don't want them to stumble,' Cai said.

Wading up to their waists, the effort quickly became exhausting.

Remounting, the two set off pushing the horses once more. At times they were forced to weave in and out of the now densely packed pine. Ducking below low branches when they saw them, or receiving a painful whip if they didn't. Neither slowed, nor made any attempt to hide their passing.

If we can survive until dark, we have a chance, thought Cai.

But the hard pace began to tell on the horses and when they started to blow, Cai knew they had to slow.

'We'll have to walk them again for a while.'

The pain in Cai's back was excruciating. Avitius looked worn out. Removing his canteen, he took a long pull before passing it to the standard bearer.

'If they're chasing us as hard as we're running, they'll be in the same condition,' Cai said.

'You've never been much good at bullshitting, Cai.' Avitius shot him his familiar toothy grin.

'Aye, well.' Cai smiled back at his old tent mate. 'If we can keep ahead of the blue-faces until dark, we can give them the slip.'

'Maybe.'

They ran alongside their mounts for another hour, continually looking over their shoulders, expecting their pursuers to burst through the undergrowth with each passing moment. Avitius was tiring badly

'The horses have had enough rest,' Cai said. 'Time to push on.'

For the rest of the afternoon they repeated the cycle. Riding the horses hard until they tired, then they would run alongside them, for as long as Cai thought Avitius could take it.

In the early evening, as the sun lowered towards the west, they came to an outcrop of tall rocks. Dismounting Cai scrambled up the face of the brown, moss-strewn sandstone.

Keeping below its summit he carefully peered between a gap made by a pair of great stone slabs. He spotted their pursuers immediately. They were close. Less than a mile. But only four riders? A flash of colour caught his eye further away. A second group, walking exhausted mounts. Cai turned away and slid rapidly back down the surface of the rock.

'Why're you grinning?' Avitius said.

'Because, brother, we're about to even up our odds.'

Cai held tightly to his shield, a javelin grasped in his right hand. Would the lead group take the bait? Where the hell are they?

Adela snorted. 'Easy my love, your time will come,' Cai whispered.

'They're near,' Avitius hissed, hearing them first.

From where the pair hid within dense undergrowth, the approach of the lead group would be concealed. But the Novantae were careless of the noise they made. The horses were walking. Voices were raised, but at first the conversation couldn't be discerned.

'Slow your talk, I can't understand you.'

Cai's heart thumped harder. It was the voice of Barra.

'Clean your ears out, Novantae,' the other voice sneered. 'The Roman's trail leads this way. They're pushing their horses hard again.'

'Their desperation drives them,' Barra said. 'We're close and if your ugly little ponies can keep up, we'll run them down before dark.'

'It's your men that are lost in the woods behind us, not mine. Only your stolen Roman horse allows you to keep up with the Damnonii.'

The talk continued, but it gradually became unintelligible as the group passed by.

'They've gone for it.' A grin creased Avitius's face.

Cai nodded, gripping the shaft of his spear tighter. The wait for the second group would test their nerve.

Despite a gentle evening breeze, sweat trickled under Cai's leather-and-chainmail-covered back. Both men were assailed by the biting insects that so loved this time of day.

'Where're the idle bastard's?' Avitius grumbled. 'It's been ages since the first lot passed.'

'Patience, brother,' Cai said, but he was becoming concerned. If the lead group uncovered their ruse and doubled back too soon, it would be the end for them.

Both men looked at one another, hearing the sound of crows rising in alarm. Cai raised his spear and Avitius nodded. Minutes passed, before finally low voices could be made out, accompanied by the slow rumble of horses' hooves.

'We'll not catch Barra and those unwashed cattle-humpers before dark now.'

'Shut your moaning, Bethna. The Romans will be dead before night falls. If you'd ever had the honour of joining the hunt with our lord you'd know he seldom misses his quarry.'

Cai sat unmoving, listening to their approach. Finally turning to Avitius he mouthed, 'Now.' Both men burst from either side of the thicket, driving their mounts hard at the warriors. The group of four, stared in their direction, open-mouthed, not comprehending what they were seeing. That indecision allowed Cai and Avitius to close on their enemy.

Each cast their javelins at the same instant before the Novantae could react. Cai's target, a bald-headed warrior with a great rotund belly, raised his hand instinctively and was killed instantly as the spearpoint penetrated deep into his armpit.

The warrior closest to his now-fallen comrade was shocked into action. Drawing his long sword he roared an incoherent warcry. But again too late. Cai had already freed his long lance from its scabbard as Adela ate up the ground. He drove the long point of the iron lancehead into the helpless warrior's groin, his small shield unable to deflect its impetus. The Novantae's warcry became a scream of agony.

Glimpsing movement to his left, Cai instinctively raised his shield. A sharp pain jarred his arm as a heavy sword blow clashed against the shield's rim, the force of it driving him onto Adela's neck. The experienced war-horse leaped clear, giving Cai time to right himself, but he was forced to release his spear.

He drew his spatha, barely deflecting another vicious downward cut from this new, determined assailant.

But now Cai and the Novantae faced one another. On a different occasion he might have found the sight of his adversary comical. He was huge. His long, well-groomed hair, tied in two braids, hung across his shoulders. But on the small, shaggy horse he looked almost childlike, despite the mass of swirling tattoos covering his chest, the patterns weathered with age.

He sneered at Cai, displaying a single tooth like a weather-worn milestone, standing tall within the dark crevice of his mouth. Both kicked their mounts in the same instant, clashing swords as they passed one another. Belying his size the warrior turned his mount quickest. This time, Cai could only partly deflect the follow up cut, crying out as pain lanced along his ribs. The blade had sliced through his chainmail and leather jerkin. Cai gasped again as the warrior jerked his sword in an effort to free it. But it was caught.

Gritting his teeth, Cai sliced downwards with his spatha, carving the blade deep into the warrior's arm at the elbow. The Novantae howled and reflexively pulled his mount away. The big man stared in open-mouthed shock at his forearm, hanging loosely, as blood pumped over his troos, his sword hilt released, Cai's presence forgotten.

Cai turned sharply in his saddle, hearing a horse's tortured screams. Avitius's mount kicked and thrashed on the ground, a spear buried deep in its rump. The standard bearer had been thrown clear but lay unmoving. Two warriors lay dead nearby. A third had dismounted and advanced towards the prone standard bearer, sword in hand.

An incoherent sound erupted from Cai's throat. He kicked Adela hard, driving her across the short distance. The Novantae had raised his sword to finish Avitius, but spun around reflexively at the sound of the charging horse. A look of horror crossed his face, an instant before he disappeared under Adela's hooves.

There had been six assailants. How had he missed the other two?

The Novantae now lay unmoving, with the exception of the big warrior whose arm he had almost removed. He was slumped across his horse's neck as if asleep.

Feeling the sharp pain in his ribs, Cai realised the warrior's sword was still tangled up in his chainmail. He pulled it free, cursing at the jolt of pain before tossing the iron blade aside.

Dismounting, Cai ran to Avitius. The old warrior lay on his back, eyes closed, but his chest still rose and fell. There was little time to check for injuries, the lead party of warriors would have heard the clash of the battle. They would soon be upon them.

Moving quickly, Cai retrieved an undamaged javelin from the body of a Novantae. Then using much of his remaining strength he lifted Avitius, hauling the standard bearer across Adela's back and after much cursing, levered him into a slumped sitting position. He remounted with difficulty, pulling the unconscious Avitius against him. Adela snorted, objecting to the extra weight.

Once Cai sat steadily, his arm wrapped around Avitius, he nudged Adela into a trot. It was still hours until nightfall.

43

Adela splashed into the stream. Cai let her find her own way along its shallow bed.

He held tight to Avitius, his right arm curving around his waist. The old warrior's head lolled from side to side. After a while Cai's arm began to tire and he swapped to his left.

'Shit.'

His hand dripped with blood. Avitius had a wound he hadn't seen and needed dressing. There was no choice but to push on until dark.

As if the gods now laughed at his foolishness, Cai heard the first shout. The bodies had been found.

Leaving the streambed, he turned Adela east once more. After a short time the forest floor became thickly covered, intermingled with hawthorn, holly, ash and hazel, making passage difficult. But Cai knew the undergrowth could be his ally too.

They entered a glade, perhaps a hundred good strides across. The sun had disappeared, unnoticed by Cai. The light was fading. If he could just stay ahead of them for another hour.

But the shouts came again, much closer. Darkness would come too late.

Twisting left and right in the saddle, he took in the forest around him. It looked the same in all directions. Until he spotted a darker, denser looking patch. *That will have to do*.

He nudged Adela into a trot around the glade, continually changing direction.

Once he was satisfied he walked her towards the darker bushes. Dismounting he pulled her deep into the interior of the thicket, with Avitius slumped across her neck.

Loosely hanging the reins around a hawthorn, he gently lowered Avitius, laying him against the moss-covered trunk of a wide oak. The standard bearer let out a low moan, but didn't wake. Moving to Adela's side, Cai slid one of the javelins from the scabbard, cleaning the dried blood from the spearhead. Once done, he crouched low pushing his way back amongst the thicket. He grabbed a handful of damp, fragrant dirt, smearing it over his face and hunkered down to wait as the forest became darker still.

'Over here, I've found them.' The shout came from the now unmistakable voice of Barra. Cai couldn't see him clearly through the underbrush, but could discern movement.

'They think they're so clever.' Cai heard the frustration in this new voice. 'They must be close, why else go to so much trouble?'

'It's just another trick to disguise that they are still running for home,' Barra said.

'No. Novantae. The tricksters are here. This is new for them. And they're on a single horse, one of them is wounded. They'll be listening to us right now.'

'Let's dismount and split up, see if we can flush them out then,' Barra said.

'What? Alone? The light is failing, are you mad? You saw what they did against six men out in the open.'

'I didn't know the Damnonii were such women,' Barra said, his voice dripping with contempt. 'Frightened of the dark are you?'

'Watch your mouth, Novantae. It isn't my men that lie dead in the forest back there. Six defeated by two.'

'Have it your way,' Barra said. 'I'll search on my own. If they're here, I'll find them myself.'

There was more unintelligible grumbling before the four finally dismounted. Cai crept forward, carefully moving a piece of thornbush aside. Even in the poor light he saw the unmistakable frame of the Novantae warchief. Cai froze as Barra seemed to scrutinise his hiding place, pointing directly at him. He let out a long, slow breath as Barra's gaze passed on, indicating other parts of the glade to the others, as they made their plan. An agreement made, three began moving, fanning out, swords drawn. The fourth watched the horses.

One of the Damnonii walked with careful, deliberate steps towards Cai's thicket. Like the dark warriors they had encountered on the first day, his tattooed head was shaven and his chest bare.

Cai edged back, deeper into the dense bush. Both hands gripped tightly to the shaft of the javelin. Taking a deep, calming breath, he adjusted his hand hold. Ready.

The thicket in front of him rustled as the warrior pushed through. Cai crouched, his thighs burning. His wounded side ached, but he didn't dare move. When the Damnonii was almost upon him he suddenly turned away, moving towards where Avitius lay. As if the old standard bearer sensed the danger, a rasping moan escaped his lips.

The warrior froze. Listening. But didn't call to the others. The undergrowth rustled again. If it had been daylight the Damnonii would already have seen Avitius. But in the half-light he was just another root-like hump on the ground. Adela snickered at the stranger's presence. The warrior's silhouette froze once more.

Cai sprung from his hiding place. The Damnonii turned in time to see the silent scream on his attacker's face, but had no chance to shout an alarm as the point of the javelin was rammed into his throat. The warrior's hand went reflexively to its shaft as blood gurgled from his lips. His eyes rolled upwards until only the whites could be seen, before slowly slumping to his knees. Cai used the shaft to ease him onto his back, the Damnonii rasping his last breath.

Abandoning the javelin, Cai moved to Avitius's side, stepping back in fright at seeing the old standard bearer's eyes fully open.

'Fuck me I hurt,' Avitius croaked.

'I'm sorry, brother,' Cai whispered. 'I'm going to have to hurt you some more. But you must be silent.'

Avitius groaned as Cai raised him to his feet. Half carrying the older man to Adela, he lifted him into the saddle.

'We have to find somewhere to lay low. It's nearly dark, so we shouldn't have to go too far. I can see to your wounds then, brother.'

'I'll be fine,' Avitius rasped, 'let's go.'

Cai led Adela. Leafed branches shushed as they passed through the undergrowth. They had gone no more than a hundred or so paces when he heard the call. A question. The dead Damnonii's name perhaps? It came again, this time more urgent and accompanied by the rustling sound of men stumbling through dense bush.

Cai prayed the sound of his own passage wouldn't carry. The ground was soft underfoot; perhaps it would mask it? The darkness was now nearly complete.

'Run, Romans. Run.' The shout, some way behind, not Barra's voice. The Damnonii. The pursuers crashed through the undergrowth, cursing as they were caught or tripped. To his surprise the sound was moving to his left. They couldn't tell what direction he had taken. Gradually the noise of the pursuit faded.

But Cai dared not stop. He pushed on, an occasional moan coming from Avitius, letting Cai know he still lived. After a while he heard the trickle of what must be a small stream. Moving carefully between broad trunks, feeling his way along their gnarled bark, he came to its bank.

'Let's get you down, brother.' The old veteran hissed as Cai helped him from Adela's back. He propped Avitius in a sitting position against a dark trunk.

Cai then led Adela to the stream, which turned out to be little more than a single stride across. Cupping his hands he tested the water. It was good. He filled his canteen and left Adela to find what grazing she could, knowing she wouldn't wander. He felt his way back to Avitius's side.

'Are you still with me, Vit?' Cai asked

'I'm still here,' Avitius said, his words strained. 'It's been many years since you called me that.'

'Let me see to your wound.' Cai started to lift up Avitius's chainmail vest, but was stopped by a firm grip.

'Just sit with me awhile, Cai, will you?'

'But you've lost a lot of blood, I need to bind it.'

'It's too late for that, brother.'

'But—'

'Sit,' Avitius said. Cai's heart sank

He felt his way along the tree trunk, easing himself down beside the old veteran, moving against him to share whatever warmth he had with this friend. Their heads were close together. There was silence between them for a time and Cai thought he might have fallen asleep, until Avitius cleared his throat.

'Thank you, brother.' He spoke quietly, but with less of the earlier strain.

'For what?'

'For putting up with a cantankerous, insubordinate old bastard like me for so many years.' He wheezed a laugh before becoming quiet again for a moment.

'And for letting me lead a warrior's life. To the very end.'

'It hasn't been so bad has it, Vit?' Cai responded, feeling his throat tighten.

'Not so bad!' Avitius coughed harshly.

‘Here, take a drink.’ Cai held his canteen to Avitius’s lips, who nodded his thanks.

‘So few of us left, from the lands of our home. So many friends lost.’

‘True,’ Cai said. ‘But some have taken their diploma and farm in the lands of the Carvetti. They’ll have sons of their own, who will come to us one day, heads filled with their father’s tall tales of glory.’

Avitius wheezed a laugh. ‘Aye, poor buggers.’ His laugh turned to a coughing fit which took some time to pass.

‘Do you remember that sadist of a Centurion we had, when you and Adal first joined our section as snivelling youths?’

Cai laughed. ‘Arcan. Aye, how could I forget. I felt his staff across my shoulders often enough.’

‘And do you remember what Adal did after you took one too many beatings, for his liking?’

‘He sneaked into the bastard's tent one night, when he was out drinking with his mates and took a shit on his bunk.’ Cai almost couldn’t finish what he was saying, he was laughing so hard. Even the pain in his side couldn’t stop it. Avitius wheezed a laugh, blowing long and hard through his teeth.

‘By the gods, I’ve missed him,’ Avitius said.

Both men lapsed into silence for a while. Apart from the occasional rustle of a floor dweller in the undergrowth or a snort from Adela, the forest was still.

‘I know he’s waiting to welcome me, with a cup of ale in hand.’

‘It’ll be the first time he’ bought a round then,’ Cai said.

Avitius wheezed again. ‘Aye, too true,’ his words were becoming laboured. ‘But I’ll be glad to see him and share stories around the campfire once more. I’ll tell him how I managed to stop you from making too many fuckups while he’s been gone.’

‘I’m sure he’s been watching and shaking his head in dismay.’

‘Aye.’ Avitius's voice was now difficult to hear even with their heads so close. ‘But we’ll wait for you by that fire, brother.’ Avitius coughed again before he could continue. ‘But don’t come too soon. Live a long life with your woman.’ Avitius was quiet again.

‘I’m tired, Cai. I think I’ll rest for a while.’ The old warrior lay his head gently on Cai’s shoulder with a sigh.

'Sleep well, brother,' Cai whispered. 'I'll take first watch.' Avitius murmured a response that Cai couldn't make out. He stared into the darkness, listening as his old tent mate's breathing slowed, gradually becoming shallow and ragged, until finally he could hear it no longer. And for the second time in his life, Cai wept for the passing of a friend.

44

Cai awoke to a snort of warm breath against his cheek. He opened his eyes to see the dark outline of Adela's long nose. She nuzzled against his cheek, snorting once more.

'Alright my lovely, I know it's time to go.'

During the night he had carefully laid Avitius's body by the stream, placing the standard bearer's spatha on his chest, wrapping his cold hands around its hilt.

He had then taken some dressing from his saddle, with the intention of binding his own wound. But the excruciating pain prevented him from removing his mail. Instead he had stuffed strips of the cloth into the gash. It would have to suffice. Exhausted, Cai had fallen asleep with his back against the tree's broad trunk.

Now his joints ached. Cold and dampness permeated every part of him. It was still dark, but birdsong told him that first light was not far away.

Pain lanced in his side as he attempted to rise. Groaning, he tried again. Leaning against the dark trunk, he slowly got to his feet. Moving stiffly, at first, his muscles slowly loosened. Cai took a long drink from his canteen, before refilling it from the stream, splashing some of the icy water over his face.

He went to Adela's waiting silhouette, slowly stroking her nose.

'Well, girl, it's just you and me now, and it's time we were away.' He looked up at the star filled sky. 'Divine Epona, help us survive this day' he whispered.

He turned one final time to look at the dark shape lying by the stream.

'Happy hunting, my friend. Say hello to that grumpy bastard for me.' Taking Adela's rein, Cai led her across the stream, heading eastward.

At first the darkness made progress difficult. But gradually the forest revealed itself.

'We'll have to chance it.'

Taking hold of Adela's long blonde mane he prepared himself for the sharp stab of pain. Taking three quick breaths he leapt. The instant, searing agony forced him to release his hold. He fell to the ground, muffling his cry as soon as it left his mouth.

Cai lay on his side, waiting for the pain to subside. Rising cautiously he stood by Adela's head, sending long slow strokes along her neck.

'Right girl, I'm going to need a little help from you now.' Gingerly bending over he took hold of Adela's left leading leg, just above her hoof. Lifting it he tucked it under and was relieved to see her respond.

Adela tucked her head to her chest, lowering into a kneeling position. Gratefully Cai swung his leg across her back. Patting her neck, he whispered in her ear as she arose once more.

'Thank you, girl,' he said softly. 'What would I do without you?'

As the light grew Cai nudged Adela into a trot, clenching his teeth against the cry of pain that threatened to release with every stride. Weaving between huge oaks, pushing through dense undergrowth, progress was slow. Then he heard them.

As the rays of the sun's dawn light broke through the canopy, the first shout came. He recognised no words, but the excitement in their tone was unmistakable. They had found his trail. They were close.

'Well, my sweet. Let's make sure the price for our lives is a high one.'

Cai began searching the ground ahead. Upon seeing the wide, dry stream bed he smiled to himself. The side of its left bank was steep, perhaps three times as tall as a man, topped with more of the tangled blackberry bush. Horse and rider entered the rock strewn bed, passing the high bank. After a short distance he turned and drove Adela hard to the bank's crest, immediately doubling back along it to seek the concealment of the thorny barrier.

For a while all Cai heard were the sounds of the forest. Adela snorted, nostrils flaring.

'Patience, girl,' Cai whispered. 'They'll be with us soon.' He lifted his helmet from the saddle horn, running his hand through its white plume. Satisfied, he placed it on his head, tying the chin straps firmly. He drew his left arm through the shield holds, before lifting his spatha part way out of its scabbard, before letting it drop back once more. Finally he drew his remaining javelin from its sheath. He was ready.

'Mighty Cocidius. Give me the strength this day, to bring honour to my tribe and my cohort.'

Adela's ears pricked at the rumbling sound of hooves. Cai heard the murmur of voices. It was difficult to judge distance in the forest but they were close. Follow the trail, you bastards.

'He's using the river bed to disguise his trail. Does he think we'll be so easily fooled again?' The Damnonii's voice.

'He's close, the sign back there is fresh,' Barra called.

Cai peered through the mesh of thorny branches. If the three riders had looked up they would have seen the white flash of his plume. But they didn't. The uneven rocks of the stream bed forced the group to move in single file. Cai gripped his spear tightly as he watched them pass his hiding place. First the big Novantae, Barra, followed by a Damnonii warrior. Finally the rearmost rider came into view. He kicked Adela hard, the war horse leaping instantly through a small gap in the brush and over the bank's edge.

The steepness of the descent forced Cai to lean back in his saddle. Through vision darkened by pain, he cast the javelin. The warrior, startled by the sudden noise, only had time to turn his head. His look of shock became one of agony as the spear point passed deep into his back below the shoulder blades, his cry silenced as it ruptured his heart.

A shriek, part scream, part warcry pierced the air and before Cai had time to draw his spatha. In a blur of black, the Damnonii drove his mount directly into Adela. The force of the impact caused the mare to lose her footing on the uneven ground. In desperation Cai tried to stay upright but it proved in vain as both horse and rider hit the ground. Instinctively Cai threw himself clear, only to land hard amongst the rocks of the river bed, striking his head.

His ears rang. His senses were stunned. His body screaming with agony, he made an effort to rise but his body betrayed him. Cai fumbled for the pugio at his hip and through the fog in his head, he heard laughter.

The dark Damnonii stood over him, sword in hand. Forlornly Cai tried to pull the dagger from its scabbard, feeling fresh pain as the warrior's boot crushed his hand.

'It's too late, Roman. Time to suffer for the pains you have put us through.'

'Domelch, wait.' Cai heard Barra's voice but could not see him.

'Go take a piss, Novantae, if you're too faint hearted for it.'

Cai's vision began to clear. He saw the sneer on the Damnonii's tattooed face. He snorted and spat down on Cai's prone body, a dribble of phlegm trickling down the warrior's chin.

'Roman turd,' he said. Without another word he raised his sword, two-handed. Cai watched the blade rise in an arc. Only to see the warriors' look of hatred turn, in an instant, to one of shock and incomprehension. He stared dumbly down at a bloody sword point that protruded from his chest.

'I told you to wait, Damnonii,' The words from Barra were the last Cai heard, before darkness took him.

45

Pain filled Cai's head. It throbbed in continuous waves, pulsing in his ears. In the darkness he became aware of distant sounds, the chatter of birdsong, the trickle of water and the crunching of footsteps through undergrowth.

'Roman.' A familiar voice. 'Roman.' A touch of his shoulder this time. 'Drink.'

Cool water hit the back of Cai's throat, immediately choking him, spluttering the water back up again. Cai's eyes flickered open, pain pounding through his head, forcing him to close them tight once more. A groan escaped his lips.

'So you live, Roman.' He knew that voice.

Slowly this time, he opened his eyes, to be greeted by the sight of low overhanging branches, filtering soft sunlight through their broad leaves.

'Here, drink more.'

The face of the Novantae warchief appeared, blocking the light. He held a water skin to Cai's lips. This time Cai drank deeply. The warrior disappeared from view, letting the light drift across him once more. He turned his head away from the light, wincing as pain lanced through his head.

'You cracked your skull. Your shiny helmet took most of the blow, otherwise you would be dead.'

And there was Barra, across a campfire, sitting on a moss-covered fallen oak. He hadn't changed much since their last meeting. His long red hair was not as well groomed, showing the ravages of two days hard riding, but he was unmistakable. The curling snake tattoos on his arms framed his scale armour which reflected the dappled light. He stared back at Cai, slowly pulling the lengths of his drooping moustache through pinched finger and thumb.

Cai croaked an attempt to speak and watched as Barra stood and walked to his side. Carefully placing his hand under Cai's neck, he raised Cai up, so he could take another drink from the canteen.

'My thanks,' Cai rasped.

Barra shrugged, his scale armour chinking with the movement.

Cai raised his hand, trying to touch the back of his head, expecting to feel the wound, but instead found it had been dressed.

'You were bleeding,' Barra said, in answer to his quizzical look. 'I've also bound the gash to your ribs. But I could only clean it with water, so you may still get the fever.'

It was then Cai realised he was not wearing his chainmail shirt or his leather jerkin, just his filthy, sweat stained tunic.

'Why?'

'Why didn't I let Domelch finish you?' A smirk briefly crossed his face. 'I told you once before Roman, I owe you a debt.' The big Novantae stared into the fire. 'Besides, I've greatly desired to put my sword through that filth since the day I met him. Only diplomatic niceties prevented me.'

'All not happy in the great alliance of the sheep-humpers, is it not?' Cai said, not sure why he wished to antagonise his rescuer.

'Watch your mouth, or I may just forget my debt and finish what Domelch started.'

Cai bit back a response, knowing it served no purpose. Eyes closed again, he listened to the crackle of the fire and the trickle of the stream. A thought came to him.

'Where's my horse?' He stared over at Barra, who twitched his head.

'To your left, Roman.'

Turning his head carefully, to his relief Cai saw Adela's tan-coloured hide amongst the trees, head down chomping contentedly alongside the white stallion.

'A good horse. She stood over you when you lay in the riverbed. Perhaps I'll take her for myself and breed her with Enbarr.'

'Adela's fussy. She doesn't like her mates to stink of barbarian.'

For the first time he heard Barra laugh. A deep throaty sound of genuine mirth.

'Just because you wear their clothes, *Nervii*, doesn't mean they look upon you as any less barbarian than the free peoples. Just tamer. You smell more fragrant from those hot baths your kind are so fond of. How does it feel to give up your freedom in return for a few women's comforts?'

Cai smiled, 'The hot water of the bath house, at the end of a long day on horseback, is a gift from the gods. Why don't you pay us a visit one day. Try for yourself?'

'I'll be at your fort soon enough, Nervii. We—,' Barra didn't finish

Cai levered himself into a sitting position, his head throbbing. For the first time he noticed the smell of cooking meat and glanced at the fire. What looked like a partridge was roasting on a stick overhanging the low flames. His mouth instantly filled with saliva and his stomach growled. Barra laughed once more.

'Do you like the look of my bird, Roman? If you're a good boy, I might let you have some.'

Cai pulled his eyes from the bird.

'So what next?' he said. 'Are you going to bore me to death then leave my body here to rot?'

The Novantae poked the fire, stirring up the flames. 'You returned my nephew to me, so I will return you to your fort. Unharmed. Or at least with no further harm. That will see my debt paid.'

Cai shuffled across to the fallen tree trunk so he could sit unaided.

'How long?' Cai asked.

Barra idly tossed a twig into the fire. 'We leave after we've eaten. If you can stay on your horse and don't bleed to death from your wounds. I'll get you across the Anam, and near to your fort before the last light fades from the day.'

'Your concern for me is touching, Novantae. I think I can manage to stay on Adela, without falling off too often.'

Barra grinned. 'We'll see soon enough won't we. *Nervii*.'

After sharing the meat, washed down with more water from the stream, Barra helped Cai over to Adela. Cupping his hands the Novantae hoisted him into the saddle. The pain caused by the sudden movement was excruciating and Cai was relieved that a grunt was the only sound to escape his lips. He watched as Barra stuffed his damaged chainmail shirt into a leather pouch and hung the crested helmet across his white stallion's Roman saddle.

Barra noticed him staring.

'I need them to show my people I killed you,' he said. 'There would be too many questions to answer if I returned with news of Domelch's death, without proof that I had dealt with his killer. Besides, I like your helmet and its pretty feathers. It'll make a fine drinking bowl for our victory feast.' Cai snorted, but said nothing.

Mounting up, Barra turned to Cai. 'Can you guide your horse or do I need to lead you?' There was no malice in his voice, this time.

'I can handle Adela. She'll follow your white without direction.'

The Novantae nodded, nudging his horse into a walk and out of their camp. The thumping in his head and the pain in his side competed to be the first to unman him.

For a while, there was silence between the two men. Cai observed the warleader as they travelled. He rode with a relaxed, almost languid manner, with reins held in his left hand and the thumb of his right hand hooked through the leather belt of his green and checkered troos. The warrior's long red hair curled down his back, its colour reflected in the well-maintained scale armour.

'Where did you steal that armour from Novantae?'

Barra rumbled a laugh at Cai's attempt to get a rise out of him.

'I took it from the still warm body of one of your men of the legion. He and his party had been cutting timber for part of the daemon Urbicus's new wall. You Romans love to build walls, don't you?'

'Why were you so far from home?'

'Home? Have you so soon forgotten what Rome did to my home?' Barra turned his stallion to face Cai, rage in his eyes. 'After my people's defeat at our sacred hill, you Romans didn't stop, there did you?' Barra gripped his sword's pommel, the whites of his knuckles clear for Cai to see. 'Your Sixth Legion moved up the valley of the Anam, burning our villages and taking what slaves they could. But I had already sent our women and children away. Most escaped capture. But Rome made sure we had no home to return to.' Cai watched Barra visibly attempt to calm himself before continuing.

'When what was left of our men caught up with their families, I sent them west, deeper into our great forest.

'But I journeyed north, with my hearth warriors, to ally ourselves with any tribe who had the heart to continue the struggle against our common enemy.' Barra stared into the distance, remembering. 'We fought Rome for another three years. We learned the lesson of our sacred hill. Never again did we commit to battle against the full strength of the legions. We used our land to our advantage instead.

'There were some successes, but in the end it wasn't enough.

We'd had little chance to grow and harvest our crops and we went hungry much of the time. We withdrew into the land beyond the Clutha and let Urbicus build his wall.'

The anger returned to Barra's eyes. 'What is it that Rome wants with the land of the free peoples? We have mountains, forests, lakes and precious little else. We have little gold or lead to mine. Why are you here?'

It was a question Cai had asked himself in his darkest moments. But he knew the answer.

'Because,' he said, 'our emperor commands it.'

Barra spat, never taking his eyes from Cai. 'That's the answer of a slave.'

Cai shrugged 'I'm a soldier. I go where I'm ordered. And you've seen my men in battle, Novantae. We don't, in truth, fight for a distant faceless emperor. We are brothers. We fight for each other. You saw this for yourself on that hill of yours. We would have fought to the end. Are these the actions of slaves?'

Barra snorted, turning his mount once more and spoke over his shoulder. 'It's lucky for you then, that your General rescued you from destruction, isn't it?'

For a while they rode in silence. But eventually Barra slowed, allowing Cai to move Adela alongside his big white.

'My brother died that day,' Barra said, still staring straight ahead. 'At the hands of that big Centurion in the centre of your line. I watched from the edge of the forest. I don't understand why your leaders make such targets of themselves?'

The memories of the battle came flooding back, and Cai was lost in them for a time.

'We wear such helms so we are visible to our men and they take heart. All know that only the bravest, those who have stood in the front rank in battle many times, get to wear them.'

The pain in Cai's side flared. The ride was sapping his strength.

'That Centurion you speak of was a brother to me. From my own village. He also died that day, so if you seek vengeance, you're ten summers too late. And lucky it is for you too.'

The effort of the exchange made Cai's head throb fiercely once again. Lifting his canteen from the saddle horn he took a long drink.

'The boy Herne is your brother's son?' he asked. The warrior acknowledged with the briefest of nods. 'Beren, the boy you saw when you came for your nephew is the son of that Centurion.'

Barra looked at Cai in surprise.

'Well, Roman, it seems our sacred hill still casts its long shadow. You have adopted the son of your friend?' Cai heard no malice in the question.

'No. I watch over him and try to guide him where I can.'

'War has made it difficult for me to take a woman,' Barra said. 'But it's good to have a young soul to guide through life, I think?'

Cai found himself nodding. 'It is.'

They rode on in silence. As the day progressed Cai began to recognise landmarks, including the brooding presence of the mountain of Criffel. His side chafed with each movement and he felt lightheaded.

'Drink this.' Cai felt his head being lifted and a canteen put to his lips. Much of the cool liquid spilled down his chin and onto this tunic. 'Take it slowly,' Barra said.

Cai opened his eyes to see the vague outline of Barra's drooping red moustache. He was lying on the ground amongst long grass. But had no memory of dismounting.

'The binding on your side has come loose. You're bleeding again. All I can do is redress it and hope you don't die on me before we reach your fort. Can you stand?'

Cai grimaced. 'There's only one way to find out.' The Novantae lifted Cai with little effort, walking him to a nearby tree.

'Raise your tunic, so I can get at the binding.'

Barra worked quickly to remove the blood-soaked cloth. Cai tensed as the warrior poured water from his canteen into the wound, rebinding it with a fresh strip.

'I know you hurt, but we can't delay further. It's another half day's hard riding. If you fall again, I'll have to tie you to your horse.'

'Do what you must,' Cai said, his words slurred. His strength was almost gone. Barra retrieved Adela, stroking her neck when she became skittish at being handled by a stranger.

'You're a fine lady,' Barra whispered. Without pause he lifted Cai onto her back, who this time cried out at the sudden jolt of pain.

'We'll be moving quickly. Hold tight to your saddle horn. I'll take the reins.'

They set off at a trot. Around Cai, the forest spun, but he held tight to the saddle. His world coalesced into a fight to stay on Adela.

He did not notice the passage of time. But at one point he became dimly aware of the sound of water, then splashing as Adela entered it.

'We're crossing the Nid river,' Barra said. Hold onto your horse's mane, she'll have to swim part of it.'

Cold water covered Cai's feet, quickly rising to his thighs, until he could feel himself floating out of the saddle. If he let go of her, he thought, it would be the end of him. The water began to subside and he heard the sound of Adela's hooves crunching across shingle.

'We'll reach the Anam valley soon,' Barra's voice came from a great distance. 'Hang on.'

'Wake yourself, Roman.' *He knew that voice.*

Cai opened his eyes at the shock of cold water on his face. He lay once again in long grass, Adela's long nose hanging over him. He tried to sit up but found he couldn't move his arms apart.

'Stay still while I will untie you,' Barra said.

'I'm tied?'

'You fell from your horse and I couldn't wake you. So I had to tie you to her.'

'How long?'

Barra strugged, throwing the bindings into the grass.

'We're here, Roman.' Helping Cai to his feet, the Novantae indicated a gap in the thicket in which they had halted. Cai could just make out the Sack's western turrets, with the village nestled below them.

Without ceremony, Barra hoisted Cai into the saddle once more, where he sat frozen, waiting for the wave of agony to pass.

'I owe you my life,' Cai said, his voice barely a murmur.

'You owe me nothing Roman. I've paid my debt, that is all.'

'Nevertheless, you have my thanks.'

The big red-haired warrior nodded once and handed the reins to Cai.

'We'll meet again, Roman, you can be sure of that.'

Not giving Cai time to respond, Barra slapped Adela's rump,

propelling her through the thicket.

Cai held on, the ground a blur around him, until eventually Adela slowed to a halt. Raising his head he saw the open gates to the village and felt hands lifting him from the saddle.

'Are you alright, Cai?'

Cai thought it was curious that the blacksmith was talking to him.

'Of course he's not alright you fool. Help me lift him.'

'Alyn,' Cai mumbled.

Then darkness fell.

PART 3

46

The Sack

Lucius sat behind his desk in the principia. As Tribunus he had his own residence, but having no wife or children, he preferred the headquarters building's bustle and had set up sleeping quarters behind his office. These days the praetorium was only used on the rare occasions it was necessary to entertain dignitaries.

Fingers steepled, he observed the two men sitting before him, cups of wine resting almost untouched in their hands.

'The lads from the First Hispana,' Facilis said, 'are on their way from Exploratorum; they'll be here before last light. Advanced centuries arrived a short while ago. They've already made a start on the cohort's camp.' He took a deep swallow from his cup before continuing. 'I spoke to one of their Centurions. He reckoned when he left the fort the navy boys were already preparing to sail down the Isca to patrol the Sula. If the Damnonii have allied with the Novantae, then they must have slipped around the northern wall by sea.'

'Which,' Lucius said, cutting across the First Spear, 'means they have boats and might try crossing to Carvetti lands and outflank us.'

'There are only two available boats,' Facilis continued. 'From what he knows, two others are in dry dock and not serviceable. But it might be enough to at least give us some warning. If they attempt it.'

'The estuary is a lot of water to cover with just two boats,' Lucius said. 'We'll just have to hope the visibility remains fair. How go the preparations for the Sack's defences?'

Facilis grinned.

'We'll have some nasty little surprises ready for the blue-faces. I've had sections of axemen out in the woods and we've pretty much cleared the ground outside the Sack of bramble bushes to fill the ditches. The bastards will be in a world of shit before they even get near our walls.'

'Try not to have too much fun, First Spear,' Lucius said, with a lopsided smile.

'Well, we wouldn't want to make it too easy for them now, would we sir? We also have a few caltrops to sprinkle across the causeways but we could use more. I've asked the smith but he and his lads already have their hands full.'

Lucius scratched the day old growth on his chin.

'We're going to need many more,' he said. 'Enlist the village smith. He won't like it, but tough. Just be prepared, he's got a foul temper on him.'

Facilis grinned back.

'Have you considered how best to situate our scorpions?' Lucius asked.

'Aye, sir, I propose we deploy them initially over the porta praetoria. It seems likely they'll first chance their arm with an assault on the main gate. But I've ordered the two crews to practise disassembly and rapid relocation to any of the turrets.'

'Very well.' Satisfied Lucius looked at the man sitting next to Facilis. 'And you, Nepos?'

The old Decurion was quiet, as was his way, considering his words. His milky eye stared back, blindly.

'Turma strength patrols have ranged north and west,' he said. 'There's no sign of the enemy. Nor, unfortunately, of the Praefectus and his men.'

All three looked at one another, it had been nearly three days since they had seen Cai and knew what that likely meant.

'He's a hard man to kill,' Facilis said, with vehemence. 'I'd wager a month's pay, we'll see him soon.'

Lucius looked at his wine cup 'I pray it is so.' He turned to Nepos once more. 'What of the garrison at the town of the Carvetii?'

'I have a dispatch from the Praefectus of the Petriana.' Nepos handed the tablet to Lucius. 'His cohort is understrength. Aren't they all? He has around four hundred cavalry in the field. He'll deploy as you suggested, to watch the coastline along the western end of the Sula. But he'll position the bulk of his force to watch the sands at the eastern stretch to deal with any attempt to cross the estuary at low tide.'

'Well,' Lucius said, 'that's all of the forces at our disposal on the move. We must pray to Fortuna that we are given time to complete our preparations.'

'What of the messengers to Deva and Eboracum, sir?' Facilis asked as he placed his now empty cup on the desk.

'Assuming each section met no trouble as it passed through the lands of the Brigantes, they should reach the legions any time now. But it'll be a long, hard march. Even if they force the pace all hours of daylight, it may be five or six days at best before they reach us.'

Lucius stood to retrieve the wine jug, refilling their cups, before continuing.

'I've sent three section strength units north to alert the forces on the new wall and the garrisons along the route. If they aren't intercepted by the Novantae we may get some support before the legions reach us. But we can't rely on it.'

He took a deep swallow from his cup. You're drinking too much again, he thought.

'Gentlemen,' Lucius said, 'we have to assume we're on our own and we must plan how we deploy our forces accordingly and in a way that will buy time.'

'And what is the plan, sir?' Nepos asked expectantly.

'I've given it some thought over the years. How could we defend the Flour Sack against an insurrection of the Novantae tribe?' We have two cohorts at our disposal, which is better than one. Sufficient, I think, to take on the Novantae. But perhaps not if more allies have joined them, as we fear.' Lucius took another long gulp from his cup before continuing.

'Our objective,' he continued, 'must be to delay the enemy from moving south into Brigante lands, long enough for the legions to arrive. Which likely means holding out for several days. To have a chance, we can't just hide behind the Sack's walls waiting for them to attack us. We must meet them in battle outside of the fort.'

Nepos's one good eye widened in surprise. 'Sir?' he said.

Lucius spent some time outlining his plan. As he finished, Facilis let out a low whistle.

'Well, sir,' he said. 'I see why we'll need more caltrops. A great many more. Not to mention cart loads of additional timber. I see one kink though.'

'Just the one, First Spear?' Lucius said, raising his lopsided smile.

'The village,' Facilis said. 'If we're forced to retire to the fort, their homes will give the enemy cover to assault the western ramparts.'

'You're right. Very well,' Lucius said, his tone resigned. 'The settlement buildings must be pulled down, but not burned. We'll leave a tangled mess that'll prevent them from easily massing for an attack.

'Aye, sir.'

'There are a number of retired veterans in the settlement too,' Lucius continued. 'Inform them, and any other able man, they've been conscripted into the empire's forces for the duration. The women and children can be sheltered within the barrack blocks.' Lucius rose from his chair. 'Very well—' All three officers froze at the sound of multiple hobnailed footsteps, double timing around the stone paved floor of the principia's covered walkway.

'Not bad news I hope,' Nepos said in his gravelly voice.

Moments later the doorway to the room was filled by the outline of three men. Two troopers supported a third larger man, who swayed unsteadily between them. All eyes were drawn to the thick mat of congealed gore on the big trooper's chainmail shirt. His dirt spattered face carried a look of exhaustion.

'Hrindenus!' Nepos exclaimed.

'Get him a chair,' Lucius said. Nepos took hold of Hrindenus's arm, lowering him into his own chair.

'Here lad, drink this.' Nepos placed his wine cup into the Tungrian's shaking hands.

Hrindenus drank greedily, much of the red liquid escaping in rivulets from the sides of this mouth. Nepos filled the cup again.

'Were there others?' Lucius spoke to the two troopers, now standing by the doorway.

'No, sir. He was on his own. Just him and his horse. The beast is in a worse condition than he is. He asked to be brought directly to you, sir.'

'Very well. Dismissed.' Lucius waited until he heard their footsteps retreating cross the atrium. 'What happened, Hrindenus? Where are the rest of the patrol?'

'I haven't seen any sign of the other lads, sir,' he said. 'Not since the Praefectus ordered us to strike out in pairs to get the message to you. The bastard's nearly had me too, this morning. They did for

Caratallus though. But he went down fighting like a Tungrian. Gave me the chance to give them the slip.'

'You've done well, lad.' Nepos placed his hand on the big man's shoulder. 'Tell us the message.'

Hrindenus took another great swig of wine and told the tale of his and Cai's infiltration of the Novantae settlement. When he finished there was silence in the room. Facilus spoke first.

'Three tribes?' he said, incredulous. 'It's worse than we feared. I've heard stories about the Damnonii. Real savages.'

'Were you able to estimate their numbers, Hrindenus?' Lucius asked.

'It was difficult, sir.' Hrindenus looked glassy-eyed at Lucius. 'Most of them were camped amongst the trees or across the other side of the lake. But when it got dark we saw countless campfires. The Praefectus thought there might be as many as ten thousand warriors.'

Lucius blanched. Looking across at the other two officers, seeing they shared his shock. 'You've done well, Hrindenus,' Lucius said. 'Get yourself across to the bathhouse and get cleaned up. We'll need you back. Nepos, can you get food brought to him and have Castellanos check him over?'

'Aye, sir.'

'Have none of the lads made it back then, sir?' Hrindenus asked.

'Not yet. But if you made it, there's a good chance more will.'

Nepos patted the exhausted trooper on the shoulder. 'Come on lad, let's get you sorted. Can you walk unsupported?'

'I think so, sir.'

Lucius watched as Hrindenus hobbled through the doorway, followed at his shoulders by Nepos and Facilis. He smiled briefly at the incongruity of the scene, reminded of two elderly aunts fussing around their favourite nephew.

He sat back in his chair and stared up at the timber joists of the ceiling.

'Jupiter's balls. Ten thousand.'

47

As the evening light began to fade, Lucius left his office to review preparations for himself.

Now striding towards the porta praetoria, he passed between the rows of cavalry barrack blocks. He smelled the sweet aroma of hay and dung, so familiar in his daily life.

As he neared the quartermaster's office Lucius was pleased to see a group of veterans were waiting to be issued with equipment. All still carried their old swords and some wore used but well maintained chainmail.

He picked out Decurion Salvinus in deep conversation with one of the veterans who had his back to Lucius. Upon seeing his approach Salvinus waved Lucius over.

'Look who I found, sir,' Salvinus said, a broad smile on his bearded face. 'I caught him trying to sneak in and rejoin.'

'Mascellus, you old goat,' Lucius cried out in delight. 'How did they drag you away from that farm of yours?' The former Decurion must have been well into his sixth decade, but still looked strong. His complexion, ruddy from so much time spent out of doors, was framed by a short silver beard and shoulder length hair, only showing a few streaks of grey in amongst the gold so typical of the Nervii people.

'I wasn't going to miss the chance of a scrap with the blue-faces, was I, sir? Besides,' he said, nodding towards Salvinus, 'us veterans need to show these youngsters what proper soldiering's about.'

'I see you kept your kit in good shape. Just in case we called you back, eh?'

'Aye, sir. The armour fits a bit snugly these days, though.' Mascellus patted his considerable paunch that pressed against his armour. 'The missus makes fine honey cakes and I enjoy eating them.'

Lucius spent a few minutes talking to the group, a mixture of retired cavalry and infantrymen. He could recall all of their names and knew them to be good men. He left encouraged. Now he would be able to distribute more veterans amongst some of the less experienced men, to stiffen their resolve.

On passing between the last blocks, he exchanged salutes with the sentries on the porta praetoria, noting with satisfaction the activity beyond the big oak gates. But instead of exiting the fort he turned towards the southwest turret, his route taking him along the base of the steep turf embankment of the fort's ramparts.

As Lucius approached the entrance to the turret, he halted at the clattering sound of multiple booted feet as they noisily descended its steps in haste.

'Move you laggards. If we get beat by that other lot, I'll have you cleaning out the latrines for a month, do you get me?' Four double-timing soldiers rushed out of the turret's entrance. The first had the wooden frame of a scorpio slung over his shoulder, followed immediately by another carrying its stand. Next came a heavily panting bear of a man who carried a full basket of the short bolts under each arm. Taking up the rear was the crew commander, an Optio by the name of Mantus, who tapped the end of his long wooden staff against his helmet in salute at Lucius's presence, but didn't stop.

'Move you big lump or you'll find the wrong end of this up your arse.'

Lucius smiled to himself as he watched the four men disappear up the narrow route between the fort's western wall and the internal buildings. I like an officer who knows how to motivate his men, he thought.

Taking the turret's wooden steps, two at a time, he reached its platform.

The sun had now set. But in the late evening gloom the ground outside the fort was alive with activity. Like the ant colonies he used to toy with as a boy, in the heat of summer. Men, stripped of their tunics, worked within the ditches and in the long grass that ran towards the stream beyond.

'Divine Fortuna, let there be time.'

His thoughts were interrupted by shouts coming from the village. He tried to discern the cause, but even from the turret's elevated position his view was blocked by the peaked roofs of the homes and workplaces within. He shrugged to himself. His men must have started already.

At that moment, a cavalryman came into view, riding hard along the outside of the village palisade towards the Sack's main gate. Lucius ran along the battlements to intercept him.

As the trooper crossed the causeway through the outer ditches, Lucius called from above the gate.

'Trooper Gallus! What's so urgent?'

The horsemen pulled up, confused, but quickly came to himself.

'Tribunus, sir. It's the Praefectus. He's returned.'

Euphoria washed over Lucius. 'Where is he?' Why wasn't Cai here himself?

'He's injured, sir. They've taken him to Alyn's home. It was her who ordered...asked me to fetch the medicus.'

'On your way then, Gallus. Quick as you can.'

The trooper kicked his horse into a trot, heading towards the hospital in the north of the fort.

'That damned Greek had better be sober,' Lucius hissed to himself. He ran along the fort's battlements. Bemused men pressed themselves against the parapet to allow their Tribunus to pass. He careered down the steps next to the western gate, not seeing the salutes of the sentries as he ran through the gateway and across the wooden walkway bridging the two ditches separating fort and village.

He was greeted by a scene of chaos in its main street. The inhabitants, whose homes and businesses opened out to its paved surface, were now spilling out onto the thoroughfare and arguments had broken out with the soldiers, who had apparently now communicated his order.

Lucius ducked quickly down a narrow passageway between two long dwellings and into the alleyway at their rear. He weaved between buildings until finally reaching the lane leading to Alyn's home.

A familiar sight came into view: Adela, Cai's horse. A trooper was removing her saddle as Lucius took in the sight of the bedraggled and exhausted state of the mare. He stroked her neck.

'You've been through it. Haven't you girl?' he said.

'Me and Gallus was dismantling the gyrus as ordered, sir,' said the trooper, 'when we heard this ruckus. We spotted some of the folks from the village standing around a horse. I could tell a mile off it was Adela here, I'd know her colouring anywhere. At first we thought she was riderless. But when we ran over we could see the Praefectus being held up by that big lump of a smith. The Praefectus kept asking to be brought here. Almost delirious like.'

'Very good, trooper. Take this lady to her stable and get her fed and cleaned up.' Without waiting for a response, Lucius knocked on the door. It was flung open by an excited Beren.

'Tribunus Lucius, he's back,' Beren grabbed Lucius by the hand, dragging him through the doorway.

'So I've heard.'

'Lucius! Is Castellanos with you?' Alyn said as she appeared from behind the screen that gave her sleeping cot privacy. It was the first time she'd used his given name in all of the years he had known her and he was slightly taken aback. Her Latin was better than some of his own troopers.

'No, but he won't be far behind me. How is he?' Lucius asked, as he crossed the room.

'He sleeps. But I fear it's more than just exhaustion.'

Lucius knelt by the cot's side. His friend lay propped up, his legs covered by a blanket. Cai's arms and torso were uncovered and were laced by dozens of cuts and bruises. But he was immediately drawn to the deep gash in his side.

'I cut away his tunic,' Alyn said, her voice anxious, 'it looks like the wound has been kept clean. But there's a red swelling around it and I fear his blood may be poisoned. He has no temperature yet, which I pray is a good sign.'

Alyn leant over the cot, continuing what she had been doing before Lucius arrived, cleaning the filth and encrusted blood from Cai's face. As the damp cloth touched his forehead, his eyelids fluttered open. It took a moment for his eyes to focus, but soon looked directly into Alyn's. He smiled weakly.

'Hello, my love,' Cai whispered. Alyn harrumphed, but as she turned away Lucius could see the tears that glistened in her eyes.

'So you've decided to stay in the land of the living, brother?' Lucius said. Cai turned at the sound of his friend's voice.

'Lucius,' he croaked. His voice became strident. 'I must tell you of what we saw.' Cai tried to raise himself, Alyn's firm hand on his shoulder preventing him.

'Still yourself,' Alyn said. 'You'll open your wound further.'

'All is well, brother. Trooper Hrindenus returned some hours ago. He told us all about your nighttime adventure at the Novantae settlement. So we've kicked over a large hornet's nest. But thanks to you we're now preparing for their sting.'

'Hrindenus? Good. Who else has returned?'

'None yet. But there's time,' Lucius said. Cai closed his eyes.

'Avitius—' Cai saw Beren standing behind Lucius. Almost imperceptibly he shook his head.

There was a double rap at the door and it swung open. The doorway was filled by the tall frame of Castellanos, the physician.

'I seem to have spent rather a lot of time, recently, tending to the sick here,' he said. Without invitation, the medicus bustled in, making his way to Alyn's now crowded cot.

Lucius backed away, making room, gently pulling Beren with him. Alyn remained.

'Can we have more light in here?' Castellanos asked.

Alyn turned to her son. 'Beren, bring a taper from the fire please. Then you will attend to your evening chores.' The boy grumbled but moved quickly. Shortly after Alyn had lit two more oil lamps, holding one low for Castellanos to see by.

'I'll need to prod you a bit, Praefectus,' he said. 'It'll hurt like Hades, but it's necessary. Are you ready?' Cai nodded and immediately groaned as Castellanos explored the wound. The medicus making noncommittal sounds. Next, he lowered his head to the gash, sniffing it with his long nose, like a hound in search of its master's kill. Finally he held the palm of his hand against Cai's forehead.

'Good.' The Greek stood tall, stretching his back. 'Well, the wound seems clean enough, it doesn't smell foul, but only time will tell if the blood is tainted. Whether an ague sets in, we'll find out in a few hours.' Cai nodded his thanks.

'I need to stitch it up and apply a poultice. I can give you some juice of the poppy to help with the pain.'

'No poppy,' Cai croaked.

Castellanos shook his head. 'So be it.' The medicus searched the contents of the dark wooden box he had brought with him, retrieving his needles and some gut. Cai turned his head away.

'Would it help to have an arm to grip onto, brother?' Lucius asked. Cai gave a brisk, single nod. Lucius moved to his friend's side and they clasped each other's arm.

'Right then. Here we go,' Castellanos said. Cai hissed as the physician squeezed the two sides of the gash together between finger and thumb, swiftly making the first pass of the needle. Cai hissed, gripping hard to Lucius's arm. Castellanos worked quickly and soon had the wound closed and dressed.

'Are you sure you won't take some poppy? It'll help you sleep, which you need.' Cai shook his head firmly.

'I'll prepare a drink of cloves; it will help.' Alyn moved away from the bedside for the first time since the medicus had arrived. Lucius followed, speaking quietly.

'We must abandon the village, Alyn. I've given orders to pull down every building. I'll instruct the men to leave your home until morning, but you must leave then.' Alyn looked at Lucius, tears brimmed in her eyes, but she said nothing. 'All women, children and the old, will be found room in the barracks. You must gather what food and valuables you can carry.'

Finally she nodded. 'I'll bring what herbs I have. Castellanos may welcome my help, in the coming days.'

'Perhaps,' Lucius said, 'but the sights you'll see will cause you much grief.

'We women must become accustomed to grief, Lucius.' Her words were without rancour.

'You must rest now,' Alyn told Cai once he had taken the cloves.

Castellanos cleared his throat. 'Yes, perhaps we should move you to the hospital.'

'No. I'll be fine here.' Cai's voice was still strained, but a little stronger, Lucius thought.

'Well, we need you back as soon as you are able, brother. Your presence will lift the men.' Lucius pretended not to notice the look Alyn gave him.

'I'll be back. I just need a night's rest.'

'Well, you're in good hands my friend, so I will let you sleep.' Lucius turned to the Greek. 'Are you finished, Castellanos? I'd like to talk to you about the preparations for the wounded.'

'I'll return later to check on the dressing,' the medicus said, as he and Lucius left.

For the first time since his return, Alyn was alone with Cai. Sitting gently on the side of the cot, she slowly caressed his cheek.

'You have returned to me,' she whispered.

Cai smiled up at her. 'I told you I would, didn't I?'

'Yes. And now you must rest.' She continued to gently stroke his cheek, until, despite the pain of his wound, he drifted into a warm sleep.

48

The five senior officers crowded around the mound of sand at the centre of the principia's atrium. Facilis and Nepos stood on either side of Lucius, their stalwart presence reassuring. The other two Lucius knew a little, having collaborated with their cohort over recent years.

Tribunus Salvius of the First Hispana was a grizzled veteran who had transferred from the Twentieth Legion for the promotion. His short cropped grey hair and lean physique gave him an air of competence. Salvius had accepted Lucius's leadership, in part because of his social status, but also his ten years of experience in the tribunate.

The final member of the party was his First Spear, Pudens, he came with a fierce reputation, both as a fighter and disciplinarian.

Lucius had sketched a map in the sand. The columned walkway that surrounded the atrium was still in darkness, but the early morning light was sufficient in the open area to see it clearly enough without the aid of a lamp.

'Let's go over the plan one more time,' Lucius said. He borrowed Facilis's vine stick to use as a pointer. 'The Nervana will defend the ground from the edge of the stream that flows past the Sack's east facing ramparts, anchoring its flank against the water's steep bank. From there its centuries will be formed up in three ranks, covering the ground as far as the road that approaches the village main gate.' Lucius prodded with the vine stick before handing it to Salvius to continue.

'The Hispana's centuries,' he said, 'will join the Nervana at that point, then arch around the village. Our flank will butt against the southwest corner of the Sack's outer ditch.' Salvius pinched his nose in thought, looking long at the patch of sand. 'Are we not exposing the Hispana's flank to too great a risk? Will your little tricks be sufficient to slow the enemy?' He looked pointedly at Facilis.

'They are strong, sir,' Pudens interjected, upon seeing Facilis bristle. His Latin was accented but precise. 'I walked them myself, before last-light. In combination with the slingers on battlements they are a formidable barrier. But may I make one suggestion?' He looked at Lucius who nodded. 'Perhaps we could redeploy one of the scorpions to the southwest turret, instead of both being over the gateway. It could still support any assault on the southern ramparts, but also assist the Hispana's flank if it comes under pressure.'

Lucius nodded. 'A good suggestion. Can you see it done, First Spear?' he said to Facilis.

'Aye, sir. The Novantae and their friends are in for a nasty surprise. After a bit of gentle persuasion the village smith has been churning out caltrops. The lads have already sown so many in the long grass there's barely a piece of clear ground for a field mouse to stand on. If they get through those, the lilies await them.'

Lucius smiled to himself. Salvius was nervous about his flank. Recognising this too, Facilis, in his colourful way, had made the defences sound impregnable. But they were not.

'Our lines will be under continual pressure.' Nepos's gravelly voice was sharp in the stillness of the early morning. 'The blue-faces only need to break through one part of the line and the whole defence will crumble.'

'There's a reserve century for each cohort, bolstered by a turma from the Hispana. Their role will be to react swiftly to shore up any weak points. Are you clear on the part you must play in this, Nepos?'

'Aye sir, with my Tungrians and the cavalry from the two cohorts, we'll keep the blue faces looking over their shoulders.'

'We're going to need you, brother,' Lucius said. Both men exchanged a look of understanding. 'My command post will be in the northwest turret. From there I'll have sight of most of our front.' Lucius placed a hand on Salvius's shoulder. 'I'll need a section from the reserve turma to act as messengers during the battle. These men must be able to retain and communicate orders verbally. They'll be crucial to our survival beyond the first day of engagement.'

'I'll handpick them myself,' Salvius said.

'That'd be appreciated, brother. Now gentlemen, if there's nothing further? Let's get about it. Make sure your officers understand the plan. They in turn must communicate it effectively to their own units. Our men must have hope to hold on to. They need to believe the twentieth and sixth are on their way and this isn't simply a doomed last stand.'

All five men held grim looks, but said nothing more.

'Marcus,' Lucius said, 'would you join me on an inspection of the defences?'

'Of course, sir,' Salvius said.

Lucius and Salvius rode through the north gate and across its six ditches. Lucius noted with satisfaction that all were lined with a tanglement of the thick thorn bushes so abundant in this land. They took the military road for a short distance, until they were flagged down by an Optio leading a working party.

'Take care from here, sirs'. There are lilies for a spear's throw, from this point.' Lucius looked closely, pleased he could barely see the depressions in the ground.

The two walked their horses along the edge of the hidden defences, towards the stream that would be the extreme of their right flank. It was narrow. A man taking a run at it could jump from one side to the other. But its banks were steep, perhaps the height of a trooper on horseback.

'I would like a bit of heavy rain to fill it,' Salvius said, 'but it's still a difficult obstacle to overcome.

At last some damned confidence, Salvius, Lucius thought. The two spent a while in discussion before returning along the front once more.

'Your man Pudens seems to know what he's about,' Lucius said.

The Tribunus of the Hispana made a rumbling noise at the back of his throat. 'I've found in the time he has served under me that Pudens is rarely wrong. Much to my annoyance on occasions.' Salvius lapsed into silence for a time. Lucius sensed something preyed on his mind.

'Speak, brother. This is the moment to get any concerns out in the open.'

Salvius's look of surprise told Lucius he had hit the mark. They were approaching a squad of men on foot, returning to the fort. Salvius halted his mount, turning in the saddle to face him. Lucius saw the warring emotions playing across his face. He kept his voice low as the men marched by.

'We will do what we must to stop our enemies here,' he said finally. 'But—' Salvius's horse became skittish and he leaned forward to pat its neck. When the animal was calmed he turned to Lucius once more. 'You have met them in battle before. If they assault in the numbers we fear, can we survive this?'

Lucius lifted his water canteen from the saddle horn, taking several long swallows, in part to give himself time to think. Salvius shook his head when Lucius offered the bottle.

'There's no doubting their courage,' Lucius said. 'The Novantae are fierce in battle, at times seeming driven to the point of madness.' He looked north along the old military road in the direction of the hill, now hidden from view by the rise. Remembering.

'If our enemies are led well,' Lucius continued, 'our position will eventually be overwhelmed. How long we can delay that ending will depend on the courage of our men. And how well *we* lead them.' Lucius looked pointedly at Salvius. 'If the blue-faces don't come today. If either the Twentieth or the Sixth left on the day our messengers arrived. *If* they arrived. By my estimate, we must hold out for four days. So we have a chance, brother.' His voice now became harder. 'But come what may, we *will* do our duty before the gods. If they demand our lives, then so be it.'

49

The sound of men shouting pulled at Cai's consciousness. His wound throbbed, but the pain was distant. The shouting became more urgent, jolting him awake, and in the faint morning light, he saw her.

Alyn lay next to him. Her long dark hair rested on her shoulder, some loose strands had fallen across her cheek. She exhaled the long slow breaths of sleep, her lips slightly parted. Her hips were covered by the same blanket that lay across him. Despite the pain of his wound he did not move for fear of waking her. He wanted this moment for himself.

His eyes moved down her body. She wore the same long green dress from the evening before and he watched as her chest slowly rose and fell, her arm draped across her waist. Her eyelids fluttered open.

His breath caught. Her soft, grey eyes watched him for an instant before a slow languid smile lit up her face. Alyn reached across the small space between them and gently stroked his face.

'Good morning,' she said. The words came as a whisper. He returned the smile.

'Good morning.'

Hearing the dryness in his voice, she rose and poured water from a jug set to the side. Cai rolled gingerly onto his back and lay staring at the wooden beams above. Alyn reappeared, placing a cup to his lips. He took long, grateful swallows. With the tips of her fingers, she gently wiped away a drop that escaped across his cheek.

Alyn lay down next to him once more, her head next to his, her lips brushing his ear.

'How do you feel?' she whispered, her warm breath sending a tremor across his body.

'Better,' he said, with a smile.

'Are you in pain?'

'Only a little,' he lied.

Cai felt her smile against his ear, before Alyn rose to stand at the side of the bed. She looked shyly down at him. By the gods, you're beautiful, he thought. He watched as she released the ties at her shoulders. The dress fell, momentarily delayed by the curve of her hips, until she finally stepped out of its folds. Alyn stood for an instant longer, their eyes meeting.

'Do you like what you see?' Her tone challenging.

'How could I not?' he replied.

Shivering slightly in the cool early morning air, she slipped quickly under the cover and lay against him. She rested her head on his chest, listening to his heart beat. For a time she did not move. Cai raised his free hand to stroke her long, silken hair. She raised her face to his, kissing him full on the lips.

Alyn shivered again, but this time not from the cold.

'Are you sure?' he said quietly, remembering Beren lay asleep on the other side of her home. In answer she kissed his neck and a gasp escaped his lips as he felt the light touch of her nails playing over his stomach. He moved his hand slowly down her side to the soft curve of her hip. Alyn pushed his arm back gently.

'Not yet,' she whispered, moving her caress from his stomach and along his thighs. Again playing her nails lightly across his skin, as she kissed his neck once more, before slowly over long agonising moments, she moved her lips down to his chest. His desire to take hold of her was unbearable. Finally, unexpectedly, Alyn slid her hips over his and he was inside her.

Their foreheads touched and hands interlaced above his head. After a short while her breath became husky and her body began to tremble. She whispered his name. He could no longer hold back.

Afterwards they lay together, legs entwined her head resting against his shoulder.

'Did I hurt you?' she asked.

'Only a little.' He laughed into her hair.

They slept for a while, until Cai was woken once more by shouts and the noise of hammering and breaking of wood.

'What's going on?' He asked.

'They're pulling the village down!'

He turned to her in surprise. 'Your home too?'

Alyn nodded. 'We're to take what little we can carry and move into the barracks.'

Cai wanted nothing more than to lie there in the warm bed, with this beautiful woman. But knew he could not.

'I must go,' he said, his voice full of regret. 'I have to see that my men are ready.'

'I know, my love. But you must eat first, you're still weak and who knows the next time you'll get the chance.' She squeezed him once more and stood. 'I'll clean and rebind your wound too.'

When Cai was dressed in his troos and a fresh tunic, which, he guessed, had once belonged to Adal from the way it hung loosely on him, he sat on the edge of the cot, wincing at the effort. Beren had risen and was chattering away excitedly.

'Will I be given a sword do you think, mam?'

'No, you will not. You're too young.'

'I'm not a child. I have ten summers now.'

'Your mam's right in this, Beren.' Cai appeared from behind the wicker screen.

'Cai!' Beren ran over to his friend, throwing his arms around his waist. Cai's face was caught between a grimace of pain and laughter at the boy's joy.

'Well, it's good to see you too, my friend.' Cai ruffled the boy's hair, which hung in wild tangles down his back. Kneeling, he looked directly into Beren's eyes.

'Your mam's right, young trooper. Besides, I have a special job for you.' The boy looked at Cai expectantly.

Cai had noticed his spatha laying next to the hearth. He'd assumed Barra had taken it as his prize. But the Novantae had surprised him once more by leaving the sword untouched. His pugio also still hung from his belt. Cai removed the dagger and its sheath and handed them to Beren, who took it with wide eyed wonder.

'You're not yet strong enough to wield a spatha,' Cai said, 'but I need you to help protect your mam if the time comes. Do you understand what I am asking, Beren?' The boy nodded solemnly, staring at the sharp blade, before sliding it back into its sheath and tucking it into his own belt. He looked at Cai, his young chest swelling with pride.

'Thank you, Cai.'.

Alyn and Cai looked at one another, struggling not to laugh at the boy's solemn acceptance of the duty.

'Well then,' Alyn said, 'two men of the Nervana must break their fast before attending to their duties.' She placed yesterday's bread and a slab of cheese on the table. 'The porridge will be ready shortly.'

The three sat around the small table. Alyn and Cai saying little, just responding to Beren's almost incessant questions and enjoying the simplicity of this rare time alone. But the noise from outside could not be entirely ignored. As the sun broke over the eastern edge of the village's palisade, light spilling through the open window of Alyn's home, Cai knew he couldn't linger.

He stood, a little shakily, taking hold of Alyn's hand. They both knew there was nothing more that needed to be said between them.

'I'll send men to help you move into the barracks.'

'No, I need only take a few things. Anything of value I'll bury beneath my apple trees.'

Cai nodded. 'If you have need of anything, send Beren to find me.' He placed a hand gently on her cheek and smiled. 'Thank you.'

'For what?'

'For rescuing an old soldier and giving him something to live for.' Tears filled her eyes, but without waiting for a response he turned to Beren. 'Make sure you look after your mam. The days ahead are going to be hard but we men of the Nervii are made of tough old leather.'

'Yes, sir.' Beren saluted smartly.

'Good man.'

Cai and Alyn shared one last, lingering look, before he turned and left her home.

Chaos greeted him. Most of the village was now little more than a great forest of tangled wood and thatch. The only other building still untouched was the forge, which bustled with activity. The burly smith shouted continuously at his apprentice, as the hapless lad ran back and forth continuously at his master's bidding. As he passed the forge's open doors, Cai saw a great heap of caltrops.

'Lucius *has* been busy.'

The iron points gleamed dully in the morning light. The four-pointed devices could be tossed into the long grass and one of the wicked barbs would always point skyward.

By the time Cai reached the fort's western gate he had begun to sweat. The pain in his side was aching appallingly. At first the sentries didn't recognise him in his dishevelled state.

'You alright, sir?'

'Fine,' Cai said, more irritably than he'd intended. He continued through the gateway, wincing as he was barged into by someone emerging from alongside the barrack blocks.

'Sorry, sir. I didn't see you.' It was one of the grooms, his face flushed red. It took a moment for his name to come to Cai.

'Lenius.' A sudden thought came to him. 'Where's my Adela?'

'She's in her stall, sir. At the back of your quarters. I cleaned and brushed her myself.' The boy was speaking without drawing a breath. 'She was in a frightful filthy state, but I soon got her sorted out. All nice and shiny now, and well fed.'

'Lend me your shoulder, Lenius. Let's go and see her.' The two walked along the pathway between the back of the barrack blocks and the turf ramparts of the western wall. As they reached her stall, Adela's blond-maned head appeared out of the open upper door. He patted her neck. Her coat shone, despite the cuts and abrasions.

'Hello girl. We've been through it, you and I,' Cai said, as he continued to pass long, slow strokes along her neck.

'You've done well, lad, my thanks for looking after her.' The boy flushed with pleasure.

'It was no bother, sir. We can't have our best horse not *looking* her best, can we?'

'Indeed, Lenius. Now help me along to the principia.' He patted Adela one more time.

Cai dismissed the groom at the entrance to the headquarters building. Trudging around its colonnaded walkway he spotted the pile of sand at the heart of the atrium.

'I thought that might be you, Praefectus.' Cai turned quickly at the sound of Lucius's voice and immediately regretted it, wincing at the jolt of pain in his side.

'Your wound is bleeding again, brother.' Cai looked down and saw red spots on his tunic. 'You should go see Castellanos and get that looked at again.'

Cai waved the words away. 'I've had enough of being prodded by that Greek scab-lifter.'

Cai gave Lucius a searching look. He clearly hadn't slept much in recent days.

'You look like shit, sir,' he said.

Lucius laughed heartily at the gall of his friend. 'Whereas you,

Praefectus, are fresh and raring to go, eh?' Cai smiled, nodding at the pile of sand.

'So is that the plan? Care to explain it to me, sir?'

'I will,' Lucius said. 'But let's get back to my office and find you a chair before you fall down.'

'It's a solid plan,' Cai was sitting opposite Lucius in his office. 'And it might even work, if ladies in the Sixth or Twentieth can get themselves out of their nice warm beds, then double time it up here.'

'Our survival depends on it,' Lucius said. 'If the gods are with us we should hold out for a few days. But beyond that?' He shrugged.

'I'll lead the reserve turma. The enemy will come hard at any weak point and—'

'You'll not be leading the reserve.' Lucius held up his hand to forestall the objections he could see about to tumble from his friend. 'You're in no fit state to ride a horse for long. Never mind staying in the saddle in the thick of it for a day, under the sun's heat.' He could still see the emotions warring across Cai's face.

'You'll lead the defence of the south and eastern ramparts,' Lucius said. 'We've prepared the ground in front of both, but in the end, they *will* reach our walls. They must be held, or our whole plan fails.'

Cai sat in sullen silence for a while, but he understood the wisdom of what Lucius asked.

'I have at least one piece of good news for you,' Lucius said.

Cai played along. 'Oh? And what would that be, sir?'

'Our old colleague Mascellus has presented himself for duty.'

'Ha! I hope he hasn't tried to get back into his chainmail. The last I saw him his belly hung low over the belt of his troos.' The news did cheer Cai. Mascellus had been one of his best.

Lucius laughed. 'It is rather a snug fit, but a few days sweating on the ramparts will see it loosen.'

Lucius could see his friend had reconciled himself, if grudgingly, to his unwanted role.

'Now get yourself off to the medicus, Praefectus. And that's an order.'

50

Cai spent the morning inspecting the defences. Outside of the ramparts, preparations were proceeding well. However, no attention had been paid to the fortification of the walls themselves. He sent parties of the civilian volunteers, led by the newly promoted Mascellus, to the two stream beds, with orders to gather fist-sized stones.

Next, he explored the armoury and was amazed to find a cache of ready-made lead sling balls of different weights and sizes. He had seen the damage the vicious, acorn shaped projectiles could do to a skull. There were even the little buggers with a single deep hole on one side that made a sound like an angry wasp when released. He doubted the Novantae had forgotten them.

In the early afternoon Cai looked down from above the porta praetoria. Parties of men moved back and forth across the causeway, some bent over under the weight of heavy sacks of stones.

'Get a move on you slackers,' Mascellus shouted. 'The more of these beauties we have, the more skulls of those sheep-humpers we can dent.'

Cai grinned. The old Decurion had slipped easily back into the ways of command. He pulled at the neck of his new chainmail shirt. The tunic Alyn had given him did not fully protect his skin from the metal links. He would have to go in search of a leather underjerkin as soon as time allowed.

Cai spun at the sound of a throat being cleared behind him. He was met by the salute of the Tungrian, Hrindenus.

'I was told to report to you, sir.'

'Hrindenus. So, it's true, you made it out of that damned forest in one piece. How are your injuries?'

The big man smirked. 'A bit better than yours, from what I've heard, sir.'

Cai snorted a laugh. 'Good. Were you told why I wanted you?'

'No, sir. Decurion Nepos just ordered me to double-time over here to see you.'

Cai turned to look over the battlements once more, Hrindenus moving to stand beside him.

'You'll be aware the Nervana's ala has lost its Vexillarius?'

'Aye, sir.' Hrindenus spoke quietly. 'I was sorry Avitius didn't make it. I liked him.'

'He was an insubordinate, cantankerous old bastard who drank too much.' Cai couldn't keep the fondness from his voice. 'Well, you're the new standard bearer, until I decide otherwise.'

Hrindenus stared open mouthed at Cai, until he remembered himself.

'Me, sir? But I'm a Tungrian. How can I be the Vexillarius in a Nervii unit?'

Cai grunted. 'Look around you. How many Nervii do you see? Avitius and I were amongst a shrinking group of those who came to Britannia from our tribal lands. Now the cohort is a mongrel bunch, serving the Emperor on the edge of the world.'

Hrindenus looked on the point of objecting again, but Cai cut him off. 'Go fetch your kit and bring it to the principia'

'The principia, sir? Shouldn't I be moving into the cavalry barracks?' He nodded to the rows of buildings immediately below them.

'You won't be joining the lads for a while. I've been given charge of the defence of these ramparts. I want you at my side day and night.'

'If I'm not to be astride my horse, sir, what will my duties be?' Hrindenus asked, bemused.

'I want you to be visible, Hrindenus,' Cai said. 'I want the Novantae to see the size and fierceness of the warriors who await them. You'll be my guardian when these helmet plumes make me the focus of attention for the enemy. Which they will. And finally, if it comes to it, you and the ala's standard will be the rallying point when the defence becomes desperate.'

The Tungrian grinned, still somewhat taken aback. 'My thanks, sir. I'll do all I can to be as good as Avitius.'

Cai guffawed. 'Tungrian, I expect you to do a damned sight better than that.'

The rest of the day passed in a blur of activity. Not long after sunset, Cai joined Lucius and Facilis in the northwest turret as the light was fading.

'Well, by the gods, the blue-faces appear to have given us an extra day,' Facilis said, in his usual cheerful manner, at odds with his face's perpetual fierce expression. 'Perhaps they'll give us another.'

Lucius stood with his hands clasped behind his back, looking north along the military road. A century marched in good order towards the fort, axes slung over their shoulders. Four horse-drawn carts stacked with timber lumbered in their wake.

'I'd give a year's pay to make it so, brother,' Lucius said. 'But our enemy knows now that we're onto them. They must act before our colleagues in the legions arrive to pull our arses out of the fire.'

'We're ready,' Cai spoke from behind the pair. 'Our defences are prepared and we have a plan. Let them come.' Lucius heard the testiness in his friend's voice.

'How's your wound, Praefectus?'

'Hurts like a bastard, thanks for asking, sir. It's just a scratch, that bloody Greek— what was that?'

A mournful, wavering sound, floated towards them on the evening breeze from the north. Then another arose from the west as if in answer.

'That,' Facilis said, 'is the sound of our enemy. It appears they've finally arrived.'

The sound grew in volume as more horns joined their sisters. The three officers watched as a turma of the Hispana appeared over the rise on the road, moving at a gallop. Lucius turned at a rumbling sound coming from the direction of the porta praetoria and saw another patrol crossing the stream, towards the fort's main gate. Thirty men and horses, blowing like they were riding for their lives.

'First Spear,' Lucius's voice sounded calmer than he felt. 'Send a messenger to Tribunus Salvius with my compliments and ask that he bring the Hispana, at double pace, to the agreed positions?'

'Yes, sir.'

'And First Spear, we'll need four centuries ready outside of the southern ditches. The Hispana may need support as they vacate their camp.' The mournful sound from the multiple horns gradually ceased, until only the one in the north remained. Then that too finally stilled.

'The Novantae have returned to their hill, by the sounds of it,'

Cai mused.

'It would appear the hunted have become the hunters, my friend,' Lucius said. 'It's us this time, penned in by overwhelming numbers and snared in a trap of our own making.' Despite the seriousness of their situation, Cai heard humour in his friend's voice.

'Why are you so cheerful?' he said.

Lucius didn't respond immediately. Instead, watched the thirty riders of the turma cross the causeway and pass through the northern gateway.

'I don't really know. Perhaps it's that the gods have finally taken notice and are playing with you and I.' Cai looked at this Roman, whom he loved as a brother, shaking his head in bewilderment.

'Have Alyn and the boy got themselves situated?' Lucius asked, changing the subject.

It was Cai's turn to laugh.

'I spoke to her for a little while this evening. It appears she's already ensconced herself in the hospital. I'm not sure who's in charge now, her or Castellanos. I don't think the place has ever looked so clean. Our wounded will be well cared for, I think.'

'I fear we'll be in great need of her services,' Lucius said. 'If she keeps that bloody Greek away from his wine jug, so much the better.'

'Beren wants to take a place on the parapet,' Cai said, his voice filled with pride. 'The Optio of one of the scorpion units sent him off with a flea in his ear. Something about asking too many bleeding questions.'

'A fine lad. There's no doubting who his father was, that is for sure.' Lucius placed his hand on Cai's shoulder. 'But I also see your guiding hand, brother.'

'Aye well, I don't know about that.'

'If we survive this,' Lucius said, 'I can finally return to my homeland for a time. I hope to see my brother. It's been too long.'

'Will you return to the cohort?' Cai asked.

The last of the riders entered the gate and Lucius turned to look at his friend.

'I know I haven't spoken to you further about this, there has been too little opportunity of late. But I just don't know yet myself and I suppose I won't until I find what awaits me.'

Both men turned at the sound of heavy footsteps ascending the turret's wooden stairway. Hrindenus appeared on the walkway and snapped a salute.

'Sirs, the patrols have reported the enemy have appeared in force approaching both from the north and west.' The big man paused to catch his breath. 'They've halted about two miles from here and appear to be making camp.'

'Thank you, Hrindenus,' Lucius said. 'Were they able to get a count of numbers?'

'It's not clear, sir, as much of the enemy's force was still concealed by the forest. But it would appear our estimate from the visit to their lake may prove to be wishful thinking.'

Hrindenus shifted his gaze to look beyond the two officers. Both turned to see what had distracted him. It took Cai a short time to pick out the group of four horsemen, lined up side by side, straddling the width of the military road. Even at a distance and in the fading light he recognised the long red hair of the big Novantae war leader, sitting tall on his white Roman horse.

51

'Tell me,' Cai asked, 'how does a Pannonian come to be serving in the Hispana at the arse end of the empire?' The light from the torches above the open gates gave Puden's eyes a sunken, almost feral appearance.

'If we survive the coming days, I'll gladly stand you a jug of wine and tell you all about it.' The words were spoken without rancour, but Cai sensed he had touched a tender spot.

'Fair enough. But you won't be putting your hand into your money bag when you're in the Sack's officer's mess, let me tell you.'

All across their front, half of the men were standing-to, whilst the others rested or ate cold rations. Fires had been forbidden. A changeover would take place at the end of each watch. Cai knew it would be tiring for the men, but hoped they would get at least some sleep.

A rumble of massed horses sounded in the darkness, to their fore. Soon afterwards shouts and jeers came from across the stream.

'Roman slaves?' Pudens said, 'Did I hear that right?'

'Someone else called me that recently,' Cai said. 'If it's what they believe, so be it. Especially if they are convinced that slaves will not put up much of a fight.'

The horsemen moved on. Shortly afterwards warcries and insults could be heard to the north as the horsemen progressed around the edge of the auxiliary's perimeter.

'Our enemies appear determined to keep us from sleep this night,' the Pannonian said.

'Most men, I've found, don't sleep the night before a battle,' Cai said. 'At least not well. So it's all the same. It might unnerve a few of the lads though.'

Pudens cleared his throat. 'My Tribunus,' he said, 'is concerned about our left flank. He feels we may be putting too much faith in our clever traps.'

'His worries are understandable. But there's nothing for it. We have to concentrate our main strength somewhere, or face being overwhelmed everywhere.' Cai thought he had managed to keep the frustration from his voice. 'Besides, don't forget my lads will also be covering the open ground from the ramparts. You have my word, brother. We'll do all we can to support the Hispana when the time comes.'

'Thank you. I know you will. And you're right. Our plan is made, we've rolled the dice. Now we must see how they land.' Pudens held out his arm to Cai, who clasped it firmly.

'May Jupiter, best and greatest, guide our sword arms in the coming days.' With that said, the Hispana's First Spear walked away into the darkness towards his cohort's lines.

Shit, that's all we need, a jumpy Tribunus. Cai watched Pudens's retreating back until it was swallowed by the night. He hoped the Hispana's First Spear would be able to give his commander some backbone, as he was indeed correct. The left flank was the weakest point. He expected it would get the enemy's full attention come morning. All Cai could do was to make the cost to the enemy a high one. But the Hispana must play their part well. Shaking his head he strode back into the fort.

'Close the gates.'

'Praefectus, sir.' Mascellus's voice was instantly recognisable and in the gloom of the fort's interior Cai saw the veteran sitting with a group of men on the covered walkway of one of the cavalry barracks blocks. 'Care to join us for a bite to eat, sir? The bread is freshly collected from the oven. Although the cheese is a bit past its best.'

Cai was about to refuse. He needed to speak to Lucius. But he also guessed the old Decurion's intent, and besides, he *was* hungry and who knew when he would get the chance to eat again. Walking over, he saw the group was a mixture of retired veterans, returned to duty, and some of the civilian men from the village. Two or three looked little more than boys.

'My thanks, Mascellus,' Cai said, 'that would be most welcome.'

'I was just telling the lads here about the time we had our last proper scrap with the Novantae.' Mascellus tore off a chunk of bread and handed it to Cai, who took a bite. As he chewed he had the opportunity to look the men over. In the veterans' demeanour he saw the usual mix of emotions: some trepidation at the coming day, but mainly calm acceptance. But amongst the civilians he sensed fear. Nodding his thanks to Mascellus at a proffered canteen of water, he took a long swallow.

'Well,' Cai said, 'there's no doubting their fierceness and courage. They caused us a good deal of trouble at their hill, I can tell you.' He watched as some of the civilians looked at one another, the fear in their eyes now plain to see. 'But. That same fierceness is their greatest weakness. They are reckless, their courage blinds them to all else and was their undoing that day. It always will be, when they come up against a disciplined formation of the Emperor's army.'

He now pointed at each of the civilians with the hand that still held the hunk of tbread. 'But you men are lucky. You have with you a group of warriors of the Nervii, whose bravery and skill in battle is unmatched. Watch what they do and listen to what they tell you. That is how you will get through this. You and your families.' This time he saw some of them look meaningfully at one another. He hoped his words had helped. Cai nodded at Mascellus, who grinned back. 'My thanks for the food.' Cai resumed his walk through the fort, in search of Lucius.

He found him in the northwest turret. Although at first, as he reached the top of the inner steps, he couldn't see him in the darkness.

'Are you there, sir?'

'Over here,' Lucius said.

Cai felt his way along the parapet until he could discern Lucius's outline, hunched against the turret's edge. The night sky was clear and the stars stood out in the near total darkness. But the lights that drew Cai's attention were the campfires of the tribes. They encircled the Sack from the north all the way around their western side, finally disappearing amongst the trees to the south. The east remained eerily in total blackness.

'There's a lot of them, aren't there?' Cai said.

'One or two.'

Cai hawked and spat over the tower's edge into the ditch below.

'Barra, the Novantae who saved my arse, is cool headed. If his words hold enough weight with the Damnonii and Selgovae then I think we're really in for a shitstorm, brother.' Cai moved so he too could lean against the turret's edge, their shoulders almost touching. 'But. I've also seen the Novantae and Damnonii close up.

There seems little love between their peoples. The Damnonii are fanatics in battle, right enough. But I think once the battle commences they will be almost impossible to control. We must take advantage of that when the chance arises.'

In the distance a cacophony of sound began to gradually rise.

'It seems our enemies are trying to drink themselves into new heights of bravery,' Lucius said. 'Let's just hope they find oblivion instead.'

For a time both men gazed at the massed fires, as the increasingly chaotic noise washed over them.

'I'm worried about Salvius.' Cai saw Lucius's silhouette turn to face him

'How so?'

Cai relayed his discussion with Pudens.

'Well, he'd better damn well hold that left flank,' Lucius said, 'or we'll very quickly find ourselves penned inside this fort, like cattle. Those that make it.'

'Pudens strikes me as a good man,' Cai said, 'if a bit morose.'

Cai felt Lucius's hand clasp his shoulder. 'I expect neither of us will be able to rest, so why don't you go and visit that woman of yours? I doubt there will be time once the hard fighting starts.'

'Aye, perhaps you're right,' Cai said, feeling a little awkward. 'What will you do?'

'Oh, I think I might visit with Salvius one more time. Let me see if I can stiffen the backbone of our colleague.'

Cai entered the hospital. Soft lamplight gave just enough illumination to see his way. The Greek had been busy, cramming more beds into the available space, barely allowing room for an orderly to shuffle between them. As his eyes adjusted to the gloom he made out what looked like a bundle of cloth lying in a cot in the far corner. He moved carefully, conscious of the noise his hobnails made on the wooden floor.

The bundle of clothes rose from the bed at the sound. It was Alyn. Her long dark hair hung messily over her face.

'Hello my love,' she whispered. Cai noticed the sleeping figure of Beren next to her in the cot. She moved carefully, so as not to awaken her son. Wrapping her arms around Cai's neck she kissed him firmly on the lips. Cai held her tightly. Their kiss lingered, until finally she let her head rest against his shoulder.

'I'm sorry,' he said. 'I didn't mean to wake you.'

'You didn't. Sleep wouldn't come. I was just listening to the breathing of my son, wondering how many more times I would do so.' Before Cai could speak, she placed her fingers across his lips. 'Cai, I know what war is and you cannot make promises. Nor would I want you to. We are in the hands of the gods.'

She led him to the cot next to Beren's and they lay together entwined in each other's arms. For a time they spoke in whispered words to one another, Cai still filled with wonder that this beautiful woman desired him. Eventually they simply lay quietly in the peace of the room and Alyn drifted into sleep, Cai watching over her. With his arm wrapped around her, he felt the steady rise and fall of her chest, letting the warmth of her body revive him.

Finally, knowing he must go, he arose carefully and walked quietly from the room. Turning one final time at the doorway, he looked upon her, a bundle in the corner once more.

Out in the open air, Cai could hear the wild sounds of the tribal revelry. He was about to head back to the ramparts, but a hint of movement stopped him. Someone was sitting in near darkness on the barracks walkway, across from the hospital entrance.

'Good evening, Praefectus.' It was Castellanos.

'Medicus,' Cai returned. The Greek had been stationed at the Sack for two or three years now, but Cai didn't know him well. He thought Castellanos liked a jug of wine overly much, although there was no doubting his skills. 'Sleep hasn't found you either, I see.'

'I sleep little these days. You would think, having seen the results of battle on men's bodies so many times before, I would be used to it by now.'

'I wasn't aware you'd seen active service before,' Cai said. Castellanos chuckled quietly at the surprise in Cai's voice.

'Ah yes. I was a junior medicus during the bloody Judean campaign, on the staff of our great General, Quintus Lollius Urbicus. Our Emperor liked Urbicus's handiwork so much he dispatched him to Britannia, to do his bloody work here too. I and a number of my colleagues were part of a small group he brought with him. Well, at least he liked to give his men the best medical care, those that survived, that is.' Castellanos took a long draw of liquid from a skin. The Greek noticed Cai's look of concern and laughed once more.

'Don't worry, Praefectus, it's only water. But it was indeed the grape that was my undoing in the end. You see, I'd swapped one murderous campaign for another in this god's awful land and the nightmares that followed me from Judea would not let me sleep. So I took to having a drink or two to help ease things. Which, I'm sure you know, is not really conducive to good discipline. So, to cut a long tale short, I was insubordinate one time too many and found myself left behind when the great Urbicus finally left these shores.'

'May I?' Cai took the skin from the Greek, taking several swallows. Nodding his thanks as he handed it back.

'Any who've seen so much death are changed by it,' Cai said. 'But I think when you're charged with saving the lives of men, men who are often grievously wounded, you must fail more often than you succeed. Which in many ways must be harder than for someone like me, whose purpose is to kill.'

'Perhaps.' The medicus spoke almost imperceptibly.

'The hospital is in a fine state of readiness,' Cai said, changing the subject. 'Is there anything you need?'

'It's certainly never been cleaner. Your lady has seen to that. She's been bossing my orderlies around like a newly promoted Centurion.'

Cai smiled. 'Yes, that sounds like her. I suspect she'll be an asset to you, brother. In the days ahead.'

'Of that, there is no doubt.' Castellanos stood and Cai took it as the signal the conversation was over. He turned to leave.

'Thank you,' Castellanos said. Cai stopped, turning back.

'For what?'

'For calling me brother.'

52

As the first hints of light began to show in the east the sounds from the camps of the tribes began to slacken, gradually falling to near silence. Cai stood in position over the portus praetoria once more, watching as the lights of the distant campfires began to wink out, one by one.

'I hope the bastard's have thick heads.' Hrindenus appeared at Cai's side. He wondered, not for the first time, how such a big man could move around unheard.

'Do you have the Nervana's standard, Vexillarius?'

'Aye, sir. I've left it by the gate ready to be fetched.'

Cai looked at the sky. It would be a cloudless morning. 'A good day for slingers I think.'

'And their bowmen, sir.'

'Cheerful bastard, aren't you, Vexillarius? Just like the previous—'

The low, undulating sound of a horn blew its mournful call from the north, quickly picked up by others from the south and west.

'Stand to!' Cai bellowed, hearing his command relayed throughout the fort and beyond. There was a cacophony of noise as men strapped on sword belts, gathered their shields and spears and donned helmets. Centurions' and Optios' could be heard chivvying tired men into action. But both cohorts were soon in position. They formed a solid, curving barrier of shields, three ranks deep, on the ground outside the Sack.

The military road south was now discernable as it disappeared on its journey to the Wall and the lands of the Carvetti beyond. The route crossed a ridge not more than a half a mile from the fort and it was there the first of the enemy appeared.

Cai watched as dark shapes emerged. They came in ones and twos at first, but quickly coalesced into a single mass. The horns, which had stopped their call briefly, started up once more, as if a great beast had sighted its prey. The horde moved slowly from the ridge and onto the level ground of the floodplain that ended atr the stream, a short distance from the Sack's ditches.

Lenius, the groom, appeared, panting at Cai's side. He snapped off a smart salute. 'Sir, the Tribunus said to tell you the enemy has appeared to the north and west.'

'Thank you, lad. Return to the Tribunus and inform him a large enemy force has appeared to our south, but not yet from the east.'

The tribesmen progressed across the open ground, slowly separating into numerous groups, both walking and mounted. Their horsemen moved with no sense of formation, many mixed in with those on foot. All the while the horns continued their low, wavering music, interspersed by the chaotic chants of the warriors.

With each passing minute, the improving morning light revealed more of the field and the faces of their enemy.

'So many,' Cai said.

'It's those mad Damnonii bastards.' Hrindenus's deep voice grumbled at Cai's side. It took his older eyes a moment longer to pick out the dark tattoos, the swirling designs covering bared chests and, in many cases, their faces and shaven scalps. The barbarians from north of the empire's new wall looked fearsome. A few individuals scampered ahead, yelling unintelligible challenges at the defenders.

'Eager fuckers, aren't they?' Hrindenus said, 'Let's see how keen they are once they've sobered up.'

Cai thought he could now distinguish some of their leaders. One in particular caught his eye. Surrounded by his hearth warriors, even on his grey pony he didn't look big, unlike most chieftains. He was skinny, a long black beard hanging straight and lank over his ill-fitting chainmail shirt. He wore a helmet that shone silver and from Cai's position it looked very familiar.

'Well, I'm having that back,' Cai said.

'Sir?' Hrindenus said, puzzled.

'Never mind.'

Cai slid his bronze ceremonial helmet onto his head, its three white swan's feathers standing proud. He hoped he wouldn't lose it; it was his most valuable possession. The cumbersome face plate was still wrapped by its cloth in his quarters.

The skinny chieftain held his arm aloft, sword gripped in his fist. Gradually the horde came to a halt just out of bowshot range, on the far side of the stream.

Cai turned his gaze west beyond the remains of the village. More of the enemy were emerging out of the early morning mist that had formed on the higher ground like a ghostly apparition. Looking now at his men along the parapet, he was pleased to see most held looks of determination.

'It's time to play your part, Vexillarius,' Cai said.

'Yes, sir.' Hrindenus turned to leave.

'Remember. I want to feel the hairs on the back of my neck stand on end.'

It was time to prod the hornets' nest once again, he thought, and filled his lungs.

'Scorpios, prepare!'

Even in the din created by their enemy he heard the rapid metallic clicking sound as the torsion arms of the bolt throwers were rachetted.

'Open the gates.' Cai shouted. Hearing the creak of the heavy oak doors he turned to look over the causeway, watching as Hrindenus marched smartly along its narrow length. The Nervana's standard rested against his shoulder, with its white horse on a black background, a silver vertical lance to the animal's front and rear. The Tungrian came to a halt midway along the outer ditches.

'Scorpios. When I give the order I want you to skewer that skinny, bearded bastard on the grey horse. The first team to do it gets a jug of wine on me.' He heard a cheer go up, not just from the two crews but from the men standing along the fort's southern wall.

The men on the ramparts watched in awe as Hrindenus drew his spatha. He held it in his right hand and the standard in the left. Slowly he raised both aloft and let out a fearsome warcry directed at the waiting tribesmen. A wave of noise broke from the Damnonii, who screamed back their anger at this challenge from a lone warrior.

'Scorpios, release!'

The aimers of both crews pulled the retaining levers and the deadly bolts flew, almost unseen, towards their target. The first overshot the Damnonii chief, passing through the skull of a horseman behind, bone and brain spraying those nearby. The second punched into the chest of the chief's horse. The skinny warrior was thrown backwards as his mount collapsed onto its haunches.

It was unlikely the chief was dead. But that, combined with Hrindenus's challenge, had the desired effect. A great tumult of noise broke from the massed Damnonii, who, by an unspoken command, charged towards their antagonists.

'Right, in you come, Vexillarius!' Cai shouted down to the Tungrian. Hrindenus began to walk slowly backwards, still holding the standard and sword in the air. Taunting.

'Gate section, once he's inside, close them up.'

Many Damnonii horsemen had overtaken those on foot and were already nearing the bank of the stream. They had taken the bait. Charging headlong towards the Sack's entrance, they ignored the ranks of the Hispana to their left.

'Mascellus, ready your slingers!' Cai shouted, but he knew the old veteran had been awaiting this order.

'Slingers!' Mascellus's voice carried along the parapet. 'Prepare your volley.'

The men, lined up at intervals along the parapet, placed a lead shot into their strip of leather and began to spin them rapidly over their heads, accompanied by the brisk metallic rattle as the scorpios were reloaded. Cai nodded to Mascellus.

'Slingers. Release!' the old veteran yelled, his voice carrying along the parapet.

A dark wave of lead flew, quickly becoming invisible to the eye. But the sound was startling, like a swarm of insects. An instant later, they struck.

Some of the metal projectiles splashed harmlessly into the waters of the stream; most did not. They hit the unprotected bodies of the riders or their horses. Some were thrown from their mounts. One horse crumpled, its legs collapsed beneath it, tossing its unfortunate rider into the shallow stream bed. The scorpios continued to send volley after volley into the mass, now impossible to miss. Often the bolts claimed more than a single victim. One, shot from the east turret, passed through the top of the skull of a mounted warrior, before pinning another riding behind to his saddle after passing through his groin.

Tortured sounds of terrified horses rent the air. They began to fall, throwing riders, rolling and thrashing in an attempt to escape the pain. The caltrops were doing their deadly work. Riders to the rear began to pull up in confusion. Some rode up the stream bed, seeking a way around the injured and dying horses.

The screaming horde of men on foot were catching up with the floundering horsemen. Some tried to force their way through panicked animals, adding to the mayhem. Others, in their battle frenzy, flowed around the edges of the living barrier, oblivious to the danger hidden in the long grass. All the while, lead slingshot from Mascellus's men took a bloody toll.

Cai watched in grim satisfaction, as the ranks of the Hispana's flank stood firm and untouched, anchored against the Sack's outer ditch. He could no longer hear the reloading clink of the scorpions. The cacophony of noise from below was now too great. But they continued to spit their bolts into the helpless cavalry.

The screams of agony renewed as the warriors on foot reached the hidden caltrops. Men fell, mewling, as unprotected feet were pierced through by the wickedly sharp iron points.

But the press of the Damnonii behind, unaware of the hidden threat, continued to push men forward over the ground the Nervana had prepared for them. Mascellus and his men were relentless, as volley after volley of lead projectiles struck the enemy, whose front lines had become compacted.

Nevertheless, it was inevitable that the first warriors finally got clear of the tall grass and its hidden menace. But the red mist of their hatred and blind desire to finally engage with their enemy meant most did not see the depressions in the ground to the fore of the ditches.

'They really are mad,' Hrindenus said, as the Damnonii came on.

An instant later the legs of some vanished into the ground, accompanied by more shrieks of agony as limbs were shattered or impaled on the points of the wooden stakes hidden below. The lilies caused terror and panic in the leading groups as the unrelenting pressure from behind drove them, helplessly, onto the deadly traps.

The morning light had brightened. The floodplain beyond the stream could now be clearly seen. His heart sank. Dark, tattooed men continued to flow over the distant ridge in seemingly unending numbers.

53

Lucius observed the battleground, casting his sight from south to north. The Novantae and their Selgovae allies had halted some distance from the leading ranks of the auxiliaries. The tribes were making a tumultuous din. Some warriors cavorted, making a great show in front of their fellows, but they did not advance. The assault on the fort's southern defences had been underway for some time, but still the enemy here hadn't moved.

'What are they waiting for?' Lucius said, not for the first time, as he struck the parapet with his fist.

When the tribes had first emerged from the mist, Lucius had thought they were organised into irregularly sized divisions. But eventually it became apparent they were most likely family groups. The blue-faces liked to fight and die alongside their fathers, sons, brothers. The only exception were their horsemen. They were amassed to the rear of the main force.

Well. Someone understands the value of cavalry, Lucius thought.

His own men were a marked contrast to their enemy. They stood rock steady in their centuries, staring back at their enemy in eerie silence. The reserves, the turma from the Hispana, were in place, standing by their mounts just outside of the fort's northern causeway, awaiting his orders.

'What have I missed?'

He heard footsteps behind him.

'Tribunus, sir.' Lucius turned to see the groom, Lenius, making his salute.

'Report.'

'Sir,' the boy said, gasping for air. 'The Praefectus reports the enemy have taken heavy losses.' He took another deep breath. 'But have now reached the gate.'

'Thank you, Lenius.' Lucius saw the lad flush with pride. 'Inform the Praefectus that we're still awaiting the enemy here to make their move.' He watched the groom as he disappeared down the turret steps, taking them two at a time. He shook his head. So much like his brother Marcus once was. Full of boyish enthusiasm. He pushed the memory away.

'What are they waiting for, an invitation?' Lucius said into the empty air. He didn't have to wait much longer for his question to be answered.

He whipped his head to the east at an eruption of sound. Warriors were emerging from the steep banks of the stream and were tearing into the side of the flanking century. The clash of steel and the battlecries of men carried even above the din of the battle below the southern ramparts.

The Centurion had reacted, attempting to wheel his men to face the threat.

'Too late,' Lucius said to himself, as a seemingly endless flood of the blue-faces clambered into view.

Lucius turned to the nearest trooper. 'Get down to the reserve turma. Tell their Decurion to engage the enemy emerging from the stream.' The messenger saluted and began to run towards the turret steps. 'No, wait.' Lucius called. The turma had already mounted and was on the move. 'Good man.' Their commander had seen the danger and was getting his men into the fight.

'Single file!' The order carried to Lucius. The turma quickly resolved into one line and advanced at a canter. In short moments the thirty horsemen reached the fight. As they approached the rear of the century, now battling desperately for its survival, the Decurion began to wheel away. The manoeuvre was repeated, one at a time by his men. At the extreme point of the turn the Decurion threw his javelin, emulated in quick succession by those behind. The short spears looped over the heads of the Nervana's embattled flanking century. For a second they seemed to slow at the top of their arcs before plunging towards the enemy emerging from the stream. The effect was immediate. Most found a victim as the spearpoints penetrated unarmoured bodies. Agonised screams of men mingled with those assaulting the shields of the auxiliaries. Some were thrown back into the stream bed by the impact of the javelins, to be trampled or drowned in its waters.

Lucius watched as the turma wheeled once more. The Decurion drew his spatha, its long blade glinting in the light of the rising sun, the motion emulated by his men. A single word burst from thirty throats.

'Hispana!'

The sound became an incoherent howl as the unit broke into a charge, the ground rumbling as great clods of dirt were thrown into the air.

An instant before the impact of the charge, Lucius turned reflexively to a wall of sound that burst from the main Novantae horde. They were finally on the move, one mass heaving across the ground.

Warriors ran, heedless of those around them, roars of hatred escaping gaping mouths. There was no order to it. The Novantae and their Selgovae allies ran as if in competition to reach the enemy lines first. Lucius's men stood steady, waiting. Optio's moved along the rear of each century, the junior officers ensuring all was ready.

The cohort's slingers were in action on the Sack's southern ramparts, so the charging tribesmen would be unimpeded for a time. But not for long.

The fort's immediate surroundings had, many years since, been cleared of woodland. To the east and south the land was farmed by the cohort, but to the north and west it had been left fallow, dense scrub grass growing to almost waist height in places. Each year Lucius had ordered it to be cleared for horse-feed. But not this year. That laxness now appeared to have been a gift from the gods.

The lead warriors, those that had been cavorting in front of their lines, were the first to reach the long grass that rippled gently in the morning breeze. Some merely broke ankles as a leading leg plunged into the concealed cavities. Others were not so lucky as feet, shins or thighs were impaled on the sharpened wooden stakes. But the effect was the same, whatever the harm.

The agonised sounds of these first, unfortunate men went unheard, so great was the tumult of sound as the main body followed, howling in their headlong assault.

Lucius stood transfixed as they plunged into the scrub. From his position it looked like a wave crashing against the rocks, as the leading ranks fell from sight. Some stumbled into the hidden pits whilst others were tripped by those already skewered by the barbs. This time the shrieks of agony could be heard across the battlefield.

Lucius turned his attention to the century that straddled the road and saw the Centurion's plume of Facilis bobbing as he gave the command. The front rank drew back their spears in readiness. An instant later forty javelins flew in an arc, plunging into the midst of the compacted Novantae. Men fell, dead and dying. A writhing mass, acting as a tortured barrier to those behind.

In frustration many chanced the long grass on either side of the road, where more of the deadly lilly pits awaited. The effect was the same.

A second volley followed swiftly. The trajectory, this time, was flat and direct. The spears flashed across the now shorter distance between the two forces. The result was calamitous for the Novantae as more bodies were added to the writhing, human rampart, upon the road's metalled surface.

The centuries on either side of the road joined the fight. Both sent a flight of spears into the unprotected side of the chaotic column. The road had become a killing ground. Dead and wounded to the fore stalling the advance. More warriors took their chances with the grassland, trying to gingerly pick their way across the overgrown field. Some, in one's and two's, reached the Nervana's solid line of shields, only to be quickly dispatched.

The lilly pits had done their job well. But Lucius knew it would be a short respite. The tribes would quickly learn and the real, grinding fight would begin.

54

The putrid stench of blood, guts and shit hung heavily in the air. Bodies carpeted the ground, most dead, but some still lived, trapped under the weight of the rapidly cooling flesh of their fellows. Many of the black carrion birds flapped hungrily upon this unexpected feast.

The Damnonii had reached the main gate on three occasions. Each assault was greeted by a withering hail of sling shot and hand flung stones. The enemy had been unprepared. None carried ladders, or any kind of ram and had been reduced to battering impotently against the heavy oak of the iron-bound gates. Finally, as the dead littered the base of the ramparts, their war horns had blown.

The tattooed warriors had withdrawn, followed by the jeers from the parapet. But the defenders had not gone unscathed. One of the retired veterans took an arrow through the cheek, but he would live. One unfortunate had his jaw broken, when a stone he had just thrown was returned from below. But thankfully, so far, no deaths.

As he had expected, Cai’s swan-feathered helm had attracted the attention of their bowmen. Hrindenus's close attention with his shield had twice saved him. But their good fortune could not last.

The Damnonii had regrouped. Only to turn their attention to the ranks of the Hispana. Time and again, throughout the remainder of the morning, they had assaulted the cohort’s lines. On each occasion the auxiliaries had held firm, but at a dreadful cost in lives and wounded.

After the last attack had failed to break their enemy, the host had withdrawn across the stream, where they now stared back menacingly, like a hound straining at the leash. The warhorns blew their baleful music once more and, as if released from their yolk, a roar broke from every throat and the Damnonii advanced once more.

Cai watched impassively as they plunged into the stream and out the other side, sweeping across the open ground. Warriors tramped over the bodies of their dead, uncaring if they were friends, fathers, or brothers.

'Thank the gods we got away from them in that damned forest,' Hrindenus said. The ever present Tungrian shook his head in wonder. 'I can't tell if it's blind courage or they've been drinking some poison that just turns them to madness.'

'Or both,' Cai said. 'I must admit though, for the first time I'm glad to be standing behind a high wall.' He licked his dry lips. 'But the time will come, when we must lock shields and smell their stinking breath in our nostrils.'

'Comforting words as usual, sir.'

Cai gave the Vexillarius a sharp look. 'Just make sure you're by my side with the standard when the time comes. I'll need your strong arm and thick skull.'

The thunderous crash resonated across the field as the Damnonii slammed into the Hispana's line. War cries and screams of pain mingled in the air, the grinding of close quarter fighting beginning again. The enemy determined to break the wall of oval shields, the auxiliaries equally determined to hold.

The scorpio crews continued their barrage from the turrets. The metallic rattle of their reloading arms an ever-present background accompaniment to the chaotic sound of the battle.

Mascellus continued chivvying his slingers, but they were tiring, and with the blue-faces engaged so closely with the Hispana's ranks, the men on the Sack's southern ramparts had resorted to using less effective overhand lobs, aimed at the Damnonii's rearmost ranks.

'Pudens has ordered the reserve forward,' Cai said. 'The Damnonii know the flank is the weak point.' Cai watched as the retained century bolstered the ranks of the flanking units. But the lines continued to fray. The enemy had seen the opportunity and the pressure was unrelenting.

'The flank's going to fold.'

Above the tumult of the battle, a deep rumbling noise arose, 'Sir. To the east.' Mascellus shouted from further along the parapet. Cai leaned between a crenelation and saw a line of horsemen. They crested the ridge above the floodplain, before galloping down its shallow slope. Two more turma strength lines followed, moving swiftly.

'Crybaby!' Hrindenus shouted, excitedly, as he squinted into the sunlight.

Even at a distance, Cai could see he was right. It was Nepos. The grizzled, battle-scarred Decurion was riding at the centre of the leading line.

At first the cavalry went unnoticed by the Damnonii, so intent were they on breaking the Hispana. But as the vibrations underfoot rose in intensity, heads turned. Initial puzzlement quickly turned to shock and then fear.

Some of the dark tribesmen turned to face this new threat. But others, trying to escape the onrushing horsemen, pushed further into their massed ranks, causing panic.

'Get at them, Crybaby,' Hrindenus yelled, drawing laughter from the men on the ramparts.

Nepos's leading turma looked like it was intent on charging directly into the Damnonii's massed ranks. Only at the last instant did the line wheel, all thirty men using the momentum to cast their javelins, before galloping their mounts along the edge of the enemy's line. Cai watched in admiration as the second line executed the same manoeuver. Followed swiftly by the rear turma.

The battlefield churned with screaming, writhing men. The rearmost of the Damnonii horde was in chaos. The agonised sounds were heard, even by those in their battle madness as they assaulted the Hispana's shields. Panic spread as warriors realised they were caught between two forces.

'He's coming again, sir.' The big man couldn't contain himself and thrust the cohort's standard into the air.

'Now, that's how you manoeuvre cavalry,' Cai said, upon seeing the old Tungrian wheeling his men once again. Now all three ranks moved into close formation a short distance from the Damnonii. Nepos drew his spatha.

'Tungriiiii!' The warcry broke from the throats of Nepos's men, turning into a roar as they kicked their mounts into a gallop. Swords raised high and shields held tightly, they thundered towards the Damnonii. A peppering of arrows flew from the horde, but to no effect that Cai could see, as an instant later the cavalry crashed into the blue-painted tribe, driving deep into their ranks, cutting and slashing as they went.

'Oh balls.' Hrindenus groaned.

'What?'

Cai looked at the standard bearer, and then in the direction he was staring.

For a fleeting moment, Cai thought a huge herd of.cattle was stampeding, so large was the fast-moving mass of the beasts. The air reverberated with the sound of their approach.

Mounted warriors, more than thrice the number of Nepos's force, swarmed across the ground, baying their battle cries. Not Damnonii, but Novantae. And there, to the fore, was the large white mount of Barra, his distinctive scale armour reflecting the sun's light. The horsemen were forced to loop around the rear of their retreating allies, slowing progress.

'Run for it, man.' Cai shouted, too far away to be heard.

But Nepos had seen the threat too. He gave the signal to withdraw, not an easy thing to do in the midst of the enemy. Troopers began to detach themselves from the fight, but even so a number were pulled from their mounts as they tried to withddraw.

At last the Tungrians pulled clear, galloping away in the direction they had first appeared, vanishing over the rise with the Novantae in pursuit. Barra was less than a spear's throw from the rearmost turma and gaining. The Tungrian's would have to ride for their lives.

But their intervention had not been in vain. Unnerved, the Damnonii were stepping back from the Hispana's embattled line. Pudens seized the opportunity and the cohort advanced, driving into the confused ranks of tribesmen. War horns sounded once more, and the host began to withdraw quickly and in disorder. Splashing across the stream, carrying their wounded with them. Most of them.

The Hispana's line halted. The auxiliary's taunts following the retreating backs of the enemy.

'What the fuck? Why have they stopped?' Hrindenus said, his voice filled with frustration.

'Pudens knows his men, Vexillarius. They're exhausted.' But inwardly Cai seethed. The Damnonii were on the run and there had been an opportunity to deal them a damaging blow.

'Let's hope the Nervii don't tire so easily then, eh sir.'

55

The Nervana was being assailed along its entire front. Lucius had watched as the blue-faces had filled the lilly pits with the bodies of their dead, allowing the living to finally engage with their enemy in force. The centre of the cohort's line, straddling the roadway, continued to be under the heaviest pressure.

The assault from the steep-sided stream had been dealt with, but at a high cost in casualties. However, his men had made the blue-faces pay their own price. A long mound of corpses was building at the feet of the cohort's front ranks.

'Sir, to the west.'

Lucius was shaken by the sight of the host of enemy horsemen, whose brooding ranks had stood unmoving throughout the day, finally in motion, riding hard to the south. What had they seen? In moments they disappeared, hidden by the line of the village palisade.

Lucius paced the turret in frustration, growling at one of the messengers who stood in his way. It was now long past noon and his men were tiring. A steady stream of wounded had passed through the rear ranks, where the medicus and his team attended to them, assisted by some of the women from the village.

Lucius saw the familiar sight of Alyn as she helped a wounded man across the causeway. He shook his head in wonder at her boundless energy. The dead had been laid, as best they could, in front of the ditches. There was no room in the fort's interior, but the smell was becoming appalling.

'Sir, the Damnonii are withdrawing.' Lenius, the groom, had appeared at his side, panting.

'Slow down, trooper. Take a breath and make your report.'

The boy swallowed. 'Sorry, sir. The Praefectus reports Decurion Nepos engaged the enemy with three turmae. He has been forced to retire by enemy cavalry, but the Damnonii are now withdrawing.'

'That's better, Lenius. Wait here a moment.'

Lucius returned his attention to the battle before him. Their situation was worsening. The Nervana's centre was starting to buckle, men forced to take backwards steps. Gaps would soon appear. He grabbed one of the waiting messengers by the arm.

'Get to the Centurion of the reserve century, tell him he's to move immediately to support the centre.'

The trooper disappeared down the turret steps, running to his waiting horse. Lucius turned to the groom, speaking urgently.

'Tell the Praefectus the scorpios are to be redeployed immediately to the north turrets. Off you go.'

For the next few minutes Lucius observed the battle, feeling like a spectator at the arena. He watched the eighty men of the reserve century double-timing across the open ground to bolster the centre of the line. The reserve turma waited in its original position, but its ranks were depleted. Only eighteen remained on horseback by Lucius's count. If this continued, he would have to signal a withdrawal.

'Move you idle bastards. You lot get out of the fucking way.'

Lucius looked down the turret stairwell and saw men struggling up the steps, red faced and puffing heavily. The first, a burly looking soldier, carried the cumbersome scorpio frame over his shoulder, followed closely behind by another with its wooden stand. Two more followed, carrying baskets of the short bolts. Last came the Optio, blowing hard.

On reaching the top of the turret the squad immediately began reassembling the weapon. The Optio studiously ignored Lucius until the scorpio was operational.

'Optio Tranquillis reporting the scorpio is ready, sir.' The crew commander gave a smart salute. His team heaved in great gulps of air whilst leaning against the turret's parapet.

'Thank you, Tranquillis. That was well done. Now I have a job for you.' Lucius signalled the Optio to stand with him at the parapet's edge.

'As you can see,' Lucius continued, 'the lads straddling the road are in trouble. I want you to search for targets where the line is most under pressure. Look for any bastard wearing armour or a decent helm, they might be important men. But have a care, I don't want any of our men taking a bolt in the back of the skull.'

'Will do, sir. My lads have honed their skills all morning on the Damnonii. Let's see how the Novantae like it up 'em.'

'Good. Send one of your crew across to the other turret with the same message.'

The rapid clinking of the scorpio's metal teeth being rachetted was loud in the confines of the turret. Lucius watched in fascination as the arms of the weapon were pulled inwards, straining under the torsion of the rope springs. Once ready the loader placed a bolt into the groove of the slider and the Optio began searching for targets.

'Right, Pollonis me lad. See that big sheep-humper with the shiny helmet, a few paces back from the fighting.' Tranquillis pointed to a position towards the centre of the Nervana's line.

'I see him, sir.'

'Well let's see if you can give him a haircut.' Pollonis pressed his shoulder into the crescent handle and sighted along the frame of the weapon, a metal arch at its end helping to narrow his line of vision. Resting his right hand lightly on the release bar, he let out a long slow breath. The release was so sudden that Lucius didn't see it. The arms flashed forward with a dull thunk, the bolt racing towards its target. Lucius tried to watch its flight, but it proved impossible.

Cheering erupted in the tower from the scorpio team and the waiting messengers. Lucius looked for the big Novantae with the shiny helmet; he hadn't seen the bolt hit home, but the warrior was no longer in sight.

'Right lads, that's enough joviality, we've got a job to do,' Tranquillis said. The rapid clinking sound started again as Pollonis wound the crank handle.

'Keep them at it, Optio,' Lucius said.

'Yes, sir.'

Lucius left the tower, signalling the small group of messengers to follow. He strode along the north-facing ramparts to the turret above the gateway, the best view he was going to get of the fighting on the roadway. Even with the reserve now committed the situation was becoming perilous. For a distance of around fifty paces there was no longer a third rank.

'Get to Decurion Salvinus of the reserve turma.' Lucius spoke to the nearest messenger. 'He is to dismount and join the rear rank of the century straddling the road.'

Moments later the messenger galloped across the causeway, quickly reaching Salvinus. The last of the Nervana's reserve was now committed.

The lines were holding, but for how long? The heat had been steadily rising throughout the day and lines of sweat trickled down Lucius's back beneath his leather jerkin and heavy chainmail. But it would be far worse, he knew, for the men down there.

Flashes of reflected light, coming from the northern rise where the road disappeared from view, caught his attention. His heart sank at the sight of more enemy horsemen appearing on its summit.

'Gods, help us,' Lucius said into the tumult of sound below him. 'That's all we—'

He stood transfixed as the horsemen ordered themselves into lines.

'It's Decurion Nepos's men, sir,' the trooper behind him said. 'Must be.'

He was right, Lucius realised. But they had not gone unnoticed by the enemy. The now familiar deep warble of the war horns of the tribes sounded across the battleground. Warriors towards the rear turned, wondering at the cause of the warning.

'Nepos must have split his command,' Lucius said.

He estimated there were only three turmae forming up. What are they planning? A short time later he knew.

'Shit! Someone, thinks he's fucking Alexander.' Lucius gripped the parapet in frustration.

Two riders had trotted their mounts forward, halting a short distance from the main body. Next each turma moved up behind, the first forming two diagonal lines the others filling in the gap between. A wedge.

The formation moved forward at a walk, each trooper holding their long lance. The walk quickly became a canter. Suddenly, with a great collective bellow, the long lances were lowered and they charged. More painted warriors turned to face this new threat.

The cavalry's commander was using the road to keep his men centred as the wedge struck. The sound of breaking bones and lances from the impact was matched only by the screams. A number of horses stumbled and fell, throwing their riders. But, for most, the formation's impetus took them deep into the throng.

Many troopers had lost or abandoned their spears, drawing spathas to hack and slash at the packed ranks around them.

The shock of the impact had an instantaneous effect. Hearing the chaos behind them, the enemy assaulting the Nervana's line began to step back.

'Advance.' Lucius shouted impotently.

The gap between the auxiliaries and the Novantae grew, but the ranks of infantry remained stationary, staring dumbly at their enemy. Suddenly, as if a fog had lifted, they saw their salvation. A tired cheer broke from the throats of the blood-spattered front rank. They began to advance. But men tripped and stumbled over the dead and dying of the blue-faces piled before them, impeding progress. The lines became ragged as men individually tried to pick their way forward. Dangerously wide gaps appeared.

Lucius watched as a big red headed beast of a man rallied the warriors around him.

'Move.' Lucius pushed past the waiting messengers and ran along the ramparts towards the tower, taking the steps two at a time.

'Optio!' Lucius shouted as he reached the top.

'Sir?'

Lucius pulled Tranquillis by his arm, to the edge of the tower's parapet.

'See that break in our line?' Lucius pointed frantically.

'I can see that big ox trying to get at it, sir.'

'Good. Bring him down.'

Tranquillis turned to his crew. 'Right, Pollonis, time for you to be a fucking hero again.'

Lucius didn't wait as he ran for the tower steps once more, hearing the sound of the scorpio being reloaded behind him.

On reaching the parapet he stopped. The cavalry was in trouble. What Lucius had feared, on seeing the wedge forming, had come to pass. The Novantae and Selgovae in their fury had wrapped around to the rear of the turmae. They were cut off. The horsemen fought frantically in individual battles for survival.

Assailed on all sides, troopers were being run through with sword and spear or simply hauled from their mounts, to be hacked to death on the churned earth. Lucius saw the white-crested helm of their commander. His contorted face, pointing his spatha to the east. One by one the remaining cavalrymen began to fight their way out towards the stream. They hacked, cut and kicked out furiously in their desperation.

The first troopers plunged down the steep banks of the slow flowing water, before struggling out on the other side. The warhorns blew once more, taking on an urgent tone, with short, high-pitched blasts. The losses to the cavalry force had been high. But at least it had served a purpose, as the centuries of the cohort continued the slow advance into the chaos, their lines closed again.

Like a turning tide the withdrawal of the tribe's was inexorable and soon they began to run, many stumbling on the blood-slick ground. Family groups lifted their wounded, carrying them from the battlefield.

The auxiliaries halted and watched on. Too exhausted to pursue further or even cheer their own survival, individuals lowered their shields to the earth, holding onto their topmost rims, to prevent their own collapse.

It was a reprieve. Shading his eyes, Lucius took in the position of the sun. There were still several hours until darkness. There was time for them to come again.

'But they'll be licking their wounds for a time yet,' Lucius said hopefully, to himself.

The enemy's withdrawal was encouraged by the unrelenting accuracy of the scorpio crews. Eventually even they fell silent, as the tribesmen passed beyond effective range.

Exhaustion weighed heavily on Lucius's shoulders. He had slept little the night before, and doubted he would get any sleep in the coming hours.

The battlefield was carpeted by the dead in every direction. Not a carpet, he thought. More like a grim, badly cut harvest. A dark cloud of the ever-present carrion birds flocked above this new banquet of gore.

Tearing his eyes away from the bleak scene, Lucius turned to the interior of the fort. Long lines of the wounded were passing through the gateway, helped by their mates and some of the civilians. A few could walk, but many had to be carried. The medical orderlies passed amongst them and he was not surprised to pick out Alyn, once again, at the heart of it. Most were being directed towards the largest of the granaries. Its large interior had been emptied for the purpose, the hospital now overwhelmed. But it wasn't enough.

His eyes were drawn to the white swan feathers of a parade

ground helmet. Cai weaved his way through the shuffling lines of the wounded along the Via Praetoria. He saw the look of joy on his friend's face as he came across Alyn, and watched them embrace. He was glad they had this opportunity. It might be the last.

56

Cai had left Mascellus in command of the main gate. His side ached. He had barely noticed the wound in the midst of the fighting, but now, as he passed between the cavalry barracks, the pain of it forced him to walk with an awkward, halting stride.

Reaching the main granary, he was compelled to weave his way between the walking wounded, slowing his progress. He could have more easily walked around the ramparts, but this way he might catch a glimpse of her. As he approached the principia he stepped over the drain at the roadside to avoid the continual influx of shuffling men.

And there she was. Even amongst this chaos, elation warmed him at the sight of her.

'Alyn.' he called above the din of the human traffic.

She turned from the soldier she had been tending, the work-worn look on her face changing instantly to joy. Uncaring she leapt into his arms and he held her tightly, ignoring the jolt of pain in his side. She pulled away a little to look into his face, her grey eyes glistening.

'I was so worried about you,' she said, a tear escaping to run down her cheek. 'There have been so many wounded, I feared I might see you amongst them.' The words tumbled out. Cai took hold of her blood-encrusted hands, squeezing them gently.

'I would say never fear, but I know you will.' He lowered his voice so as not to be overheard. 'Our position is not good, my love. We may be able to hold on for another day, but beyond that, I don't know. When the time comes, you and Beren must stay close to Castellanos and I will find you.' Alyn nodded, saying nothing, simply pulling him close once more.

'How's Beren? Is he keeping out of mischief?'

'He's been helping me in the hospital. I thought to shield him from the worst of it, but without a word, he simply took a pail and started fetching water from the well for the wounded, even helping them to drink.' She said, smiling.

'A brave lad.' He squeezed her once more before releasing her. 'I must go, Lucius is waiting for me. I'll try to see you again tonight if I can.'

'Go,' Alyn said, smiling, before turning quickly to support a wounded man whose friend was struggling to keep upright. Cai watched her for a moment longer before resuming his weaving journey.

He found Lucius in conversation with Facilis. The First Spear was blood spattered and looked haggard.

'If they come again today,' Facilis said, 'I'm confident we will hold out until dark. But it'll be a miserable night for the men.'

Cai came to Facilis's side, clasping him firmly on the shoulder. 'A hard day, brother, but your men did well.'

Facilis gave a weary nod. 'You and your lads had a tough time of it too, from what the Tribunus tells me.'

'Aye, perhaps,' Cai said, 'but we were standing behind high ramparts hurling rocks at those tattooed bastard's, thank the gods. We didn't have their rancid spittle on our faces.'

'That time will come I fear, my friend,' Facilis replied.

All three turned at the sound of purposeful strides approaching along the wooden walkway. Cai and Facilis saluted Salvius, the Tribunus of the Hispana.

'Ah Marcus, thank you for joining us.' Lucius spoke as if they were about to have a congenial evening in the officer's mess. Salvius carried his helmet, his short-cropped, almost white hair looking as if it had been plunged into a bucket of water.

The veteran former Centurion nodded to each of them. 'I'm glad to see you made it through the day, brothers.'

'The Praefectus kept me apprised of the strong defence the Hispana put up against the Damnonii,' Lucius said.

'True enough,' Salvius said. 'Our Nervii brother here got them all riled up first.' Salvius grimaced at the memory. 'The blue-faces wasted many lives in fruitless attempts to take the gate, before turning their attention to us. Nevertheless our losses have been heavy. If not for Nepos's timely intervention, it could have been worse.'

'Our force, gentlemen,' Lucius said after a pause, 'is no longer sufficient to maintain our current order of battle. To my mind we have two choices; shorten our lines somehow or withdraw behind our walls. What are your thoughts?'

'Sir, if I may?' Cai said. 'If we withdraw into the Sack, we will hasten our end. The tribes will be able to focus their assault and eventually overwhelm us. If we hold at least some of the ground outside, we can delay them further.'

'But our losses will be murderous. Wouldn't that *hasten* our destruction?' Salvius interjected, not able to keep the consternation from his voice. 'Surely withdrawing gives us the best chance of survival.'

Cai responded calmly, although he thought the Hispana's Tribunus might be losing his nerve. 'Sir, if we can delay them a further day before falling back on the Sack, that's another day we buy for the Sixth or Twentieth to reach us.'

Salvius didn't respond, staring blankly at Cai. So he pressed on.

'I would suggest the Hispana moves its flank to the settlement's gateway ditch. It'll shorten the line by a third. Two centuries will be needed within the village to defend its south-facing palisade. It will also ensure those outside have the opportunity to more easily withdraw, when the time comes.'

Lucius nodded. 'Can you make it work, Marcus?'

'Yes, sir,' Salvius said, after a delay that Cai found disquieting.

'First Spear,' Lucius said, turning to Facilis. 'The Nervana too is stretched thin. We will anchor our flank against the Sack's ditches outside the northeast turret.'

'Bastard!' The three officers looked at Facilis in consternation, before realising he was staring out across the parapet.

Just outside the scorpio's range was a lone warrior, mounted on a large white horse. His long red hair hung from beneath his helmet, the bronze scale of his armour reflecting the light of the late afternoon sun. Barra gripped a long Roman cavalry lance in his right hand, which he raised skyward, bellowing an incoherent warcry that carried across the battlefield.

Dismounting, the big Novantae thrust the spearpoint into the soft ground. The severed head pierced by the butt-end now clear for the fort's defenders to see. Even at that distance the watching officers could discern the long grey hair and milky eye with its red teardrop scar.

57

Lucius sat at his desk, staring unseeing at the hunk of two-day old bread. The wine cup he held, now empty and forgotten.

He had not long returned from the main granary, which now more closely resembled a butcher's shop. The moans and cries of the wounded had been interspersed with agonised screams, as Castellanos and his orderlies went about their grisly duty. The supply of the juice of the poppy had long since run out.

Night had finally fallen. The tribes did not come again. Instead they had settled for keeping their enemy from rest. He had lost count of the number of times horsemen had ridden out of the night to loose off a hail of arrows or sling stones. Only one man had been hurt, an arrow buried in his calf. But the effect on the men's nerves was worse. The image of the old Tungrian's head on the spear flashed into his mind once again, and once again he felt the creeping hand of despair.

The familiar sound of hobnails on the stone floor pulled him from his dark thoughts. It was not the usual, purposeful stride of someone entering the headquarters building, but halting and irregular.

Cai appeared in the doorway. His long fair hair was matted, his eyes looked dark with exhaustion. Lines of pain etched his forehead.

'Sit, before you fall down.' Lucius rose to pour another cup of wine, refilling his own. 'That's the last of my stock. We'll have to drink that swill from the officer's mess after this.' Cai took the offered cup but said nothing. 'Have you eaten?'

Cai stared at Lucius as if the answer to the question was beyond him, eventually shaking his head. Tearing the hunk of bread into two, Lucius handed one to Cai, dipping his own into the cup of wine. Both men chewed in silence for a time.

'Tomorrow will be harder,' Cai said.

'It will. When they see the Hispana have shortened their line, I believe they will hit the southern wall and the porta praetoria hardest. They'll know we are weakened, but time is counting against them. Our main gate will seem the quickest route to victory.

The morning will be hard for you, brother.'

Cai moved in his chair to find a more comfortable position. His wound continued to chafe.

'We'll hold,' he said. 'With your permission, I'll have the scorpions redeployed to the southern turrets. We've nearly exhausted our supply of bolts but there's enough to do some damage to their first assault.'

Lucius nodded his assent. 'Facilis is making a count of the walking wounded. Anyone who can still hold a sword will be formed into a makeshift reserve. You'll be able to call upon them as you see fit.' Cai heard the weariness in his friend's voice.

'Why don't you try to grab an hour's shut eye, Lucius? I'll wake you if anything happens.'

'I'm not sure I can. But perhaps you're right.' Lucius drained his cup and shuffled to his narrow cot set up in the corner, sitting heavily on its edge. 'By the way, how is our new standard bearer shaping up?'

Cai snorted. 'Well he's certainly as insubordinate as Avitius, I'll have to knock that out of him. But one thing is certain, I'm glad to have the big lump beside me on that damned wall.'

Lucius smiled, laying his head down. Cai continued to sit where he was, chewing the last of the stale bread. After a few moments he heard the gentle snoring of his friend.

'Sir.' Cai's shoulder was roughly shaken. Jolting upright, he stared into the face of Hrindenus.

'What is it man?' Cai said irritably.

'Sorry to wake you, sir. It sounds like the blue-faces are on the move.' Cai glanced over at Lucius's empty cot.

'Where's the Tribunus?'

'I saw him heading towards the north gate, sir. In the company of the First Spear.' Cai rubbed at his stiff neck before accepting the waterskin the Tungrian handed him.

'Keep that close,' Cai handed the skin back. 'We'll be grateful for it as the day wears on. Let's see what our painted friends are up to, shall we?'

In the half light, they strode towards the main gate, passing the largest granary on the way. The makeshift hospital was now eerily quiet.

Reaching the cavalry barracks, Cai saw the reserve of the walking wounded was gathering. Some talked in hushed tones to one another, whilst others sat quietly preparing for the day ahead, sharpening sword edges or picking out the gore from their chainmail. Anything that would distract them from thoughts of the day ahead. They were a mongrel bunch, Cai thought. A mixture of infantry from both cohorts, even a small group of grooms who chatted nervously.

'Wait here,' Cai said to Hrindenus, before stalking along the covered walkway of the last barrack block. Reaching the end, he entered the horse stall at its front. Adela whickered in greeting.

'Hello, beautiful girl. I'm sorry to leave you alone like this.' He moved his hand in long slow strokes along her neck, before moving to her nose, allowing her to nudge into his neck. 'You want to ride out to meet them, don't you, my sweet? I do too. But it won't be too much longer.'

A short while later, he climbed the steps at the gate onto the battlements. Cai looked upon the shadowed field before him. A sentry standing nearby hawked and spat over the parapet. The sudden sound caused a cacophony of angry croaks, as disturbed, the massed ranks of crows and ravens rose and rippled across the battlefield, like the shaking of a great black cloak.

The foul stench of the dead made the bile rise in Cai's throat. The carrion birds always went for the softest parts of the body first, spilled guts, open wounds and of course the eyes. The dark sockets of the dead now stared up at him in reproach. Mascellus had asked to remove those at the base of the ramparts, so the men did not have to suffer the clouds of flies that would appear as the day warmed. But Cai wanted the enemy to have to climb over the bodies of their kin to get at the defenders above.

He was drawn to the bodies of two warriors that had fallen into the innermost ditch. The first, an older man, with long red hair interlaced by stripes of grey, whose matching bushy beard was matted with blood. The second lay against him, almost in a sitting position and from the look of his hairless chin, was perhaps older than Beren by five or six summers. Was this father and son? Their empty eye sockets seemed to look upon each other.

Cai heard shouted orders and curses, from within the village, as men of the Hispana, who were to defend the palisade, were chivvied into their new positions. A clinking sound came from the turret as one of the scorpio crews greased down the moving parts of the bolt thrower. The Optio spoke quietly to his men, as if fearful of waking the dead on the field below.

The walkway on either side of Cai began to fill with slowly shuffling men, many yawning as they went. He gave a nod of satisfaction that most carried a long cavalry lance along with their shields. *They'd need them today.*

'Did you manage to get some sleep, Hrindenus?' Cai asked.

'Aye, sir. I grabbed a couple of hours in the roof space above the horses. Always the warmest place to be, if you can't have your own bed.'

'True enough.'

Cai continued to look out across the ground beyond the Sack. 'Make sure the standard can be seen by the men and our enemy, at all times. Tie it to the walkway railing if necessary, but make sure it continues to fly.'

'Yes, sir. I know just the spot.' The big Tungrian set off along the walkway, the heavy wooden pole of the standard resting across his shoulder. Then the sound Cai had been unconsciously dreading broke through the stillness of the morning. The war horns of the three tribes.

For a while the sound carried mournfully across to the distance to the defenders, like a lament. But as the tribes neared the battlefield the tone changed, picking up in intensity until it became more like blasts of the cornicen's of the legions.

Cai observed the first of the enemy emerge on the ridge, a wall of silhouettes. He moved along the battlements, speaking to individuals and groups of men who congregated to watch the warriors advance.

'We've given the blue-faces a beating already, we'll do it again. Use your lances to throw them off when they attempt to scale the wall. Don't forget to drink when you get the chance.' He noted with satisfaction that Mascellus was doing the same.

'Well brother, are you missing your farm yet?' Cai said as he reached the old veteran.

'Not for a minute, sir. I'd forgotten quite how much I love knocking a bunch of youngsters into shape. And they're all good lads too, even if most lack the good looks of the Nervii.'

As Cai mounted the wooden turret over the gate, he saw Hrindenus had strapped the standard's pole to its parapet. The embroidered white horse rippled gently in the light morning breeze. The Tungrian now held his oval shield, his long cavalry lance leaning against the turret's edge.

'It looks like the bastard's have been busy during the night.' Hrindenus said.

'So it would seem,' Cai said. 'They've finally learned we won't open our front door just because they knock politely.' Cai had also seen what the Damnonii now carried. Ladders. The war horns reached a new peak and instead of the expected cacophony of individual warcries, a great chant arose from the still shadowed ranks, a single word. Death.

'Decurion Mascellus, prepare your men.' Cai bellowed

'Slingers, make ready.' Each man along the wall pulled a leather sling from his belt and took a lead ball from the small pile at their feet. Cai raised his arm in signal to the scorpion crews, who stood ready.

He could feel the power of the enemy's chant reverberating in his chest.

'Get on with it,' Hrindenus hissed.

Then as suddenly as it started the chanting ceased, to be replaced by maniacal screams. The Damnonii were on the move.

'Slingers, prepare.'

Mascellus's command resounded along the wall. Each man began the swift rotation above the head.

'Release!' The old Decurion timed the volley perfectly. In the low light, the acorn shaped balls flew invisibly, striking the leading warriors as they approached the stream's bank. Blue painted men were thrown back, or collapsed as bodies were broken. Cai saw the top of a shaven skull disintegrate in a shower of bone and brain, the body taking two more steps before collapsing.

The scorpios' fired independently. Ordered to target any who wore armour. Not an easy task, especially in the poor light. Mascellus ensured his men kept up a continual barrage, but the Damnonii were relentless.

The swiftest had reached the first of the bodies of their dead. Some slipped in the slick offal the crows had spilled. Others fell screaming as feet were pierced by the caltrops Mascellus's men had resown during the night.

'Target the ladders.' Cai shouted.

There were many, most carried between two men. The first pair to reach the causeway charged along its length. An instant later the leading carrier fell, dead or unconscious, struck by a lead ball. The slingers exacted a heavy price as warriors were funnelled along the narrow approach to the main gate. Some tumbled into the thorny tangle at the bottom of the ditches, as men barged others out of the way in their desperation to reach the illusory protection under the Sack's walls.

'Right lads, time to crush some skulls,' Mascellus shouted, as he hurled a fist-sized river stone down upon the Damnonii as they moved along the base of the turf ramparts.

The first ladder slammed against the wooden parapet. Cai saw the trooper next to it prepare to throw his lance.

'Don't you throw that bloody spear. Get that ladder off my wall.' Cai shouted in frustration and watched as the trooper, with the help of the man next to him, heaved the wooden struts sideways.

But ladders continued to appear along the length of the wall, the defenders hard pressed to fend them off. Bowmen below targeted any who showed their heads over the parapet. Cai saw Mascellus ram the bloody point of his spear through the eye of a warrior who had reached the ledge between a crenelation. The dead weight of the body almost snatched the lance from his grasp before he could wrench it loose. Mascellus threw the ladder away from the wall. A veteran held a shield to cover the Decurion. An instant later, two arrows struck it.

'I think it's time for us to join the men, Vexillarius,' Cai said.

'Aye, sir. Especially as our enemies seem to have noticed your pretty swan feathers,' Hrindenus grumbled, knocking an arrow shaft from his shield. But Cai was already disappearing down the tower steps, shield in hand. 'That madman's going to get me killed.'

Cai drew his spatha as he reached the walkway.

'Bastard!' Cai heard Mascellus's shout as he reached his side, seeing him thrust his lance once again. A Damnonii's squeal was cut off as the spearpoint punctured his throat. Cai raised his shield as Mascellus tried to wrench free the bloody metal point. A jarring pain shot along the length of his arm as an arrow head pierced its rim.

'My thanks, sir. That would have stung a bit.'

Cai grinned. 'Let's get this off the wall, shall we?' He nodded at the ladder.

'Not you, sir.' Hrindenus stepped between Cai and the ladder, barging him against the guard rail at the walkway's rear. The big Tungrian dropped his shield and took hold of the ladder's wooden spars. With a mighty heave, he pushed it away as a second warrior had started to climb.

'What the hell, Vexillarius?' Cai said, caught between astonishment at the man's strength and anger at his insubordination. Hrindenus shrugged.

'You're no good to us with an arrow through your brain, sir.'

Cai's response was interrupted, as a soldier, a short distance from them, was thrown backwards as he tried to fend off a ladder. Only Lenius's intervention prevented him from disappearing over the railing and into the fort's interior. The groom held the soldier upright, both arms wrapped around his waist, as the man's slick fingers fumbled impotently at the shaft protruding from his windpipe. The auxiliary's eyes bulged as a great gout of blood disgorged from his mouth. He stopped moving. His now dead weight forced Lenius to lay him on the walkway. The boy crouched by the body, white-faced at the sight of the blood pooled on the rough planking.

Hrindenus went to the groom's side, grasping his arm and raising him to his feet. 'Come on lad, you can't stay here.' The Tungrian lifted the dead man's shield and shoved it at the boy. 'Keep hold of this. Cover yourself when you're up here, we need our messenger alive.' The boy looked at the big man, still shaken, but nodded.

'Sir, behind you!' Mascellus shouted in alarm. Cai turned sharply as a great beast of a man leaped over the parapet and onto the walkway. The Damnonii's shaven head appeared almost black, covered, like his broad chest, with old tattoos. The warrior flashed a yellow toothed grin and screamed. He leapt at Cai, swinging his long sword in a fierce downward arc.

58

'Here they come again, sir.' The Novantae and their Selgovae allies were advancing for the third time that morning. It was no longer possible for them to charge, uncaring, into the waiting lines of the Nervana, the ground littered with the dead and dying, along with the detritus of broken spears and shields. Each warrior moved as if trying to avoid half hidden rocks beneath a shallow shoreline.

Or did they simply not want to tread on the body of a father, brother or son? Lucius thought.

He looked to the west where the enemy horsemen again watched on impotently. There had been no further sighting of the ala since their interventions on the first day. He feared the worst. From his position above the gate Lucius turned to look back into the Sack's interior. It was a grim sight. Both sides of the Via Praetoria were lined with wounded men. Some, the luckier ones, lay along the covered walkways of the barrack blocks, protected from the rising heat of the day. Castellanos and his staff had done what they could, but they were overwhelmed. Even with the help of the civilians, many had died where they lay. More would not make it to nightfall. If the garrison could hold out that long.

The warhorns blared. Warcries filled the air as the horde hurled themselves at the cohort's lines. The noise, as they crashed against the auxiliary's front rank, rippled along its length. The wall of shields bowed in many places but held. For the time being.

'Sir.' Lucius turned to see Lenius running along the walkway. Slipping to a stop, he made his salute.

'The Praefectus reports the Hispana's left flank will not hold much longer and Tribunus Salvius appears to be withdrawing.'

'Damn it.' This was what Lucius had feared. If the left flank folded the entire defence was in danger.

'You.' Lucius pointed at the nearest messenger. 'Find the First Spear, he's positioned somewhere near the north road. Inform him the Hispana are withdrawing. He is to reorganise the Nervana's front, falling back to the position we discussed.' The trooper saluted and was gone. Putting his hand on Lenius's shoulder, Lucius gripped it tightly.

'How's the south holding up, trooper?' The boy puffed his chest out.

'Only one of them made it over the wall, sir. A giant, he was. Nearly did for the Praefectus.' The words tumbled out of the boy in his excitement. 'But the Vexillarius barged the Praefectus out of the way and stabbed his spatha into the Damnonii's belly. It was unbelievable, sir. Herc tossed him back over the wall, like he was nothin'.'

'Good man. Now get back to the Praefectus and tell him I want his slingers to cover the Hispana's withdrawal. Understood?'

'Yes, sir.'

The boy disappeared along the walkway, running at full pelt. 'That boy'll break his damned neck one day,' Lucius said to himself. He quickly turned to the south at a roar from the Damnonii. They know they've got us on the run.

He could see panicked men of the Hispana streaming through the village's gate. Lucius grabbed his shield and ran along the walkway as recklessly as the boy had just done.

'Move!' he yelled at any who got in his way. In seconds he reached the western gateway, crossing the wooden bridge over the twin ditches.

A group of men were running through the village's main street, aiming for the safety of the Sack's ramparts.

'You!' Lucius roared, pointing his spatha at them. 'Stand where you are.'

The soldiers of the Hispana, eight of them, instantaneously came to a halt.

'Where the fuck do you think you're going?' The men looked at Lucius, shamefaced as he walked up to them. 'That's right, you were just about to get back into the fight, weren't you? Now, follow me.' Seeing their hesitation, he turned on them once more. 'At the fucking double.'

Stunned into action, the group trotted in Lucius's wake, back towards the village's gateway. More men were stumbling through the ruins of the village and were co-opted into his makeshift force. By the time they reached the open gates he had twenty or so men.

Halting outside the palisade he reviewed the scene before him. The left flank was crumbling, its formation nearly lost. Men were fighting for their very lives, some singely in frantic duels with the enemy. Salvius was nowhere in sight, but Lucius made out the helmet plume of Pudens. The line was gradually stepping back as the Hispana's First Spear tried to execute a withdrawal. Lucius had to act, before it was too late. He would have given anything for the chance to take a piss.

'Form two lines on me.' Most reacted quickly, but a few were paralysed by fear. 'Move your arses or I'll give you something to be frightened of.' Lucius jabbed his spatha at the reluctant men. Finally Lucius looked left and right along the line, satisfied they were ready.

'Prepare to advance. And I want you to make some noise. Advance!'

Lucius stepped off and clashed the flat of his sword against his shield's iron boss, mimicked by the rest of the small formation. As Lucius had hoped, the Damnonii saw the approach of this new force and were, for a few precious heartbeats, uncertain as to how to react.

'Prepare!' Lucius shouted at the top of his voice, hoping the tremble in his voice was not heard by his men. They approached the rear of the most desperate fighting. Lucius saw the shield of one of the Hispana's men shattered by the swing of a great sword, the soldier driven to his knees by the force, his scream of fear cut off as his head was removed by a vicious scything strike of his assailant's blade. The flank finally broke and gleeful warriors surged through.

'Charge!' Lucius's two small lines ran across the final few steps. A big Damnonii appeared in the breach, his black beard trailing in four long braids across his barrel of a chest. The skulls of small creatures were threaded to the end of each, causing the braids to swing from side to side. He fixed his sight on Lucius's plume.

Despite his size he moved quickly. Lucius braced. An instant later the warrior slammed into his shield. The impact numbed Lucius's arm and drove him into the man in the rank behind. Fortunately the soldier had been ready for the collision, firmly shoving his shield against Lucius's back, preventing him from falling. His assailant's sword cracked into the metal-lined rim of his shield, Lucius's ears ringing as the power of the swing carried it through, glancing from his helmet. The warrior howled a warcry. His breath smelled strangely sweet.

Lucius drove his shield boss at the warrior's face, who stepped back quickly, avoiding the blow. The big man swung his sword again, two handed, in a powerful downward arc. Lucius raised his shield in time, but the force of the blow drove him onto one knee. He had lost all feeling in his arm and felt panic rise as he realised he couldn't raise his shield once more.

The Damnonii grinned, seeing his chance, thrusting his sword at his enemy's exposed chest. Lucius twisted instinctively, attempting to deflect the blade with his spatha, crying out as the sword point pierced his chainmail rings. As the warrior freed his sword, red hot pain lanced across Lucius's ribs.

Lucius awaited the killing blow. But it did not come. He looked up. The warrior no longer held his blade. Instead, he pressed both hands to his neck in a vain attempt to stem the flow of blood pouring through his fat fingers.

'Up you get, sir.' The man in the second row hauled Lucius to his feet. He hadn't seen who had finished the big man, but he nodded his thanks anyway.

Lucius stepped back into line, trying to ignore the agony pulsing along his side. Immediately he was forced to deflect a spearpoint with his spatha. This new assailant, shorter than the last but with a bull-like neck, stepped back momentarily then came again, jabbing overhand at Lucius's face. Without thinking Lucius pushed the shaft of the spear aside with his shield and cut down with his spatha onto the exposed hand of the warrior, who for an instant looked dumbly at his fingerless hand as blood flooded down his wrist. Lucius drove his blade deep into the Damnonii's exposed armpit, twisting it free as the body collapsed to the churned earth.

He stole a glance over his shield rim. They had almost closed the breach in the line.

'Forward.' he yelled.

The two ranks moved as one, taking a step into the massing warriors to their fore, punching their swords points at any exposed flesh. Gradually, step by hard-fought step, the small band advanced. Other men from the remnants of the Hispana's flank, joined the line, seeking its haven.

'Jupiter, best and greatest, help us,' Lucius prayed, the words coming unbidden.

The Damnonii, incensed that their opportunity was being stolen from them, redoubled their efforts. Uncaring, their massed ranks drove in blind fury against the shields of the auxiliaries. But it was too late, the breach had been closed.

Glancing to his right, Lucius saw Pudens had continued the cohort's desperate withdrawal, Lucius's part of the line would have to match it, or their efforts would have been for nothing.

He spoke over his shoulder. 'Soldier. When I give the order, you will take my place. Understood?'

'Yes sir.'

For a while longer he was forced to defend himself, taking a sword cut on his shield rim before slicing his spatha deep into his assailant's groin. As another leaped over the body of the dying man, Lucius saw his opportunity. He stepped forward, punching his shield boss into the face of this new enemy, hearing the satisfying crunch of nose cartilage. He followed through with another heave of his shield, shoving the Damnonii backwards.

'Now!'

They executed the move, practised so many times on the parade ground. Sliding quickly into the second rank, Lucius was able to look along much of the rear of the Hispana's formation. The line was kinked, as Pudens withdrew the centre and the flank remained stationary. He would have to act fast. His throat felt like it was full of sand. He hawked and spat. Filling his lungs, he bellowed the order.

'Formation will prepare to withdraw, by the count.' Lucius waited a few heartbeats longer.

'Formation withdraw!' The front rank punched their shields forward as one, buying them an instant of grace. 'One.' Lucius yelled. Both ranks took their first almost ponderous step back. 'Two.' The Damnonii, thinking that their enemy was beaten, reacted with a new state of frenzy.

But the cohort's discipline held. Across its front the Hispana's line withdrew towards the village's gate. Lucius gave another silent prayer that Facilis was reorganising the Nervana. As the line shortened, men were able to peel away and withdraw behind the settlement's palisade.

Satisfied that an orderly withdrawal was now secured, he commanded a nearby Optio to continue the count. Lucius was now only a stone's throw from the gate. He made a run for it.

Crossing the causeway, through the two outer ditches, he came across a Centurion of the Hispana organising the gate's defence.

'Centurion, when you're done here, get more men up on the palisade around the gateway, along with anything they can throw at the enemy. When our rearguard is withdrawing across the ditches, they will be in a world of shit. We must give them what cover we can. *And* that gate must be shut behind them at all costs, when the time comes.'

The Centurion peered at him, from a face almost entirely caked in the dark red of drying, congealed blood, his expression obscured.

'I'll see it done, sir. Those wretches are not getting through those gates.'

'That's a Baetican accent, if I ever heard one. 'What's your name, Centurion?'

'Vericundus, sir. And you're right, sir, I was born near Acinipo. My father still has a farm there.'

'I know it well. I've been to the theatre there often. Well I know a Baetican will get the job done. Perhaps we can share a cup of wine and reminisce about home, when all this is done.'

'Yes, sir. That'd be welcome.'

Lucius nodded one final time and left, jogging back through the ruins of the village towards the Sack, unaware his countryman stared at his retreating back, all the way to the fort's gate.

59

'The Hispana must be in deep shit for the blue-faces to get so excited,' Cai said.

'At least they've left us alone for a while.' Hrindenus wiped his bloody spatha on the troos of the dead Damnonii, before sliding it back into its scabbard.

It had indeed been some time since the last attempt on the ramparts had been seen off. At times Cai had thought it inevitable that his men would be overwhelmed. But the weakening lines of the Hispana appeared to have drawn the Damnonii's full attention.

The scene before the main gate was grim. Bodies littered the base of the ramparts, filled much of the inner ditch and almost entirely hid the causeway's approach to the gateway.

Despite it now being weeks beyond harvest time, the weather was unseasonably warm. Clouds of flies had emerged to torment the living and dying alike. Lenius wretched and made a dash for the tower's parapet, emptying the contents of his stomach over its side. Lifting his head once more, he wiped the residue from his mouth with his bare arm.

'Sorry, sir. It's the smell.'

'You have to be alive to smell it lad.' Hrindenus handed him his water skin. 'Besides, I would be doing the same if I had anything left to puke.'

'Let's make the most of our short reprieve, shall we?' Cai said. 'Lenius, find Mascellus. Tell him I want men out scavenging for whatever weapons we can use to throw back at the bastard's when they come again. Especially spears.'

'A good lad that one,' Hrindenus observed, as the groom vanished down the turret steps.

'Aye, he can handle a horse too,' Cai said. 'Let's hope he comes through this.'

Another great wall of sound burst from the Damnonii. 'That doesn't bode well.' Cai leapt onto the edge of the parapet to try for a better view.

'By the gods, Lucius!'

'Sir?'

'It seems the Tribunus has reacted in person to our message about the Hispana's withdrawal.'

Cai's attention had been drawn to the plume of Lucius's helmet as he gave instructions to a Centurion at the village's gate. Before setting off at a run, weaving through the ruins.

'Keep an eye out here, Hrindenus.' And before the big Tungrian could respond Cai disappeared from the tower and into the fort's interior.

'Fucking officers,' Hrindenus grumbled.

Cai ran along the intervallum between the ramparts and the rear of the cavalry barrack blocks. Wounded soldiers sat or were propped against the turf walls seeking their shade.

'Make way!' he yelled. Some tried to move their legs, but many were beyond caring, forcing Cai to hurdle more than one prone body. He reached the western gate as Lucius staggered through, a pained expression etched onto his face.

'Sir.'

Lucius stopped, giving his friend a lopsided smile. 'Well, Praefectus, the Damnonii haven't managed to see you off yet, I see?'

'It'll take more than a few of those painted bastards to send me to join my ancestors,' Cai said. He noticed Lucius held his left arm against his side. 'You're injured.'

'A big brute tried to take my head off, but I think he may have broken my arm instead.' Lucius winced as he tested his arm once more.

'What of the Hispana? Are they holding?' Cai said, lowering his voice.

'It was close. But Pudens has them withdrawing in good order into the village.'

'Pudens? What of Salvius?' Cai said. But Lucius's only response was a shrug and shake of his head. 'Well, we've made them pay and we still hold the Sack.'

'Yes…' Lucius paused, lost for words. 'They have us in their grip,' he said finally. 'By nightfall, if we can hold, both cohorts will be packed in behind these walls. The blue-faces will be close enough to bring fire.'

'Then it's fortunate the Sixth rebuilt our fort's buildings of good stone.' Cai's attempt at mirth sounded forced. 'Aye, but you're right. I'll organise parties of bucket men, have them standing ready to go where needed.' Cai winced at the pain in his own side.

Lucius snorted. 'It seems we're both a little battered. I'm not sure this life agrees with us.'

Cai laughed and both men looked at one another a moment longer.

'Well I'd best go and make sure Facilis isn't in too much trouble,' Lucius said. 'May Fortuna keep her hands over you, brother.'

Climbing up onto the parapet, Cai strode along the walkway facing into the village. He barely noticed the battle cries from the Damnonii, so long had they endured them. Looking over the misshapen ruins he could see a sizable force of the Hispana's men crowded around the gateway and palisade. As he watched, a trooper was propelled from the wooden wall onto the street below. The enemy's bowmen were now within range.

Upon returning to the tower over the main gate, he saw Hrindenus standing next to the Nervana's standard, deep in conversation with the ever present Lenius. The boy looked up at the Tungrian in open mouthed wonder.

'You two look as thick as flies on a dung pat,' Cai said. Hrindenus turned, a fleeting look of annoyance crossing his face.

'I was telling the lad about our little adventure in the lands of the Novantae. I was just getting to the interesting part.'

'Tungrians like to exaggerate their prowess, Lenius. Now the Nervii, they're real warriors.'

'I beat you back, didn't I, sir?' Hrindenus quipped.

'I'm surprised that poor beast of yours managed to carry your great lump of a body all that way, Vexillarius.' Lenius looked from one to the other, not sure what to make of the pair. 'Well, at least you didn't let any Damnonii over the wall while I was gone.'

'No, sir. They've left us alone. Unless you count those poor wretches down there?' Hrindenus nodded beyond the wall, where the anguished cries of the enemy wounded could still be heard. In a low voice, he asked, 'How bad is it, sir?'

'We're hanging on. Just.' Cai leant his elbows on the parapet and stared out towards Criffel's distant peak. 'Before nightfall, we'll be penned in behind our walls,'

'That'll make it a bit cosy.'

'Aye…' Cai closed his eyes as if succumbing to sleep, but quickly roused himself. 'The dead are becoming a problem. We have nowhere to put them.'

'We could build a great pyre, sir,' Lenius chirped. Hrindenus cuffed the boy around the head.

'We'd end up burning the fort down in the attempt,' Hrindenus said. The boy's ears burned red. 'We could drop them into the ditches by the east ramparts, sir. The tribes have let that side be. We can give them a proper send off once those idlers in the Twentieth get here.'

'Unless the Sixth beat them,' Lenius said, enthusiastically. Hrindenus snorted but said nothing more.

Cai looked to the south and said a silent prayer.

60

The turret's scorpio crew were now spectators of the battle before them. They had long since exhausted the supply of bolts. Lucius had returned from the north gate, having organised the support of the Nervana's withdrawal. Facilis and the last of his men beyond the ditches were now so near that the First Spear's shouted orders could be heard, even above the Novantae's din.

For the last half hour, Facilis had been calmly executing the gradual retreat towards the fort. The blue-faces, smelling victory, threw themselves at the auxiliary's shields with abandon. But the formation still held, three ranks deep, as its flanks progressively shrank. Men continued to stream into the fort as they were released from the left and right.

A century was formed up, standing ready on the causeway that led to the gateway. The point of greatest peril was close. Their Centurion stood before them.

'Right, me lads. Not one of those sheep-humpers is getting through us. Do. You. Hear. Me?' The command was met by a roar from his men. As it died away, he nodded in satisfaction and taking his position at the end of the second rank.

Lucius observed Facilis as he moved to the rear rank, in preparation to give the final order. The arched formation, outside of the ditches, was now less than fifty men across and reduced in size step by step. The First Spear turned suddenly, pointing his blood caked sword at the century that waited on the causeway. Its Centurion responded instantly.

'Rearguard, prepare.' he bawled.

The eighty men drew their swords, tightening grips on shields. The force outside the ditches was now just wide enough to cover the entrance to the causeway. Facilis raised his sword above his head before slashing it downwards.

'Testudo!' the Centurion bellowed.

In the instant that followed, the rearguard century transformed from ten ranks, eight men wide, into a single box-like formation, shields clashing as they came together.

'Nervana. Prepare to withdraw.' Facilis bellowed, delaying

another instant.

'Withdraw!'

The men of the front rank punched their shields into the faces of the Novantae. Then without ceremony, they ran for it, all thirty or so men. The nearest warriors, surprised by the sudden move, hesitated. Facilis ran along the causeway. 'Now!'

'Rearguard, advance.'

The testudo moved as one, like a living thing. The formation left just enough room for Facilis and his men to scurry past on either side. Even so Lucius saw two men brought down and hacked to death by the onrushing horde.

'Testudo halt.'

As the command was given the first of the enemy crashed into the shields of the rearguard's front rank.

Over the years, Lucius had watched Facilis drill his men. The testudo, inexplicably to him at the time, was one of the drills that was practised most. Now he understood.

The initial impact drove the front rank back a step. Just one step. The ranks behind held firm. Then the reaping began. For to Lucius, that was what it resembled. The harvesting of men's lives. Warriors died on the swords of the front rank. Some were simply barged into the ditches, to be impaled on the sharpened stakes, or ensnared in the morass of harvested bramble bushes. Spears and arrows, loosed at close range, assailed the testudo from both sides. A spear impaled a soldier's calf, the wounded man was replaced and quickly pulled to the rear. Warriors shrieked in frustration.

Lucius looked along the battlements. 'Mascellus, ready your men,' he shouted. The old Decurion raised his spatha in acknowledgement.

'Right, ladies. I want to see broken skulls when I give the order.' Age had not robbed Mascellus of the power in his voice. His men were grouped over the gateway. The last of Facilis's men had passed through and the First Spear turned back.

'Now Centurion.' he roared.

'Testudo will withdraw by the count.' The Centurion's voice boomed once more. 'One.' The rearguard began its slow backwards walk, like a scaled beast returning to its lair. 'Two.'

The soldier to the fore of the Centurion collapsed, an arrow embedded deep in his eye. Without thought, the Centurion leapt forward, punching his shield boss into the snarling face of a warrior who had tried to take advantage of the short-lived space. The officer's broad helmet plume immediately drew the attention of the tribesmen along the face of the outer ditch and it wasn't long before his shield resembled the body of a hedgehog, so many arrows protruded from it. But still he continued the count. 'One. Two.'

The rear ranks of the testudo were passing under the gateway.

'Now!' Mascellus yelled. As one, his men threw their fist-sized stones into the packed ranks of the Novantae. The impact on unprotected bodies was ruinous. The rocks crushed skulls, cheeks and collarbones. Men fell, dead or unconscious. Some, without shields, leaped into the ditches in a forlorn attempt to escape the deadly hail. But the pressure from those pushing from behind was relentless. The gates to their enemy's fortress were open, the route to their victory was close at hand. The packed ranks were driven along the causeway's narrow length.

Mascellus left the parapet and shouted down to the Optio commanding at the fort's entrance.

'Prepare to close the gates.'

Ten men stood at either gate, ready to shove. Others held the locking spar. Lucius gripped the pommel of his spatha. The testudo continued its slow withdrawal, the front rank frantically holding the Novantae at bay, but the press continued unabated. How would they get the gates closed with such a weight of numbers?

But the warriors were now only a few paces from the stone throwers on the parapet. Mascellus's men couldn't fail to strike a target. Bodies began to pile up in front of the retreating formation.

'Prepare.' The Centurion bellowed. 'Now!' The front rank of the testudo drove their shields forward. Simultaneously the rear ranks abandoned the formation and ran the last few steps to the fort, the front rank following hard on their heels.

'Close the gates.' Mascellus bawled. A short gap, of barely a spear's length, had opened between the running rearguard and the warriors The great oak doors were swinging shut. The Centurion was last to reach the gateway, diving through the rapidly shrinking opening. The gates crashed shut. Men were lifting the spar into place just as the warriors outside slammed against the heavy oak doors. The impact forced a narrow gap to open up once more. A shrieking Novantae sprung into it, desperately thrusting his spear.

Facilis stepped forward, driving his sword in a fierce uppercut under the warrior's chin, its point burst from the top of his skull. The First Spear used his sword's hilt to drag the deadweight of the body into the Sack's interior.

'Push you slackers.' he yelled.

Men from the rearguard added their weight to the others and the doors slammed shut. The spar dropped into place. A cheer of relief erupted from all around the gate.

But it was a different tale for the enemy now trapped outside. A wail arose from massed throats. They had failed. Driven on by Mascellus, the men over the gateway continued to shower rocks onto the warriors below. Some tried in vain to turn back, but were prevented by the press from behind.

The warble of the war horns struck up and reluctantly the warriors outside the ditches slowly withdrew, shouting curses at the defenders as they went.

'Sir,' Lucius turned at the shout from Mascellus. The old Decurion held a smooth grey rock in his raised hand and shook his head. The supply of stones from the streams was spent.

61

The mansio was ablaze. Great black gouts of smoke billowed from the inn. The two-storey wooden frame was feeding a fire that would likely burn long into the night, lighting the ground around it. It has been two hours since the tribes had abandoned the assault on the north gate and instead had settled for destroying anything outside the Sack and its village.

The sun had set, but there was still an hour of light left in the day and the doleful music of the warhorns filled the air once more.

'Sir.' Lucius jumped with surprise. The groom had appeared at his side.

'How do you do that, Lenius?'

'Sir?'

'Never mind, make your report.'

'Sir, the Praefectus wishes to report that the Damnonii are approaching from the south once more.' The boy looked exhausted and his lips were dry and cracked.

'Here, drink this.' Lucius handed him his water canteen.

'Thank you, sir.'

'Where are you from, Lenius?'

The boy blushed, but answered quickly. 'My father's home is on the coast of the Sula, near Petrianis. He's a fisherman.'

'Didn't you want to follow your father's path to the sea?'

'I've always loved horses, sir,' Lenius said. 'Ever since I was small, I watched the cavalry that patrolled along the coast. My father wasn't pleased when I shook the hand of the recruiting Optio who came to our village. I've not seen my father since the day I left. I hope he's forgiven me.' The boy's voice trailed off.

'Well, when we've finished with the Novantae you shall have leave to visit him. Take one of our horses too. Show him the man you've become and I can assure you he *will* be proud.'

Lenius's face reflected disbelief, but a broad smile broke across his young face.

'Thank you, sir.'

Lucius nodded at the boy and coughed gruffly. 'Now then, get yourself back to the Praefectus.' Shaking his head, as the boy raced along the walkway. 'So like Marcus'.

The war horns kept up their haunting music, the sound becoming progressively louder as the Novantae and their Selgovae allies appeared. As they approached the battleground, the black carrion birds rose into the air, screeching angrily at being disturbed again from their feasting. Although, thankfully, Lucius no longer noticed the rotting smell of death.

Pudens commanded the Hispana in the village, the cohort a shadow of the one that had marched to join the Nervana. Lucius doubted they could hold out in the ruins for long. There had been no sight of Salvius since that morning. No one had seen him fall.

'A fine evening, sir.' Mascellus had joined him on the western wall.

'Indeed, brother. A pity about the view, however.' Lucius looked at the old veteran. The ruddy face of the farmer had been transformed, his skin sallow, beard filthy and ragged. 'Your mail hangs a little less snugly on you, my friend.'

The Decurion gave a deep belly laugh. 'That'll please my good lady wife. She's been on at me about having to continually let out my troos.'

'Did you get her away to safety?'

'Aye. If there's such a thing. I sent her and the boy to be with her sister's people, along with a couple of my field hands, so she'll be as safe as she can be. Although I have to admit, I miss her cooking. Three-day old bread doesn't have much to recommend it.'

'Well, as soon as the legions get here, we will be able to release you to your familial duties,' Lucius said. Mascellus smiled but didn't answer, simply nodding before moving along the ramparts, talking quietly to the men as he went.

The Novantae had halted a short distance from the village palisade. Wisps of smoke arose from within their massed ranks, accompanied by flashes of light. Lucius had been expecting it, but his stomach filled with dread nonetheless. Fire.

In flights of ones and twos, flaming arrows appeared from within the mass of the enemy. No great volleys as he had seen the Hamian's achieve, but with the wreckage of the wooden buildings inside the palisade, they didn't need to be. Arrows disappeared amongst the ruins. Some landed ineffectively on the internal roadways, quickly extinguished. But others fell into the morass of timber, flames quickly taking hold.

Parties of men had been detailed to delay the fires spread, but it was a hopeless task. The flights of arrows continued unabated. Black smoke arose in places throughout the village. Gradually Lucius's view of the ground in front of the palisade became obscured.

He turned at shouts of alarm from the direction of the southern rampart, as the first flaming arrows landed amongst the cavalry barracks.

'The sheep-humpers are getting brave, now they believe we've nothing left to throw back at them.' Hrindenus echoed Cai's own frustration. Arrow after arrow had plunged into the Sack's interior. Some of the first had fallen amongst the wounded, who lay outside the barrack blocks, striking a few unfortunates too slow, or unable, to take cover. Cai had given the order to move as many as possible to the relative safety at the base of the fort's eastern wall.

'It appears the blue-faces have got their fighting spirit back.' Cai watched some of the Damnonii cavorting ahead of their bowmen, calling challenges to the defenders, thumping spears and shields against their tattooed chests. Cai coughed once, which quickly turned into a choking fit. The fires in the village were burning fiercely. There was little wind and the black acrid smoke had drifted lazily over the fort, settling like a stinking fog.

Lenius handed the water skin to Cai, who nodded his thanks. Arrows continued to sail across the ramparts, but most clattered harmlessly against roof files or the stone-built walls of the cavalry barrack blocks. Those that did find a wooden surface had so far been quickly dealt with by the sections of water carriers. The few remaining horses were becoming panicked. He had been able to visit Adela briefly and even his fearless mount was unsettled, unable to move amongst the sound and stink of battle.

'It does look like they fancy their chances,' Cai said, as the Damnonii lifted their ladders.

Hrindenus hawked and spat a great, sooty globule over the wall.

Cai looked along the battlements. His men were standing ready. He had reorganised them into pairs. The first held a lance to repel any who successfully scaled a ladder. The other carried a shield to protect the pair against enemy bowmen.

All looked exhausted. Few had eaten that day, but all knew what had to be done. If the Damnonii breached the wall, none of the defenders would see another sunrise. A blast of sound reverberated from the Damnonii war horns. They were on the move, screaming their rage as they raced towards the waiting auxiliaries. They splashed into the stream, jostling to be amongst the first to cross the causeway.

'Prepare!' Cai's shout cut through the tumult of noise. An instant later the first warriors reached the base of the turf ramparts. But his men had not been idle whilst they had been waiting. They began to drop their improvised projectiles, gathered from the ruins of the village. Roof beams, brickwork and all manner of debris was dropped onto the heads of those below, shattering skulls and breaking bones. It did not delay the Damnonii for long.

A ladder's struts struck the parapet in front of Hrindenus. The big Tungrian took hold of its top spar in one hand, the other still held his shield. With a grunt and mighty heave, he shoved it away. He yelled out in pain, looking dumbly at his hand. An arrow had pierced his palm, white fletched flights standing proud, the arrowhead protruding four fingers width from the back of his hand. Blood dripped from the wound, soaking into the wooden walkway.

Cai moved quickly. Taking hold of Hrindenus's wrist. 'Kneel down, hold your hand still against the walkway,' Cai said. The big man obeyed without speaking. In one swift move, Cai drew his spatha and sliced it through the wooden shaft, the flights falling at his feet. A short stump still protruded from his palm.

'Right. After three.' Cai spoke quietly. Hrindenus nodded, closing his eyes.

'One.' Cai yanked the arrowhead free.

'Bastard.' The big man cursed. Another ladder thumped against the parapet.

'Lenius, find something to strap his hand.'

Cai sheathed his sword and leapt for the ladder. Heaving with both hands, it barely budged. Two Damnonii were already climbing, their weight pinning the ladder in place. The nearest grinned at Cai's failure, his grey and pointed teeth giving him a wolflike expression. Cai drew his spatha once more, just as the head of the dark wiry warrior appeared at the top of the ladder. Cai sliced downwards but the Damnonii was nimble, raising his square shield to take the blow. The sword cut deep into the leatherbound wood and became snagged. The warrior's grin broadened. He yanked hard, pulling Cai off balance. The two were almost face to face as they wrestled to get the upper hand, Cai could feel himself losing control. He'd have to let go of the sword.

The Damnonii shoved hard with his shield, reaching for the parapet with his free hand. He gripped its edge, bellowing a shout of triumph. Instantly his face transformed to a look contorted with pain and shock. His grip was lost, along with his fingers. He fell backwards, crashing into the next man on the ladder, all the while looking dumbly at the stump of his hand.

Cai turned to see Lenius, blood smeared spatha in hand, staring at the space where the warrior's head had been. After freeing his sword from the shield, the warrior had released as he fell, Cai placed his hand on the boy's shoulder.

'Well done, lad.'

'I don't remember getting any thanks for the number of times I've saved your arse, sir,' Hrindenus said, but moved before Cai could respond.

'Here lad, help me get this off our wall.' The two grabbed the ladder, the Tungrian shoving hard with his good hand. The ladder slid along the rampart face, crashing to the ground below.

'Sir, look!' Lenius shouted. Smoke had begun to drift over the parapet from the base of the gate.

'Bollocks. They're learning.' Hrindenus risked a look over the wall. 'They've got burning straw stacked against the gate, and more on the way.' Cai was startled by the sight. Pairs of men were running along the causeway bearing more bundles of straw between them.

'Shit. You two grab some of that rubble and start dropping it on the heads of those bastards.'

'Water carriers.' Cai shouted down into the fort.

'Sir.' came the answering shout, an Optio appearing from between the nearest barrack block.

'Get your men to start soaking the gate and pour water under it as well. I want a river flowing out of the fort. Do you understand?'

'Yes, sir.'

The junior officer ran off giving orders as he went. Cai cursed himself. He should have anticipated this.

Dark clouds of pungent smoke billowed over the ramparts and into the Sack's interior.

62

Waves of intense heat assaulted the western ramparts. The cracking sound of splitting timbers filled the air as they were consumed. Men coughed, mouths and noses covered by neck scarfs, as smoke now pervaded the fort's interior. The Hispana were withdrawing. Pudens was pulling his men out whilst he still could. The last of the exhausted men were hurrying over the bridge into the Sack. Well, not quite the last.

Twenty volunteers manned the wall around the village's main gate, to give the lie that the Romans still defended within. The horde held its position. Waiting for the fires to do the work for them.

'Right, brother, let's get the rearguard out of there,' Lucius said. Pudens, standing alongside him, nodded to the Hispana's Vexillarius. The cohort's black bull standard was raised high and waved in a circular motion by the standard-bearer. The signal to withdraw.

'I hope they can see it,' Pudens's exhaustion made him sound even more morose than usual. 'The smoke keeps obscuring them.' The Pannonian had barely taken his eyes from the village gateway.

'They've seen it,' he said with relief at catching a glimpse of the answering raised hand.

'Who commands?'

'Centurion Vericundus. A good man. He was first to volunteer.' Pudens coughed into his neck scarf.

'Vericundus. The Baetican?' Lucius looked towards the village gateway, obscured once again by thick smoke. 'We must do something for that man. If we survive.'

'Indeed,' Pudens spluttered, through his now hacking cough.

A blast of heat hit them, like opening the door to the fort's smithy. The wind had strengthened, whipping the fires to greater intensity.

'How are they going to make it through that?' Lucius said. A wall of flames engulfed the settlement.

'They'll find a way,'

But Pudens's optimism was forced. The fate of his men appeared sealed. Burn to death or wait for the enemy on the palisade. But whatever their end, the men in the Sack would not see it. The flames and smoke now blocked all sight of the rearguard.

'Tribunus, sir. To the north wall.' The shout came from Tranquillis, the Optio of the scorpio section, still stationed in the turret. Both Lucius and Pudens ran along the crowded walkway.

'Move,' Pudens screamed. Men pressed themselves against the guardrail. Reaching the turret doorway Lucius took the steps two at a time.

'Along the side of the village's palisade, sir.' Tranquillis made way for Lucius in the turret's corner. There,' he pointed. Moving in single file along the thin strip of ground separating the palisade from the inner ditch, was the rearguard. Vericundus took the lead. It was a move born of desperation. The line shuffled slowly, trying to ensure each soldier could link shields with the man in front.

The Novantae followed, like a malignant shadow. They loosed arrows erratically, but could hardly miss at such a short range. Lucius saw they had already taken a toll. The bodies of two soldiers lay unmoving in the village's ditch. It seemed no shield was free of a shaft.

A soldier near the column's centre cried out and stumbled, an arrow piercing his heel, only prevented from falling by the hand of the man behind. In obvious agony the soldier stumbled on.

There was nothing to be done. If they could reach the corner of the palisade they would have the protection of the gap between the village and the Sack's ramparts. But how many of them would make it? he thought, as two more men were brought down, collapsing into the ditch under the deadly hail.

The men along the parapet began to shout encouragement.

'C'mon lads, you can make it.' Tranquillis shouted. Soon everyone who had a view was shouting, reminding Lucius of the crowds cheering on their favoured gladiator at the arena. Another man fell. If any were to survive they must throw all caution to the wind.

Leaning over the turret edge Lucius yelled, 'Run for it Vericundus.' The Centurion, now less than a spear throw from the turret, heard the shout.

'Run boys. Run.' Vericundus hollered over his shoulder. An instant later all remaining men of the rearguard were pounding along the base of the palisade. Gaps appeared between the shields, exposing them to the enemy onslaught. But the quicker pace made them a harder target.

Another arrow struck Vericundus's shield. An anguished cry escaped his lips, his face contorted, but he continued to run. The Centurion reached the corner of the palisade, directly below the turret. Halting he grabbed the second and third man in line, forming a shield wall.

'Good man,' Lucius shouted. This tiny barrier of shields now gave protection to the rest of the small band, as each man turned the corner. The shouts from the defenders on the ramparts reached a new level, as each man made it to safety, some shaking shields and swords at the enemy, taunting their failure.

As the last surviving soldier rounded the corner, the three-man wall began to withdraw, taking measured backwards steps under the Centurion's steady leadership.

Lucius ran from the turret, making his way to the western gateway, reaching it as Vericundus and the last of his men staggered into the fort. Pain creased his features. Lucius moved to his side.

'Well done, Centurion, I think we can allow you to release what's left of your shield.'

'I would do it gladly, sir,' Vericundus said, in a hiss. 'But the fucking thing is pinned to my side.' A bubble of blood appeared between the Centurion's lips.

'You and you,' Lucius commanded, pointing at two men standing nearby. 'Help the Centurion to the medicus. We need this man strapped up and back with us as soon as possible.' He watched as Vericundus was helped away. He doubted he would see the Baetican again.

Soon after, Lucius surveyed the wreckage of the village from the parapet as it continued to burn fiercely.

'The barbarians can't come at us from that direction until long into the night. Perhaps not before first light,' Pudens said, at Lucius's side.

'Let's hope so,' Lucius said. 'Your man Vericundus is a good officer.

'He's certainly turning out to be,' Pudens said. 'Though I don't know him well. He was sponsored into the cohort only recently. Has influential connections by the looks of it.'

‘I fear the arrow he took has punctured a lung. If we were near a legion hospital he would have a chance, but in this place...’ Lucius shrugged.

Both men shared a moment of understanding.

‘Right, brother,’ Lucius said. ‘Get yourself to the north ramparts. I’m going to see how the Praefectus is getting on with our Damnonii friends.’

Thankfully the breeze had shifted direction once more, the smoke from the fires drifted to the west and away from the Sack. A small mercy.

The fort's interior was filled with a great crush of humanity. Many of the walking wounded shuffled along the Via Praetoria or between buildings, in search of somewhere to rest or simply to take cover. The most seriously wounded men were sheltered within the barrack blocks and granaries. When the arrows had first started to rain down, he had ordered the principia and praetorium be used too. Lucius caught a glimpse of Alyn as she moved between buildings, Beren, her constant shadow, water bucket slopping in his hand.

There was still a little of the sun’s purple glow, silhouetting the summit of Criffel, but light was quickly fading. As he approached the south-facing parapet, an eerie sight greeted him. The massed body of the Damnonii tribesmen were standing in silence beyond the stream. The fires from the village lit their dark tattooed faces. They appeared every bit like an army of the dead.

The Nervana’s standard fluttered on the tower above the main gate. Lucius made his way towards it, stopping several times to talk to men he knew.

‘You still live, Oraphus? It’ll take more than a few Damnonii to stop you, will it not? How is your arm, Septimus?’ And so it went. The men were responsive enough, but their exhaustion made them listless.

Finally he climbed the turret over the main gate, and there, looking out over the scene below, stood Cai. A thin veil of smoke rose in front of him. Hrindenus and Lenius were in deep conversation nearby.

‘How goes it, Praefectus?’

Cai turned, eyes bloodshot and face blackened with soot. His fair hair hung filthily over his shoulders, his beard greasy with grime.

The three swan feathers of his helm were now a dirty grey, bent in different directions. But through the black of his face, Cai's grin shone.

'The Damnonii tried to burn the gate,' Cai said. 'It was close, but we dropped enough masonry on their heads to build another fort with.' He hawked into the ditch below. 'They appear to have given up for the day. When their attempt to destroy the gate failed, they just faded away, without even a signal from those damned horns of theirs.'

Lucius stuck his head out over the parapet and was greeted by a nightmare scene. Bent and charred limbs lay crushed beneath wood and brickwork that extended out onto the causeway. The putrid smell of burning flesh and hair, mingled with the charcoaled smoking timber, was appalling. His attention was drawn once more to the Damnonii. Their dark shadows had started to shuffle towards the west, like a cohort of shadows.

'Perhaps they've given up. Surely even they must sleep.' Lucius heard the desperation in his own voice. He was too tired to care who heard it. Turning, he rested his back against the parapet, propping his aching arm on its edge. 'No. They'll fear the legions are closing in. Their time may be short.' He looked at Cai. 'I would speak with you, brother.' Cai followed Lucius to a corner of the turret, out of earshot.

'You don't think we can survive another day,' Cai said. It was not a question, just a simple statement of the truth. Lucius looked at Cai, giving his head the slightest of shakes.

'If I commanded such numbers,' Lucius said, 'tomorrow at first light, I'd send the full force through the village. I'd fill the ditches with rubble overnight and assault along the length of the western ramparts.'

Lucius looked out over the battlements, the ground before them faintly lit by the dying flames from the village. Fleeting movements of carrion birds could be seen as they hopped from body to body.

'Our only hope is that the Twentieth or the Sixth make an appearance tomorrow, before we're overwhelmed. So we must do what we can to buy them time.'

'What do you have in mind, brother?' Cai said.

'We'll use the buildings of the fort to our advantage.' Lucius outlined his plan.

'Well, it's certainly a plan,' Cai said, as he scratched his matted beard.

'A plan of the forlorn,' Lucius said. 'What of Alyn and the boy? Perhaps there is a way to get them out during the night? She rides, does she not? We could get them out of the east gate.'

Cai removed his helmet and liner and scratched his scalp vigorously, then wiped his soot covered brow with his wrist.

'It has crossed my mind,' he said, 'more than once. But I don't think she'd go. She's a proud woman. Besides, even if the Novantae have feared to attack the eastern defences, they'll be watching.' He slid his helmet back on. 'But I'll try to talk to her about it.'

'I'd take your chance now my friend, while there's time.'

63

Cai walked into the dimly lit interior of the Sack's largest granary, its raised, solid stone floor now crammed with the wounded. A continuous low moaning was punctuated by the occasional cry of anguish. He didn't want to linger in this place of death. He saw the flame of one of the lamps flutter. An orderly was moving from man to man, but there was no sign of Alyn.

'She's in the first of the infantry barrack blocks, across the way from the praetorium.'

Cai turned to see Castellanos standing in the doorway.

'You look like you've ridden through the fires of the underworld,' Castellanos said with a weary smile. 'Here, splash some of this across your face, before you seek her out, just in case she thinks a daemon has come to visit her in the night.' The medicus handed Cai a water skin that had been hanging by the door. Cai poured the water over his face, washing away the dark streaks of soot.

'My thanks, Castellanos.' Cai handed the skin back. 'You don't look so great yourself. Perhaps a few days' sleep might help.' Cai tried to make his voice sound light.

'I fear sleep. I see the dead I've failed.' The medicus held a haunted expression, his eyes sunken and dark.

'You've done your duty, brother. More men will be able to carry on the fight tomorrow, because of you and your men. You've provided comfort to those who could not survive their wounds. No man and no god could ask more.' Cai gripped the Greek's shoulder as he moved past him. He walked swiftly across the Via Principalis, past the praetorium and into the barracks.

On entering the first block he saw a bundle of blankets to the side of the door. The bundle suddenly moved and a child's foot popped out. Bending down, Cai carefully uncovered the boy's head and was momentarily startled by how much Beren now resembled his father.

'I'm sorry, my friend, I said I would protect them, but I've failed you,' Cai whispered, before replacing the blanket.

He walked along the building's narrow passageway, looking into each room that in normal times would accommodate a section of eight men, but now had double that number of wounded both on the bunks and filling every available space between. In the end room he found her sitting on a stool next to a bunk. Alyn's head rested against the wall, eyes closed, snoring gently as she held the hand of a wounded man. Cai looked at the soldier, his eyes stared blankly at the underside of the bunk above.

It was then he noticed her other hand resting upon her lap. It held the bloody hilt of a pugio. Partly congealed gore still glistened on the dagger's blade.

'He is of the Cornovii tribe,' Alyn whispered. 'His name is Conovora and he had nineteen summers.' Her quiet voice was flat, devoid of emotion, but Cai knew better. He placed his palm gently against her cheek and looked into her soft grey eyes. 'He was in so much pain, I had to—' The words came in a sob.

'You look beyond tired, my love,' Cai said. Tears pooled in the corner of her eyes before spilling down her cheeks, two streams racing to her jaw line. 'And I think these eyes have seen a lifetime of suffering in recent days.' She nodded, unable to speak. Cai pulled over another stool and sat down beside her, their backs against the wall, looking over the bunk of the dead youth. He gently peeled back her fingers and took the pugio from her. Alyn lay her head against his chainmail covered shoulder. Both were silent for a while.

'I can get you and Beren out,' Cai whispered. 'It would be a risk, but perhaps better than staying here.' Alyn squeezed his arm tightly and for a time she didn't speak.

'You have not said, but I know you made a promise to watch over us.' Alyn held her fingers gently to his lips to stop him interrupting. 'But I cannot abandon these men in their time of need, nor leave the people of the village to their fate, whilst I make my escape. It would be cowardly and I could not abide it.' She wiped fresh tears from her cheeks. 'Your promise to Beren's father has been fulfilled, I am yours now, no longer the wife of Adalfus. My fate will be the same as yours.'

'But what of Beren?' Cai said, unable to hide the anguish he felt.

'He has both the blood of the Nervii and Carvetii running through his veins,' she said. 'I don't wish him a warrior's death at such a young age, but nor would I ask him to live with the scar of knowing he had left friends in his beloved Nervana to die.' The lump in Cai's throat prevented any further response. He simply rested his head against hers in acceptance.

They stayed there, arms entwined, for a while longer, saying little, simply listening to each other's slow, deep breathing. But finally Cai knew he must leave.

'When the time comes,' he whispered, 'take cover near the eastern gate and I will find you.' She raised her head from his shoulder and met his lips, a soft caress of farewell.

'I love you,' she whispered into his ear

'And I you.'

'Tribunus.' Lucius's eyes snapped open as his shoulder was shaken. The face of Castellanos was close to his own. Lucius, slumped in his chair, was sure he had only just fallen asleep, but the room was in near darkness, the oil lamps had burned out.

'What is it, medicus?' Lucius said, not hiding his irritation. The Greek looked pale, his skin drawn, dark rings hanging heavily below his eyes.

'I'm sorry to wake you, but the Centurion Vericundus is asking for you.'

'The Baetican?' Lucius said. 'I don't have—'

'He is most insistent.' Castellanos cut across Lucius. 'He is weak, close to the end. He seems almost frantic to speak with you.'

'Very well,' Lucius grumbled. 'Does he wish me to pass on a message to his family?'

'He wouldn't say. He will only talk to you.'

'Where is he?' Lucius asked, rising wearily.

'I've found him a cot in the main granary. I'll take you.'

Upon reaching the doors to the huge building, Castellanos turned to Lucius.

'He's in great pain. I have no milk of the poppy to ease it.' Lucius nodded in understanding. 'Have a care with your footing. There's little room and we are low on oil for the lamps.'

The medicus led the way. It was a nightmare vision. In the gloom, the ground seemed to writhe of its own volition. The space was filled with the low sounds of men in misery. Nearby an officer, mumbled sporadic orders to imaginary troops. Some simply wept or called for their mothers. The smell was appalling. Lucius had become inured to the reek of death that pervaded the battlefield, but this was something else, the foulness made him gag.

The medicus led him to a cot against the rearmost wall. Without a word Castellanos indicated the prone Centurion and left to his duties. Vericundus's eyes were shut. Only the red bubble playing at his lips gave an indication he yet lived. His dark hair was sweat-dampened, and spots of moisture covered his brow.

Lucius knelt by the Centurion's head. 'Vericundus,' he whispered. The Baetican's eyes fluttered open. At first he did not appear to see, but suddenly his eyes focussed recognising Lucius. He became earnest.

'Sir.' The word hissed, a look of agony creasing Vericundus's face. 'It was I.'

'What was you, Centurion?' Lucius said, not understanding.

'It was I who attacked you…by the Sula.' Vericundus's words were so low Lucius thought he had misheard. 'I had no choice; he said he would evict my father from his farm and see him destitute.'

Lucius was bewildered. Vericundus was the masked rider? It made no sense. He could not reconcile this courageous commander of the village's rearguard with the lone assassin. But he knew Vericundus's time was short so spoke gently. 'Tell me everything, brother. From the beginning.'

When the Centurion spoke again his words came as a whisper, Lucius lowering his ear to the dying man's lips. Even then the words were halting, hissed through his growing pain. Lucius listened, not interrupting as Vericundus told his tale until finally his words faded to silence.

Lucius looked upon his compatriot. The Centurion's eyes stared. Unmoving. His last breath taken. Lucius sat back on his haunches, stunned, his tired mind running wild. The memory of his father's blood-soaked tunic came to him and he was consumed with rage, his fatigue forgotten.

He had a new enemy to kill.

'Jupiter, best and greatest, give me the courage to do my duty and if the time comes, bring honour to my family with my death.' Lucius whispered his prayer into the near darkness. The village that lay before him and the fort behind had become almost silent for the first time in days, as if taking a last deep breath. Quiet enough, he hoped, for his prayer to be heard.

'And if I should live, grant me the chance to avenge my father.'

The first hint of morning light had revealed the smouldering, charred remains of the village. The fires had finally died down during the long night. And the enemy had not been idle. Bowmen had sent continual, if erratic, volleys of flaming arrows into the heart of the fort. Many of the roof tiles had been removed from the cavalry barrack blocks during the night, at Lucius's order. Without their baked clay cover some of the buildings had been set aflame; and the few remaining horses evacuated to the courtyard of the praetorium.

Hidden by darkness, the enemy had made short work of the palisade, forcing the big timbers into the ditches below the Sack's western ramparts. Roof tiles, thrown by the fort's defenders, had ensured the work was not without loss, but in the end there was little that could be done to prevent it.

Footsteps scuffed along the parapet, sounding heavy with weariness. The outlines of four men, so familiar to him now, appeared out of the gloom.

'A fine morning, brothers,' Lucius said.

'Better now we don't have that cursed smoke choking us half to death,' Facilis said in a croak. There was none of the usual joviality in the First Spear's voice. A deep fatigue left little room for it. His normally solid figure seemed shrunken.

Lucius's most senior officers gathered around him, close enough that he could discern their faces. For the first time since he was a green, untried officer, fresh to the Nervana, he found himself lost for words. Instead he met every man's eyes in turn, acknowledging their presence with a nod. Pudens's dark complexion was inscrutable, but the Pannonian had proven his worth and would be a welcome presence on the ramparts. Facilis, when the time came, would be fierce in the bloody grind of the battle to come, an example to his men, who loved him for it. Mascellus, the affable old Nervii warrior who had retired to a quiet life on his farm and could have taken his wife and goods and left for the south with honour intact, had instead chosen to stand shoulder to shoulder with his brothers. Finally Cai, his friend, standing before him with his usual lopsided grin. If this was to be his last day on Earth, then it was a comfort to know Cai would be with him.

'Brothers,' Lucius began. 'The legions will arrive today, or they won't. That is in the hands of the gods, so we must look to what is in our gift to do. Our enemy knows they are running out of time. The signs are they will throw their full weight behind an assault on our western ramparts. Our purpose and duty today is clear: we must buy our legions time. We have our plan, we know what we must do.' Lucius let his words sink in before continuing.

'But there *is* hope, brothers. We know the overblown pride of the ladies in the Sixth and Twentieth will have them double-timing along the roads, in a race for bragging rights over who rescued the province.' Lucius was pleased to hear the murmur of amusement his words evoked. There was life in them yet.

'Are there any final questions?' Each man either greeted the question with silence or a gentle shake of the head. 'Very well then. May Fortuna be with us.' He grasped each of their arms in turn as they left to take up their positions. He came to Cai last, but before Lucius could take his arm, his friend embraced him.

'There's nothing more for you to say, Lucius. We'll either share a cup in the officer's mess tonight or be sat by the hunting fire with Adal and that old goat Avitius, whilst they laugh at our failure. Either is an ending I welcome.'

'Yes, that doesn't sound so bad, does it?' Lucius said.

Alone once more, Lucius strolled along the western rampart, looking down into the Sack's interior. The still shadowed spaces between the long lines of barrack blocks were slowly filling with the silent, shuffling outlines of men, the remnants of the two cohorts. Few appeared to be without a wound. They would form deep ranks of shields in this final line of defence. Once the wall was breached. And it would be breached. Cai commanded the south, Facilis the north, covering the infantry blocks and the praetorium.

He rested his elbows on the parapet's edge. Beyond the wreckage of the village's main gate, the massed fires of the enemy camp burned brightly.

'Get a move on, you bastards.' Lucius whispered into the chill air of the early morning.

As if in response, the war horns sounded their mournful music, calling forth the ragged battlecries of the tribes. He turned his attention to the battlements. Men stood a pace apart along its full length, roof tiles were stacked at intervals between crenellations. Each man on the parapet held a spear, a mixture of cavalry lances, the shorter throwing javelins and in some cases the rough-made spears of the enemy, scavenged during the night from the battlefield. They were as ready as they could be.

The first of the enemy's fire arrows began to rise, burning brightly against the near darkness.

'Cover!' Pudens warning bellowed into the fort's interior.

'Shields!' Cai's shouted order, taken up by the other officers who led the units wedged between the barrack blocks. Men raised their oval shields, overlapping with those around them.

Most arrows were shot from so close a range within the village they sailed over the buildings nearest the western wall. Lucius heard the scream of a horse, whether from fear or pain he couldn't tell. He hoped it wasn't his beloved Epona.

The war horns continued their unearthly warble, closer now, entering the remains of the village, leading the dark horde. The tribes gradually filled its interior, looking to Lucius like oil spilled from a flask, the dark contents slowly oozing across the ground. The sound from the horns rose to a new urgency, accompanied by massed war cries.

'Prepare!' Pudens shouted from his position a short distance to Lucius's left. The blare of the horns finally reached a crescendo, then abruptly stopped. For a time there was complete silence inside the Sack and across the village, both sides reluctant to be first to commence the slaughter.

A single battlecry shattered the silence. The host moved as one, running and scrambling across the wreckage of the village, yelling and howling as they came. When they neared the ramparts, Lucius discerned groups of warriors carrying ladders. Many ladders.

64

‘No more arguments, Lenius,’ Cai said, ‘you will not be in the line of defence.’ The groom looked crestfallen. ‘I’m promoting you to acting Vexillarius.’ The boy's head snapped up, a bewildered look on his face.

‘Sir?’

‘You’ll stand with the Hispana’s standard bearer by the eastern gateway. That’ll be our rally point, if the time comes. And you’ll defend that rag with your life. Do you hear me, Vexillarius?’

‘Yes, sir,’ Lenius said, his chest puffing out. Hrindenus coughed, disguising the laugh that tried to force its way out.

‘Right then, lad,’ Hrindenus said, ‘off you go now and don’t lose my fucking standard.’ They watched the boy’s retreating back, turning to look at each other, grinning broadly. The hail of arrows had stopped moments before and both men now stood at the rear of Cai’s force.

‘Right Hrindenus, it sounds like the blue-faces are trying to get over the wall. Let's get ready to give them a warm welcome.’

The pair marched briskly along the Via Principalis to the point Cai had positioned his century-strength unit. They stood in their ranks, before the western gate, wedged between the walls of the praetorium and the first of the cavalry’s barrack blocks, ten men across and eight deep. As Cai approached, some of his men spoke quietly to one another, others cast concerned glances towards the ramparts above.

Hrindenus shouldered his way into the centre of the front rank, the Tungrian standing a head taller than those to either side of him. Cai strode to the roadway in front of the waiting formation, turning to face them. He had been careful to ensure the men defending the gateway were drawn from the Nervana; he wanted those that stood with him to be men he knew and trusted.

Even so, the faces that stared back at him were a ragtag bunch. Most had some kind of strapping. One soldier’s head was so heavily wrapped with a dressing he couldn’t wear his helmet. Their eyes told a tale though. All had the dark, sunken look of exhaustion. But little fear, only acceptance of what was to come.

The noise from the battlements had intensified, the screams and the clash of steel fierce. His men would soon be face to face with their enemy, in a last-gasp fight for survival. Cai cleared his throat, spitting onto the roadways surface.

'You are men of the First Nervana Germanorum,' Cai shouted over the tumult from above. He had their attention. 'Your standard carries many battle honours, including one for defeating those very bastards outside our gate. We will not dishonour the memory of our cohort this day. They will break upon our shields like waves against rock. None will pass. Understood?'

'Yes, sir.' came the massed response.

Cai raised his shield and held it firmly on his left arm. Still facing his men he drew his spatha. He rapped the blade against his shield boss, starting a steady rhythm.

'Nervana! Nervana!' Cai's chant was taken up by the eighty men.

'Nervana! Nervana! Nervana!' the voices accompanied by the ring of sword on shield. Cai nodded with satisfaction and moved to stand in the front rank on the right of Hrindenus.

'Pretty speech, sir,' Hrindenus muttered. Cai ignored him keeping up the steady chant. He wanted the enemy in the village to hear what awaited them when they broke into the fort. And know fear. He watched the fight on the walkway above the gateway. The enemy had gained a foothold, confirmed moments later as a body hit the roadway in front of him. The auxiliary made no sound as he fell.

His hand had cramped and, in the brief respite, Lucius relaxed his grip on the spatha's hilt. The pain in his shield arm had been agony at times and he had come close to releasing it more than once.

Somehow, they had so far held the ramparts. Warriors had gained a foothold in numerous places and the walkway had rung with the clash of steel and curses of individual battles.

All had been flung back, but it was relentless. Despair filled him as more continued to spill across the village's remains, like ants on a bird carcass.

More ladders thumped against the parapet's edge. Men worked in pairs to dislodge them, but fatigue made it increasingly difficult.

He lept into action as the struts of another ladder appeared in front of him, realising with alarm that he now stood alone.

'More men up top, now.' Lucius roared at the Optio at the base of the steps, knowing it was already too late, he could not push the ladder away on his own. So he waited. An axe arched over the parapet from an unseen enemy, in an attempt to clear his path. But Lucius had been ready. The warrior's bearded head appeared, only to fall back, mouth open in a silent scream, Lucius's sword point buried in his eye socket.

Men of the reserve reached the walkway as Lucius wrenched his blade free.

'Get this ladder off my wall.' he yelled. Breathing hard, he looked along the battlements. Pudens was in trouble.

'You lot,' Lucius called to a section of replacements. 'Get to the First Spear.' Sending the men running along the walkway. He kept two with him.

An arrow thumped against the shield rim of the soldier closest to him, its point punching a finger's length through. All three instinctively ducked, anticipating more. But none came. Another ladder hit the edge of the wall. 'Right,' Lucius said. 'Here we go again.'

He turned, startled, as a roar like that of a bear came from along the ramparts. A huge Novantae stood, legs apart, on the parapet's edge. His great muscled arm swung a broad headed axe in huge arcs across the faces of the defenders. Two already lay unmoving below him. A blow connected with Puden's upheld shield. The force drove the Panonnian against the guardrail. The warrior held no shield, but unlike many of his tribe, he wore a chainmail shirt, deflecting some of the desperate sword thrusts from the men around the First Spear. Another swing struck a soldier on the side of the helmet. He dropped to his knees, stunned.

Pudens tried to rise, only for the warrior to leap from the parapet and stamp down heavily on the Pannonnian's knee. Pudens screamed.

'You two, get that ladder off the wall.' Lucius ran along the walkway.

The big man howled as a spatha cut deep into his bare arm. Blood flooded freely from the deep gash. But the soldier had overreached in his desperation and the Novantae grabbed the wrist of his sword arm and tossed him over the battlements and into the ditch below, as if he were a small child.

Another blue-painted warrior leapt from the ladder behind the big Novantae and more ladders struck nearby. Lucius gripped tight to his shield, the pain in his arm forgotten, an incoherent howl torn from his throat as he crashed into the big warrior. The Novantae, now off balance, swung his axe as he fell, striking a glancing blow against Lucius's helmet rim. His ears rang and his sight was filled with bright dots of light. His vision cleared just in time to see the axehead swung once more. Reflexively Lucius raised his shield, preventing his own decapitation. But the impact threw him against the guardrail, the force of it carrying him over its edge. He frantically tried to grasp for the wooden post, but it slipped through his sweat and blood-slick fingers.

'Shit.' The stone paved ground of the fort sped towards him.

65

The fighting on the wall had become desperate. Cai had watched his friend battling ferociously over the gateway. For a horrifying instant Lucius had stood alone, the men around him dead or as good as. Cai stood by, frustrated as a continual stream of replacements ascended the steps to the ramparts. He wanted to join them, but knew he could not.

Moments before, Lucius had disappeared, hidden by the roof of the nearest barrack block as he ran along the walkway. More warriors were clambering over the parapet. The fight over the gate was almost lost.

'Right lads, this is it. Prepare.' Cai's shout was followed by the sound of eighty shields rattling together. He was jostled as Hrindenus did likewise alongside him. 'No man takes a step backwards, unless I order it.'

The fighting along the walkway disintegrated into fierce, individual duels. Three warriors broke free and leapt down the gate's stairway. It didn't take long for their plan to become clear. Cai smiled at the curses of frustration of the three as they approached the gateway. Its thick oak doors had been sealed and reinforced that morning by all manner of timber and rubble.

'Well if it isn't our Damnonii friends,' Hrindenus said. The three had the familiar shaven heads and were tattooed from head to waist. 'Come to me you, Damnonii cowards,' Hrindenus yelled. The three spun around, eyes wide in terror at what they saw awaiting them. An impassable wall of shields. The three had a brief exchange, before disappearing along the intervallum and out of sight, in search of easier prey.

Hrindenus rumbled a laugh. 'They'll find no joy that way, only our pissed off First Spear.'

But more men leapt onto the platform above, uncontested, spilling down the steps in front of the waiting century's position, pooling before the gate.

'They're only men,' Cai shouted. 'Men who think wearing

armour is a weakness. So we'll make them pay for their stupidity.'

The Damnonii numbers continued to grow in the space before Cai's force, shouting challenges at the waiting formation. Their numbers swelling, warriors paced impatiently like wolves waiting for an opening to attack their quarry. The auxiliaries stared back. Silent.

A short, wiry warrior stepped to the fore and looked directly at Cai, a sneer of contempt breaking across his face as he saw his plumed helm. For a few heartbeats their eyes locked. Cai noted the snake-like tattoo that coiled around the man's skull. There was madness in those eyes.

As if prodded by some unseen hand the warrior suddenly thrust his spear and small, square shield aloft, shrieked a piercing cry and flew on light feet towards Cai. The others stormed behind, their combined warcries joining his.

The Damnonii closed the space to the Nervana in an instant. When the first of the warriors were no more than two paces away, the front rank of the auxiliaries punched their shields forward, a grunt of expelled air released as one. The metal shield bosses crunched into their enemy's faces, followed up with a swift stab of their spathas, aimed at stomachs, ribs, throats or groin.

The wiry warrior had tried to jab his spear over arm at Cai's face at the instant of impact, but was deflected by the top rim of his shield. In his desperation to get at Cai the Damnonii's crashed side on, exposing his tattooed ribs.

'Bastard.' Hrindenus yelled, as he drove the point of his spatha deep. The warrior's scream turned into a tortured shriek as the big Tungrian levered his blade to release it.

Even as he fell dead at Cai's feet, another smashed against his shield, barging him into the soldier in the second rank, who quickly used his shield to push him back upright once more and into the face of the warrior.

The Damnonii was bigger than the last, but much older, and spewed foulness from the black hole of his near toothless mouth. As more of the enemy flowed over the ramparts to join their brothers, the press between the two forces meant both sides struggled to wield their weapons.

But not Hrindenus. The big Tungrian used his formidable strength to deal swift killing strokes, slicing, sawlike, at the exposed flesh of any who were unfortunate to have to face him. Warriors slid from his shield and for an instant a space opened up in front of him, leaving his sword arm free. Without thought Hrindenus stabbed upwards into the throat of Cai's assailant who had been attempting to pull his shield down with his bare hands. Blood poured from the wound, spouting to the rhythm of his dying heart, the warm liquid splashing across Cai's face and flooding along the blade of Hrindenus's spatha.

'I've saved your arse again, sir,' Hrindenus shouted, the battle joy upon him.

Cai saw the look on the toothless warrior's face turn from snarling hatred, to shock and finally peace as the light died in his eyes. The body however, did not fall. The press from both sides held it in place, the old man's head swung from side to side in a parody of life.

The crush prevented Cai from using his weapon, but afforded him time to glimpse across the heads of the Damnonii. The flow of warriors from the wall had turned to a flood. If he didn't act soon it would be too late.

'Nervana will advance at the count,' Cai yelled. 'One.' The shields of each rank pressed into the backs of the men in front of them and shoved, taking a small but perceptible step. 'Two.' Again Cai found he could take a half step forward propelled by the force of the men behind. The body of the toothless warrior finally fell.

Finding he was able to move his sword arm, Cai stabbed forward. Tortured screams filled the air. The forward motion enabled the men in the second rank to lend a hand, stabbing their swords overhand across the shoulders of their comrades. 'One.'

'Bastards, bastards, bastards,' Hrindenus bellowed continually, in time with each thrust of his spatha. Cai heard a metallic ring against his helmet. An instant later the pressure from the shield in his back slackened as the soldier behind him collapsed, the unseen spear point buried in his throat. But Cai felt the pressure reasserted as the third ranker stepped forward over the crumpled body.

Risking another look at the ramparts, Cai saw bowmen shooting erratically into his century's closely packed formation. He hoped his men had spotted them too and were tucked behind the protection of their shields. The crush was too great to order testudo, it was more likely to cause chaos than to protect them. Nor, he realised, could he press their short advance much further or they would cross into the intervallum, exposing their flanks to the enemy, who now filled the narrow pathway at the base of the ramparts.

'Nervana halt.' Cai yelled over his shoulder.

An arrow thudded into his shield, its point halted a finger's width from his eye. They were in a perilous position, assailed to the fore and from above. Footing was also tricky. With the number of bodies at their feet the ground had become slick.

Cai was exhausted, the weight of his sword dragging at his arm. The other front rankers would be feeling the same. He must rotate the ranks, but he was no Centurion who practised the manoeuvre regularly. But he had try it.

'Front rank, prepare to retire to the rear,' Cai shouted, before taking another deep breath of air. 'Now!' The men in the front rank shoved their shields forward into the press of bodies, creating an arm's length of space, immediately stepping back into the embrace of the formation. The second rank held its ground, now becoming the new front line. Cai moved side-on between the shields of his men, more than once stumbling on an unseen body, until finally reaching the open space at the back of the formation. The men from the former front rank were doubled over, taking in huge gulps of air.

Raising his shield, Cai looked over the heads of his men and saw with some relief the manoeuvre had worked: their lines still held firm. An arrow clattered against the road surface behind him.

'Those feathers on your helmet are going to get you killed, sir. But more importantly they're going to get me killed,' Hrindenus said, standing next to Cai as he raised his shield higher to cover his commander.

'You wanted the fucking job, Vexillarius.' Cai turned to look back along the Via Principalis. Lenius stood near the east gate, alongside the standard bearer of the Hispana. Holding the wooden shaft of the cohort's standard in his left hand, his spatha in his right 'He looks the part, doesn't he?'

'Aye well, he's better over there out of the—Bollocks.' Hrindenus exclaimed, feeling the impact of an arrow against his upheld shield. Cai laughed at his discomfiture.

'Well, at least if they're aiming at us, the rest of the lads are being left alone,' Cai said. The Tungrian gave him a sideways glance and muttered under his breath as more of the enemy crossed the western wall.

66

Lucius cried out at the fierce pain in his left arm. His eyes snapped open.

'He's awake, sir.'

A face loomed over Lucius. It was one of the Nervana's double-pay men, but Lucius's fugged brain couldn't bring his name to mind.

'Are you back with us, sir? You gave us a nasty fright there, falling from the battlements like that. We just managed to pull you back behind our lines before the blue-faces got to you.' Lucius stared, finally remembering the name of his saviour.

'Help me up, Polionis,' he said. Raising his sword hand, he was pulled to his feet. Lucius's head pounded and the bright morning light hurt his eyes. The sound of battle filled the air, the smell of burning still lingering alongside that of the butcher's shop. He was at the rear of a formation holding the narrow space between two cavalry barracks blocks. The top of the southwest turret was in sight, so he was not far from the main gate.

'How goes it?' Lucius winced once more at the pain in his arm and shoulder.

'We're holding our own here, sir. But from the din I think the lads on the south wall might be in a spot of trouble.'

'Right, I'll take a look. Keep your men at it, Polionis.' Lucius walked unsteadily for the few short steps it took to reach the Via Praetoria. Bodies of the dead had been piled along the roadway's length, its drainage channels carried away blood like rainwater.

Fierce fighting was taking place on the parapet to the right of the main gate. The defenders were gradually being driven backwards. If the enemy reached the steps, they would attack the rear of the defenders.

Still dazed, he looked along the parapet, searching for the helmet plume of any officer who might be leading the defence. There were none. Reaching for the pommel of his spatha, he cursed. His scabbard was empty.

Lucius ran towards the gate, with no weapon and his shield arm held uselessly to his side. He leaped over the detritus on the roadway. Blackened wooden spars, smashed roof tiles and all manner of broken kit littered its paved surface.

He slipped, losing his footing, falling headlong, flinging out his injured arm instinctively. He cried out at the searing pain and lay sprawled on the ground. Levering himself back onto his feet, he staggered towards the steps by the gateway.

In moments he reached the parapet. All was in chaos. Lucius stood at the rear of auxiliaries fighting a desperate defence. In the confined space of the walkway the sound of screaming men from both sides was deafening.

Below, a century defended the space between the turf ramparts and the first barrack block. But the defenders on the parapet were being relentlessly forced backwards, allowing bowmen to loose arrows and hurl detritus onto the century's now upturned shields. They couldn't last much longer.

Lucius looked back along the walkway towards the east turret. It took a second to spot what he had hoped to find. Near the base of the turret steps, stacked against the parapet wall, was a bundle of lances. He grabbed the rearmost man by the shoulder, who spun around, wild-eyed, sword raised, ready to skewer whoever held him. Upon seeing an officer he quickly came to his senses. The noise was so great Lucius was forced to shout into the soldier's ear.

'I want four men. Now. Bring them to me at the turret. Understood?' The auxiliary nodded with a look of relief at the sight of his Tribunus. He immediately started grabbing men and shoving them bodily in Lucius's direction, who was already running along the walkway.

In a matter of moments four men faced Lucius, all looked filthy and exhausted. The fight continued to rage beyond them.

'Drop your shields, grab one of these.' He pointed at the stack, 'we're going to start skewering blue-faces,' Lucius ran back towards the fighting, lance in hand. He only hoped he could wield it one-handed in the narrow space.

Reaching the rear of the fighting, he shouldered his way through the crush. Soldiers cursed as they were shoved bodily out of the way, but finally Lucius got close enough to the enemy.

Raising the lance overhand, he thrust it over the heads of the embattled front men. His first strike punched into the mouth of a dark-haired warrior, whose battlecry became a strangled gargle.

Blood streamed from his mouth and dripped down his long-plaited moustache. The spearpoint became stuck. Lucius frantically jerked the spear shaft, his arm burning with the effort. It came free.

The others had joined him, taking his lead. Immediately the effort of the spearmen began to have an effect, as they drove their lance points into any exposed flesh of the enemy. The relentless pressure eased. The auxiliaries were holding their ground once more.

Then disaster struck. A soldier in the front rank, who held the space against the walkway's guardrail, stabbed his sword viciously upwards. The spatha's point punched under the jaw of a Novantae and into his brain, killing him instantly. But the force of the blow threw the now limp body over the guardrail, sending it crashing onto the upturned shields of the men below.

Their Centurion, who fought frantically in the front rank, had formed this mixed unit of soldiers and some cavalry of the Hispana into a ragged testudo to defend against the projectiles from above. The impact of the warrior's body on the shields was calamitous. The formation's centre broke up. An attempt to reform was quickly made, but the opportunity had been spotted by the enemy.

Two warriors leaped from the walkway, bellowing warcries, and into the terrified auxiliaries below. All was now chaos. The formation began to disintegrate further. Lucius watched impotently as more men jumped from the walkway. His eyes were drawn to the bronze scale armour worn by one. Stunned he realised who it must be. Barra, the Novantae war leader.

The big red-headed warchief landed in the centre of the broken testudo. Momentarily disappeared between shields, as if swallowed by the waters of a lake. An instant later he reappeared, swinging his sword in a wide scything strokes. The nearest men leapt away from this fierce warrior, who had appeared so suddenly amongst them. All cohesion was lost as the rear ranks began to, slowly at first, back away. But quickly panic set in and men, looking left and right for a way out, finally ran for their lives. Some streamed along the Via Praetoria, seeking an escape where there was none.

Lucius watched as Barra, his long red hair flowing behind, disappeared from sight amongst the buildings on the fort's eastern side, followed by many of his tribesmen. The end was near.

67

'That doesn't sound good.' Hrindenus voiced Cai's own thoughts. The frenzy of sound, coming from the southern section of the Sack's interior, had changed. His men had been holding, but the fear that the enemy would break through elsewhere was ever present.

Cai ran to the corner of the barrack block, where it joined onto the Via Praetoria.

'Shit,' Cai spat. Men of the cohorts were running, panic stricken along its length, closely followed by groups of warriors. They had been overrun.

He glanced towards Lenius, expecting to see the young groom standing ready, as he had been all morning. Hrindenus flew past Cai: he had seen it too. The groom was fighting for his life against a bear of a man, the Hispana's standard bearer lay unmoving at his feet. It was an uneven match, but Lenius fought bravely, driving the point of his spatha across the warrior's sword arm. The man stepped back, a look of shock contorting his face. For an instant, Cai thought Hrindenus would reach the boy in time.

But hope turned to despair as a sword was driven into the groom's chest, puncturing chainmail and leather. Unseen, a second assailant, had taken advantage of Lenius's distraction. This new warrior's plate armoured shirt stood out amongst the chaos around him.

'No!' Cai heard the anguished yell from Hrindenus, still some way from the groom. The big man kept on running, but it was already too late, Lenius collapsed to his knees. Barra planted his foot in the groom's slumped shoulder, kicking him onto his back, tearing the standard from the boy's loosening grasp. With a whoop of triumph the Novantae war leader disappeared from sight, running behind the eastern buildings. Followed by an almost continual line of warriors emerging from along the base of the ramparts.

The fort was lost. The enemy was behind them. The standards were captured, their rallying point overwhelmed. Cai thought desperately. What could they do? Withdraw his unit into the principia and fight a final defence from within its four walls?

He turned back to his men, preparing to give the order. The words caught in his throat at the sight before him.

His men were still in a vicious fight against their front, but tribesmen no longer swarmed over the battlements. Or rather, they did, but in the opposite direction, back into the ruined village. The Damnonii who beset the front ranks sensed something was wrong. Some new peril.

At first those at the rear disengaged in ones and twos, running for the western gateway steps. But this trickle soon turned to a flood.

'Nervana advance,' Cai yelled from the rear. His men, just moments before all but done in, found new strength. They pressed forward with a triumphant roar.

Cai turned. Hrindenus had reached Lenius and was kneeling by the body of the groom. The big Tungrian, uncaring of his own safety as warriors still emerged from the fort's south. Most however, only intent on escape.

Just one thing could have the tribes fleeing at their point of victory. He cocked his head, listening – and heard, above the battle's din, the faint but unmistakable sound of a cornicen.

But rather than relief, icy fear filled his mind. Alyn. Where was she? Had she and the boy been able to hide themselves? Cai had told her to wait by the east gate. He prayed she had not attempted it.

Hrindenus cradled Lenius's head. The boy's eyes stared glassily at the sky, filled with the black dots of carrion birds. Cai put his hand on the Tungrian's shoulder.

'Come, Hrindenus,' Cai said, 'we'll grieve for Lenius, but not yet. We must recover the standard before he gets away.' Hrindenus looked up at his commander with a look of confusion. 'Barra killed him and took the standard. The war leader of the Novantae.'

'The one who spared your life?' Hrindenus spoke, not hiding his anger. Cai nodded.

'Get up, Vexillarius.' Cai glanced upwards, drawn by movement on the battlements over the eastern gate. The sight that greeted him was like a blow to the stomach. For there stood Barra, silhouetted by the sun at his back. The two men locked eyes. Cai's hand went to the pommel of his sword as a smile flickered across the

Novantae's face. In a fluid movement his erstwhile rescuer shook the Nervana's standard once at Cai , then turned swiftly and leapt over the parapet, disappearing from sight.

Jolted into action, Cai grabbed the neck of Hrindenus's chainmail shirt, heaving him to his feet and propelled him towards the praetorium. He must get to Adela before Barra escaped or the cohort faced the shame of the loss of its standard.

The entrance doors to the Tribunus's official residence had been smashed in. One lay on the paved floor; the other hung by a single hinge, partly blocking the doorway. Fortunately, this had prevented the horses from bolting from the colonnaded courtyard where they were held.

Hrindenus kicked the door. With a crash of splintering wood the hinge gave way. Six horses milled within the small space, open to the sky. They were unsettled, tossing their heads and snorting great gouts of air.

Adela's blond mane and tan hide stood out amongst the others. Cai pushed through to where she stood. He patted her neck as she nuzzled his face in welcome. The horses had been left saddled, wasting no time, he led her out of the building.

'I wouldn't, if I were you?' Cai said. Hrindenus stood by Epona, Lucius's black mare. 'Unless you want a broken neck.' Hrindenus chose a nearby grey instead.

They left the praetorium, stepping out into chaos. Auxiliaries ran from building to building, some still burning, carrying wounded from their interiors or searching for any enemy who may have lingered.

The long, high pitched sound came again. Multiple cornicen's, it seemed. Still distant, but closer now. Mounting Adela, Cai guided her along the Via Decumana to the northern gate, but the chaos forced them to move at a walk.

'Get out of the way. Move!' Cai shouted in frustration. Groups of exhausted men congregated on the roadway, some staring blankly as if their spirits had already passed to the otherworld. Some celebrated their unexpected salvation from certain death only minutes before, ecstatically greeting friends who had somehow survived. All barely noticed Cai's shouts.

Cai was considering using the flat of his spatha to bash a few heads, when he spotted Facilis. The Nervana's First Spear sat on the veranda of a barrack block, head bowed between his knees.

'Facilis,' Cai shouted. At first he did not hear. 'Facilis.' This time the First Spear raised his head as if waking from a dream. Seeing Cai on horseback he gave a questioning look, confusion written across his face. 'They've got the standard, brother. I need to get out through the north gate.'

Shaking himself, the short, fierce First Spear leapt to his feet.

'Clear the way you slackers. Let the Praefectus through or I'll bury boot up your arse.' Facilis's command would have been heard from one end of the Sack to the other. The soldier's moved. In short order the two riders were able to kick their horses into a canter.

'Open the gates,' Facilis bawled once more. A group of soldiers ran to the gateway, lifting the thick oak cross bar, swinging the doors open, revealing the ground beyond. The ruin of battle blanketed the land. Bodies lay everywhere, interspersed with broken spears and shields, like a stunted and long-dead forest.

A glint of light caught Cai's attention and was in time to see Barra disappear over the rise along the military way. His bronze armour stood out as he drove his white Roman horse hard, accompanied by two other riders.

To Cai's frustration he found they could not immediately kick the horses into pursuit. Bodies littered the causeway. He dismounted, leading Adela through the dead. As they crossed the final ditch, the way became less impeded. They remounted.

'What about the caltrops, sir?' Hrindenus shouted from further back.

Cai ignored the Vexillarius, nudging Adela into a trot. Black carrion took flight in great screeching puffs as the two riders passed.

Bodies of both auxiliary and enemy alike blanketed the field in broad lines, silently marking the stages of the Nervana's withdrawal. A dog Cai recognised from the village nuzzled his bloody snout into the rent of an auxiliary's chainmail shirt.

Closely watching the partly hidden surface of the road, the two gradually negotiated their way through, avoiding hidden perils. But it felt a lifetime before they reached clear roadway. But at last Cai was able to kick Adela into a gallop. She responded enthusiastically after days of being cooped up.

Glancing west, Cai saw the dark mass of the tribes fleeing

towards the Anam. Perhaps hoping its deep, slow-moving waters offered sanctuary from pursuit. Some were on horseback, but most on foot, many encumbered by their wounded. The Sixth or the Twentieth, whoever were the Sack's saviours, could deal with them.

Cai turned away, his only thought now to run down Barra. He dared not think beyond that.

'There are three of them,' Hrindenus shouted from behind.

'I know.' They continued to pound along the road, pushing the horses hard. 'Divine Epona, give our horses wings.' The words of the prayer were snatched away by the wind of their passing.

The forest edge emerged on the eastern horizon, Cai estimated they must now be close to two miles from the Sack. But they were yet to catch sight of their quarry. Panic began to rise within him. There had been no sign of tracks leaving the road, but it could only be a matter of time before they turned west, deeper into Novantae lands.

'Why're they running to the north?' Hrindenus yelled. Cai had wondered this too. Why flee along the road, rather than join his tribe in escaping over the Anam? Then it came to him.

'He doesn't want to risk being trapped,' Cai shouted over his shoulder. 'He knows many of his people will be run down by the legion.'

As the road crested another rise, the familiar flat-topped summit of the Novantae's sacred hill came into view. And there along the arrow straight road were the three mounted warriors, not more than a quarter of a mile ahead. Cai curbed Adela at the top of the rise. The Novantae were riding their horses abreast of each other at a walk. They were conversing as if merely returning from a day's hunt. Barra rode at their centre, balancing the staff of the Nervana's standard across his shoulder.

'It looks like our friends aren't expecting trouble,' Hrindenus said, his voice a low rumble. 'Should we ride over and see if they'll give us a warm welcome?'

Drawing his spatha. Not taking his eyes from Barra, Cai hissed, 'Let's kill them all.' He kicked Adela hard, into a gallop, swiftly descending the rise, with the big Tungrian trailing.

The three riders turned sharply at the sound of hooves clattering on the road's surface. Cai laughed at the look of shock on Barra's face. The warrior's set off. Driving their mounts hard.

But Cai was elated. They had closed the gap to little more than a long bow shot. Sitting low over Adela's neck, her mane whipping his face, the distance steadily shortened.

Despite carrying the standard, Barra was noticeably pulling ahead of the other two. His larger horse outpacing the others.

The Novantae's hill was looming large, filling the horizon. Suddenly, inexplicably, the three left the road, making directly for it, lifting up great clods of turf as they crossed the soft pasture. Barra had pulled perhaps ten horse lengths ahead of the nearest rider, with the third trailing badly, his mount tiring.

Knowing he was about to be caught, the warrior pulled up sharply to face his pursuers. The horseman had just enough time to deflect the wild swing of Cai's spatha, but could not react to the curved slice from Hrindenus's blade that removed his head. Wasting no time to look at their handiwork they continued the pursuit of the remaining two.

Cai could feel Adela was starting to struggle. But he had no choice. He had to continue to drive her hard.

The distance between Barra and the second warrior was growing, and, perhaps understanding he was not going to reach the hill's summit before he was run down, the rider suddenly changed direction towards the sanctuary of the forest.

Cai pointed his spatha towards the fleeing horseman. Hrindenus veered away..

Barra was approaching the old siege camp of the Sixth legion, which hugged the ancient hill's southern edge. Pushing his exhausted mount to a final effort, the warchief passed through the camp's southern entrance, its gates and wooden palisade long dismantled. Horse and rider struggled across the slick, boggy ground of the rutted interior, finally reaching the northern gateway, just as Cai neared the southern.

He slowed Adela to a trot. It was clear the Novantae was no longer intent on escape.

'Well done girl, we're nearly finished,' Cai said as he passed one of the old turf-covered ballista platforms, now more closely resembling a burial mound of the ancients he had seen throughout this land.

Adela's head swung from side to side as she struggled up the hill's southern ramparts. Cai let her pick her own way until they reached the ruins of its west-most entrance. The hill's summit was deceptive. When observed from a distance it appeared unusually flat. As if sliced by the sword of a long-dead giant. However, when upon it, the hilltop undulated with hiding places to surprise the unwary.

But Cai guessed where Barra was headed, confirmed by the signs of hoof prints amongst the thick heather and tufts of scrub grass. He looked across the overgrown hilltop, the wind stiffening from the direction of the Sula. It was difficult to imagine a fierce battle had taken place here only ten summers before.

Turning Adela towards the hill's western end, he approached the small rise which had once been surrounded by a thick wooden palisade. Where the Novantae had made their last stand against the Sixth legion. Some tumbled and rotting timbers still showed through the undergrowth, like contorted and broken teeth. There by the ruins of its entrance was the white horse. It was untethered and cropped contentedly at the long grass, snickering at the approach of another horse.

Sheathing his spatha, Cai dismounted and patted Adela's neck, letting her rein drop so she too could move freely. He removed his helmet and liner, allowing the strong breeze from the Sula to cool his sweat-soaked hair. He inhaled deeply, smelling the salty air and readying himself for what came next.

Replacing his helm he strode across the uneven ground, passing the fire-blackened ruins of roundhouses. Barra was standing by the edge of the hill's escarpment, looking towards distant Criffel. The sun had not yet reached its zenith, light reflected from the back of his bronze armour, despite much of it being coated with dark stains. The shaft of the cohort's standard had been thrust into the soft ground nearby. The white horse banner rippled with each gust of wind.

'Look at this land, Roman.' Barra spoke not taking his eyes from the view beyond. Cai stopped some ten strides from the Novantae.

'What of it?' Cai said. Barra turned to face him.

'Beautiful is it not?' Barra continued as if Cai had not spoken. 'The land is fertile, the sea plentiful and the hunting is beyond compare.'

'I've known better,' Cai said with disdain.

'What I don't understand is why you Romans want it. Our lands hold nothing you value. No mines of silver or tin. You can't grow the grape for your wine. What is it you want?'

Cai stared at Barra, his red hair straggling below his helmet, his long drooping moustache giving him a mournful appearance. His left hand rested on the pommel of his sword, strapped to his hip by a silver-buckled belt.

'I told you once before, Novantae. I am a soldier. I care nothing for such questions. You picked a fight you couldn't win, just like the last time we fought on this hill.' Cai saw the flash of anger in the warchief's eyes.

'Well then. What is it *you* want, Roman?' Barra sneered.

'I am of the Nervii and you have my cohort's standard. I will take it back and avenge the boy you killed to steal it.' There was a quiet hiss as Cai slid his sword from its scabbard.

'It gave me no honour to kill one so young, but he would not let it go. He had spirit. He fought with courage, but poorly. Perhaps you should not have put one so young in such peril.'

Cai knew Barra's barb was intended to rile him, but he didn't care. He roared a guttural warcry and hurled himself across the space between them. Barra drew his own blade in time to deflect Cai's downward scything blow. Both men pulled apart, Cai taking a deep calming breath. They began to slowly circle each other, neither speaking, both closely watching the other.

Barra moved first, feinting a downward hack that he turned quickly into a low slice aimed at Cai's knee, forcing him to leap backwards away from the blade.

The Novantae now had Cai on the defensive, forcing him to retreat with a series of vicious left and right slashes, continually changing the angle of attack. All Cai could do was parry and continue to fall back. The clash of the blades rang across the barren hilltop. A final lunge by Barra struck a glancing blow on Cai's left shoulder. His chainmail took the worst of it, but nevertheless a shock of pain jolted through his arm.

But fortune intervened. Barra, in his determination to get at his enemy, overreached and stumbled, his leading leg caught in the dense undergrowth. Cai was able to wheel away and prepare to face the Novantae once more. Both panted heavily. The pain in Cai's shoulder throbbed. The pair circled once more, but Cai could feel his own exhaustion. Days without sleep and constant fighting weighed heavily. He must finish the fight quickly.

He feigned a thrust at the Novantae's groin, turning it to an upward slash at Barra's face. The warrior instinctively leapt backwards, but his heel tangled in the undergrowth and he fell heavily onto his back. Cai moved quickly, before the other could recover. He stamped down hard on Barra's sword hand, with the sound of a snap as the studs of Cai's boot crushed the clenched fingers. Barra cried out.

Cai held the point of his spatha at the exposed throat of his enemy, the blade drawing a thin line of blood as he pressed it against the pale flesh. He looked down at the warchief who returned his gaze, eyes creased with pain. But Cai saw no fear there, only resignation.

'Get on with it, *Nervii.*'

Both men held eye contact for several heartbeats, before Cai finally eased his foot from Barra's hand. The other closed his eyes in anticipation of the death stroke. But Cai backed further away and sheathed his sword.

'Enough of death, Novantae. Enough,' Cai spoke wearily, into the increasingly strong gusts of wind. A look of confusion crossed the warchief's face as his enemy walked to the hill's steep edge. Cai looked down at the pastureland below. There was now no sign of the Nervana's stand, where his friend had fallen, all those years ago.

He heard the rustle of footsteps through the undergrowth behind him, accompanied by a muffled hissing sound as Barra slid his own sword into its scabbard.

'What is it you want from me? In return for my life?'

Not taking his eyes from the old battlefield, Cai spoke in a flat, emotionless voice. 'I want nothing from you, Novantae. I have recovered our standard and honoured the dead. Now go.' For some time Cai could feel the warrior's eyes on him. But finally he heard the rustle of footsteps as the warchief crossed the hilltop towards his waiting horse.

Cai continued to stare at the vista below him, but he no longer saw it. Old memories played through his mind and realised his words, spoken in anger to Barra, were true. He had seen enough of death.

'What do you think, brother?' Cai whispered. 'Is it time?' He looked for a sign, but saw only clouds as they blew in along the Sula. He imagined he could hear Adal's laughter in the wind.

He caught sight of a rider on a white horse crossing the open field below, moving at a walk towards the edge of the forest. As Barra neared the first of the great pines he curbed his mount, turning her to face back towards the hill. Whether or not the Novantae could see him, Cai did not know, but as he watched the warchief bowed his head once, holding it for a second, before turning again to be swallowed by the forest's dark depths.

Cai walked beside Adela, along the hilltop and down to the remnants of the siege fort. As he crossed over its deep northern ditch he heard the thunder of hoof beats coming from the east. Hrindenus came into view, the big Tungrian looking unruffled by the day's events.

'You got it back then?' Hrindenus nodded at the standard strapped to Adela's side.

'As you can see. And it would be nice if you called me sir from time to time.'

'What of the Novantae who stole it? Sir.'

'He escaped into the forest.' Cai looked away. The Tungrian deciding not to press further.

'Well, my one wasn't so lucky,' Hrindenus tapped the pommel of his sword. Cai nodded, remounting Adela.

'Let's get back. We have a cohort to salvage.' The image of Alyn came into his mind and he kicked the horse into a trot, guiding her quickly towards the military road. He didn't dare push Adela hard, so it took longer to cover the four miles to the fort. On reaching the brow of the last rise, they pulled up, taking in the sight before them.

To the south of the Sack, on the flood plain beyond the stream, there were hundreds of legionaries digging the surrounding ditch of their camp, the large command tent already starting to rise at its centre. The men of the Nervana and Hispana had started piling the enemy's dead into mounds, ready for burning. Black clouds of crows bounced enthusiastically on and around the gruesome heaps.

It seemed to Cai that this was a single Legion, but he couldn't yet see any standards. Was it the Twentieth or the Sixth who had come to their rescue? He shook his head. All he cared about was finding Alyn and Beren. The rest could wait.

A pall of misty, grey smoke hovered stubbornly above the fort, as the two men descended towards the north gate. Cai slowed Adela as he saw they were going to be intercepted by a mounted patrol. No, not a patrol, he realised. Its leader was helmetless, head heavily bandaged, covering his left eye. But Cai recognised him nonetheless.

'Betto!' he shouted, as the small group of riders approached the pair. 'I'm glad you made it through.'

'You too, sir,' said the Duplicarius, smiling.

'You look like you've been in the thick of it. How do the rest of the turma fair?

'This is it, sir.' Betto's voice dropped.

'Only five?'

'Aye, sir…there must be more survivors from the ala scattered around, I suppose. The lads put up a hell of a fight though. We kept the blue-faces looking over their shoulders. We made a nuisance of ourselves at night when our numbers were too low to take them on in daylight...But I suppose it wasn't enough in the end?'

'It was more than enough,' Cai said, with some vehemence. 'The cavalry bought us time to hold on.' Cai looked over Betto's shoulder to the floodplain. 'Who are our rescuers anyway?'

'The Twentieth, sir.'

'So the Boars have the bragging rights.'

Betto and his men fell in behind Cai. The roadway to the fort had been cleared. Ordered lines of the two cohort's dead had been arranged outside of the outermost ditch.

'So many dead,' Cai said. Hrindenus said nothing. No response was needed. There was still so much debris and rubble strewn across the Sack's interior they were forced to dismount at the gate and lead the horses.

'Sir.' A weary looking Optio commanding the gate section hailed Cai and saluted. 'The Tribunus requested you attend him in the principia immediately upon your return.'

Leaving Hrindenus to take care of the horses he made his way to the headquarters building, passing the infantry barracks on the way. On the covered walkway of one of the blocks he saw Mascellus and Salvinus sitting side by side on the wooden planking, legs dangling into the drainage ditch. They passed a wineskin between them, not the first by the looks of them.

Where did those two old scoundrels find wine?

The buildings on the eastern side of the fort appeared to have survived, largely, intact. But in the west, many were blackened shells.

More bodies were piled along the Via Decumana, awaiting removal, the smell of burnt wood only partly masking the odour of decaying flesh. As he passed the final set of blocks, Cai's attention was drawn by the unexpected wailing cries of women. Two, mother and daughter from their look, were bent over the body of a man of middle years. Other civilians from the village milled around, unsure what to do, or where to go.

On entering through the arched entrance to the principia, rather than head straight to Lucius's office, he crossed to the well. Retrieving an already filled bucket that had been left on the well's low, round stone wall, Cai removed his helmet and without ceremony plunged his head into the cool water, staying submerged for some time, savouring the feeling of relief. Then slicking his hands through his dripping fair hair he rung out its ends. He drank deeply of the remainder, uncaring of the filth that had washed into it.

Helmet now under his arm, Cai went in search of Lucius, hobnails crunching on the broken roof tiles and masonry strewn across the atrium. The scene that faced him as he reached his commander's office brought him up with a jolt. From the doorway he saw Lucius and Castellanos bent over the body of a boy, who lay in Lucius's narrow cot. Beren.

His friend turned.

'No, brother. He lives,' Lucius said, upon seeing the look of grief on Cai's face. 'He only sleeps.'

'He's taken a blow to the head,' the medicus spoke without turning. 'But he'll be fine after a few days' rest. Though his head will hurt like Hades for a while.' Castellanos carefully raised Beren's head as he wrapped it in a dressing. A wave of relief washed over Cai, replaced an instant later by dread.

'Where's Alyn?' he asked, knowing she would be by the boy's side, if she was able. Lucius walked around his desk to Cai, placing a hand on his friend's shoulder, speaking quietly.

'Beren told us she was taken as the tribes were fleeing,' Lucius said. 'He tried to defend her, which is why he has that lump on his head. He's a brave lad.' Lucius paused seeing his friend's look of panic. Cai tried to pull away, his only thought to get to a fresh horse and find the woman he loved. But Lucius held him.

'No my friend,' he said, 'you can't go after her now. You won't find her in all of the confusion and it will likely mean your death if you did.' Lucius tried to keep his voice firm. Cai tugged his shoulder free but Lucius grabbed his arm, gripping it tightly and staring down the look of anger that crossed his face.

'The Twentieth is pursuing the tribes across the Anam,' Lucius continued. 'But they'll soon disappear into their great forest. We *will* go after her, brother. I swear it. But your death will not help her.' Both men were face to face and continued to stare at one another for long seconds, until finally the frantic look in Cai's eyes was replaced by one of despair.

Collapsing onto a chair, Cai placed his head in his hands, overwhelmed by exhaustion and sorrow.

68

The night was warm and sultry. The rider had set off from the coast that morning leaving the ship at the port of Malaca, where he hired a horse and departed for his destination without delay. He had moved his mount at an unhurried pace. Knowing how long the journey would take, he did not want to exhaust the animal.

The temperature had gradually risen, but for a while he had the welcome, cooling breezes from the sea that had remained in sight for much of the morning. But as the mountains had finally closed in around him the heat of the day had risen, forcing him to remove his travel cloak. Mid-afternoon had been the most difficult time of the journey as the heat soared, impelling him to shade beneath a copse of broad pine trees close to the road.

He had rested there, eating the food bought for the journey, waiting until the sun was an hour past its zenith before continuing. But finally he had arrived.

Leaving the road he walked his tired horse along a broad, well maintained trackway lit by occasional oil lamps, accompanied by the buzzing cacophony of the cicadas. Pine trees lined both sides of the route, their broad canopies creating a long dark tunnel. The track continued to rise for a time and as he turned a final bend the bright lights of the villa shone from its perch on the hillside.

Shortly afterwards he entered the main gateway and was received by two slaves. The first, a dark-skinned boy, led his mount away. The other was finely dressed and in his middle years. Dark, almost black hair hung in ringlets across his brow and was matched by a well-oiled beard, clipped to a point at his chin. He indicated with a flourish of his arms that the rider should follow him.

Entering the villa through a door clearly used for visiting tradesmen, he trailed the slave in his wake of pungent perfume. The rider had seen this one on his previous visit. The duties for his master were clearly diverse. They passed through what looked like storerooms or perhaps the cells of slaves, before finally reaching a long corridor that ended in a curtained doorway.

Pulling the curtain aside the slave indicated with another flourish that he should enter and turn to the right.

'The dominus wishes you to attend him in his study.' The slave's Latin was impeccable, with the hint of an accent. Cappadocian perhaps?

'Thank you, Silvanus,' the rider said, remembering his name.

He entered a large atrium. At its centre was an intricate fountain, a statue of the goddess Athena at its heart. Water made a tinkling sound as it sprang from multiple sprouts, entering channels that carried it around the open area. Creepers climbed the columned walkway framing each of its three sides. A light from beyond a door standing slightly ajar radiated onto the passage. He walked to it and knocked once.

'Enter,' came a brusque command.

Pushing the door fully open he saw his patron, or at least his back, hunched over as he worked at some hidden task. He sat at a huge intricately carved desk, its polished wood dark with age. The desk faced a tall window, open to the night breeze, nothing but darkness beyond. But in daylight, it would enclose a view of olive plantations as far as the eye could see.

'So what message is so important you could not commit it to parchment?' the rider's patron said, without taking his eyes from the scroll he read.

'It appears our old friends the Faenii, or at least the eldest son, have supporters in high places. One supporter in particular, who has the ear of the Emperor, has agents who have been making enquiries about our acquisition of the father's former lands.'

'What?' Rising from his chair, his patron turned to face the rider for the first time. Grey jowls wobbling at the sudden movement. The folds of his white tunic struggled to contain the huge girth of his belly. A head shorter than the rider, his nearly bald head glistened with sweat. 'Explain yourself. What high placed ally could an insignificant family like the Faenii possibly have?' Derision dripped with his words.

'The Numidian.' The rider kept his voice low.

'What? Him? Why would he take a nobody under his wing? That makes no sense.'

'Nonetheless, my source is exemplary. I wouldn't have made this journey if I didn't think more than our enterprise was at risk.' The rider saw a flash of fear cross his patron's face, quickly controlled. The fat man waddled to a small table set against the wall next to the open window. It held a tall flask. He poured wine into two intricately coloured glass cups, passing one to the rider.

'I thought of the Faenii boy as a minor inconvenience to be got rid of. Now I fear we must be more rigorous in our dealing with him.'

'What of the assassin you sent? He may yet be successful,' the rider said.

'I would have expected to receive a message from him by now. No, we must assume he has failed.' The fat man took a long swallow of wine, a red drip escaping his lips to meander across his chin, his fat belly catching it, staining his tunic.

'My source passed on other information. Urbicus has instructed the boy to meet his agent in Baetica.'

'So he's finally going to leave that shit hole in the arse end of the empire. Did your source say where he was to meet this agent?'

'Italica.'

'Well then, let's be sure our people are there to give him a warm welcome home.'

Acknowledgements

Any author will acknowledge that they could not do what they do without the support of their closest family. My eternal thanks go Jenny, Mike, Robbie, Tess and Abbie for their unfailing words of encouragement.

I have also been delighted by the helping hand and guidance offered by the wider writing community. I would like to acknowledge two fabulous writers in particular who have helped make my writing better. Marian L Thorpe and Matthew Harffy. Buy their books too, they're excellent.

For my talented nephew Arran, taken from us much too soon, you were ever on my mind as Beren ranged the countryside around the Sack.

Finally to Jenny for the last 35 years. Where you found the patience I will never know. But I'm forever grateful that you did my love.

Author's Note

Edge of Empire: Siege is a work of fiction. There are both deliberate and inadvertent historical inaccuracies throughout. In part to fit the story narrative but also because of sparse detail and dates in the written record. Most of what we know of Quintus Lollius Urbicus's campaign has been left in the landscape of southern Scotland. But Lucius and his cohort of Nervians did exist and if you would like to know more of this period I strongly recommend the following reading;

Birrens (Blatobulgium) by Anne S Robertson. Covering her extensive work at the site and enabled me to provide the detail for the Sack.

The paper written by John H Reid and Andrew Nicholson Burnswark HIll: The opening shot of the Antonine reconquest of Scotland? Published by The Journal of Roman Archaeology. The paper offers compelling insight into what may have been an assault of exemplary force against the hillfort of the local tribe.

For ballista geeks (like me) I highly recommend Roman Imperial Artillery by Alan Wilkes. An introduction to the ballistas of the Roman army.

Lucius Faenius Felix and Cai Martis will return in Edge of Empire: Hunt.

Alistair Tosh.

Printed in Great Britain
by Amazon